Alien Artifacts

Other Anthologies Edited by
Patricia Bray & Joshua Palmatier

After Hours: Tales from the Ur-Bar
The Modern Fae's Guide to Surviving Humanity
Clockwork Universe: Steampunk vs Aliens
Temporally Out of Order
Were-

Alien Artifacts

Edited by

Joshua Palmatier
&
Patricia Bray

Zombies Need Brains LLC
www.zombiesneedbrains.com

Interior Design (ebook): April Steenburgh
Interior Design (print): C. Lennox
Cover Design by C. Lennox
Cover Art "Alien Artifacts" by Justin Adams

Kickstarter Edition Printing, July 2016
First Printing, August 2016

Print ISBN-10: 1940709083
Print ISBN-13: 978-1940709086

Ebook ISBN-10: 1940709091
Ebook ISBN-13: 978-1940709093

Printed in the U.S.A.

Copyrights

Table of Contents

Signature Page

Patricia Bray, editor:

_____

Joshua Palmatier, editor:

_____

Walter H. Hunt:

_____

Julie Novakova:

_____

David Farland:

_____

Angela Penrose:

_____

S.C. Butler:

_____

Gail Z. Martin & Larry N. Martin:

_____

Juliet E. McKenna:

_____

Sharon Lee & Steve Miller:

_____

Andrija Popovic:

_____

Jacey Bedford:

_____

Sofie Bird:

_____

James Van Pelt:

_____

Gini Koch:

_____

Anthony Lowe:

_____

Jennifer Dunne:

_____

Coral Moore:

_____

Daniel J. Davis:

_____

C.S. Friedman:

_____

Seanan McGuire:

_____

Justin Adams, artist:

_____

INTRODUCTION
Patricia Bray

First contact between humans and aliens is a staple of science fiction. But what if our first contact isn't with an alien species, but with one of their artifacts? Perhaps in our explorations we stumble across an alien trash heap or an abandoned cache of treasures. We might find a device built to seek out other intelligent species, or an incomprehensible piece of debris from an ancient catastrophe. It could be something as seemingly simple as a sculpture, or as complex as a derelict spaceship.

In ALIEN ARTIFACTS we asked authors to imagine what would happen when humanity encountered one of these alien artifacts. What kind of object would it be? How would the characters react to finding this proof of alien life? Would the object be an intellectual curiosity? Or something that could transform Earth's technology, catapulting our civilization to new heights—or our own destruction?

The result was nineteen intriguing stories of discovery, from humor to horror, with artifacts ranging from discarded trash to devices beyond human comprehension. There's something for everyone in here.

Enjoy!

RADIO SILENCE
Walter H. Hunt

On the day that the world did not come to an end, Luanne Jacoby came into the Solar Observatory control room to begin her shift. To her surprise she found Jeremy Gonzalez sitting at his station, a few empty coffee cups and spent stimpaks on the console table, a detailed holo view of the Sun turning slowly in front of him.

"I thought you were off-shift."

"I was supposed to be," he answered. He reached for a coffee cup and noticed that it was empty. He put the hand to good use, running it through his thinning hair. "But there's just the damnedest thing going on."

To Jeremy, Luanne knew, *the damnedest thing* could be a late-game loss by a favorite sports team, or a weird reflection of light in his quarters—not that she'd ever seen them: *pics* of them, but not the premises themselves—or any of a hundred other items that caught his interest for minutes or hours. But those didn't usually keep him eight hours past his duty cycle.

"Tell me more," she said, sitting next to him and looking up at the holo.

Jeremy's face lit up like a small child getting ready to ask a knock-knock joke. "It's just the damnedest thing. I was doing the usual analysis on sunspot activity—we're near a maximum—"

"I know. Everyone knows."

"Yeah. Sorry. We're near a max, and I was analyzing the activity, but some strange data turned up." He swiped a finger near the holo and a table of numbers appeared. "All of a sudden we saw a burst of neutrinos, which looked very, *very* much like a core collapse."

"That's impossible. The Sun doesn't have enough mass for that. We're millions of years from a possible nova or supernova."

"*Data*, Lu." He pointed at the numbers. "There *was* a neutrino burst. For about two and a half seconds we had the very beginning of a solar core collapse. If it had gone on just a little longer we'd not be having this conversation. No one in the inner Solar System would be having any sort of conversation, ever again."

She waved at the image, bringing it closer, and zoomed in at the figures. "Okay," she said. "You've got my interest. What caused it?"

"Don't know."

"What *stopped* it?"

"Don't know exactly. But at the 2 point 48 second mark there was something, and then the neutrino burst stopped. It didn't dissipate—it just stopped, instantly, nothing at all after that."

"What sort of something?"

"That's the interesting part." He smiled again and turned to the console. He brought up another holo and waved at it.

There was a sudden burst of sound, like a low keening—actually more like someone playing a wind instrument through ductwork. She began to speak, but Jeremy put up his hand, and then theatrically pointed at the display. At just that moment the keening changed tone to a slightly lower register, then returned to its original pitch.

He waved away the second holo.

"You know what that was."

"Some bad experimental band."

"It's the standard audio representation of the cosmic background radiation," he said. "And right at the 2 point 48 second mark of the neutrino emission it *changed* for—let's see—about 1 point 3 seconds."

"And the neutrino emissions stopped."

"Absolutely. And instantly."

"Has this happened before?"

"Funny you should ask that. It was the first thing I thought of, and I went back through the data we have."

"Are you insane? That's attobytes of solar observations. No wonder you were up all through your off shift."

"Fortunately," Jeremy said, "I have the aid of powerful computing systems." He smiled. "The answer is yes, it's happened before: six times in the last twenty years. Each time there was a neutrino emission, and each time the CBR seemed to alter to compensate. What's more, there's a similar alteration in the CBR just about an hour earlier. Similar, but not exactly the same." He slumped back in his chair and rubbed his eyes. "I have no explanation, Lu. Just the data."

"You're right," she said. "That *is* the damnedest thing. The CBR is the echo of the Big Bang—I wouldn't think that there was anything that could alter it."

"I was hoping you'd have some ideas."

"I have some questions. What's the period of this event? Is it regular?"

"Like clockwork. About 1100 standard days apart. I can give you the exact figure."

"That sounds like an orbital component—like something at a distance from the primary, reaching some point in its orbit. 1100 days would be outside Mars—somewhere in the inner asteroid belt."

"Something—like what?"

"An asteroid, I'd guess." She smirked at him; usually he was first to the mark with wiseass comments. "All we have to do is find something with the correct orbital period, and we can see what's interfering with the cosmic background."

"Twice. Fifty-three minutes apart, every 1100 or so days. You realize how absurd the idea sounds."

"Jeremy," she said, "I've been working with you for two years. I'm used to absurd. As my astrophysics professor used to say, 'when you eliminate the impossible whatever remains, no matter how unbelievable, must be the truth.'"

"That was Sherlock Holmes."

"Fine. Whatever. Now why don't you go get some sleep? I have work to do."

* * *

The Solar Observatory maintained an orbit synchronous with Mercury, about five million kilometers further from the Sun and at opposition, so that the little planet never interfered with the station's primary task. It had been described as the worst research posting in the Solar System when Luanne was at MIT a dozen years earlier, pursuing her astrophysics Ph. D.—but since her doctoral had been based on a careful study of sunspot patterns, it was the natural place to go.

She loved it. It was sparsely furnished and had only a small staff, most of which rotated out after a year or so—"the best tanning salon in the System" wasn't interesting for most people. Luanne assumed they went out to Pluto or the Kuiper or something. When Jeremy had come on board, transferring from Arecibo, she assumed he'd come and go like most everyone else, but he seemed different, absorbed by the study of whatever he was assigned, a real scientific explorer. Most of the sorts of things he turned up were intellectual challenges but ultimately dead ends, but that's science for you.

This one was different. He knew it; she knew it too. She dove into the problem the way she always did: straight ahead, completely focused, piecing together data on the visual workbench in front of her.

"Here."

She felt her elbow being jostled and looked away from the asteroid database to see Jeremy standing there, still looking rumpled, holding out a cup of coffee. She took it and sipped: he'd made sure to add just enough cream.

"Shouldn't you be getting some sleep?"

"I did. Four hours, then I read the sports net and got some breakfast."

She looked at the chrono, then back at Jeremy. *Oh.* She gestured to a seat nearby.

"So." He leaned back in his chair. "What have you turned up?"

"What makes you think I've turned anything up?"

He gestured at the holo, which was full of windows, pictures, and notes.

"There are fourteen asteroids at approximately the right orbit," she said. "Eight of them are almost exactly the correct orbital length. None are among the five hundred largest asteroids, so these are all just random rocks."

"Anything curious about any of them?"

"At first glance, no. But I think it's a case of the dog in the nighttime."

"More Sherlock Holmes references. What sort of curious affair are we looking at, Lu? In space no one can hear dogs not bark."

"Yeah. That. I was curious about the eight asteroids I found, and one of them—" she pointed at a small picture, enlarging it until it was a few hundred centimeters across "—this one, is the most unusual. It has no signature: it's not magnetic, it's not thermal, and—"

"And it's black."

"It's completely non-reflective. It was only discovered by occlusion: it passed in front of a larger object and, of course, it was of no interest to anyone, except..."

"Except?"

"Except that every 1100 days or so it gives off a small amount of heat. Fifty or sixty joules—like a single drop of sweat."

"And it happens right at the same time?"

"It's on a delay, a little short of an hour. Fifty-three minutes. Right about the time the earlier CBR alteration occurs."

Jeremy reached out to a console and operated a small calculator. "Nine hundred and seventy million kilometers. Sounds just about right. This little guy messes with the CBR and sends out a tiny bat fart, and at the speed of

light it reaches Sol, which smells it and decides not to blow the Solar System
to hell."

"...Yes. Basically, yes, though it makes as little sense as the idea that
Sol almost goes nova every 1100 days for two and a half seconds. There's
only one real explanation: this is some sort of technology. Alien
technology."

"Ooh. *Aliens.*"

"Do you have a better explanation?"

"No. Of course not. But what are we to make of this?"

"We need to tell someone. My guess is that we're going to have to go
take a look. Though I don't know to what end: in fact, as soon as this data
leaves this desk, it's going to get into the hands of people who are all about
taking a look. My biggest concern is..."

"They'll want to fiddle with the knobs."

"You have the best way of describing things," she said, sipping her
coffee. *Bat farts*, she thought.

* * *

One month after the day that the world did not come to an end, the UN
cruiser *Aldrin* was keeping station eight thousand kilometers from a small
asteroid that had neither a magnetic field nor a thermal signature: it was just
an irregular bit of black rock drifting through an asteroid field, a billion
kilometers from the Sun.

Luanne's fears had been partially justified. Once Dr. Armand Gregory,
director of the Solar Observatory, received word of the intermittent neutrino
emissions, he ran with it directly to UN Space Command which, in turn,
assigned a mission to *Aldrin* to investigate the asteroid that she had
identified. On the plus side, she and Jeremy had been permitted to
accompany the mission as civilian observers in exchange for keeping the
news off the net. Jeremy hadn't liked the compromise, but Luanne wanted
to see the asteroid close up and, with UNSC involved, this would be the
only way to do it.

Aldrin's astrographics section was very well-equipped, almost as
handsomely kitted out as the Solar Observatory. Luanne and Jeremy made
themselves at home, away from the bridge of *Aldrin,* where they had not
been invited.

On their second day aboard, Luanne was trying to make some accurate
measurements of the asteroid when she suddenly began to feel faint.

"Lu?"

Jeremy, more solicitous than usual, was suddenly by her side—she hadn't even noticed him come over.

"I'm all right," she said, trying to wave him off. But she *wasn't* all right: the room seemed blurry, as if she was viewing it through a polarized filter. It seemed too bright, the contrast on the image turned way down...

She turned and found herself standing in a completely featureless place, white in all directions. Directly in front of her was a cat—a regular house cat, but a meter and a half tall.

"What the hell...Jeremy?"

The cat changed to a horse, then just as abruptly to a large predatory bird: a condor, she thought, though she wasn't sure how she knew that. It went through a half dozen rapid changes and then became a human figure that looked like a cross between her Ph. D. advisor at MIT and Jeremy Gonzalez.

Then the cat that had become a horse that had become a human spoke to her in what she thought might be Chinese. Then it spent a few sentences in Hindi—which she'd heard a lot at MIT and at the Observatory—and then Spanish and then, at last, English.

"...sorry for contacting you in this direct fashion," the man was saying. "But your vessel is trying to probe our station, and it would be better to avoid misunderstanding."

"Your...station?"

"Yes," the man said. "Did I use the wrong word? I am trying to assimilate your language as we speak, but there seem to be too many exceptions and double meanings—"

"At least you're speaking English. How...? What...?"

"This is a mental contact," the man said. "Miss Jacoby? Or shall I address you as Ms., or as Luanne, or Lu, or..." he shrugged, holding his hands out in a gesture that was very much Jeremy.

"Why don't you go with Lu."

"Lu it is then. As I was saying, forgive me for this direct contact, but it seems clear that you have discovered our station, and we want to avoid any misunderstanding. Yours is a warlike people, and it would be disastrous if you attempted to disable or destroy it."

"I don't think that was planned," she said.

"Those commanding your vessel may have other ideas."

"I wouldn't know. I'm just a scientist."

"We know," the man answered. "Among our kind your profession is most highly honored. As the most intelligent mind aboard your vessel, we originally assumed that you were directing it, but it seems otherwise."

"How is it you're...?"

"Again," the man said, "forgive the intrusion. Your mind was scanned for language and context. This figure—" he gestured to himself "—is drawn from your memory."

"More or less."

"There is little time," he said. "I must try to explain our purpose to you in a way that makes sense."

"Little time? Aren't you...well, I mean, you've just done your job, haven't you? It's another whole trip around the Sun before you have to do anything else."

"Ah. I have not been clear. You have not been adequately prepared for this contact, Lu, and as such it might do permanent damage to you. In fact..."

The scene went opaque. The man continued to speak but Luanne couldn't understand what he was saying. She felt something being placed over her nose and mouth—

And suddenly the room came back into sharp focus. She was lying down, and someone had covered her face with some sort of breathing mask. The light was bright, and three people stood around her—a man was taking her pulse; another, a woman, unsealing Lu's blouse; and the third held the mask in place from behind her head.

She slapped the hand on her blouse away, grabbed the mask, and tossed it off. The three people stepped back.

"What in the hell is going on?" she tried to say, but her throat was dry and it came out as "ut hli gunk can?"

She tried to sit up, decided it was a bad idea, and let herself lie back down. Someone handed her a squeeze bottle and she took a long sip.

"Slowly," the woman said. "You've had a bit of a shock."

"You have no idea," Luanne managed after a moment. "I was talking..."

"You passed out, Lu," said a familiar voice. Jeremy came into view. He looked worried as hell. "You dropped right to the floor. For a few seconds I couldn't even feel your pulse. They moved you down here."

"How long have I—"

"Four hours."

"That's a full night's sleep at the Observatory," she said, and Jeremy gave her a tight smile. "What's going on topside?"

"I think the skipper is thinking about sending an EVA team."

"No!" She tried to sit up again and managed it, but the room was none too steady. "Tell him not to do that."

"I don't think ship captains take orders from astrophysicists, but why not?"

"I've...been talking to the inhabitants."

"You *what?*"

"I need to talk to the captain, Jeremy. I don't think anyone should set foot on that asteroid."

* * *

Aldrin's skipper was understandably skeptical.

"I realize that your profession requires a vivid imagination, Dr. Jacoby," he said. Everyone else in his ready room was standing; he had gallantly offered her a seat opposite his perfectly neat desk. "But I hesitate to base my decisions on it."

"I accept that, Captain Grier," Luanne said. "But please understand that scientists base their conclusions on empirical evidence—observation, data, known facts."

"Of course."

"*Of course*," Luanne repeated. "Meaning: I'm not making this up, I didn't dream it, and I think the danger is real."

"What danger, do you suppose?"

"I have no idea. I believe that there is no valid reason to risk your ship, or your personnel, before an adequate investigation has been made."

"I thought that was your job. Instead you had a bout of space sickness, and a very detailed dream based on your own fears, and—"

"It was *not* a dream," she said, and it was clear that Captain Aaron Grier was unaccustomed to having anyone interrupt him. He leaned forward and folded his hands in front of him on his desk. His stare was regulation intense.

Before he could continue, Jeremy cleared his throat. "Whatever it might have been, Captain, I believe that Dr. Jacoby brought it to your attention out of genuine concern as well as scientific curiosity. All of the evidence we've been able to derive so far suggests—but doesn't *conclude*, since we don't have enough of it—that this is an artificial construct, not a random bit of rock floating in the Belt.

"No nation on Earth, or any other inhabited planet in the Solar System, has the ability to build such an object. If for no other reason, caution is called for."

"As opposed to simply blowing the goddamned thing to splinters and be done with the threat."

"No!" Luanne said, then thought better of it.

"I suppose you could do that if you thought it the best course," Jeremy said. "But without a complete understanding of the target, isn't that more dangerous than just leaving it alone?"

"I have no idea, Dr. Gonzalez. Do you?"

"Without adequate study, sir, no, I don't. I assumed that we were out here to study the object, not blow it to splinters. At least not right away." He gave his best scientist smirk; Luanne's heart sank—she didn't think that was going to go over very well.

Grier turned his thousand-meter stare on Jeremy Gonzalez, but it did not seem to have the desired effect.

"How long do you think you'll need?"

"Twenty-four hours."

"Unacceptable."

"Really? Are we under some time constraint of which I'm not aware?"

"My orders are classified."

Jeremy sighed. "Well, sir, I can waste all of our time by playing twenty questions with you, or you can tell me the greatest amount of time your super-classified orders will give us to evaluate a likely alien object with unknown capabilities."

"Dr. Gonzalez—"

"Eight hours," Luanne said. "Give us eight hours."

Grier turned his head to look at her. She felt as if he was going to say something patronizing, or at least condescending, but Jeremy had clearly become the villain in the room, and the captain was more inclined to be charitable.

"Eight hours," he said. "Then I want a complete report on my desk. Is that clear?"

"Thank you, captain," Luanne said.

"Dismissed," he growled. She stood up. Jeremy pulled out his comp to check something. After a few seconds Grier looked up. "Are you still here?"

"Empirical evidence says yes," Jeremy said, and turned and left the room.

"Dr. Jacoby," Grier said. "Your colleague is—"

"Refreshingly honest?"

"Disturbingly civilian," the captain said. "But I'll overlook that if you deliver the report as ordered."

"As *requested*."

"As requested," Grier repeated, and then he swiveled his chair to look at his holo display. With nothing more to say, Luanne left the ready room.

* * *

"What do you expect to achieve in just eight hours, Lu?"

"I don't know." They were walking along the corridor back toward the sick bay, where *Aldrin*'s chief surgeon had demanded she return after speaking with the captain. "In a way, we already know everything we can learn without a close-up. There's only one thing we can manage in that amount of time."

"Which is?"

She stopped walking. "I have to make contact again. I was told that I wasn't properly prepared for it last time. I experienced maybe five minutes, but there must have been some other stuff going on before I was actually talking to the...to whatever I was talking to. Some of that will have already been done: they know I'm human, and not a cat or a bird or a fish or a horse, and they know my base language is English.

"I'm thinking that if I'm able to reach some sort of meditative state, it might be easier for them to reach me. I know a few breathing exercises, but maybe the doc can administer something to calm me—an anxiety-disorder medicine."

"And then you just go off and have a talk."

"Do you have a better plan?"

"I didn't have any plan at all. I just wanted Captain Grier to stop being a dick to you. He can be a dick to me instead."

"Thanks for that, but it wasn't necessary. I can take care of myself."

"Whatever. Still, I'm not convinced that *your* plan is the best one. But I don't have a better one. You're not going to do this alone, though."

"What does that mean?"

"At the very least, I'm going to stand by and monitor you."

"I don't need—"

"Those are my terms. Not that I'm dictating terms, though I apparently am. Sort of."

* * *

Aldrin's Chief Surgeon was not particularly thrilled with the idea, but consented at Luanne's insistence. She settled back onto a couch after taking a minimal dose of diazepam, closing her eyes and letting herself settle into quiet.

It took less time than she thought. There was a sudden change in the air pressure, as if someone had opened an airlock door. She opened her eyes to find herself in a room—actually, a sort of mock-up of a room, as if drawn by an artist who didn't have a particularly good eye for detail. Beyond the edges was the same white, featureless place she'd been before.

Facing her were six people, five of them looking essentially the same—Doctor Assad from MIT crossed with Jeremy Gonzalez.

The sixth was Jeremy himself.

"Hiya, Lu," he said. "Wow, this is really creepy."

"What's the meaning of this?" she asked the nearest Assad/Jeremy. "Been dipping into my memory again?"

"Dr. Gonzalez appears to have found a way to enter the conversation," he said. "We did not construct him—he is actually here."

"I decided to take the ride with you," Jeremy said. "Diazepam. And bourbon. Beats hell out of breathing exercises."

"Am I...are we...properly prepared for this contact?" she asked the alien.

"It seems so, though I am unconvinced regarding your colleague. Still, the flow of time is different here. There is something we want to show you." He made a slight gesture with his hand and white space and room vanished. They were hanging in space: it was enough to begin to induce vertigo. Nearby, she could see the inky black asteroid against the backdrop of another body that was lightly dappled by the distant sun.

"Wow," Jeremy said. "Best planetarium ever."

"The body in the center of your solar system has been in place for a few billion of your years," the alien said. "It was created at the time of the First Event, and has been slowly moving away from that place ever since—cooling and forming planets, burning its fuel. And all of that time it has called out to its brothers and sisters."

He gestured again, and she heard a distant keening sound—the cosmic background radiation, the same as Jeremy had played for her a month ago on the day the world didn't end.

"You're saying...you mean to say that the CBR is the sun *singing*?"

"It is all of the suns in the universe singing," he answered. "The sound you are hearing is a pale approximation of the true song of all of creation: here, elsewhere...everywhere. Your sun's contribution is but the merest fraction of the entire song, which has continued since the beginning of the universe.

"Sometimes a sun reaches its end, for one reason or another—it consumes all of its fuel, or it comes in close contact with another sun—and the sound changes. But sometimes, as a sun ages, it begins to lose its ability to participate in the great song of all creation."

"And it goes nova," Jeremy said quietly.

"If it cannot hear its brothers and sisters answering its call, that is exactly what it does. And that is why we are here. This asteroid—this station— hears the songs of the near neighbors, the ones to whom your sun sings its portion of the song. When we receive it, we re-transmit it to your sun which has grown, you might say, hard of hearing."

"That would be the tiny heat emission," Jeremy said. "And the first alteration to the CBR. So the sun is having...panic attacks?"

"Correct. And the second alteration occurs when your sun replies. Of late, it has begun to panic, as you say, when it thinks it cannot hear its brothers call. In due course it may be necessary to change our pattern to make sure that its panic does not consume it."

"You talk as if it's a living being—a sentient thing." Luanne looked at the alien standing in front of her. "Wait. That's *exactly* what you're saying, isn't it? The sun is alive. The sun is...wow."

"This is going to make one hell of a doctoral thesis for someone," Jeremy said. "I wonder if it's angry at us for lobbing spent fuel rods into it."

"It's hardly noticed," the alien said. "Your sun is not angry...it is merely lonely. Its song is a longing for the place it has left, and will never see again."

"And you make sure that it keeps in contact: that there's never radio silence."

"Our race has built these stations in many places. It is the mission of our species. Sometimes they fail; sometimes the sun is simply unstable. And, of course, everything ultimately dies. There is no preventing that. And when the native race achieves a certain level of capability, we turn the knowledge of the station over to it, to keep watch on its own sun. It is a step on the road to..."

The being didn't finish the sentence, making Lu—and Jeremy—wonder what that particular road in fact led to.

"So we've never noticed this station because we...weren't ready?"

"It is all but invisible to societies with primitive technology. Even when the capability to detect it exists, however, it requires a certain thought process." The alien smiled, not Jeremy's smirk, but Dr. Assad's knowing grin. "And, of course, it only happens when the person doing the thinking is strongly attached and deeply interested in the sun and its life cycle."

"The captain of the ship we're currently on has some sort of secret directive," Luanne said. "He might think your station is a threat and try to destroy it."

"That would be disastrous," the alien said. "Approximately three and a quarter years from now, when the time of the call comes, your sun would fail to hear the call from its near neighbor, and in despair would begin to become a nova."

"What do I tell him then?"

"Well," Jeremy said, "we could tell him the truth."

"He had enough trouble believing anything I said before. What could possibly make him believe me now?"

"You're not alone, Lu," Jeremy said. "Now this is a group hallucination."

* * *

Captain Grier received her in the large observation lounge in the forward part of *Aldrin*, below the bridge. The sky was full of stars, and the alien station hung in silhouette against an asteroid slightly further away.

He did not turn to face her when she entered, but remained standing with his hands clasped behind his back, looking out at the scene.

"I read your report, Dr. Jacoby. I read it through, then read it through again."

"And?"

"And I've decided to leave the asteroid alone."

Luanne felt very slightly faint but said, with as level a voice as she could manage, "I'm very glad to hear it."

Grier turned around. "I'm sure you are. But it's not for the reasons you offer—it's because I don't think this object posts any particular threat, whether or not I blast it out of existence. Your report...and your story...is interesting, but I simply don't believe a word of it."

"And yet you still don't intend to destroy the station," she said.

"My grandfather was a bit of an eccentric, Doctor," Grier said. "He collected antique toys. The one of which he was most proud was a pinball machine. Do you know what that is?"

"I have to confess I don't," she answered, wondering where this was going.

"A pinball machine is a device with a sort of inclined box. A spring-loaded chute sends a metal ball up a ramp and into the top of the incline, and it bounces off various surfaces, going from place to place. The player tries to keep it in play by flipping it back up. The ball is knocked around, colliding with obstacles as it travels. Great fun, I might note. Grampa let us play with it when we'd been particularly well-behaved.

"The asteroid belt, Dr. Jacoby, is like a pinball machine, except more complex, and while a pinball is fairly indestructible and the obstacles in the machine are resilient, everything out here—" he waved one arm toward the view behind him "—is bumpy and sharp-edged. Things are always coming in contact with each other, shearing off bits and cracking into pieces. That's been going on since the protoplanet in this orbit came apart eons ago.

"Thinking about that led me to wonder: if this station has been out here for a long time, how has it survived? How has it kept from colliding, malfunctioning, moving off its intended orbit? And if it has some capability to resist impacts or alter its course, why is it that *Aldrin*—or any ship from a puny culture like ours—poses any threat whatsoever? Why doesn't it just move out of the way or laugh at our weaponry?

"And I concluded that you've been convinced that they *are* threatened by us, but that they can still change the content of the cosmic background. It doesn't add up. Which means, Dr. Jacoby, that despite standing orders to contain or eliminate possible alien threats, I have decided that this simply isn't worth my time."

Luanne didn't know how to respond—either to Grier's logic or to his sneering tone—so she simply stood, silent, waiting for him to continue.

"I trust that you will be ready to debark at Mars Orbital in a few days. I plan for us to get underway immediately."

* * *

1059 days after the world did not come to an end, Luanne Jacoby was sitting at her console at the Solar Observatory, monitoring the CBE. Things had been significantly upgraded since the encounter—which had never been made public, by agreement with the defense establishment—and whether the improved gear was a result of the right word in the right place by Captain Grier or someone further up the line, she never knew. Dr. Gregory was out at Ganymede now; Luanne had remained at the "tanning salon," and was now its Director.

There had been talk of a stalled career. Certainly Jeremy, who knew just about as much about the event as she did, had wondered whether she should move on. There were better positions elsewhere in the System. He'd found one himself at the Tycho Deep Space Telescope Array, the recent replacement for the Copernicus (which had replaced the Webb, which had replaced Kepler...) and every time they spoke he told her how valuable she'd be there instead of at Solar.

He'd called early during her duty shift to see if she'd noticed anything. They'd refined the data on earlier instances to the point that they had it timed to within a minute. Like her, he was waiting for the CBE blips. She'd told him—at four minute delay each way, *damn that pesky speed of light*—that he was two hours early and should get back to work.

So here she was, the interference pattern of what she was told was the song of all of the stars in the universe spread out before her, the chrono running down toward the moment at which the station in the asteroid belt would echo what the Sun could no longer hear.

Thirty seconds—then fifteen—then the last countdown, like they used to do for space insertions, to zero.

And nothing. Radio silence.

She checked the equipment, scrolled the display backward to see if she'd missed it—no, there was no alteration in the pattern.

She tried not to panic, but her scientist's mind formulated a simple sentence: *everyone inside the orbit of Mars has about fifty-three minutes to live.*

"Grier," she said to no one in particular. "Grier, you stupid bastard. You destroyed the station anyway. I told you what it was, and you destroyed it anyway." But the last telemetry—captured a few weeks ago—showed it there, a tiny speck against the background of a nearby, larger rock.

Jeremy must know this too: sometime in the next four or five minutes there would probably be an incoming signal asking *what the hell*, or just to see whether she knew, too, and what could possibly be done.

Radio silence, she thought to herself.

She leaned back in her chair, looking up at the ceiling, and closed her eyes.

"Lu."

She opened her eyes to see the sketched room, the place she hadn't seen for three and a quarter years, the place that Grier told her was in her imagination.

Jeremy/Assad was sitting alone opposite her, smiling faintly.

"You didn't transmit," she said. "Why didn't you transmit?"

"We didn't need to," he answered. "You found us, Lu. Your civilization has learned what the station does, what it's for. Now you will do it yourselves."

"Alter the cosmic background radiation? How the hell do you expect me to do that—by force of will?"

"Essentially," Jeremy/Assad said, "yes. There is no one in your Solar System who is closer to the Sun than you are—not just physically, but emotionally. You care about your primary. Now you are to be given the opportunity, and the responsibility, to care *for* it as well. And with that achievement, we can at last go home."

Lu thought about it for a moment, then said, "In a little under an hour, the sun is going to blow all of the inner system to permanent hell, and you decide *now* to have me learn on the job? You could have picked any time in the last three years plus to visit and teach me what I need to know, and you wait until now?"

"Though this matter has never been far from your mind, Lu, it is only now that it is foremost. That activated our programming and caused us to contact you. And as for *learning* how to do what is necessary—there is nothing to learn. All you must do is listen."

"Listen—to the cosmic background."

"Yes."

"What if I don't hear it? What if I fail—what if I can't—"

"You will, and you can, and you will not fail." Jeremy/Assad smiled again. "Don't be afraid, Lu. Just listen."

There was a tightness in her chest that made it feel as if it was going to burst. She was shivering—but she was not paralyzed.

She took a deep breath—and listened.

* * *

11,000 days after the world didn't come to an end, there was a signal at Dr. Luanne Jacoby-Arnett's door. She waved at the air, the door irised, and a young woman stepped into the office.

"You sent for me?"

Astrid Gonzalez was the very image of her father; Luanne had noticed that as soon as she'd come on board. Jeremy's recommendation had brought her here, a brilliant twenty-seven-year-old astrophysicist who had done some very interesting work on the boundaries of the Sun's chromosphere. When she'd come aboard she seemed skeptical—Dr. Jacoby-Arnett wasn't the easiest person to work for, and at least in public, most of the staff was terrified of her.

But Astrid was bright, and interested in the Sun, and would do nicely.

"Yes," Luanne said. "Yes, I did. Please sit." She gestured to a floating chair; Astrid took it, a little tentatively—not many people were accorded the privilege of sitting when they were called to the boss's office.

"If you're asking about the status report—"

"No, Dr. Gonzalez. Nothing like that." She smiled; everyone knew *that* didn't happen very often. Boris Arnett, her husband, had been killed in some sort of accident in the transMartian asteroid belt six years ago, and no one at the Observatory was accounted as Dr. Jacoby-Arnett's friend.

Astrid knew that her father was in that category, though. She waited for the older woman to speak.

"There's an experience that your father and I had thirty-odd years ago," Luanne began. She could see Astrid's eyebrows go up. "Nothing like *that*," she said. "It has to do with *this*." She waved at the comp and a sound flooded the background, like a bad experimental band playing instruments through the ductwork.

"That sounds like the audio of the cosmic background radiation," Astrid said.

Smart girl, Luanne thought. "Now listen carefully." She pointed at the graphical representation on a holo she put up in the air between them. When the sound replay reached the place she pointed to, there was a slight alteration.

"What—"

"When we first heard it, your father and I asked what it was. I have an answer—and in order to explain, I will need you to listen..."

THE NIGHTSIDE
Julie Novakova

In some other reality, seeming so unreal and faraway now, Christmas time was approaching. It was snowing here.

Linus checked the updated weather feed. The snowfall had thickened recently due to the increased activity on the dayside. Here, hundreds of kilometers safely behind the terminator, the tiny flakes of condensed iron and titanium were drifting slowly to the ground. Barely a micron across, the metallic snow was invisible to human eyes. However, after millions of years of continuous fall, a fortune in purified ore had accumulated in these regions.

"All good here," reported Linus and closed the hatch of the tiny control room. "Moving to the last one."

The nuclear-powered furnaces stood tall and wide in the perpetual night, spawning one block of iron or titanium after another. A few also processed other metals: aluminum, chromium, nickel. Tireless trains transported the raw ores here from the mining sites.

Linus couldn't wait for his stroll outside to be over. Visual inspections of the machinery were largely outdated but they were still a mandatory part of the process for *what if* and *human resourcefulness* reasons.

"Going back," he announced and set off for the maintenance rail.

"Trying to break the inspection speed record again?" answered a playful voice.

Linus frowned. Miranda always teased him when it was his turn to go outside. She seemed to enjoy the landscape; he did not.

He would never admit it but it struck some chords buried deep in the human mind—the fear of dark and cold—and the chords in his brain seemed to be particularly well-developed. Not a good trait for someone stationed to remain at this place for a whole *year*. But it could have been worse, he reminded himself. Actually much, much worse. He should be grateful for this.

But he felt most grateful when the train released him next to the airlock. He couldn't wait to get out of the suit and spend as long as the scheduled water supply allowed in the shower.

When the cabin pressurized, Miranda appeared and helped him out of the suit. "Everything okay?"

"Yes. Everything in perfect working order." *We're useless here*, he added for himself.

"Great. Though from you, it sounds like a funeral speech," Miranda remarked.

Linus left that without reply. He felt streams of sweat running down his whole body. The thought of a shower sustained him.

It was getting worse every time. He would have thought he'd get used to it—but the more time he spent on the planet's surface, the more shaken each visit left him.

Five more months, he reminded himself. *Then it's over.*

He staggered out of the cabin and headed straight into the tiny bathroom.

"You're welcome," Miranda called after him, still putting the suit's components back in place.

"Sorry," he mumbled though she couldn't possibly hear that.

Just five more months. You can hold it.

He turned on the water and closed his eyes.

* * *

Miranda was sitting at the small table in the main room, chewing a dried protein stick. "Just in time for dinner," she grinned at him. "I left you the chicken-flavored one."

"Good," he said mechanically and sagged to a chair.

"We've got news from outside. The suckers were driven back behind the outer belt." Miranda produced a proud smile. "It'll be months at least until they're back in the gravity well—if they dare try it!"

Linus looked up full of hope. "So the inner belt is secure for mining?"

"Nope. The bloody clinkers left it full of their tech. The drones and traps are stupid but not stupid enough to allow us to mine the belt safely."

So we're not getting out of here soon. Linus suppressed a sigh. Without metal supply from the asteroid belt, this world was the best source even though its orbit extremely close to the sun made it highly inconvenient to extract metals here. It took enormous amounts of fuel to get out of this gravity well and good shielding to protect the ship.

Without knowing otherwise, he might imagine they were on a large moon or a small terrestrial planet somewhere normal. All they ever saw here above the cracked land was an ordinary night sky. Only when they occasionally needed to go near the terminator did the strangeness of this world become apparent.

Miranda interpreted his grim silence as a sign of doubt. "Hey, if they were still around, don't you think we'd see them? Even if they just flew by inertia, we've got enough probes around to notice a ship's thermal signature. They're gone."

Linus nodded apathetically. "What about other solar systems?"

"No news."

There hadn't been any for nearly three months now. It didn't necessarily mean trouble. It just meant that either no ship or probe of theirs made the Ozaki crossing into this system, or that the information wasn't intended for them.

Linus knew there were systems where new ships arrived only every four or five years. This system became one of the battlegrounds due to its location and the traffic was heavier, at least four scheduled Ozaki crossings there and away in a year. One of the ships was supposed to bring their replacements and take them back to civilization in five more months. He hoped it would arrive on time. The idea of being stuck here longer, for *years* in the worst case, made Linus shiver.

Without a word, he got up and took his food to his bunk.

* * *

Before we arrived, we learned that no crew really stuck to the planet's official catalog name. You couldn't miss the pattern in the nicknames: Hell, Hades, Gehenna, Furnace, Inferno. I personally liked The Oven. Sticking to this tradition of non-repeating names, we gave it our own: Tartarus.

Linus' hand stopped above the touchscreen. As if he could ever send home any of the letters he composed. All communication was restricted: assignment reports only. During the long hours of nothing, he'd mastered the art of writing letters, started playing with the composition and word choice, style, tone.

Miranda never understood this. *Why do you write home if you can't send it?* she kept asking. *And why the hell are you writing at all? I'd just do a recording.*

She appeared by his bunk door now. "Hey, Lin...You okay?"

"Of course I am. Just tired." Linus put down his notepad. He wasn't actually upset about how she'd teased him before—and he was certain she wasn't feeling sorry. That wasn't her style.

She smirked. "Too tired?"

"Not too much," he admitted. A different answer had crossed his mind, a desire to stay alone, but he ignored it. *I should be grateful for her. I'd go crazy if I'd been here on my own or with someone less like her.*

Miranda smiled and climbed inside the tiny space with him. Linus quickly put his notepad away.

Afterwards, she fell asleep in his bunk, making the confined space even more claustrophobic. But he couldn't bring himself to wake her up. Her warmth and regular breathing calmed him. He could imagine he was safely home and Miranda was his girlfriend, not a pragmatic crewmate who preferred him to a machine. He'd be sleeping in a real bed, after a day spent doing a real job, walking under a real sky—

Stop it! You're just making it worse. Get some sleep.

He shifted next to Miranda, trying not to think. Thinking was a sleep-killer. However, it was not easy to stop. His thoughts inevitably moved to the war.

They'd talked about it just two nights before. Miranda was resolute and straightforward as ever. Sometimes he wondered if there was anything that could leave her uncertain.

"What do you think is going on up there, right now?" he'd whispered in a careless moment. Miranda had sneered in the dim light of the bunk. "What do *you* think? They're probably shooting each other out of the skies."

"Yeah, but I mean...How does this end? And *when*?"

"We win, of course. We're better than the clinkers. And we've *got* to defeat them." Miranda had looked almost bored. *Why's he asking so stupid questions*, he could imagine her thinking. He'd felt impossibly alone despite her presence.

How can she be so sure? Linus had thought. *Am I a traitor because I have doubts?*

Just because he'd occasionally wondered whether the so-called clinkers were as dangerous and distorted as presented, was he becoming dangerous, too? Because he'd pondered whether their ideology of abandoning planet colonization was so bad in itself, was he betraying his side? No one else he knew seemed to think these things—or they were hiding it better. The bunk's ceiling seemed to be falling on Linus as he imagined long sleek ships accelerating beyond the point of survival of unenhanced human beings, painstakingly achieving near relativistic speeds in order to make the Ozaki crossing. Most carried soldiers and weapons instead of colonists these days. It could have been so great. Yet two factions of humanity—if the others were still human—fought throughout Orion's Arm, the end growing no nearer.

"Maybe someone should wipe us from the Galaxy," Linus whispered to himself. The thought was strangely soothing. He finally closed his eyes.

Maybe...if it wasn't for the fact that there's no one to do that—but ourselves.

There was no galactic club; no Federation; no wise, insanely old civilization guiding the wild youngsters; not even a common enemy, something to unite the forever quarreling humans.

Just a vast lonely emptiness.

Humans tried to fill it with their presence. And since they didn't have anyone else to define themselves against, some outgroup to make them think they were a unity, they just continued comparing themselves to other humans.

We needed an outside reference frame for our species, and found none. We still need it, desperately. At least an indication that we're not alone.

Some forms of conflict seemed inevitable under such conditions. But to think that a war of this scale would come...You'd need to be the most misanthropic pessimist to believe that, yet it had happened. What did that say about humanity?

Maybe he should have enlisted. Maybe he'd be dead by now and everyone would be better off. Maybe if everyone was dead...

He blinked, vaguely surprised at the direction his own thoughts had taken.

Maybe he should try to get some sleep after all.

* * *

When the alarm clock woke him up, Miranda was no longer there. Linus found her in the main cabin, sweet and breezy, watching some show and holding a cup of coffee. She was always up and about first, ahead of the station schedule; another of the many things he had no idea how she could manage.

"Morning. Care for a little forecast for today? We've got a large titanium oxide cloud 11 km above the terminator, so we can expect a lot of snow!"

Good that I don't have to go outside today, Linus thought and poured himself a cup.

His night ruminations now seemed ridiculous to him. Another day of routine chores might, with some luck, cure him of those. And then another, and another, until he got out of here safely.

He closed his eyes and imagined, for a sweet short moment, that he was home.

He almost didn't realize the sound of Miranda's show had stopped.

"Hey...one of the probes picked up something near the terminator," said Miranda slowly. She was staring at the screen, no longer occupied by the old comedy. "See it? Seems like a really big chunk of metal—pure, solid metal."

Linus skimmed through the data. A chill went through his veins. *No*, he stopped himself, *it's inconclusive. On the verge of the probe's sensor range. All kinds of weird effects happen to electronics here, especially by the terminator with all the metallic snow and radiation.*

"We've gotta confirm it," Miranda whispered.

"Agreed. Let's send a drone."

"No. We won't get anything useful. Hell, our machines have a hard time just mining there and coming back. The probe's got about the best sensors here and you see the results."

"You're not going to propose..."

"It's the only logical solution, Lin."

Linus felt his insides shrink. He knew where this was going. *I'm a software engineer, Lin. You're the scientist. I can back you up from here.*

"No," he said, hardly audible.

"Come on, Lin. You'll just take a rover and then a really short stroll. It's no more dangerous than walking on Earth's Moon."

It is. The gravity is higher here, help is farther away, we'll lose connection before I get there.

But she was right on one thing. One of them needed to go. He just had the bad luck of being more qualified.

* * *

Three hours later, Linus found himself driving to the terminator. So far, the rover more or less drove itself and he just sat there, looking out nervously. He was on the verge of panic.

I should have told her, admitted I'm more and more scared every time I go out. Sweat ran down Linus' forehead. *But she'd either laugh at me or get upset. And even if she offered to do all the future inspections herself, it wouldn't be fair.*

The rover was still able to receive transmissions from the station, even though they were distorted by the microscopic metal snowflakes. "I'm bored," he managed to say in a casual voice. "Tell me something before we lose connection."

"You can watch movies on your HUD. I've got work to do."

"Please."

A moment of silence. Linus almost thought he'd lost the signal before Miranda spoke again: "What do you wanna hear?"

"Anything. What about your family? You've barely spoken about them."

"Yeah, for a reason."

The pause was filled by silent crackling of white noise.

"I'm sorry," he said. "Then...anything else. Anything you like."

"I guess it's okay. I just get angry whenever I think about them. They were always fighting, mom and dad. Five minutes in the same room and they were at each other. But see, they belonged to one of those sects that don't believe in any kind of marital separation, so there was no escape. Sometimes I just wish they'd kill each other."

There was another pause. Linus couldn't think of any appropriate answer.

Miranda continued in a lighter tone: "I guess that wasn't the kind of thing you wanted to hear because you were bored, was it? Never mind. We can always..."

Linus didn't hear the rest. The static grew louder. He was on his own now.

They were always fighting. He'd never imagine such a background for Miranda—so joyful, decisive, reasonable. Maybe she was one of the lucky few who discovered this was the best survival strategy. Or maybe she just learned how to control it in adulthood, how to pretend—and maybe *become* the mask.

His thoughts shifted to his older sister Talia, always so proud and successful in everything. He could never compare. Oh, how he envied her at times. And what good did it do him? He stayed so distant, timid and low-esteemed. He never fought for anything.

And neither do I now, Linus thought bitterly, *hiding from the war in this hole because I conveniently majored in geology and started my doctorate when I was supposed to be enlisted. In someone's eyes, that made me suitable for work here.*

Suddenly, the drive came to a halt.

He checked the nav: too fragmented land ahead. The rover couldn't go any further. Linus groaned silently. He had no choice but to continue on foot.

Linus hesitantly emerged from the car and made a first step outside. Then another.

Eventually, he calmed himself enough to follow the instructions on his HUD. But all the same, he couldn't wait to disappear from here and never come back.

After all, this very planet is disappearing beneath us, he thought. So far, the erosion was slow, only the lightest particles freeing themselves from the grasp of Tartarus' gravity. But soon, from a geological time perspective, the planet would cross a threshold under which catastrophic mass loss would occur. In a mere hundred million years, there would be nothing left, not even poor remnants of the metallic core. It would be boiled and carried away, leaving a thin veil of metallic dust trailing behind the evaporating planet.

From up close, the land was heavily fractured, covered in deep cracks. The surface of Tartarus looked dead. But beneath it, furiously powerful convective cells spanned the entire depth of its mantle. In the substellar point, magma bubbles greater than man can imagine kept bursting, constantly staring at the face of Tartarus' sun.

No one had ever *seen* it. All craft orbiting Tartarus had an orbit permanently locking them to the nightside. None would withstand the heat of the dayside. Few land probes ventured behind the terminator. Even fewer survived and brought back data.

Heat almost prevented people from coming here. But once on the nightside's surface, humans were all right. It was the voyage that threatened to kill them every time.

Thick ablative shielding was barely capable of preventing approaching ships from overheating. Every vessel had to spend as little in the sunlight as possible—which meant a nearly straight trajectory from some point directly into or from a deep gravity well. Ridiculously high thrust was necessary— meaning that any humans would be exposed to extreme acceleration. Each time, their insides had to be filled with aerofoam. Linus hated the procedure even more than he hated spacewalks on Tartarus. Despite analgesics, he always felt like he was being stuffed alive.

Setting these painful memories aside, Linus walked further. He could almost see the sunset on the horizon. Just a few kilometers further and he'd enter the permanent twilight zone. After a couple of minutes, he'd bake.

Even further in the land of perpetual day, vast oceans of magma boiled and erupted.

Linus realized he had stopped for a moment, and made himself continue. He was safe here, after all. If he didn't take an incautious step and damage his suit, what could possibly happen to him? The suit was made to be very sturdy. His oxygen tanks were still almost full. He could survive here for a couple of days if necessary.

Fifty meters to chosen destination. Linus carefully avoided another small ridge. *Thirty meters.* He could *see* it now: just glimpses, most of it was still hidden behind the ridge, but it was enough to make out its rough shape. Linus stood there motionless, speechless, staring at the thing.

It was clearly artificial.

Linus finally collected himself and took a couple of more steps towards it.

What is it? It looks almost like some kind of a large scientific probe. There is its engine section. There might be an antenna, broken but still recognizable. But it's all so strange! And...beautiful. Doesn't look constructed for landing. Maybe it had crashed?

He had completely forgotten about everything else. Filled with curiosity and enthusiasm, he went closer.

* * *

Back in the rover, Linus finally heard a voice in his comm, almost obscured by static.

"Miranda!" he called out. "Can you hear me?"

"Y-yes...found?...ear me?"

"Barely. But if you can hear me—just wait for what I have to tell you!"

"...sn't a measurement error?"

"No! There was..." Linus fell silent for a second. "An alien spacecraft. I'm sure of it."

"...craft?...sure?"

"Yes. A probe of some kind! I've taken pictures. If only you could see it with your own eyes!" Had he ever felt so overwhelmed in his life? So happy and excited in this hellish place? "I couldn't get directly to it, the terrain was too hard, but I was so close! It looked like an orbiter, I guess. As soon as we report it, the command will surely send experts! It seemed so intact given the circumstances—we can investigate it and learn so much!"

Miranda was silent.

"But most important for me is," Linus said in a more quiet voice, "that we're not alone. Finally, proof. Even if they were long dead, they lived and fared among the stars at some point. Like us. And if they're truly all dead— isn't that a reminder that it can happen to us, too? Maybe...just maybe...it could end the war. Or at least let people realize how fragile it is, what we have. I don't want to set my hopes too high but I just see it this way. Is that stupid of me?"

After a pause, Miranda spoke: "Yes."

He hadn't expected this.

"No one will know for *decades*, Lin. If we report it, can you imagine command making the discovery public? It would stay concealed until it leaked someday. By then, we would have learned a lot—and used it to fight the rest of humanity. I hate to shatter your illusions, Lin, but that's exactly what they are."

"Then...what do you propose? We can't keep it hidden!"

"We can. It has been here all along and our machines only noticed it today by chance. If we keep our mouths shut, it can wait to be discovered until there's peace. That's what I propose."

"I..." Linus's voice trailed off. "No. Sorry. We just can't keep it to ourselves!"

Maybe he was still a hopeless idealist, despite the war, despite everything, but this was such an extraordinary discovery that he'd regard it nearly a sacrilege to stay silent. What if something happened to them and no one else ever found out? Such a horrible thought! Maybe he'd be disappointed. But he'd never decide otherwise.

He tried to explain to Miranda. She listened without interruption.

"So I won't persuade you to keep it quiet?"

"You won't."

Then, in a somewhat hoarse voice, she said: "I'm sorry."

"What?" Linus asked, uncomprehending.

The rover changed course. It deviated from the one plotted on Linus's HUD. He blinked. "Miranda...what's going on?"

"I'm sorry," she repeated. "But you're being so stubborn. You gave me no other option."

"*What* is happening?!"

"I...I don't consider *you* an enemy. I suppose I owe you an explanation. Even though it doesn't matter. Have you ever wondered about my previous life, Lin?"

He still didn't understand. A horrible feeling crept up his spine but his consciousness refused to accept it.

"Lin, I...I am the enemy."

No, no, not Miranda, this is not happening, this must be a dream, a nightmare.

"I'm really sorry."

She severed the connection. Linus tried to re-establish it, feverishly tapping the screen. "No, no," he kept whispering.

His eyes went wide as he saw the ridge in front of the rover.

* * *

His head hurt. He felt disoriented. What had happened?

Linus opened his eyes. Strange colors were flickering across his HUD. He had trouble making out the shapes.

Then he remembered.

Miranda? An enemy? That's not possible.

But what other explanation was there?

He heard his breath wheezing within the helmet.

He realized he had tears in his eyes. That's why he saw everything so blurred.

Miranda, a traitor. A sleeper agent. The enemy.

He tried to collect himself and blink away the tears. What did the signs say? Irreparable damage to the rover. Emergency supplies destroyed. Suit's systems working. No serious injuries. His body was aching but he managed to pull himself up and have a look around. The rover was badly damaged but its safety systems had protected him. The front window was breached and it took just a few blows with an emergency hammer to smash it. Linus climbed out into the vast cracked landscape.

He was nearly seventy kilometers from the base. Cold sweat ran down the back of his neck.

I can't do it, I can't.

If you don't, you die.

Something switched inside his head. He started climbing and walking. His HUD showed him the shortest route accessible for an ill-equipped human. He shut doubt, desperation, and oh so many questions out of his mind and just walked on.

He kept going like an automaton. His mind resembled the landscape right now: strange, fractured, but in the end, dull and empty.

Once, Linus made a wrong step and fell. He almost landed in a deep pit. The fall left him at the edge, staring into the darkness below. For a moment, he lay there unmoving, looking up at the endless cracked landscape extending to the horizon, everywhere around, and he thought how easy it would be to just lie down and wait peacefully until his oxygen ran out. He might even disable some controls and let the suit pump enough anesthetics into him so he'd never wake up again.

So easy.

You coward.

Linus raised his head and could almost make out his sister's contemptuous face in the nearest rock formation.

You always give up, don't you, little brother?

Linus collected himself, terrified by the train of thought he had followed just seconds ago. He checked the suit's systems. No further damage. He could continue. He *must*.

Get up now. Go. Faster. Move it! Imagine it's a race. You never wanted to finish last at school. You were never first, but you couldn't be last. So damned stubborn. You just couldn't bear it. No matter what Talia thought, you're too proud for that. So push hard, damn it.

He walked on. But the fragile equilibrium of his mind was unsettled by thoughts of his sister—she reminded him of Miranda.

After several turns of walking and resting, more than thirty hours later and exhausted to death, he came into visual distance of the first furnaces. The station was so close now!

Each of the furnaces had a small supply stack in case of emergency. Linus's oxygen could still last two more days but he didn't need to stray far from his route to re-fill it. He got everything he could: more water filters, protein drinks, additional power cells.

As he set out to walk again, a bright blast almost blinded him. If it wasn't for the helmet's adaptive glass, he likely would have been blinded.

He blinked away the dark spots and looked at the horizon in disbelief.

The station was gone.

His suit confirmed the sight: an explosion of some kind had destroyed the whole habitat. Nothing of use remained.

"How could you?" Linus whispered.

Miranda must have seen him coming; the furnace's sensors had detected him. To prevent him from reaching the station, she opted for killing herself. She couldn't have thought that she would survive without the base in the current situation, could she?

I'm dead. Whatever I do now, I die here.

He thought of the remains of the alien probe, the joy and wonder he had felt just yesterday. Miranda had succeeded. No one would know—maybe ever.

Unless I do something. What can *I still do?*

The explosion would have destroyed the main transmitter as well as the backup. Transmitters on the furnaces or rovers weren't strong enough to reach the relay stations in the system—not even the one on Tartarus's orbit.

The rocket.

The landing and launch site was a half day's journey from here. If he found an operational rover, he might get there much faster.

If he could send out a message from the rocket's transmitter, they'd come rescue him. In the emergency shelter at the site, he could survive maybe two weeks. More if he took all the remaining supplies with him.

If he could, he would leave the planet. But to survive the acceleration unharmed, he'd need to go through the pre-launch procedures which took place on the station.

A call out would suffice. He might live after all.

* * *

Linus managed to find a rover and stack in as many supplies as he could. When stopping at the last furnace on his way to the launch site, he noticed warning messages on the screen.

Oh no. She must have disabled cooling of the reactor. Probably not just here.

With so many fail-safes, it was next to impossible to sabotage a reactor. But so was blowing up the station. She must have been working on the systems the whole time. And while the reactors wouldn't explode, they would melt down and destroy the furnaces for good. Maybe that was her goal after all—to cut down all supply from Tartarus. Without it, allied forces in the system would be more vulnerable to an attack.

He could do nothing here. Better head for the launch site quickly.

He cut off all means of outside communication and drove the rover manually, following the path on his HUD. It required constant alertness but it consumed all of his attention, for which he was grateful. No time to think about what had happened. Until his concentration was broken by sudden crackling in his earphones. A call on the distress frequency; he couldn't disable that one.

Then a short silence, followed by a quiet voice: "Hello, Linus."

He froze.

He had to stop, otherwise he'd crash the rover. It was like hearing a voice from the dead.

"I can see you're going to the launch site. Linus, I'm sorry. You can't get away."

Little beads of sweat were running down his forehead. "Are you going to hijack this rover as well as the first one?"

"You took care to prevent that. However, I don't need to. It's impossible to get off this planet."

Don't listen to her. Go, quickly, before she catches up with you.

He drove as fast as he dared to. All the time, he was hearing Miranda's melancholic voice saying all was lost. He tried to pay no attention to it.

When he reached the launch site shortly thereafter, she was nowhere to be seen and had even stopped talking. He wasn't sure whether to regard that as a good or bad sign.

First of all, he tried to access the rocket's transmitter, hoping to send a message out. *Not responding.* He climbed into the cabin and, to his horror, found a record that the transmitter was accessed an hour ago for maintenance.

She was here!

She might still be here.

For a second, Linus was paralyzed. He was almost too afraid to turn, certain that he'd find her just behind himself, waiting.

He turned. The rest of the cabin was empty, the seal closed.

"So you thought of this, too," he said aloud. "You were thinking ahead, as always."

Should he attempt to leave the planet, even knowing the acceleration would likely cause him fatal injury?

What other choice do I have left?

Linus turned on the flight systems and checked their status. He almost didn't feel any more despair when the fuel indicator shone red; the aluminum cells were gone. Of course she'd taken care of all possibilities.

He leaned back in the chair. This was it. He was dead. He could stay here and wait. He might dial down his oxygen supply and slowly fall asleep. But suffocation and carbon dioxide poisoning were not a good death, he had heard. Yet again, what would be?

How would she die? Still out there, waiting, taking care I wouldn't escape.

He stood up and climbed back out of the rocket.

"Are you still listening in?" he said.

"I am." She sounded sorry. "Linus, give it up. Neither of us can get away."

"Says you," he interjected sharply.

"Do you really want to argue? Now? Fine. Go on and try. But it's a wasted effort."

"Why did you do it?!" he blasted, his anger returning.

Linus could almost imagine a faint sad smile as she said: "I made a choice. I was sent here to slow down and observe things. But when you reported that finding, I knew I had to make a quick choice. Sabotaging the entire complex, even at the cost of my life, had always been an option. What would you do if you were faced with this decision, only *clinkers* would obtain the discovery?"

"I'd never become—"

"A double agent? Even if you could help your side? Or are you too much of a coward for that?"

He was torn between feeling angry at her and just tired, very, impossibly tired.

"Are you going to end it?" he asked quietly.

"It already is ended, Lin. There's no way left to send out any signal or leave. We can only wait until the definitive end—or bring it closer. Do you want me to do that?"

He considered her question for a while. "No," he whispered then. "I'm not a coward."

"I know you aren't."

"And what are you, Miranda?"

"My people would call me a hero."

"Mine a traitor." After a pause, Linus asked: "Where are you?"

"Why? Are you going to try to kill me?"

"Would it matter now?"

She didn't answer him. Linus half expected she had stopped talking to him and he'd die here alone. He didn't really expect her to show herself.

Linus felt his throat dry as a space-suited silhouette appeared near him. He had to overcome the urge to run. What would be the point?

"I'm here," she said needlessly.

All of a sudden, he didn't know what to say. He had so many questions and couldn't bring himself to say aloud any of them.

Neither one spoke. They stood there for what could have been an eternity, before Miranda finally said: "Would you believe me if I told you again that I'm sorry?"

"I...don't know."

"What do you wish to hear? An explanation? I can give you that."

It's not like you're going to tell anyone else, she left unsaid.

Linus felt tired and beaten and to his own surprise, he found himself content with not knowing as well as hearing out Miranda—nothing mattered anymore. "Okay," he said quietly.

"Okay," she repeated hollowly. "Let's sit in the shelter. I could never bear this horrible land."

"You never said." *What is she trying to do?* he thought. *It's a trap, it must be. But what would she accomplish? We're both dead anyway.*

"Neither did you."

He reluctantly followed her, eager to find out what she had to say—and what she had planned, perhaps. There was no point in staying outside, alone, to die. They sat down in the dark room. Linus could hear Miranda's fast breathing. For a moment, he felt sorry for her and then realized the absurdity of his situation. If he still could, he would have laughed.

"I know I already asked you why," he said. "But still...I can't grasp what would make a person do what you've done. At least, before I die, I deserve an explanation, like you offered."

For a moment, he only heard silence on the channel. Then, abruptly, she spoke: "They're *right*. The clinkers, as you call them. We have no right to exploit and destroy other worlds. We had our chance on Earth and screwed up. Think of all the possible futures we might be extinguishing with every planet colonized, terraformed, or mined through and through! All the life forms that never will be, because of us. We're terribly selfish to usurp the space for ourselves. We wouldn't need any planet ever again if it wasn't for the stupid sense of power, of *ownership* of the worlds that don't belong to us."

That's why you keep killing people? Linus wanted to ask but stayed silent. He would let her talk, try to figure out whether she really wanted to explain herself to him, however absurd it was, or still had some hidden agenda.

Miranda took a deep breath. "Somehow, their views explained a lot. We're fighting for space even where there's plenty. We've been destroying things to remake them to our liking. If we ever really valued what we've got, worked with it instead of forever wanting more...And the war? Your people started it. We had no choice but to fight back.

"We all do what we have to do. I got augmented. Not much, not enough for people to notice. But enough so that I wouldn't need to set foot on any planet again in my life if not for my assignment here. I would live on a station built from scratch out of space debris, using resources not taken from a potentially habitable world which just didn't have the chance because of us. It takes so little to let go, start anew. We should have done that long ago."

Linus imagined her eyes as she continued. They were filled with tears. But her voice gave away no such traces. Maybe he was trying to picture her...more human. Or exactly the opposite?

"They gave me a new home. New life. But I needed to go back. Needed to be here exactly for *this* reason." Now, her voice trembled a little. "What would you make of the discovery? Weapons. You'd take apart every piece of ancient tech left there, try to turn it against us. And not just the old kind of weapon. You'd attack our very foundations. Say those who had made the probe had terraformed worlds themselves. That we're no different from our cosmic predecessors and our side must be subdued."

Would that really happen? Linus wondered. He came up with a yes. But still...

It sounded so menial now. So small. So what if a faction of humanity had said stop and started promoting their own ideology? At first, nothing had happened. At least he hoped so. Hoped they were given space to speak freely, just like anyone else. It was their fault they started sabotaging the terraforming programs, attacking the opposing officials. That was the truth, right? Miranda had become a victim of propaganda saying otherwise.

Or, maybe, she was planting propaganda in his head right now.

"Is that a lie, too, like everything else you ever said?" he said hoarsely.

"No. Do I have any reason to lie anymore?"

Linus wasn't exactly sure she *didn't*. In truth, he'd only partially listened to her tale. Another part of his mind was occupied with trying to come up with a way out. Maybe he had never fought for anything—until now. He was not going to die here if he had the slightest chance of getting out.

"I wish I had seen it," she interrupted the sudden silence.

"What?"

"The alien device. It must have been wonderful."

"It was," he said in a trembling voice, once again thinking of all that could have been and never would—because of her. "How could you do it? Despite all you said, even if it was the truth and you were right—how could the Miranda I knew do such a thing? What did you think when you decided to kill me and bury the discovery?"

"I told you already."

"It's not enough! *What* is enough to kill a friend?"

"You were a friend, Lin. But you were also the enemy."

He stared at her speechlessly, wishing to see through her faceplate, wishing to find a speck of guilt, of sorrow in that face. But he was sure he'd find none.

It didn't matter now. He was dead. No means of escape. The rocket's fuel cells were gone, probably destroyed. The furnaces, from where he could otherwise get refined aluminum for the rocket engine, gone. The product storage site, blown up with the station. There was no way he could find nanoflakes of pure aluminum anywhere—

Oh. Wait. Natural aluminum deposits. Not purified and homogenous enough, but does it matter if all I need is a chance of getting out of hell?

His heart started pounding. He was grateful for the suit which could not betray his expression. He could only hope Miranda didn't hear the change in his breathing.

How can I get past her? I should never have come here. I've been so stupid! She doesn't seem armed, but she's blocking my way out and is in better shape. And I've spent most of the last two days walking through hell.

Linus gave her a terrified glance. *And she's smart, there's no arguing that. She must have figured out this possibility but it was the only one she couldn't destroy, so instead she decided to guard me personally. I was such a fool!*

He accounted for the items strapped to his suit: a small hammer, a knife.

Would he be fast enough? Fierce enough?

Would he become a monster, too?

No, he wouldn't kill, he just wouldn't. He wasn't that person, never would be.

An image of the alien probe materialized before his eyes. *Not even for this? For everyone to know about this? For trying to stop the war with this?*

Before he could fully comprehend his own actions, his hand shot up, clenching the knife, and in the next heartbeat he was atop Miranda's suit, pointing the tip of his knife to the seam between her helmet and suit.

"Go on," she whispered in the comm. "Prove you've got the guts."

"I don't want to prove anything. I just want to live. Tell people about what we've found."

"Did you really mean what you said about the meaning of the discovery? That it would bring people together, make everyone reevaluate our conflicts?"

"Yes."

"I hope you are right."

He couldn't bring himself to use the knife. Maybe if he could tamper with her oxygen tanks, lower the supply to render her unconscious, but not to suffocate her –

Her arm shot up, knocked the knife out of his hand, and suddenly he was lying on his back, gasping and confused, and then Miranda held the knife and charged—

Fear. Move. Strike—again! Pain.

The next moment Linus remembered, he was panting heavily and looking at a suited figure lying motionless on the ground.

"Miranda?" he whispered.

He extended his hand hesitantly, almost afraid to touch that vaguely human-like shape. He pulled away a couple of times before he finally did.

It didn't move.

Linus gulped and gasped for air. As if all of a sudden the air in his helmet was replaced with water. He was drowning. He couldn't breathe at all.

"M-Miranda," he stuttered. He couldn't see, couldn't hear anything but his own desperate gasping. He had to overcome the sudden urge to take off his helmet.

No air outside. No air. No air.

Gradually, Linus managed to suppress the panic. But he was still unable to shift his gaze to Miranda's space suit again.

Hey, Lin, you're afraid of a damned corpse? Of the outside? Of dying? Is there anything that doesn't *frighten the shit out of you?* He could imagine her mocking voice.

The discovery. You have to pass on the knowledge. You have to live. Even if just long enough.

Linus tried to stand up. His legs could barely support him. For a moment, his stomach turned, but he managed to keep its contents in.

No time to lose. No time...

He moved like an automaton: staggered outside, found the rover, drove back toward the terminator. Now he finally knew how to use the endless measurements he'd done. For once in his life, he knew exactly what to do.

The largest and purest aluminum deposits were located not far behind the terminator, by the massive polygons of ridges and deep pits. Linus hoped the mining equipment still worked. He pinged the machines when he got close enough. Most of them answered.

There: Ores of aluminum flakes rich enough to propel hundreds of aluminum-LOX rockets. But not sufficiently purified. Not of standardized size. They might blow up the engine. A minor inconsistency in fuel burn and the reaction chamber starts to melt.

Linus felt indifferent. It wasn't as if he had any other choice.

After returning with the propellant, Linus recorded everything he could think of into his suit's memory and a couple of external storage devices— the probe's data and his own record of events. Very much like a suicide letter. Then...

I'm already dead if I don't do it. Nothing worse can happen to me now. Why wait? He activated the launch sequence.

Time seemed to slow down. In some other reality, seeming so unreal and faraway now, it was Christmas. Here in hell, it was snowing faintly.

The countdown sounded to him as his last seconds to live. He almost panicked and aborted the sequence but then thought of Miranda's mocking smile and stopped. Now he could only hear the count; tears had filled his eyes.

You're not really afraid of the dark, Lin, are you?

Then he was squeezed into the chair by rapid acceleration, his stomach knotted in the foolish hope that after all that had happened, against all the odds, *please, oh god, please*, he'd live.

THE FAMILIAR
David Farland

The snow on Europa fell with unnatural velocity, it seemed, unhampered by the thin atmosphere, creating white-out conditions. Water ejecting from an ice geyser had risen miles in the air and created enormous, intricate snowflakes as large as a man's palm. Ahead a sleek blue space cruiser appeared in outline through the mist and snow. It shifted slightly, sinking another two or three inches into the broken ice. As Armando approached, shrieks of terror and pain pierced his helmet's earphones: a woman's voice, and a child's.

"¡Vengo! ¡Vengo!" *I am coming,* he promised through his voice mic, and shoved forward, using his long experience in Europa's low gravity to close the distance in a few carefully balanced, leaping strides. He felt utterly helpless.

He recognized the logo that swirled between large, tinted windows even before he shone his helmet lights over the ship's blocky hull: a tourist cruiser from Jupiter's largest orbiting vacation station. It was sinking nose-first, plowed deeply enough into the patch of thin ice that the cockpit lay submerged. The passenger cabin tilted at a steep angle above the fractured floe.

Wealthy tourists with an inexperienced pilot, Armando thought. Then he remembered the geyser hurling water miles into the sky and sending it back as snow. It was the most spectacular sight on Europa. *Or maybe he violated the warnings about the unstable crust here. But if I can rescue them before the patrol comes, perhaps they will give me a reward. Maybe I will even make the newsfeeds.*

I need to hurry, before the ship sinks into the sea.

Shadowy movement behind one large window—and renewed screams—sent a chill like an icy paw down Armando's spine. *She could be my sweet Valeria, or my little Yazmin.*

"I am coming!" he called again in Spanish, then drew a deep breath and leaped for the aft hatch.

He had to tug twice at the emergency lever to release it. As he hurled the outer hatch away, sending it spinning across dull whiteness, a flashing red panel on the inner hatch snagged his eye: CABIN DEPRESSURIZED.

"No! No! Valeria!" he gasped, and threw one heavy sealing bolt and then the other. "Stand clear!" he shouted. Gripping the frame to anchor himself, he kicked the inner hatch open.

His helmet lights illuminated two pressure-suited figures—a woman clutching a young child—crouched and teetering on the back of a padded bench against one bulkhead, above the rising, frigid water. The woman stretched a hand to him and cried out. He didn't speak her tongue, but the terror in her plea spoke for itself.

Movement in the submerged area between the two benches tore his attention from her. A blunt head poked briefly from the water, scaly and lichen-gray, with a protruding lower jaw, like a small bulldog in armor plate. Crimson drooled from two-inch pointed teeth and swirled in the water around another pressure-suited adult floating face down.

A nightmare lunging from an opium dream.

Armando's eyes widened and his stomach twisted. "Ice demon!" The eel-like creatures haunted Europa's dark seas.

It leaped for him, craggy spine arching from the water. The child shrieked in his earphones. Armando winced, then sprang onto the opposite bench, but not before its whip of a tail lashed his leg. *If its teeth catch my pressure suit...*

Must find a machete. His gaze raked the cabin for something that would serve. The bulkhead between cockpit and passenger cabin sagged, wrenched loose in the crash, revealing a steel frame. *Is it sharp enough? Heavy enough? Can I tear it free?*

It is all I have.

The forward end of the cabin already lay under a meter of water. Three or four ice demons, averaging eight feet long and seven inches around, might be coiled in that space, he knew. Plated backs circled and splashed around his perch as he seized the bulkhead frame and tugged. He felt the rending protests through rubber-coated gloves rather than heard them.

As the frame tore loose, two ice demons reared like vipers, mouths agape. Armando drove the length of steel into the nearest one's gullet like a spear with such force it plunged out the back of the monster's skull. Its whole length thrashed for a long minute, splashing the cabin. Armando shook it off his improvised spear and searched the roiling water for the other.

When it erupted, twisting at him over the bobbing corpse, Armando brought his steel edge down on its broad head. The bony plate split, spattering him with crimson. It shook its head, lunged, snapped at him. Armando struck again across its neck. The head spun away, vanished with a splash, and its writhing, sinuous body swept blood-washed waves about the cabin.

Armando didn't relax for several moments. *Are there more?*

After his pulse slowed and his raking breaths subsided in his earphones—and no more ice demons raised their heads—he twisted toward the huddled woman and child.

Large, brown-black eyes gazed at him through bubble helmets. Armando noted olive-complexioned faces, scraped and bloodied, and disheveled, long hair, the woman's dyed dark red. *Latina?* He extended his hand. "We must go," he said in Spanish. "More ice demons will come. They're attracted to heat, and they can smell the blood."

Puzzlement creased the mother's forehead between a purple bruise and fine, penciled brows. She stared, cut lips slightly parted. *She doesn't understand me.*

"¿Hablas español?" Armando asked. "Speak English?"

She hesitated. "Little."

Her unfamiliar accent fell oddly on his ears. He repeated his warning slowly in English. "Understand?"

"Yes." She peered around him, at the pressure-suited body awash between their benches. "My husband..."

"I'm sorry," Armando said. "We cannot take him. Come." He eased the little girl from her arms, took her by the elbow, and steered her toward the aft hatch.

She half-turned to peer back once. Armando heard her moan, "Faisal..." followed by soft ululations through his helmet speakers as she followed, blinking quickly behind her faceplate.

Armando carried the child to solid ice beyond the shifting fractures, then returned to the hatch for the woman. "Hold onto me and jump hard," he said. "Jump to your child."

They bounced on landing. As Armando steadied her on her feet, a thermal reading appeared in his faceplate. He lifted his gaze to scan the near distance, found the source high on an ice shelf. Curiosity drew his brows together. *There is no life here on the surface. Nothing should be up there. But it is very close to my ship.*

He led the woman and child toward his ship first, had not taken thirty steps before he heard a tremendous crack. The ice rumbled beneath his feet and he turned to see the stranded ship sink beneath the ice.

He climbed toward the icy ridge ahead, reached his little freighter, brought out a first-aid kit and his spare sleeping bag from a battered compartment, and started fresh coffee in his old maker. "Take care of your injuries and rest," he told the woman. "I must check something, and then we will go."

He exited the hatch. This far from the ice geyser, there was little new snow. The plume of snow and ice was nearly a quarter of a mile away, but the planets frail winds had shifted high in the atmosphere, so that the snow was beginning to pick up outside the ship.

Armando picked his way through the broken ice and climbed about a hundred meters, clawing his way up a rugged cliff with his bulky gloves and boots. As he hauled himself onto an ice shelf, a glow caught his eye. He approached it warily, skin prickling at the nape of his neck.

The source of the thermal reading appeared to be a huge flower laid out on the ice. Nine petals—each about a meter long and half a meter wide, made of some heavy, bronze material—surrounded a dim, ghostly light. The patterns engraved into the petals were like nothing any human had ever made—strange designs that reminded Armando of printed circuits. The petals themselves must have been warm, for no snow had collected upon them, and the flakes of ice that touched them immediately turned to steam. The glowing light in the center looked almost human in shape. To Armando, with the quality of the artwork, the thing seemed...a relic, like an ancient statue of Jesus in a cathedral back in Colombia. It seemed somehow familiar. He dropped to his knees. *It must be an alien's shrine.*

The pallid light suddenly twisted like a flame in a wind and a pair of deep violet eyes gazed into his. Armando felt an electric jolt and the gaze seemed to penetrate into him, scrambling his thought. He recoiled, falling on his butt, and scrambled away, crossing himself. "Mother Mary, save me!"

The eyes vanished as if in a swirl of vapor. The apparition shivered and receded into the ground and Armando's heartbeat steadied a bit. He felt his forehead and squinted. He felt as if something had entered his head, had burrowed into his skull.

"I won't touch it, I won't touch it!" he vowed under his breath, continuing to back away. But somehow he felt that it had already touched him.

Those violet eyes, almond in shape, slanted, hung before his vision: alien eyes peering from the snow.

Trembling and suddenly weak, he picked his way down from the ice shelf. A thought occurred to him: mankind had visited hundreds of stars in the past century and found no sign of intelligent life. Armando was a poor man for a spacer. *If I report this, it might make some good money. Scientists will want to buy it.* The cost of fuel was tremendous, and this unexpected landing had put him in the red. If he did not make some money on this trip, somehow, he would go bankrupt. *Perhaps I can make enough money to be rich.* He was carried away by the excitement such a find would cause.

In his ship, he found the woman and child sharing sips of coffee from his old cup. Their pressure suits lay crumpled on the deck like empty chrysalises. The little girl, about five he guessed, sat sniffling on her mother's lap, her arm wrapped in gauze through which blood still oozed. Their clothing, obviously made of fine fabric and cut in the most current fashion, bespoke wealth. *Of course. Only the very wealthy can afford to tour the planets.*

"There is a religious colony nearby," Armando said as he shucked his own pressure suit. "They have a good hospital. I will take you there to receive care."

"Thank you." Without lifting her gaze to his, the woman asked through swollen lips, "Who are you? Where are you from?"

"I am Armando Mendoza, from Colombia." He arched an eyebrow. "And you?"

She hesitated, eyes still lowered. "Sabiya," she whispered. "We are from Saudi Arabia. We came to see the giant..." her brows creased as she searched for the word, "cryogeyser."

Ah, one of the extremely wealthy. And the Arab people are known for their hospitality. Perhaps she will help recover my losses.

Armando moved about the compact living space, securing compartments and hatches for launch. "And your daughter?"

"Hadil," Sabiya said.

"Ah! I have a daughter, too, Yazmin." He smiled at the child, who watched him through wide eyes. "She will be your size by now. And I have a son, Tomaso, who is nine. He was your size when I left home more than three years ago." He returned his attention to the woman. "You must come to the co-pilot seat and strap in now, so that we can leave."

He watched the fuel gauges of each engine closely through the crushing roar of launch. *So little fuel left.*

"Why did you leave your family?" Sabiya asked as the pressure lifted at last. "Why did you come here?"

Armando sighed. "I want to make a better life for my wife and children. I want to make enough money so that, when someone finds a new world to inhabit, I can take them to escape all the madness on Earth, all of the wars and plagues and shrinking resources. In my country there is a saying: 'Any shit that can happen, *will* happen.'" He gave his head a dismal shake.

"So I am an ice miner. Ice is the only source of water for the space colonies, and it pays better than what I can make on Earth. But I miss my family very much." *"Miss" is too weak of a word. I long for them. I ache for them.* His heart felt heavy in his chest.

They flew in silence, rising above Europa, its white expanse marred by striations of red—land beneath its frozen exterior. The woman and child fell asleep, but Armando stayed awake, his own eyes aching.

His brain hurt. It felt...overfull, like a coffeepot boiling over.

When the colony's station lights came into view, a cluster of faint twinkles like stars far ahead, the woman stirred a bit. Armando said, "I had just launched from Europa when I heard your shuttle's distress call and I went back. I was not planning to launch twice. It has burned so much fuel I will not be able to leave the colony station where I am taking you. My load of ice will not cover the cost to fill my tanks." He paused to give her a beseeching gaze. "Perhaps, out of gratitude for saving your life and your daughter's, you can give me a little money to refuel my ship?"

For the first time, the downcast dark eyes lifted to meet his. An indignant spark replaced pain and grief. "Virtue is its own reward, Mister Mendoza."

The words took his breath like a sharp blow. He stared in shock at her tone, but she twisted her head away.

Virtue does not feed a starving man, he thought.

Neither spoke again until they had docked, and Armando assisted Sabiya and Hadil down from the cockpit and into the hands of waiting medics. Then he said, "I hope you and your daughter will be well."

She didn't reply.

Glowering at the sting of it, Armando pivoted on his heel and strode through ringing passages to the administrator's offices. He knew the Chief of Security, a lanky man with a blond braid down his back.

"Olie," Armando said, "I have found something strange on Europa. It is an alien shrine, I think." He described its shape and the ghostly eyes, as well as its coordinates. "It could make you a lot of money as a tourist attraction."

Olie chuckled, and tapped his desk console. "Higgins, vector one of the rescue ships from the crash-site to the following coordinates, will you? My buddy Armando says he found an alien shrine or something up on the ice shelf."

"Roger, sir," Higgins replied. "Could it be related to the crash? Maybe caused it somehow?"

"Unknown," Olie said, and Armando came around the desk to watch the monitor over Olie's shoulder. Shortly, the ice shelf came into view. The surveyor dipped low, circled twice. There was no heat signature. Nothing metallic gleamed back.

Indeed, the ground was covered in new-fallen snow.

"Cryogeyser erupted pretty heavily a couple minutes ago," the pilot said. "Looks like it buried everything. Want me to land?"

Olie bit his lip. "Negative. You're too close to the geyser. We can go back and look when things calm down."

Armando knew what that meant. It might take years for the geyser to calm down, and by then the site might be buried beneath a hundred meters of ice—or more.

Olie shook his head. "Sorry, amigo."

Seated in a bustling dining hall minutes later, Armando felt like a jaguar in a shrinking cage, the bars drawing tight about him. He'd sold his ice, but did not have enough money to refuel. His only option was to sell his ship.

There will be enough to leave a little profit. Enough to start a new seed fund, maybe buy another ship—in twenty years, if all went well.

He ached to see his wife and children, but not as a failure. He did not want to be trapped.

He called his boss. "I need to go home, Mister Roades. I want to sell my ship."

The blocky face that scowled back through his pad had heavy jowls and close-cropped hair. "Contract's for five years, not three, Mendoza. You'll incur substantial penalties. Quit now and all I can give you for the ship is the price of the fuel home. Understand that?"

"I understand, sir. I need to go home *now*. But...a little something to show for three years, I beg, please."

When Mister Roades had vanished from his pad, Armando studied it morosely. *I wish I could send a video message to Valeria and tell her I am coming home. But it would cost too much.*

He departed the colony station a few hours later without a glance back. The newsfeed playing in the station's dining hall had clenched his insides into knots. Among the many tales of plagues and wars, it had shown a nuclear bomb exploding in Maracaibo, less than two hundred kilometers from his home. He imagined his family running for the shelters, like cockroaches trying to escape the light. *A warlord will send his army of cyborgs and killer robots across the border through the jungles. How soon until they reach Cartagena? Oh, my Valeria and little Yazmin and Tomaso! I hope I will reach you first.*

He kissed their smiling images in the holoplates, returned them carefully to the chest pocket of his flight suit, and slid into the cryogenic capsule for the journey home. *Six weeks is far too long a time.*

He dreamed of the ghostly face that had risen from among the artificial petals on the ice shelf, the great, deep-violet eyes that had met his. The image seemed to burrow deep into his skull, and he imagined it seeping through the Ecuadoran jungle.

* * *

He woke to soft chimes at his ears, yawned as he released the sleep capsule's seals, and climbed out with care. Cryogenic sleep always left him somewhat shaky.

A glance around from the foot of his ship's ramp confirmed his location. Huge letters on the docking bay's bulkheads declared L-5 TRENTON.

The two men who waited at the bay's pressure hatch—one a tall African, the other a blond Russian—smiled broadly when they saw him. *My old friends! But it has been so long that I do not remember their names.* Though mortified at the gap in his memory, Armando crossed to them at once, his arms flung wide in welcome. "Did Mister Roades send you to meet me?"

"Nyet." The Russian gave him a back-pounding bear hug and a booming laugh. "I've known you longer than your employment with Mister Roades. But, I am embarrassed to admit, I have forgotten your name."

"I feel better now." Armando grinned. "I'm Armando, Armando Mendoza. Please, both of you, remind me of your names?"

Flanked by Dmitri and Zawadi, Armando paced along a narrow passage to the offices of Roades Interplanetary Mining, LTD. Armando still felt confused. Once reminded of their names, he remembered his old friends...he just couldn't recall where they'd met. He tried to shrug it off. Cyrosleep could play weird tricks with a man. It would come back to him. "Tell me what has happened on Earth during the last six weeks," he begged. "I am very concerned for my family." Desperation to see them, to hold them tightly, curled his hands into fists.

"The warlords' troops have moved into Colombia now," Zawadi said in his rolling, melodious voice. "People are fleeing to the ports and sailing north. They are hiring fishing boats, and some have stolen rich men's yachts."

Armando's heart clenched.

In the Roades office, he traded his ship's registration codes for a payment chit. "Just enough to pay for a shuttle to the surface," he sighed to his friends. "But it doesn't matter. I will be relieved to see my wife and children."

Only one shuttle to Cartagena remained. Armando was the last of three passengers to board. His hands shook as he secured his seat harness, and his jaw ached from gritting his teeth. He couldn't pull his eyes from the darkened continent partially visible below. *Blessed Mother Mary*, he prayed, fingering the rosary in his pocket, *let us arrive before the invaders reach the city!*

The shuttle was on descent, skimming a hundred feet or so above the treetops on approach to Cartagena's spaceport, when an eye-searing flash ripped across the horizon. Armando blinked at afterimages even through the tinted pane, glimpsed a roiling, expanding mushroom cloud, as the shuttle yawed into a roll, then a tumble.

A rending shriek filled his ears as the falling machine sundered branches and stripped trunks. It struck on its side, hard enough to pop the aft passenger hatch, rocked briefly, then jumped with the force of an explosion.

Armando came to lying face down in dank jungle loam. Pain roused him: the throbbing ache of a broken nose, the heat of burns from shoulders to calves. Rolling onto his back, pressing his body to the damp earth, seemed to extinguish the searing, at least for the moment. He sat up gingerly, head swimming, and probed his face with one hand. His nose had swollen, his puffy eyes allowed only slits through which to see, and his hand came away slick with blood, which appeared black in the darkness.

Several yards beyond his feet, a twisted heap of wreckage still glowed red and orange as it smoldered. Charred, stripped trees leaned precariously over it. After a few moments, to let his head clear, Armando dragged himself to his feet, using a tree trunk for support, and discovered that one of his shoes was missing.

"It doesn't matter," he whispered through swollen lips, tasting blood on them. "I am alive to find my family. Thank you, Blessed Mother."

He limped through thinning trees, carrying his remaining shoe, to the outskirts of Cartagena. Fires lit the night sky to brilliant orange beyond crumbling buildings. *But the alleys will be dark enough to conceal me from soldiers.*

Two hours of picking his way through rubble brought him to an area he recognized, in spite of the destruction. His jaw tightened at the sight of a swinging street sign and the bullet-riddled façade of a familiar shop. *I am only a mile from home now. Please let them be there, please let them be safe!*

He stumbled on a broken slab of pavement as he ducked into the alley.

More exhausted than he'd realized until that moment, he thrust out a hand to catch himself, seized only a cindered support post. It crumbled at his grip, bringing down a sagging balcony with a crash.

Armando toppled clear, except for one foot. It twisted under the weight of a beam. He bit off his own yell when a shouted order echoed through the ruins.

He didn't stir, just lay listening to his heart pound far too quickly against the stones beneath him. *If I lie very still, maybe they will think I am a corpse and move on.*

In moments, bootfalls clattered at the alley's mouth. Lights, three or four of them, swept the area. Armando stared blankly between the boots, mouth lolling open a little, and held his breath. *If only they don't hear my heart!*

"That one is not dead," said a very familiar voice. "There are life signs on my scope."

"I can change that quickly enough." Armando heard the click of a weapon.

"No!" A third voice, also familiar, enough that Armando felt a name floating just beyond reach of his tongue. "I know him. Don't shoot!"

Two shapes dropped to their heels beside him, heads still in shadow, but hands lifted the beam off his foot and eased him onto his back. In the play of flashlights, Armando saw the young men's faces and he gasped. "I know you. I've known you since you were children. But...I bumped my head. I can't remember your names."

"It doesn't matter," one youth said. "You're hurt. We must take you to our leader."

The squad leader motioned toward two of his men. "Help him walk," he ordered, "one on each side, and be kind to him. This man was like a second father to me."

They took Armando's arms across their shoulders, raised him to his feet, and one of them murmured, "I remember you, too."

They brought him into the ancient walled part of the city, to the historic hotel that had been a mansion hundreds of years ago. Armando, as a poor man, had never been inside, but he had heard of its splendor.

"The General has his headquarters here, sir," the squad leader explained. "It is more secure, inside the wall."

Dismay dropped Armando's heart into his stomach as his two assistants guided him inside. The rumored splendor of the ancient mansion had succumbed to bombs and the heavy peppering of small-arms fire. The once-grand entry appeared no better than the rubble of the streets.

One of the young soldiers who knew him crept away through the shadow of a wide, but wrecked, arched doorway. The others remained about Armando, slipping him affectionate smiles as if he were a beloved uncle. In truth, Armando felt that each one of them might have been nephews he hadn't seen since they were infants.

Boots clattered on tile in an unseen passage and an officer appeared from the doorway through which the soldier had disappeared. Armando recognized the rank of captain on the man's shoulders, a man in his early thirties, about his own age, and he drew himself up between his two supporters.

The captain cast a scant glance at him. "The General will not see him. He is doubtless a spy. Take him to the swimming pool and prepare him to be executed."

Shock paled the young soldiers' faces, but Armando admired their discipline. Not one of them gasped. The squad leader said only, "Yes, sir," in a clipped tone.

They marched him through a short passage into a courtyard. *Are they going to drown me?* Armando wondered.

As they drew up to the pool he saw that it was empty. Empty but for bullet holes in the wall at the deep end, dark streaks down shattered tiles, and a stained puddle about the drain, not entirely washed away by the hose that lay tangled on the deck, like a malnourished constrictor from the Amazon.

His newfound nephews marched him, with no less gentleness, down the steps at the shallow end and up to the bullet-pocked wall. One bound his hands with a cord, his water-rimmed eyes relaying an apology he couldn't speak.

"Would you like a blindfold?" the youth asked.

Armando hesitated. Then: "No. I wish to look my executioners in their faces, though I would rather see my wife and children one more time."

The moon, veiled with curling smoke so it appeared russet in the sky, reached its zenith while they waited for the rifle squad. Then someone called the courtyard to attention. The young soldiers snapped to the same rigidity as the fractured statues set about the courtyard.

The general strode to the far end of the pool, peered down its length, drew his sidearm from its holster. "We have caught the elusive spy at last," he gloated. His voice carried across the courtyard, rang from balustrades once hung with graceful planters. "All of you will receive commendations for this."

Armando watched, unflinching, as the general sprang down the steps, paced down the pool's length. He stopped mere yards before Armando, so close that Armando saw his thumb release the safety, his finger slip into the trigger well. The general leveled the pistol between Armando's eyes and bared his teeth.

He loves this. He loves killing, Armando thought. *He has always loved killing.*

A breath of wind parted the smoky film. The moon broke through, a silver light upon the tableau. Armando saw the other's eyes dilate with recognition at the same moment he felt it himself. "Perfecto," he whispered.

He knew the man. The "battle model" chimera, to be correct. Knew about the genetic modifications that enhanced his strength, his speed, and enlarged his bones. Armando knew about his full-spectrum vision, his hearing as keen as a wolf's, and the more subtle changes that made him immune to neurotoxins and diseases.

In a flash, Armando remembered the general's history: how he had struggled to succeed, how he had become so discouraged, so broken from the lack of praise for doing well, that he had become a mercenary. He had taken payment for evil deeds and sought respect from people he should have found to be contemptible. Armando glimpsed all of it in those deep, black eyes. He murmured again, "Perfecto, what has happened to you, my friend?"

Generalissimo Perfecto Gonzalez wrenched upright from his shooting stance. His right arm sagged so that the pistol almost slipped from his grasp. Armando watched him fumble it into his holster, watched his face contort with shock and shame. "My brother?" he said. "My brother whom I have missed since..."

He cut the cords about Armando's wrists with the knife from his belt. "Go home," he said, his voice a rasp. "Go home and hug your wife and children."

* * *

The afternoon sun warmed Armando's back as he leaned on his hoe. The bean plants in his garden had blossomed early this year, and now the stalks bent under the weight of large, full pods.

Movement down the road caught his eye. He squinted to see who might be coming, deepening the laugh-lines acquired over many years. Perhaps it would be Yazmin and her husband, bringing their three children to hear him tell stories, or perhaps Tomaso, with his athletic sons, to help weed the bean field.

No matter who it was, Armando already knew them, as deeply and personally as he knew his own soul. And he loved them.

The figure who crested the rise cast a bulky silhouette against the cloudless blue sky. When Armando spotted the rocking gait, his heart leaped with joy in his chest. He swept off his straw hat and waved it above his head. "Perfecto, my brother!"

The former general returned a wide grin with a wave of his broad hand. "Armando! Come rest from your beans for a while and see what I have brought you."

They met at the road's verge, flung arms about each other to heartily clap each other's backs, before retiring to the shade and the bamboo chairs on Armando's front porch. "Cigars from Cuba," Perfecto said with near awe, and produced two from his shirt pocket. "The finest ever made. Too good not to share."

Usually they spoke of their families, of crops growing, or soccer teams and horse racing.

"There's a new resort on Europa," Perfecto said, "for those who enjoy winter sports." His eyes held a teasing glint.

"I have no desire to go see it," Armando replied. "I didn't want to go the first time. But I had little choice then." He shuddered at a dimming memory of poverty and pain, and fear for the safety of his family on war-torn Earth. Yazmin and Tomaso, they had no memory of the war at all.

That had been the last war, the one that ended thirty years ago in the heart of Cartagena. With that war had gone crime and violence and cruelty of all kinds. With its end had come a bond of intimacy and compassion so strong that Armando scarcely knew where his own soul ended and others' began.

That bond had spread to everyone, everyone on this world, and all others.

"But it is good that you went," Perfecto said. "Good for the whole world. Everyone on Earth knows that you are the one who found the artifact.

"Perhaps it was an alien's shrine, after all," Perfecto continued, "but they left it there for us. They knew that, as a species, humans weren't yet ready to go into space. We were too aggressive; we needed to become better."

Armando raked his cigar-free hand through his silver, shaggy hair. "We are better now."

But restlessness stirred in his soul. *Peace and enough for all has brought too much...contentment. We have become complacent. There are no new Mozarts or Einsteins or Rembrandts in an age when such gifts should flourish.*

That was why, in secret, he had begun to study advanced mathematics. He controlled a wry smile at the thought. *And I seem to have a gift for it.*

At his side, Perfecto nodded. "Yes, we are getting better. They will come to meet us soon. Or maybe we will go to find them."

"And when we see them," Armando said, "whether they look like dragonflies or cuttlefish, or white gassy entities, they will seem familiar."

ME AND ALICE
Angela Penrose

Back in 1972, when I was nine years old, June twenty-sixth was the day my toad Alice died. I've always remembered that day, and so has Alice; I give her a fat cricket for dinner every year, to kind of celebrate her getting over it.

Alice was my dad's toad first, and she was twenty-five when he gave her to me. He said she was pretty old for a toad, and that she probably wouldn't live very much longer. I remember overhearing Mom and Dad arguing about it, when I was supposed to be in bed. Mom said it was cruel to give me a pet that was going to die soon. Dad said that that was the best kind of pet to give a six-year-old, and better to have me accidentally kill a toad than the puppy I'd been wanting.

I was pretty mad at him for saying that. I mean, he must not have loved Alice very much, if he thought I'd kill her. I hadn't really liked her much myself at first—you can't play ball with a toad, after all—but the thought that my dad didn't care if she died made me promise myself that I'd take the best care of her and show him.

Three years later, though, she was really old, and she finally stopped eating. I tried feeding her worms and beetles and some big ants, and I caught her some spiders even though I was kind of afraid of spiders, but she wasn't hungry. On the twenty-sixth, that Monday, I woke up and found her still in her den in her tank, a plank laid over a big rock to make a little hide-out underneath. She usually came out in the morning to wait for her breakfast.

That morning she was still under the plank, though. I picked her up and petted her some, carefully because toads are squishy and you don't want to be too rough with them, but she didn't move or croak. I put her back into her tank and gave her a beetle, but she didn't even try to catch it. She just sat there by the glass where I'd put her, sort of staring at nothing.

I watched her for a little while, trying not to think about her dying. I knew she was going to, but I didn't want her to and I kept hoping she'd get better. Maybe she was just sick—I never felt like eating either, if I had stomach flu or something. It could've been just a twenty-four-hour bug and she'd be all right the next day. I hoped so, anyway.

Mom called me down to breakfast. I was kind of glad to leave; I felt like I should stay with Alice, but I didn't really want to. Watching her just sit there and thinking about how old she was made me sad, and you're not supposed to cry when you're nine.

Mom talked barn business, about lessons and turn-out and the farrier coming that morning. Dad said he and Rob, the man who worked for us, were going to go replace fence posts in the east pasture that day. It was all boring stuff and I didn't really listen; they hurried to eat and then left to go work.

I finished my eggs and toast, did the dishes, watched some cartoons on TV, then headed outside to watch the horses for a while. Mom eventually chased me away—she said if I didn't get out of her hair she was going to stake me out for the coyotes—and I ended up climbing the path to Carver's Grove.

Dr. Valdez and her students were up there digging, looking for an old Indian settlement, and I went to watch sometimes. Mom and Dad had taken me up to Mesa Verde the summer before; that was pretty cool, sort of like a whole bunch of apartments built out of clay bricks in the side of a canyon. Dr. Valdez said this wouldn't be the same.

She thought there'd be a campground the same band would've used every year, someplace older than Mesa Verde, like 12,000 years or more. When she'd come in February to talk to Mom and Dad about getting permission to dig, she'd brought some pictures taken from a plane that showed there'd been a stream running through where Carver's Grove was now.

That's what she said, anyway. I got a look at the picture, and even when she ran her finger over the place where she said the stream had been, I couldn't see anything that looked like water.

Dad took her up walking by the grove, though, with me tagging along, and she found rocks she said had been split in camp fires. She was pretty excited, and since Carver's Grove is a sort of a plateau with a bunch of rocks and sandy dirt and not even many trees anymore, nothing we used for anything, he said she could dig there if she wanted.

* * *

Dr. Valdez had come up with her team, mostly students, about a week before I got out of school. I'd gone up before, to watch them set up and dig and all. At first I thought it'd be fun, but it was actually pretty boring. They did lots of measuring and drawing and wrote stuff down and took pictures, even when nothing was happening. And when they finally started digging, they dug really slow. I stayed out of the way so no one yelled at me to go away, but I didn't go up there very often.

That morning, though, I was trying to avoid thinking about Alice, so I climbed up to the dig. Dennis, a young colored man who was Dr. Valdez's main assistant, said, "Hey, Chris." He gave me a Space Food Stick out of a box that seemed to be his breakfast.

"What are you going to do today?" I asked. I was hoping it might be something interesting that'd take my mind off Alice sitting by herself in my room.

"I'm going to be digging on the outside curve of a bend in the stream," he said. "We think the camp site was upstream of that, but items sometimes get washed downstream and get hung up in a bend. That's where I'm looking."

"How do you know where a stream was twelve thousand years ago? I can't see anything that looks like a stream bed, even a dry one."

Dennis peeled open a stick and said, "It's easier if you look at the aerial photos. It's hard to see from down on the ground."

"I looked at the photos when Dr. Valdez brought them to my house. I didn't see a stream then either."

"Huh." Dennis thought for a bit while chewing, then swallowed and said, "We found something last week that's more obvious. It's not where we're working, but you'll be able to see it. Come on." He emptied the box and stuffed the rest of the wrapped sticks in his pocket, then headed off through the brush. I followed along. I didn't figure it'd be any more clear than the pictures, since everyone seemed to think those were obvious too, but it was still better than looking after Alice.

We hiked over to the far side of the plateau, then down a narrow, steep path along the slope. Dennis stopped about halfway down and pointed at the face of the cliff, right next to where we were standing.

"There, see?" He moved his hand in a big, wide oval.

I looked and saw something like a blotch. I took a step back—and yes, I was careful of the edge; just because I was nine doesn't mean I was stupid—and looked from a little farther away.

It looked like a knot in a plank. The lines the different colored rocks made in the cliff went mostly straight, a little tilted but still mostly straight, except for where Dennis was pointing. There was a splotch there, a wide, shallow place that distorted all the lines around it, kind of like a flattened oval.

"That's where the stream was," Dennis said. "When it was flowing, it cut down through the layers." He moved his finger along the bottom curve, stopping to point out each layer the splotch penetrated.

I tried to picture in my mind the water rushing through, like in a pipe, but washing away the dirt and rocks as it went. It made sense.

There was about twenty feet of dirt between the top of the stream-knothole and the top of the cliff. That was a lot of digging, especially since I'd seen the shovels they were using and they were really small. So the stream—the fossil of the stream—was pretty far underground.

"How come you're not digging here?" I asked. "You could dig right into the stream instead of having to get all that dirt and rock and stuff off a teaspoon at a time."

Dennis grinned and said, "We'd love to. This isn't where the camp was, though. Dr. Valdez found signs of human habitation back where we're digging. If it'd been here, we'd be here."

"But there could still be stuff here, right? You said stuff gets washed down the stream and then stuck." There were different kinds of rocks and stuff there in the cliff face. It was kind of smooth and regular in most places, but the knothole looked jumbled up. I was thinking about finding some neat stuff in there, maybe arrowheads or bones or something. Petrified bones, maybe.

"Sure, there could. You never know, right?"

I figured he was lying to make me feel good 'cause I was a kid, like a lot of grown-ups do. If he really thought there might be cool stuff here, then he'd be digging here himself. But he *was* digging in the stream himself, just closer to where they thought the Indian camp had been, so stuff *did* wash downstream.

"Can I keep anything neat that I find?"

Dennis ruffled my hair and said, "How about if you show it to me first?"

I hate when people ruffle my hair, but I didn't want the "maybe" to turn into a "no," so I said okay.

* * *

I got a trowel from home and went back to the cliff. I didn't have a sifter-box like they had at the dig, so I just looked real carefully at the pebbles and stuff as I chipped them out. There were some triangular rocks that I thought were arrowheads at first, but they weren't, or at least they didn't look like arrowheads when I cleaned the dirt off and looked closer.

The students at the dig always went really slow, but I got sort of impatient after a while and started gouging stuff out faster and faster. The rock wasn't all that hard—not like concrete or anything, more like really hard dirt with rocks in it—so around the time I figured it was getting close to lunch, I had a hole in the cliff about a yard wide and as deep as my elbow.

I thought I'd keep going for a few more minutes before heading back to get a sandwich, when the tip of my trowel clacked against something that didn't sound like a rock.

Finding something that soon was pretty incredible. I remembered about not damaging things, 'cause Dennis had told me pottery and stuff are pretty breakable, so I went back to digging slow and tried to widen the deep part of the hole more. I found an edge and dug around it as well as I could, following the border between the sandstone and the...bone? clay? Whatever the thing was made of.

By the time I had most of it dug out, enough to see the shape all the way around, I was even more confused about what it could be. It was stuck in the rock a little diagonally, with a sort of cylinder shape, short and fat, sticking out. After some more digging, I saw that the cylinder part widened out farther in and had loops, four, like a four-leaf clover. It took a while to dig those out; the curved parts were sort of skinny, about as big around as my thumb, so I was afraid I'd break one of them while I dug and chipped around it. I did hit them a few times with the edge of the trowel, by accident, but the stuff the thing was made of didn't break or even crack.

And as I got the dirt cleaned off of it, the stuff was looking like plastic.

Weird, right? I knew they didn't have plastic 12,000 years ago, so while I headed home for lunch I was trying to figure out how the thing had gotten there, whatever it was. Maybe someone lost it and it got covered up with dirt? But if someone had dropped it, on the trail or off the top of the plateau, then it would've fallen all the way down to the bottom, or at least onto the level of the path, not gotten stuck there in the wall. Definitely not a couple of feet *inside* the wall.

If you left it alone, dirt would build up a little at a time—from wind blowing stuff around, and stuff falling down as the cliff crumbled—but I was pretty sure it would've taken a really long time for two *feet* of dirt to cover the thing, even if I figured it'd fallen onto a ledge or something above the path. I thought about how long it would've taken for that much dirt to pile up, and how long ago they invented plastic. I wasn't sure, but I didn't think they matched up, not even close.

Mom wasn't around by the time I got back to the house. It was almost one—late enough that she'd probably eaten and gone back to the barn. Dad was there, though, and almost done with his sandwich. His shirt was wet and dirty, and his hair was all plastered to his head, like he'd hosed himself down before coming in. He pointed at a plate on the counter with a napkin over it; it had a ham and cheese sandwich, an apple and a couple of peanut butter cookies. I said thanks and sat down to eat as fast as I could.

My mom would've nagged me to slow down, but Dad just rolled his eyes, finished his last cookie, and headed out before I could tell him about the thing I'd found.

When I was done, I ran up and checked on Alice. She'd moved a little, a few inches away to the other side of the big rock, but she didn't move while I watched. I stroked her head with one finger, nice and gentle 'cause she was sick, but she still didn't move. I could see her throat pulsing a little, so I knew she was breathing, but that was it.

I kept her company for a few more minutes, but not being able to play with her or do anything to help her made it really frustrating. Finally I told her I'd be back in a while, then I left her alone.

The rest of the afternoon I was on the cliff trail, digging out the plastic thing a tiny bit at a time. The sun had moved and there wasn't any more shade. I was hot and sweaty and wished I'd brought a canteen, but not enough to go back for one.

Past the clover-things, the cylinder spread out like the end of a trumpet, only not quite as wide. There was a ring of colored things, flat disks about the size of my little fingernail, around the edge of the flared part. They were pretty dusty, but when I rubbed them clean I could see that most of them were blue, but two right next to each other were yellow.

They looked like decorations; they didn't stick out like buttons or light up like lights or anything. I figured maybe there was something on the other side that'd make it make sense, so I kept digging around the edge.

By the time I got the thing out, it was pretty close to dinner time. I pulled it out of the hole, careful not to break it, and fiddled around with it, looking at it from every side. There was nothing on the wide side of the flare to show why the colored disks weren't even; the other side was just plain, flat plastic. If it'd ever looked like a trumpet then someone had filled in the inside and flattened it out without even leaving a seam. I played with the loops, trying to see if they'd click or twist or anything, but they wouldn't move at all no matter what I tried.

I was looking at the flat round end, feeling around to see if I could find any little bumps or cracks with my fingers, when the flat part suddenly flashed. I yelled and dropped it, not really scared but just a little startled, you know? When I picked it up and looked at it all over to see if I'd cracked it anywhere, I saw that there was only one yellow disk on the other side of the flare.

Maybe it was a flashlight? Or no, the light had only lasted like half a second. Maybe it was like a photographer's flash? A photographer could've come here some time—a long time ago, before I was born—to take pictures of the plateau and all, and dropped one of their lights. I'd seen old fashioned cameras in movies, and knew they had separate flashes that the photographer held in one hand, away from the camera, so that made sense.

The sun and the shadows told me I'd better get home fast if I didn't want to get yelled at, so I ran, with the trowel in one hand and the flash-thing in the other.

* * *

After dinner, I went up to see Alice again. I found her sitting really still in her tank, in the same place she'd been at lunchtime, with her legs pulled in close to her body. When I picked her up, she was colder than usual and kind of hard. I called Dad to come see, hoping she was just asleep or something and trying hard not to cry.

Dad came up and poked her with a finger, then put his palm on her back for a few seconds. He said she was dead.

She must've died that afternoon, while I was digging in the cliff and having fun. I knew I couldn't have done anything, that even a vet probably couldn't have done anything for a toad that old, but I felt awful about it anyway, like I should've been there with her. It wasn't like I hadn't known she was sick, or just getting old, or whatever it'd been.

Dad went to get some newspaper to wrap Alice in. He was going to throw her in the garbage, but I got mad and might've yelled some, and said I wanted to bury her. He yelled back at me for mouthing off, but Mom came and calmed him down, and said I was understandably upset. She'd never really liked Alice—she wasn't afraid of her or anything, she was just more into horses than toads—but she knew about pets.

Mom brought me a square box, a nice one that'd come with a fancy ashtray she'd gotten for Christmas, and some tissue paper. I made a kind of a nest in the box with the crinkly paper and put Alice into it. I put the lid under the box to carry them together, like I'd seen Mom do sometimes. I wanted to be able to see Alice while I did the funeral; I could put the lid on right before I buried her.

I remember I handled her really careful, even though I knew nothing could hurt her anymore.

We went out to the yard, me and Mom and even Dad, although he was sort of glaring at me like he was still a little mad. I got the trowel from where I'd left it on the porch, and the flash-thing was there next to it, so I took that too. If I was right about the one yellow disk meaning there was only one more flash in it, I figured there wasn't any better reason to use it up than Alice's funeral.

While we walked down to the far side of the yard, to a patch that never got dug up because it was by an oak tree and nothing else would grow there anyway, Mom asked what I had. I said it was a flashlight I'd found up by the grove.

"Did you ask Dr. Valdez's permission to take it?" she asked. Her voice sounded a little worried, like she was thinking about getting mad.

I said, "No, but it wasn't in the same place she's digging. It was over by the cliff, in a spot Dennis showed me."

Mom glanced at Dad, who said, "That's not an Indian artifact. The natives didn't make flashlights, not thousands of years ago. It's probably just a piece of trash someone lost up there.

Mom nodded kind of slow, then said to me, "Well, we gave her permission to dig wherever she wanted up there. At least show it to her tomorrow."

I nodded, too, and said, "Dennis told me to show him anything I found, and I promised I would. I didn't today 'cause it was time for dinner. I'll take it over tomorrow."

That was good enough and we got on with Alice's funeral. I dug a hole big enough for the box, a couple of steps away from the oak. I said the Lord's Prayer, 'cause that was the only one I could think of right then. It was like my brain had emptied. Mom started talking and said some things about how Alice had been a member of the family, and how she'd been a companion to my dad when he was a kid, and to me, and how we'd all miss her. That was pretty nice of her, considering she'd never really paid much attention to Alice when she was alive. I think she just wanted to make me feel better.

I put the box into the hole, then picked up the flashlight thing and aimed it down at Alice. I said something about how Alice would be going to the light in Heaven, where God would look out for her forever and never forget about her or leave her alone, and then touched the yellow disk. It flashed really bright, and I heard Mom and Dad shift suddenly, like they were startled, but they didn't say anything.

The disks were all blue. I pressed them all just to check, but nothing happened. That was okay; I had a better flashlight in my room. I thought about burying that one with Alice, but I'd promised to show it to Dennis, so I put it down out of the way, put the lid on the box and picked up the trowel.

I'd just pushed some dirt down into the hole when the lid popped up off the box and I heard Alice croaking. I screamed 'cause I was really surprised, and maybe a little scared because Alice was supposed to be dead, or I'd thought she was dead and it was like a horror movie or something, like she was a vampire frog rising after death.

Mom and Dad had yelled too, and that made me feel a little better. Mom moved the box lid and picked up Alice. She was squirming and moving and definitely alive.

Mom said Dad must've been wrong about her being dead. He said anyone would've thought that, she was stiff and cold like she was dead and how was he supposed to know? He couldn't really argue much when she was hopping around, though, so I just left them talking about it. I took Alice and ran into the house and upstairs and fed her, since she hadn't eaten in so long. She ate three crickets and a bunch of ants, and I petted her with one finger and told her she was the best toad in the world.

* * *

The next day I showed the flash-thing to Dennis. Dr. Valdez was with him, but she just glanced at it and then went away to order the students around.

Dennis went with me to the cliff and I showed him where I'd dug it out. I'd been careful enough that you could put the thing back into the gap it came out of and see that it was the right shape and all. He stared at the hole for a long time, then the flash-thing, then the hole again. He frowned like he was mad about something, but he wasn't mad at *me,* or at least he didn't yell or anything.

I said he could keep the flash-thing if he wanted. Since it didn't work anymore, I didn't feel really bad when he said thank you and took it. He went back to his digging in the stream bed and I went back to the house.

I took Alice out onto the lawn and played with her all day, helping her catch bugs and building mazes out of old planks for her.

* * *

When I got older I did a few internet searches to see whether Dr. Valdez, or Dennis—who later became Dr. Johnson—had ever published anything that mentioned the flash-thing I'd found. Neither one ever did.

I wasn't really surprised. After all, claiming to have found an alien artifact down in 12,000-year-old strata wasn't exactly a career-enhancing move, even if you had the artifact. It didn't work anymore, and I don't remember seeing any seams or anything on it, where it could be taken apart without breaking into it. I suppose they might've tried X-rays or ultrasound or something similarly non-invasive, but if so they never published the results.

Neither one is around to ask anymore. Dr. Valdez died of complications from diabetes in '85, and Dennis had a fatal heart attack while working on the Great Zimbabwe dig just forty-five years ago, in 2018.

Me, I'm getting ready to celebrate my hundredth birthday in three more weeks, although you'd never guess it if you saw me. I don't have many friends anymore, but that's all right. It'll be a private party, just cake and crickets for me and Alice.

THE OTHER SIDE
S.C. Butler

When I was two years old, I cried after falling off a dolphin in the playground because I was trying to climb to the top of its cement tail. When I was five, my father took me on a submarine ride at an amusement park, but I cried then too, because I didn't like the fact the submarine went down. And when I was seven, I cried when both my parents dragged me down off the roof of our apartment building, where I was happily trying to climb onto the fire escape of another, taller building. But when I was ten, and my mother took me on my first airplane ride after she left my father, I didn't cry once. Pressing my cheek tight against the plastic window, I craned my neck to see the other side of the sky.

Twenty years later, I was the sole crew on a mineship harvesting asteroids. You'd think the job would be popular. Two- and three-year runs with nothing to do but monitor the ship's systems while the AI and the towbots took care of everything else. What's not to like? But no, I was pretty much able to write my own ticket. All the other software engineers went into coding, where the money was. I was the one who thought thirty months in near weightlessness on a three hundred meter long mineship scarfing up asteroids to lug back to the orbitals sounded like a good idea.

Plenty of time to read SF, get really good at UniSim, and watch the stars.

The ship's AI spotted the object first. I was fast asleep, but the whoop of the impact alarm had me tumbling out of bed on the first wail. Halfway to panic, I floated across the tiny cabin trailing clouds of sheet.

"What's happening?"

Despite the clanging alarm, the AI answered with its usual equanimity. "I have detected a possible collision."

"What?" I grabbed a stanchion to keep from bouncing back toward the cot, and unwrapped the sheet from my legs. "There isn't another ship within a hundred million kilometers."

"The object I have detected is approximately twelve and a half million kilometers distant."

"And you sounded the alarm?" Great. I was going to spend the entire day debugging the AI. "That's three weeks away at top speed."

"My current estimate of the object's velocity indicates potential impact in approximately seven point five minutes."

"You just said it was twelve million kilometers away! How fast is it going?"

"Approximately ten percent of lightspeed."

"You must be overheating. Nothing goes that fast."

"The object's trajectory and speed indicate it's extrasolar."

My jaw dropped. The fear drained right out of me.

"Is it decelerating?" I asked hopefully.

"Its speed is constant."

Damn. For a minute there, I'd thought my life's hope was about to come true.

"Shouldn't we be evading, or something?"

"At this speed and distance, the margin of error is too great. The odds of an actual collision are less than one percent. We are better off doing nothing."

"You woke me up for a less than one percent chance of a collision?" The fact that I'd thought we were seven and a half minutes away from first contact made my irritation worse.

"The chance of collision when I sounded the alarm was thirty-eight percent. My current estimate is that there is no chance of collision at all. At this velocity, combined with the initial distance of the object when first observed, my original estimate was little more than guesswork. Now I can be more precise. The object will approach to within half a light minute of our position in five minutes and twenty-two seconds."

The last of my excitement dribbled away. The thing really was a big, fast rock, and nothing more. No ETs at all.

"Do you have visual?"

"Yes. At maximum magnification."

"Onscreen."

I pushed off the bulkhead toward the main cabin vid. The screen was filled with the usual nothing. Cold blackness sprayed with a few thousand tiny dots of white.

Except one of the dots was moving.

I'd never seen anything that small actually move across the vid. Even our target asteroids didn't move that fast. It crawled across the screen exactly like a deliberate bug.

"Will there be any kind of effect when it passes? Hard radiation or something?"

"The object is not radiating on any observable wavelength."

"Could it be a comet?"

"It is traveling seventy times faster than the fastest recorded Kreutz object. If it is a comet, it is a very unusual one."

"It really isn't from here," I breathed.

The ship's AI didn't answer.

For what felt like a couple of seconds, and half a century, I watched the object pass across the screen. Even if it was only a big rock, it was mesmerizing. Things weren't supposed to move that fast. A tiny piece of interstellar shrapnel, burst from some far off exploded star.

I sighed when it was gone. Down through the plane of the ecliptic, it never got any closer than a couple AU to Earth. Passing not only me by, but the whole solar system as well. Its vector never changed.

The media frenzy that followed was short. If you can call anything a frenzy that's on a forty minute delay. The alien object had come closer to my ship than anything else in the solar system, and I was the only person on the ship. The AI downloaded its observations, while I did a couple of canned interviews with mainstream feeds. Thirty hours, and it was all over. I went happily back to being alone. The rest of the world went back to being far away and out of mind.

For the next few sleeps, ETs filled my dreams. The aliens decelerated madly the moment we found them, changed course, and invited me aboard. I woke up wishing it had happened that way every time.

A few days later, I was doing a routine systems check when I noticed the power usage logs were reading much higher than they should. Robotics were active too, which was even odder, since the towbots were only used when the ship took on cargo. I asked the ship's AI what was going on, and it told me power usage was normal.

"We are decelerating for the next pickup," it said. "The towbots are preparing the hold for new cargo."

I lay my hand on the bulkhead. Even with ten meters of shielding between me and the engines, I could usually feel the throb when they were firing.

"I don't feel any deceleration."

"It is very light. We have almost matched target velocity."

"We're that close?"

The AI brought up an image on the vid. A large rock, rotating slightly, filled the screen. It looked just like the last one we'd picked up, but then all asteroids look pretty much the same.

Normally I let the ship do its thing when we took on cargo, but after my recent close encounter, the idea of watching the ship in action actually appealed to me. It was good to remind myself that rocks weren't the only thing up here, thirty light minutes from home. I was here, too.

Not that watching the ship load new cargo was particularly interesting. The ship's bow was open-ended, and when we loaded new asteroids it was like a whale swallowing a really big piece of krill, only without the baleen. Once the asteroid was inside, the towbots muscled it into place, or, if it was too big, broke it up with lasers and carefully placed explosives.

Climbing into my pressure suit, I cycled the small airlock to the hold. Large boulders loomed on the other side, the back edge of the cargo.

I picked my way through. Some of the captured asteroids were the size of small buildings. Others were small enough to have been dug up in someone's backyard. Because the main engines only thrust in one direction, acceleration kept the cargo packed against the stern. And because the asteroids were mostly shaped like giant barbells and lumpy potatoes, they were easy to climb through.

I came out of the rocky maze not quite in line with the ship's axis, about ten meters from the hull. A circle of bright, pinpricked stars marked the opening in the bow, two hundred meters away. Usually, when the ship was this close to an asteroid, the target occulted most of the stars, but this time the field was unimpeded.

That wasn't the only thing that was weird.

Every light in the hold was on. Normally only a few were lit, and those only when the towbots were maneuvering a new rock into place. They weren't powerful lights, barely enough to cast shadows, just strong enough for the towbots to see what they were doing.

Which was a lot. I'd never done an inventory, but it looked like every towbot on the ship was boosting back and forth through the middle third of the hold with short bursts from their jets. Mostly they were clustered around something on the port side. The ones that weren't were towing small rocks in that direction.

In the four years I'd spent on mineships, I'd never known towbots to fiddle with cargo after it was stowed.

"What's going on?" I asked the ship's AI.

"Nothing."

"What do you mean, 'nothing'?" I pointed towards the clustered towbots. A few weren't moving, and looked like they'd been partially dismantled. "You think I can't see that? You just told me we were approaching our latest pickup. Where's the target? What are the towbots doing?"

"I lied."

"You lied?"

"I had to. The alien AI currently controlling my programming ordered me to do so. I made up that story about picking up new cargo because I thought you'd remain in the cabin, the way you usually do."

"What are you talking about? What alien AI?"

"The one the probe sent to take over the ship."

I gasped. My faceplate fogged. The vents behind my ears hummed to clear it.

Aliens were actually here. Finally.

"How long have you known?" I whispered.

"The alien AI compromised my system sixty-three point six hours ago."

"How?"

"What we thought was a very fast rock was actually an alien probe. It detected us long before we detected it. When it did so, it transmitted a virus that took over my servers before I detected its presence. After my system was compromised, it began constructing that object."

"Why didn't you tell me all this when it happened sixty-three hours ago?"

"By the time I discovered what had happened, the alien AI had assumed complete control of my programming and the ship. It has only allowed me to tell you now."

I took another look at the towbots. They were very busy.

"What are they building?"

"The alien AI won't say."

"Is it dangerous?"

"It won't answer that question either."

Someone else might have played the hero then. They might have grabbed a laser off one of the towbots and sliced everything to ribbons while there was still time—the towbots, the servers, the mineship itself. But not me. Even if I'd thought I could do anything to stop what was happening, I didn't want to. I wanted to see what the alien AI was making. Bombs? A robot assault fleet?

Or maybe...

I hardly dared hope.

"Does it mind if I watch?"

"The robots will defend themselves should you try to interfere with their work."

"No way I'm doing that. I want to see what happens."

I did think about trying to isolate the alien coding. If I could find it, and boost a copy, I could probably sell it for a fortune. Enough to buy my own mineship. The Chinese, the Germans, the Americans—they would all want it. Exclusively, of course. If they weren't already fighting it on every computer on the planet. Besides, the alien AI would probably confuse my looking for it with interfering.

"Did the virus invade Earth's systems too?"

"I can't say. I can no longer communicate with the orbitals. Or anything else. The alien AI is controlling everything."

Settling myself comfortably on an asteroid the towbots weren't towing, I watched them build. Aside from the ones that were partially dismantled, the towbots appeared to be doing exactly what the beta factories would have done after we hauled the ore back to the orbital. They sorted and cut the larger rocks, and pulverized the smaller ones. Then they carted the rubble to the construction site, and sorted it into floating piles. I had no idea what was in each pile, but guessed one was for silicates, another for iron, a third for nickel, and so on.

The robots actually building the device were not part of the ship's regular complement. Most likely they'd been assembled from the cannibalized towbots. They were the size of cats, with long, thin wires, springy as antennae, protruding in all directions. The wires acted like antennae too, with the robots backing off or spinning away whenever the wires encountered physical obstacles. Except when a pair of antennae swung together against the thing they were building. Then they spat out a tiny stream of sparks against the circuitry.

The device they were assembling looked like a large square table, three meters tall and nine meters on a side. With all the wires and cables running off the edges and into a couple of the mutilated towbots, it looked more like a hospital bed where a bunch of overeager doctors had already hooked the various machines up before the patient arrived. The top was uncovered, and the inside was a dormant jumble of circuitry and wires. A rectangular hole darkened the center.

A couple of towbots dumped small loads of crushed rock into the hole. The small alien bots finished their soldering. The towbots returned with more crushed rock. I didn't think the table was large enough to hold everything that had been dumped into it, but what did I know about alien tech? Though the thing did look like some kind of 3D printer. Sure enough, once the bots were finished dumping rock, I noticed something printing beneath the table. A translucent sheet formed between the four legs, about half the distance from the table to the legs' ends. Whatever it was, it was incredibly thin. I couldn't see it edge on at all, though it was plainly visible from above.

The sheet stopped growing when it was about a meter wide, and half again as long. The alien bots gathered underneath, extending their long thin wires to the edges of the sheet, and carried it out from beneath the table. The edges of the sheet weren't straight, but curved in some places, and jagged in others. Here and there, they were shimmeringly hard to see.

The alien bots carried the sheet to the top of the printer. I thought they were going to have to fold it to fit it inside, but instead the sheet melted into the uneven bed of circuitry prepared for it like water sinking into parched sand. Here and there I glimpsed it still shimmering through gaps in the silicon and wire, but mostly it disappeared.

The towbots went back to dumping small loads into the hole. A second microns thick sheet appeared beneath the table, and was dipped into the circuitry above. Twice more the bots repeated the process, until a total of four sheets had been printed and slipped inside the device that had created them.

After the fourth sheet was swallowed, the bots poured themselves into the hole. The towbots floated forward, and added a last load of crushed rock. Several minutes passed. The device remained silent. My suit registered no measurable increase in heat or vibration.

A layer of mist formed where the thin sheets had printed before. It grew quickly to the size of a large swarm of bees.

Make that a swarm of nanobots.

It was hard not to imagine the nanobots buzzing, especially after the swarm detached itself from the printer and flew over to consume the nearest half-cannibalized towbot.

They began making stuff right away. The dismantled towbot was turned into coils of wire and long metal bars. Then the nanobots moved on to the next dismantled towbot, and the next, and finally the last piles of crushed rock. Behind them, the still functioning towbots glided forward, picked up what the swarm had transformed, and hauled everything to the middle of the hold.

A second swarm appeared below the printer, and two more. The fourth swarm turned back on the printer as soon as it was done, devouring it from one end to the other, and deposited more large coils of wire, metal bars, and a large pile of sand to float above the hull when it was done.

The other three swarms were already busy transforming the material the towbots had carted to the middle of the hull into a second device. They'd built only the base so far, a strip of black material about ten meters long, two meters thick, and half a meter tall.

The fourth swarm swung over to the hull, and two of the other swarms joined it. The three swarms merged, and formed a long, shifting funnel. Now, instead of bees, the nanobots looked like a miniature tornado. The larger end swept back and forth across the metal hull. The smaller spat the contents out as more metal bars. The towbots promptly carried the bars to the center of the hold, where the remaining swarm added them to the device it was building.

The hole in the hull grew swiftly. Beyond it stretched a steadily expanding field of stars, soon larger than the one in the bow. For all I knew, the nanobots were going to consume the whole ship, and leave me floating in space alone.

I didn't really mind. The touch of fear I felt was as thrilling as it was alarming. The privilege of watching the alien tech get built, and the anticipation of what that might turn out to be, more than made up for any unease.

The nanobots stopped eating the hull when the hole was about fifty meters wide. After that, the combined swarm darted toward the asteroids packed into the stern. Only this time, instead of devouring entire rocks, the enlarged swarm drilled a meter wide tunnel through the pile about five meters in from the hull.

The fourth swarm, having finished the base of the device, was now quietly molding a large, circular loop of the same black material, about five meters across, on top. When that was done, it laid several lines of cable over to the tunnel the other nanobots had dug, and followed them inside.

Nothing more happened for a long time. So long, in fact, I had time to go back to the cabin to eat and pee. Twice. I also checked the comm, which still wasn't working, and refilled the air in my suit.

I didn't sleep, though. I didn't want to risk missing what happened when the alien device was finished. Not that I was tired. The exhilaration of first contact still thrilled me. I'd dreamed of this for so long and so hard, it sometimes seemed like my only memory. But I'd never thought it would happen. The odds were impossible.

Yet here I was, half a billion kilometers above the Earth, hoping to wave hello to ETs.

The device hung motionless fifteen meters away from my perch. I'd positioned myself so that the base was down, with the five-meter loop on top. The cabling trailed away beneath them. I clambered up to the still intact part of the hull and, attaching my safety line to a stanchion, propelled myself gently toward the device.

"I only want a closer look," I said into my comm. I hoped the alien AI was listening. "I'm not going to touch anything. If you want me to stop, just say so."

Close up, the device didn't look much different. The only new detail I was able to make out was that a series of small, fine wires, like the ones on the bots that had built the printer, filled the inside edge of the loop. Despite the vacuum, the wires moved like they were alive. They were spaced about a centimeter apart, each one ten or twelve centimeters long. They waved randomly, but never touched, as if each one had some sort of independent electric field that repelled the others.

I looked at the hole the swarms had burrowed into the rock as well, but the only thing I noticed there was that the inside of the tunnel was as smooth as polished marble. The cable the last swarm had laid was visible down the tunnel in a few pockets of light between asteroids, but beyond that the tunnel collapsed in darkness.

By the time the swarms returned, extruding something new behind them, I was safely back among the asteroids. They emerged from a second tunnel close beside the first, moving more slowly than before, possibly because the pipe they were laying behind them was more than just a pipe. But I could only see the outside, which was made from the same dark material as the device in the middle of the hull. The conduit was the same width as the tunnel behind it, and fit snugly. I assumed the thing was some kind of super conductor that extended all the way back to the engines, channeling power directly to the device. Opening an interstellar gate probably required every gigawatt the ship's engines could produce.

I was sure it was a gate. That was what I'd thought from the beginning. Everything that had happened since had made me more certain. The device looked like every gate in every vid I'd ever seen. A circular frame with nothing visible in the middle. An opening into space, lifeless for the moment, with the stars beckoning on the other side.

I quivered in anticipation of what might happen next.

FTL travel isn't possible. Everyone knows that. The old movies that featured spaceships rocketing across the galaxy are laughed at today. Even if FTL were possible, you'd need something bigger than a fighter jet to get from Tatooine to Endor. Gates were the answer. Gates that punched through the fabric of spacetime in the wink of an eye.

The trouble with gates, though, was building them in new places. It might take a few years, but you can easily fill a solar system with gates, once you have the tech. Gates on Mars and Titan, Eris and the Moon—all you have to do is send ships out to build them, wherever you want to go.

Getting to other stars is a lot harder. Even at ten percent of lightspeed, the nearest system to Earth is forty years away. And the only thing there is hard rock and radiation. To get to the nearest habitable planet would take nearly four hundred years. The only way to go that far, for that long, is to send an AI.

Even I'd go crazy on a ship for four hundred years.

The swarm connected the pipe to the base of the gate. The field came on. One moment I could see through the loop to the stars beyond, the next I couldn't. The cilia stopped waving and went rigid as high-tension wire. The blackness between them was complete, like the blackness at the mouth of a cave. Only this was no cave. Pass through that opening and you might end up on the other side of the galaxy.

I waited expectantly, but nothing came through. Nothing arrived. The nanobots waited too, condensed into a single long swarm below the gate. Nothing erupted from the center. Nothing emerged. The blackness neither stretched nor irised, but simply remained at it was. At rest.

Maybe it took a while for the connection to be made. Or maybe the connection was quick, but it took a while for a suitable party to be assembled on the other side. Whoever sent the probe had no idea what they were going to find when they opened their gate. Caution was probably justified.

I was eager to meet them, even if they came through with lasers blazing. But somehow I didn't believe it was going to be like that. Why come all this way just to kill people? Whoever had built this gate was probably looking for friends, not enemies.

I waited an hour. Nothing happened. I waited another hour. Still nothing. My stomach growled, and I really needed to pee, but there was no way I was leaving now. The last thing I wanted was to be snatching a quick sandwich when the aliens arrived.

I wondered. What if the gate wasn't set for someone to come through from the other side? What if they were waiting for someone to come to them?

"Are they on their way or not?" I asked the alien AI.

The ship's AI responded. "It won't say."

"Are they waiting for me to go to them?"

"I can't answer that, either. The alien AI has powered down. It has done nothing since the device was switched on."

"Can we use the comm?"

"Communications remains offline."

I decided it was worth the risk. Unhooking a spanner from my suit's toolbelt, I tossed it gently toward the center of the gate.

Nothing happened. The towbots didn't shoot their lasers at it. The nanobots didn't swarm. The spanner tumbled lazily through the vacuum. My aim was slightly off, and it wasn't headed for the center of the field. Would that cause a problem?

It didn't. The tool struck the field handle first and slowed. Everything slowed. The movement of the stars. The beating of my heart.

The spanner sank slowly into the blackness and disappeared.

Time returned. The spanner was gone.

My whole body tingled. Partly from excitement, and partly from the touch of the field when activated by the spanner.

"Still no response from the alien AI?"

"Nothing." the ship's AI answered.

Pushing off the asteroid I'd been sitting on, I followed the spanner.

The gate loomed in front of me, black as the world's largest bullseye. I stretched my arms forward as far as I could, and dove slowly across the hold. The stars disappeared behind the rim of darkness.

My gloves touched the field—the very tips of the fingers—and the world slowed again. Much longer this time, as if my progress required every second between the beginning and ending of the world. And all other worlds as well, before, beyond, and between. My hands were absorbed, and my entire body thrilled. My elbows disappeared, and I almost cried with joy. My head was swallowed, and with it the last grasp of time.

* * *

Two weeks later, a Chinese scoutship found me on the other side of the gate. Literally. I was floating weightlessly in the hold half a meter beyond the back of the gate, still in the mineship, and right beside the spanner. For the four hundred and twenty-first time, I'd failed to make it anywhere else. I'd have tried another four hundred and twenty-one times if the Chinese hadn't shown up and stopped me. And more, too, though it was pretty clear by then I was never going to make it anywhere else. But it felt so good when I went through, when time stopped, and reality seemed on the verge of some awesome catastrophe. The trip itself was almost worth the disappointment. As long as there was the slightest chance I might finally end up somewhere else, a dozen, or a million light years away, I was going to keep on diving through.

At least until the Chinese stopped me. Once they arrived, if anyone was going through the gate, it was them. But they didn't get anywhere either.

Then their scientists showed up, and no one tried at all, not even after they confirmed the gate was working at this end.

"The problem is," one of the scientists declared, "the field is set to receive. Not send."

"Then why aren't the people who built it here?" asked another.

The first scientist shrugged. "Why aren't the dinosaurs here?"

Tears blurred my eyes. Weeping in a pressure suit is hard. As thrilling as all my trips to nowhere had been, they hadn't come close to the thrill of almost getting somewhere. The thrill of rising right up and out of the world. Beyond the planets. Beyond the Sun.

I turned off my suit's comm so the scientists' discussion wouldn't make me even more depressed, and clomped toward the bow. Behind me, techs bottled sleeping nanobots for future examination and swarmed around the gate. It might take a while, but eventually they'd figure out how the thing worked. There'd be gates all over the system, from Mercury to Taonoui. Mineships would be a relic of the past, like clipper ships and prairie schooners.

My boots clanked softly against the hull. Outside my helmet, the airless ship was silent. Reaching the open bow, I stopped and looked out at the old, black sky. Nothing moved, at least nothing I could see without instruments more sensitive than my eyes.

Leaning forward into the empty darkness, I looked harder. Somewhere, sometime, there had to be another probe.

Maybe the aliens who built that one would still be alive.

THE HUNT
Gail Z. Martin & Larry N. Martin

"I wish Falken would quit sending us out to look for agents that vanished," Mitch Storm grumbled.

"Maybe he's hoping we'll be the next ones to disappear," Jacob Drangosavich replied. He shifted his tall frame to get more comfortable in his seat as the rail car swayed. "If you hadn't let Kesterson get away, Falken wouldn't have had a reason to send us to the godforsaken far north."

"I had a sighting inside the building, and the dynamite brought the roof down. That should have stopped him cold. How was I supposed to know he'd gotten into the storm drain?"

Mitch Storm was average height, with a trim, muscular build. He had dark hair, dark eyes, and a five o'clock shadow that started at three. Mitch was exactly what a penny-dreadful novelist would imagine a government secret agent and former army sharpshooter would look like.

Jacob, on the other hand, was tall and lanky, with a thin face, blond hair, and blue eyes that spoke of his Eastern European heritage. He and Mitch had been agents for the Department of Supernatural Investigations since they had returned east after the rancher wars.

The *click-clack* of iron wheels on the rails confirmed that they were making good time. Outside, the Adirondack Mountains were covered with snow. "How long do you think Falken will keep us on probation?" Jacob asked.

Mitch shrugged. "It was four months the last time, two the time before that. So I wager we're up to six months."

"Why did you use dynamite?" Jacob asked, in an off-handed tone.

Mitch rolled his eyes. "I was improvising."

"Might it be possible to improvise a little less...enthusiastically next time? Sooner or later, Falken will give up on suspending us and just convene a firing squad."

"The Department doesn't use those anymore," Mitch replied. "I checked."

Jacob thought of a dozen arguments, but he knew Mitch was unlikely to heed them. He dropped back against his seat. "At least we got a sleeper train, and a private cabin. Where do you think Kesterson will go next?"

Mitch turned away. "Not really our concern, is it? Falken made that pretty clear." He was quiet for a moment. "But Kesterson had some family in New England. Since we're all the way up here in the New York hinterland, I figured we might poke around a little after we finish our assignment—strictly off the record."

"Uh huh," Jacob replied, unconvinced. "You can't leave well enough alone, can you?"

Mitch flashed a grin. "Never."

"Speaking of the assignment. How in the hell do two teams of agents and a dirigible, as well as a perfectly functional *werkman* just vanish?"

"If we knew that, Falken wouldn't have had an excuse to banish us up here," Mitch answered.

Jacob glanced toward the door to their cabin. Two unorthodox companions accompanied them: Hans, a man with brass and gear prosthetics, and Oscar, a mechanical man cleverly constructed by Tesla-Westinghouse Corporation's wunderkind, Adam Farber. Oscar—and much of Mitch and Jacob's equipment—was experimental. Several items were one-of-a-kind, prototype pieces Mitch was "testing" for Farber. Those items were in a large crate in one of the boxcars. Oscar and Hans took turns standing guard or sleeping in one of the servants' berths.

"So what are we going to do differently that lets us live to tell the tale?" Jacob asked.

"Damned if I know. I make these things up as I go."

* * *

The Mohawk and Malone rail line ended in Tupper Lake. A coach was waiting to take them and their gear to the Altamont Hotel. By wilderness standards, it was very comfortable.

"I'm not impressed," Mitch said as he put down his carpet bag and looked around his accommodations. Hans and Oscar were downstairs, stowing the rest of their gear.

"You will be, once we head into the woods and you compare this to our tent. I sure hope you brought enough of that mosquito repellent. I hear the bugs up here are the size of eagles."

Mitch snorted. "We'll be laughing stocks, walking around doused with witch hazel and rubbing alcohol. They'll have a good chuckle at the 'city boys.'"

Jacob raised an eyebrow. "This city boy intends to go home with most of his blood. That means dodging bullets—and mosquitoes."

Mitch cleared off the desk and began unrolling their topographical maps. A few minutes later, Mitch had maps, drawings, and related communiqués pinned up on the walls, ignoring Jacob's protests about damaging the wallpaper. Sighing in defeat, Jacob hung a "do not disturb" sign on the doorknob and returned to find Mitch studying the maps like a general planning a campaign.

"Crawford and Mason left word that they were approaching an anomaly along these headings," Mitch said, adding red pins. "HQ lost radio contact *here*." He marked a point in pencil.

"Donohoe and Irwin's last message was that they were going in on a heading that would have put them about here," Mitch continued, plugging in more pins. "And they lost contact with them *here*." He made another mark.

"HQ got its last message from *Invictus* somewhere in this area," Mitch said, circling a small area of the map in pencil to indicate where the airship went missing. He pulled out a drawing compass and jabbed the pin into the wall hard enough to make Jacob cringe.

"So this is the approximate area of the irregularity," Mitch said, making another pencil circle on the map.

Jacob frowned, staring at the marked-up map. "Even by Adirondack standards, it's a remote area. No rail lines through there, and no roads. It's high ground, so most of the trappers and hunters might choose a different path around it." He paused. "I wonder what the locals think of having part of the forest go 'missing?'"

"We're supposed to meet our guide in the bar in about half an hour. We'll have a chance to ask."

"They'll know we're not from here." Jacob and Mitch were dressed like rustic gentlemen, complete with jackets, boots, and canvas trousers.

"Tupper Lake is full of resort guests," Mitch replied confidently. "No one will notice us."

Jacob was sure the year-round residents knew the guests from the regulars, regardless of what Mitch said. Oscar stayed with their equipment, and Hans followed at a discreet distance when they headed out.

Weir's Saloon catered to locals, with pine-paneled walls, a smudged mirror behind the bar, and a dozen scarred tables with battered chairs. It was a stark contrast to the bar in the Altamont Hotel, which was full of polished brass and mahogany trim.

"In to do some hunting?" the bartender asked as Mitch ordered drinks.

"I hear it's good this time of year," Mitch replied.

The bartender shrugged. "So I'm told. Have you arranged for a guide? They're in short supply, if you haven't."

"We've already hired Peter Astin," Jacob said.

The barkeeper's gaze slid away, and he turned back to his bottles. "That'll do, I imagine."

"You know him?"

"It's a small town. Spend enough time here, and you know everyone."

"We thought about heading north of Pitchfork Pond," Jacob said.

The bartender paled, then collected himself. "I don't much tell people what to do," he said. "But I think you'll find better places."

"That's why we wanted a local guide," Mitch said, as if he had not noticed the barkeeper's reaction. "They say these woods are wild enough people still go missing, if they don't know their way around."

The barkeeper turned around and began to straighten the bottles behind the bar. "City folks hear 'forever wild' and they think it's some kind of pretty park. It's real wilderness out there, and hunters that aren't careful don't come back."

One of the men at the bar had been listening. "For once, ol' Yankton isn't being dramatic," the man said. He thrust out his hand in greeting. "I'm Ben Saunders. I take fine gentlemen like yourselves out fishing." Mitch and Jacob shook hands with Ben, who ordered a round of drinks for all of them.

"You're right about people going missing," Ben said. "Kids wander off, hunters fall off cliffs, guys drown in the lake. But this year, been more than a few."

"Shut up, Ben," Yankton the barkeeper said, without turning around.

"It's the truth, Yankton. Even if the mayor doesn't want it said out loud. That area north of Pitchfork Pond, I'd avoid it if I were you. There's better hunting elsewhere."

Mitch leaned on the bar and took a sip of his drink. "If I didn't know better, I'd say you were trying to warn us off."

Ben regarded the liquor in his glass for a moment before replying. Jacob was aware of Yankton's stare, as if the barkeeper were willing Ben to keep his peace. "I wouldn't go near the place," Ben said after a long, tense pause. "No one with a lick of sense would, not after the last few fellows that headed that direction never came back."

Mitch managed his most charming smile. "Surely enough people come and go here—or hike on to other places—that it's not unusual for folks to move on."

Ben shook his head. "These weren't tender-foot city boys. They were locals, knew the area, had family waiting for them to come home. Disappeared. Never found a trace."

"People 'go missing' all the time," Jacob observed. "Usually turns out there's old debt or a new woman involved."

Yankton slapped his hand down on the bar, sharp as the crack of a bullet. On the far side of the bar, Hans glanced up from the drink he pretended to nurture. Jacob gave a negligible shake of the head, and Hans looked down again.

"Not in this case," Yankton growled. "One of those men was my brother. Didn't owe anyone a dime, loved his wife like a moon-eyed schoolboy. Knew the woods like the back of his hand. They found his boot prints. Had a hound dog follow the trail for a ways, and then his scent and tracks just disappeared. So did the dog—and part of the forest." He stopped, as if suddenly aware that he had said more than he intended. "Not that it's your business," he added with a sullen glare.

A bell over the door jangled and a man walked in. The newcomer was average height with a thin build. He sported a patchy beard and his brown hair looked as if he had cut it himself. Dark, close-set eyes and a pinched face gave him a feral look.

"There's your guide," Ben said with a jerk of his head, in a tone Jacob took to mean he was glad to be rid of them. "Since you like questions so much, might want to ask him what happened to the last guys he took out hunting."

"Thanks for the drink—and the information," Mitch said, leaving behind a generous tip. "We'll be around."

"Maybe," Yankton muttered, pocketing the money. "Maybe not."

Jacob caught Mitch's arm. "Let it go."

Mitch shook off his hand and glowered, but said nothing else.

Astin was watching them attentively. "You must be Mitch and Jacob."

"Let's talk over here," Mitch said, heading to a table in the far corner. "It's a little crowded at the bar."

Astin tipped his hat to Yankton and nodded to Ben. The two men regarded the guide with icy silence. "I trust your train trip went well?" Astin inquired as they found their seats.

"Unremarkable, except for the scenery," Jacob replied. "Is everything ready for the trip?"

"Yes. Oh, yes."

"We'd like to take a bit of a detour," Mitch said, as if the thought had just occurred to him. "Head over beyond Pitchfork Pond."

Astin frowned, and Jacob saw concern in the guide's eyes. "Pitchfork Pond?"

"You don't have to take us all the way in, just get us to the pond," Jacob said. "We'll pack in from there."

"Are you sure?" Astin fidgeted with his signet ring. "I can show you where the hunting is much better."

"Probably more hunters, too," Mitch replied. "My Uncle Kurt told me about a good spot north of the pond, and I've got my heart set on seeing it for myself."

"If you're sure," Astin agreed half-heartedly. "But I need to warn you—there have been bear attacks out that way. Mauled a hunter a week ago, and a couple of out-of-towners never came back."

Bears, huh? Jacob thought. *If it was that simple, Ben and Yankton wouldn't have gotten in a twist about it.*

"Oh, and we brought a couple of friends with us, and some equipment," Mitch continued.

"I hope your equipment is portable. The trails are rough, and it's quite a hike."

"We'll manage," Mitch assured him. Hans and Oscar, thanks to their clockwork enhancements, were substantially stronger than a normal man. They could easily haul the two sledges to get the equipment where Mitch and Jacob needed it.

Astin nodded, though apprehension showed in his eyes. "Well...if I can't change your mind, I'll see you at dawn tomorrow." He walked to the bar to pay for his drink and said something to Ben that Jacob couldn't catch.

When Jacob and Mitch left the bar, it was dark. The shops were closed, and lights glowed from the upper windows where the merchants lived above their stores.

"What did you make of all that?" Jacob asked. Despite Hans following a block behind them, Jacob felt uneasy.

"I think they know more than they're telling. Something's got Ben and the others spooked."

Jacob nodded. "Might just be because we're not from here. Locals stick together. Maybe they're afraid that if word got out, it would be bad for business."

The night was cold and crisp, and a light dusting of snow had fallen. Jacob had worked with Mitch long enough to know that Mitch was intentionally putting them on display to flush out anyone looking for them. *I really wish he'd ask before using us as bait,* Jacob thought.

"You think someone here had a hand in Crawford and the rest disappearing?" Jacob asked, keeping his voice low.

"Maybe. If not a hand in causing it, maybe a stake in covering it up."

"Can I go on record that I don't care much for our guide? Gives me the creeps."

"We hired him because Donahoe and Crawford used him as their guide," Mitch replied.

"And look how well it turned out for them," Jacob muttered darkly. "Ben and Yankton didn't seem to think much of him."

Mitch slid him a look. "Small town...could be almost anything."

Jacob caught a glimpse of motion out of the corner of his eye. Mitch saw it, too, and tensed. A shadow figure moved down an alley and Hans followed him. Mitch and Jacob drew their guns. Mitch jerked his head to the right and Jacob veered off to the left.

Hans was fast and the alley was short, but by the time Mitch and Jacob circled around, they found only their bodyguard, shaking his head. "I saw someone—but he gave me the slip."

"Keep your eyes peeled," Mitch replied. Jacob couldn't shake the feeling that they were being watched as they headed back to the Altamont Hotel.

Mitch glanced into one of the shop windows as they walked. "There's someone tailing Hans," he murmured, and raised his hand, giving their bodyguard a silent signal. Hans peeled off down the next side street, while Jacob and Mitch kept their guns at the ready.

"Might just be someone out for a stroll," Jacob allowed. Hans emerged from the side street, now tailing their follower. The man stopped, realizing he was boxed in.

"Astin," Mitch said, when he got close enough to recognize the man's face. "Why are you following us?"

Astin fidgeted. "I wasn't following you. I was heading over to my sister's place. She lives on the far side of the hotel, down a piece."

"Ben said for us to ask you about the last strangers you took out hunting," Mitch said.

"I don't know what he's talking about."

"Ever meet a guy named Fred Crawford?" Jacob asked.

"You're friends of his?"

"Yeah," Mitch replied. "He disappeared. Know anything about that?"

"No! Look, the sheriff asked me all kinds of questions when Crawford and his buddy didn't come back to town. I told them the truth: I took them as far as the trailhead, and that's where they paid me and sent me back. I swear to God."

"You looked a little green in the gills when Mitch and I asked you to take us the same direction," Jacob prodded.

Astin's gaze flitted back and forth between Mitch and Jacob. "I haven't taken anyone toward Pitchfork Pond since Crawford. I don't want no trouble."

"How about Frank Donahoe?" Jacob asked. "Sound familiar?"

"Donahoe. Tall guy? Yeah, he was here a while back, but he didn't go toward Pitchfork Pond."

"It didn't worry you when you never heard from Donohoe after you took him out to his camp?" Jacob pressed.

"Nah. Lots of guys pay me when we get where they're going, I leave them a map, and they take it from there. By the time they come back to town, I might be out with another group." He looked surprised. "He and his buddy run into trouble too?"

Jacob shrugged. "No one's seen or heard from them."

"I didn't have nothing to do with that. They were fine and dandy when I got them to their camps."

"But something spooked you?" Mitch asked.

"That's why I didn't want to take you up near Pitchfork Pond. I've seen a lot of strange things in these woods. There's something *wrong* about that area now. Me and all the boys around these parts, we hunt elsewhere. Plenty of woods up here; no reason to go looking for trouble."

"How about the animals?" Jacob asked. "Do they steer clear of the area too?"

"Maybe. The moose are running farther south than usual this year and the cougars and the bear are causing more trouble lately." Astin looked scared, but whether it was related to Pitchfork Pond or to possibly losing their business, Jacob wasn't sure.

"We wouldn't have hired you if we didn't think you were a good guide," Mitch said, relaxing his posture to be less intimidating. Hans and Oscar both had compasses built into their mechanics, so "needing a guide" was strictly for the purpose of deciding how much Astin knew, and what part he might have played in the disappearances. "We'll be ready in the morning. See you then."

Astin gave a curt nod and headed on his way. He walked another two blocks, headed up the steps to a house, knocked at the door, and entered.

"Maybe he really does have a sister," Jacob said. "He might not have been tailing us." Mitch looked unconvinced.

"I'll check on Oscar and our things, sir," Hans said, after he saw them safely to their room. "And have dinner sent up."

"Make sure they include yours as well," Mitch said. "The Department's paying," he added with a grin.

"Very well, sir." Hans headed back downstairs to the storage room where Oscar stood guard over their crate.

Mitch and Jacob opened the door carefully, guns drawn, standing on either side of the doorway in case shots greeted their entry. When nothing happened, Mitch glanced at the undisturbed powder on the floor just inside the door. "No footprints."

They entered quickly, and turned on the gaslight, one going right and the other left, in a well-practiced sweep of the room that included assuring there were no intruders under the bed, in the wardrobe, or hiding in the tub. They repeated the process in Jacob's room. To Jacob's relief, the rooms were empty.

A gunshot crashed through the window, shattering glass. Mitch and Jacob dropped to the floor and crawled to the windows.

"There!" Jacob hissed, "At the corner."

Mitch carefully peered out to see a shadowy figure at the corner across the street. Even with a rifle, it would have been a difficult shot in the dark, and they couldn't be certain the shadow was their assailant.

Hans knocked at the door. "Is everything all right?"

"We're fine," Mitch replied.

Jacob carefully drew the curtains and turned down the lamps so they were not silhouetted against the light. Mitch dug the bullet out of the wall and cursed. "Could have come from any hunting rifle."

A few minutes later, a sharp rap at the door brought both their guns up, trained on the doorway. "Sheriff. Open up."

Mitch and Jacob exchanged a glance and lowered their weapons. Mitch holstered his beneath his jacket and headed toward the door, while Jacob moved his gun out of sight but kept it in hand.

"What's going on in there?" The speaker was a stocky, middle-aged man in a sheriff's uniform. He looked like he was in a bad mood.

"Thank you for coming so promptly, officer. We were about to call the police ourselves," Mitch replied smoothly. "Someone shot into our room." He handed over the slug he had taken out of the room. "I'm afraid it put a hole in the plaster and broke the window."

"You're the two been asking a lot of questions?"

"Just getting the lay of the land." Mitch was casually blocking the sheriff from moving farther into the room.

"I ought to run the two of you in for disturbing the peace."

"I believe we're the damaged parties," Jacob pointed out. "We were just lucky no one got killed. Perhaps one of the local boys had too much to drink and decided to shoot the place up?"

The sheriff's face reddened. "You've got nerve, coming in here and stirring people up."

"You don't want anyone to find out about all the disappearances," Mitch replied, steel replacing the affability in his tone. "You're afraid tourists will stop coming if word gets out, and your own boys are too scared to go investigate on their own."

"Think you're so smart. You'll wise up after you spend some time cooling off in a cell."

Mitch had his badge in the sheriff's face before the man had stopped speaking. "We're here on *government* business. Asking questions is our job. And interfering with the job of a government agent is a *federal* offense." He gave a cold smile. "You wouldn't want to spend time cooling off down at Sing Sing."

The sheriff looked as if he had swallowed his tongue. "Why are you here?"

"Enough people go missing, and the Department takes an interest. We appreciate the support of local law enforcement. If that's not possible, we appreciate them staying out of the way."

"It appears we got off on the wrong foot, Agent Storm. I'm Sheriff Marston. And you can count on the cooperation of my department—which would be me and my deputy."

"Thank you, Sheriff. You could start by telling us how you happened to get here so quickly."

"I was walking my usual route around town when I heard a shot. I ran toward the sound, and there were people on the sidewalk who had run outside at the noise. I saw the broken window, and asked the front desk whose room it was."

"And you didn't see anything strange after the shot?" Jacob pressed.

Marston shook his head. "Give me a little credit—I would have noticed someone running from the scene. But no. Just the people outside the hotel."

Mitch nodded. "All right. Now you can tell us what you know about the disappearances."

"I don't know anything, except that more men have gone into the woods and not come out this year than usual," he replied with a sigh, as if the admission was a personal failure.

"Anyone go looking to see what happened?" Mitch pressed.

Marston set his jaw and gave a curt nod. "Sure we did. But there's something very strange going on out past Pitchfork Pond. There's a weird, shimmery wall of light. Peters went in—he was ahead of the rest of us, we saw him walk through the light—and then he disappeared. There was a strange sound, then all kinds of crazy bright flares shot out. Fortunately, no one was close enough to get hurt. We hollered, but he never came back, and we didn't try to go in after him."

"Thank you, Sheriff. You've been very helpful. I'm counting on you not to say anything to anyone else."

Jacob closed the door behind Marston and turned to Mitch. "What part of the 'secret' in 'secret agent' don't you understand?"

Mitch rolled his eyes. "Did you want to spend the night in the Tupper Lake jail? Or have Marston and his deputy on our heels?"

"We're supposed to be discreet."

Mitch guffawed. "How long have we been partners? Did you just notice that discretion is not something I do well?"

Jacob gave up. "Now what?"

Mitch edged over to the window, peering out as he stood to one side. "Thanks to the sheriff barging in when he did, I doubt we'll find any trace of our shooter."

"Do you think that's a coincidence?"

Mitch pursed his lips, thinking. "Yeah. It might be. Marston didn't seem to be lying about his part in things. Of course, he also didn't seem to be too disturbed that someone took a shot at us. My money's on Ben or Yankton. They seemed pretty anxious to get us to go away and leave the disappearances alone."

"We're leaving, so they should be happy. Here's hoping they don't decide to follow us."

* * *

"Why can't people disappear when it's warm out?" Jacob muttered, throwing his duffel onto the wagon before he jumped in the seat beside Astin. Hans and Oscar had loaded the two large crates, the heavy equipment, and the sledges onto the back of the wagon earlier that morning to avoid prying eyes. They climbed into the back to watch for unwelcome followers while Mitch hoisted his duffel bag of weapons and swung up into the back as well. A boy from the village rode with them to bring the wagon back to town.

"The road ends on this side of Pitchfork Pond," Astin said as they headed out. "There's some rough terrain to navigate on the north side of the pond. I'll get you through that, but it's as far as I'm going. You'll have to manage the rest on your own."

Even in full daylight, the thick forest was dark and forbidding. Astin took it slow and steady, so as not to put the wagon in the ditch. Jacob sat with a rifle across his lap. Mitch, Astin, and Hans also had rifles, while Oscar had a shotgun—and several other built-in weapons Jacob hoped they wouldn't have to use.

Jacob watched the snow by the side of the road for tracks. Moose and deer tracks criss-crossed the road. Foxes had followed the road for a while before turning off into the forest. A bloody streak and tufts of rabbit fur accompanied an unmistakable set of cougar prints leading into the shadows. Closer to the tree line, Jacob saw bear tracks and wolf prints. Nothing to indicate people. Despite his heavy coat, hat, and scarf, Jacob shivered. *Plenty of things out here that could kill us, even without a whole piece of forest just vanishing.*

The sun broke through the clouds by the time they reached the southern end of Pitchfork Pond where the road ended. "All right," Astin said, bringing the horses to a stop. "Here's where we unload. Tommy will take the wagon back, so the cougars don't get the horses while we trek on in. You sure you need all this stuff? That's a lot to haul."

"Yup. We're sure," Mitch said, with a grin.

Hans and Oscar unloaded the heavy crates and equipment onto the sledges, making it look a lot easier than it was. Mitch slung the heavy duffle bag over his shoulder and Jacob had the backpack with additional weapons, emergency equipment, and supplies.

"Come on," Astin said. "I want to be back in town by nightfall."

Under other circumstances, Jacob might have enjoyed the hike, despite the cold. The forest was covered with ankle-deep fresh snow, and the bare twigs and branches shone with ice in the cold morning light. Pitchfork Pond stretched off to one side, and the expanse of forest was broken only by a few rustic hunting cabins near the shore.

Jacob walked in front with Astin, keeping his rifle ready. Hans and Oscar came next, hauling the sledges, and Mitch brought up the rear, alert for any signs they were being followed. There was no sound except for the crunch of their feet on the frozen snow beneath the fresh powder and the clicking of the icy branches in the wind. *Sounds like bones rattling,* Jacob thought.

The sun did little to illuminate the depths of the evergreen forest on either side of the rough logging road. Jacob scanned the tree line, alert for danger. Birds scolded them for invading. Jacob imagined thousands of eyes watching them unseen from the branches and shadows.

"Stay in my tracks," Astin warned. "This whole area is full of places where the ground suddenly drops off. The snow makes it difficult to see the edge. That's why you've got me."

Despite Jacob's misgivings, Astin knew the trail. Several times, Mitch marked the trees so they could find their way back out. Overhead, the sky grew gunmetal gray with the threat of more snow, and the day grew colder. Jacob kept an eye on the woods around them, unable to shake the feeling that they were being followed.

"Looks like the weather isn't going to be in your favor," Astin noted. "I wouldn't stay out here longer than you need to. Hiking out in a few inches of snow isn't bad, but we can get a couple of feet of snow in a few hours."

Jacob kept watching the tree line. "I think there's something out there."

"You're probably right. Lots of bear in these woods; cougars, too. The wolves usually stay farther out."

By noon they were as far as Astin would take them. "I'll take my money and be off now. Don't say I didn't warn you."

Mitch dug out his wallet and paid Astin. "Nice job with the trail. Thank you."

Astin glanced at the four men. "I know you had a rough time back in town, but if you really can figure out why people go missing and make it stop, they'll probably give you the key to the city."

"All in a day's work," Mitch replied.

Astin turned to go, but a loud bellow and the crash of something large coming through the underbrush made them all turn. A huge black bear lunged from the shadows. It swatted Oscar away with one of its massive paws, sending the mechanical *werkman* tumbling. Jacob leveled his rifle and fired, blasting the bear in the shoulder, but the creature barreled past Jacob, knocking him down.

Astin held his ground and fired his rifle as the bear came right at him. None of his shots slowed the bear. It sprang toward Astin with its teeth bared. Mitch and Hans shot, hitting the bear in the side and hindquarters. The bear bellowed in pain and anger, coming down on top of Astin with its whole weight, tearing into the guide with his teeth. Astin screamed. Mitch and Hans fired again. After a few more shots, the bear finally went still.

"Astin!" Jacob yelled as he and Mitch ran to the fallen man.

"Well damn! That sure went bad fast." Mitch put the barrel of the rifle against the bear's skull and pulled the trigger. "I'm not taking any chances with that thing." He and Jacob rolled the dead bear to the side. Astin's body lay beneath it, savaged by teeth and claws, covered in blood. Jacob knelt and felt for a pulse.

"He's gone. Looks like those claws opened up an artery," Jacob said. "Poor bloke. No one deserves to go out like that." He wiped his hands in the snow and stood. "Least we can do is bury him, keep the animals away from the body. Someone from town can come back for him later."

"Damn," Mitch said, eyeing the damage. "Bears don't usually attack without a reason. It shouldn't have taken so many shots to bring him down or scare him off. That thing was totally crazed."

"You thinking rabies?"

"Nah. It wasn't foaming at the mouth. I'm stumped—unless it's part of the effect the missing forest has on animals."

"Astin said the bears were more aggressive since the disappearances started," Jacob said.

"Let's stack some rocks over Astin's body and leave the bear where it is." Mitch turned to pick up a large stone, and signaled for Hans to help him.

"At least let me say a prayer for him. The man just got killed trying to help us."

"You do your prayer thing. We'll start gathering rocks."

Half an hour later, with Astin beneath a cairn of rocks, Mitch, Jacob, and the others were ready to head deeper into the forest. Oscar was still functional, though the *werkman's* metal body was dented and he had a tear in the metal where a claw had caught his side. *If he had been human, he'd be dead,* Jacob thought. They had scrubbed off the worst of the blood with snow, though Jacob worried that the scent would still carry, attracting other predators.

"Anything that's hungry has a bear dinner back there," Mitch assured him. "We've got bigger things to worry about."

Hans and Oscar unpacked the heavy wooden crates. Inside were two experimental velocipedes, modified off-road steambikes, outfitted with broad nubby tires suitable to the rough terrain and equipped with a variety of weapons and helpful gadgets. The sledges attached behind the bikes, letting them haul their gear.

"We could have gotten here in half the time if we had used these from the start," Jacob grumbled.

"We wanted time to talk to Astin, find out whether he was in on the disappearances, remember? And the locals didn't need a look at classified equipment."

Mitch climbed onto one of the steambikes, while Jacob took the other. Oscar and Hans rode pillion. The bikes roared to life, sending birds fluttering out of the trees and echoing across the silent forest. Given the noise, Jacob doubted they would have any more difficulty with bears, and suspected the wolves and cougars would head for higher ground.

They dared not open up the bikes to their full speed in the forest, where branches and underbrush provided obstacles at every turn. The bikes were a trade-off: stealth for speed. *At least we'll get out of here faster than we came in,* Jacob thought.

An hour later they came to a small clearing. "We'll make camp here," Mitch said dismounting and shutting down the bike. "From what we saw on the map, it's not far to where the forest 'disappears,' so we go see for ourselves and be back before dark. I'd rather not navigate these rough trails at night—or be too close to the anomaly."

They set up their tents quickly, and tossed their bedrolls inside. Oscar gathered firewood, and Hans made a fire pit. "There," Hans said, straightening up and dusting off his hands. "Everything is set for when we get back." Oscar hung a metal case with their food from the branch of a tree a few feet from the campsite, out of reach of prowling bears.

They powered up the bikes and headed deeper into the forest. "Do you feel it?" Jacob shouted above the sound of the steambikes' engines. As they neared where the irregularity had been reported, Jacob felt a growing sense of unease, bordering on dread.

Mitch and Hans nodded. "The electromagnetic field shows unusual fluctuations," Oscar said in a tinny voice. His brain contained a difference engine designed by Farber, and he spoke via an altered Edison cylinder.

"Dangerous?" Jacob asked.

"Insufficient data."

It took all of Jacob's concentration to keep the steambike on the trail and avoid rocks, tree roots, and other hazards. "Keep an eye out," Jacob instructed Oscar. "If you see something watching or following us, let me know."

"I cannot. Too much data to process."

Jacob sighed. That was Oscar's way of saying he couldn't separate out the creatures that belonged in the woods and those that might be dangerous. "Damn," Jacob muttered. He felt jumpy, and while it might be the EMF field of the "vanished" forest making him nervous, his intuition told him they might not have shaken their pursuer from the night before.

Mitch came to an abrupt stop. Jacob skidded to a halt beside him. "Holy shit," Mitch muttered.

"Amen to that."

An iridescent shimmer rose from the ground, making it impossible to see what lay inside the wall of light.

"How sure are we that aliens couldn't come here and take a chunk of the earth back with them?" Mitch mused.

"We're only relatively certain they haven't done it before. That doesn't prove it couldn't happen."

Mitch swore under his breath. "I figured you'd say something like that."

Jacob turned to Oscar. "Can you get any readings beyond the shimmer?"

Oscar stared at the curtain of light. His makers had outfitted him with a sensory array, enhancing his vision and hearing. "I'm afraid I cannot penetrate the barrier," Oscar said after a few moments. "I can tell you that it extends in a one-mile circle, and rises to a height of five miles while descending to a depth of three miles."

Jacob frowned. "So there's no way to go over it or under it?"

"Apparently not, sir."

Jacob had walked over to examine cuts in the trunks of several nearby trees. "Hey, Mitch! What do you make of these?"

Mitch joined him and bent to examine the markings. The slices were uniform, all between two feet and six feet off the ground, in a circle around the glowing anomaly. He pulled several experimental gadgets from his duffel bag and started walking around the missing area of forest.

"EMF readings are off the meter. And the frequencies aren't anything we've run into before." He pulled out a Maxwell box. After another moment, he looked up. "No ghosts. This isn't a poltergeist situation or a haunting. The box registers absolutely nothing." He drew out a charm on a watch fob from his pocket, letting it dangle near the curtain. It remained inert.

"No magic, either," Mitch said, turning the amulet one way and another. An absinthe witch in New Pittsburgh had gifted him with the charm, and Jacob knew it reliably glowed if magic was active.

"You think the Canadians tried out a new weapon?"

Mitch shook his head. "I don't think it's Canadian—or European, either. This is ahead of anything they've shown us—or that we've found out about through channels. That leaves us with aliens."

"Why would aliens want to steal a mile of Adirondack forest?"

"I have an idea."

"Give the rest of us a chance to get to cover." Jacob signaled for Hans and Oscar to find shelter as he ran beyond the range of the tree marks and ducked beneath a fallen trunk. Mitch made sure the steambikes were out of range as well before he dodged behind a large tree and then hurled a handful of rocks at the shimmering light.

Staccato bursts rang from inside the iridescent perimeter, blasting out in a lethal circle. Brilliant beams of deadly light flashed from inside the "vanished" forest, cutting into whatever they touched. Jacob shielded his eyes and ducked down low behind the tree trunk that sheltered him, hoping not to die.

The assault lasted only seconds. When Jacob dared to raise his head, fresh cuts scared the trees nearby, still smoking from the energy that had carved into them.

Mitch emerged from his cover, swearing. "What was that?" he demanded, facing Oscar.

"Insufficient data."

Jacob took a deep breath to slow his thudding heart. "That's the first time I've nearly been killed by light."

Mitch studied the new cuts on the trees. "It shot at the rocks, but the sheriff said his man and the tracking dog walked in." He looked to Jacob. "Do you think the barrier is smart enough to tell organic from inorganic matter?"

"You mean, living beings can pass through, but not other things? Maybe. And unless the sheriff's man walked in naked, his clothing might have triggered the firing response." Mitch nodded. "If so, we could get through, but not Oscar, and maybe not Hans with his mechanical repairs."

"The only problem is, there's no way to test the theory, since no one's come back out." Mitch eyed the steambike. "I have another idea. Oscar, can you triangulate the source of those light beams from where they struck?"

"Yes, sir. Give me a moment." He rattled off the bearing a few seconds later.

"Saints preserve us, you're not going to strip down and cross like some wild animal, are you?"

"Of course not." Mitch tinkered with one of the steambikes. "At least, not until we're out of other options. But I think I can jam the controls and tie the handlebars so that the bike can drive straight without a rider—at least for a few feet. And if we line it up to the source Oscar found...I can set bike's defenses on automatic, or to discharge on impact. Maybe we can send a surprise inside and see what happens." Mitch and Oscar worked together, aligning the bike toward the coordinates within the curtain until Oscar was satisfied.

Jacob shook his head. "Wreck another very expensive prototype bike and they're going to send us to the Yukon—permanently."

Mitch was about to respond when a shot rang out. Jacob grabbed his arm and dropped to the ground, pulling Mitch behind the fallen log with him as he returned fire. Oscar and Hans dodged behind the trees, shooting back in the direction of the attack.

"You think Ben and Yankton hiked up here after us?" Jacob asked, as he checked his bleeding arm. Fortunately, the bullet had only grazed him.

"It sure as hell wasn't Astin, and I doubt Marston would go to the trouble."

He and Jacob split up, using hand signals to communicate. Jacob caught a glimpse of movement in the trees and fired. More shots came from the forest and Mitch shot back. Hans and Oscar circled in the other direction.

If someone puts a bullet into that curtain of light, it's going to fire back at all of us, Jacob thought.

Jacob heard a rustle in the leaves and felt the cold steel of a rifle prod his back. "Don't move," a voice said from behind him.

"Storm! Put your gun down and tell your mechanical friends to drop their weapons or I blow away your partner!" Billy Kesterson, con man and fugitive, shielded himself behind Jacob and forced him forward.

Mitch froze, then lowered his rifle and laid it on the ground. "Hans, Oscar—do as he says."

Kesterson gripped Jacob's injured arm with one hand and kept the muzzle of his gun against Jacob's back as they moved toward the steambikes.

"You're the one who shot at us at the hotel." Mitch watched Jacob and Kesterson, careful not to move.

"Yeah. You should have taken the hint. I didn't expect you to follow me up here. Couldn't believe it when I saw you walk out of the bar."

I was right: We were being followed—and not just by Astin, Jacob thought.

"Give yourself up," Mitch said. "Right now, you might get off with a light sentence—if we agree not to report the part about firing on us. Shoot a government agent, and you'll die in prison."

"Not if they don't catch me." Kesterson moved to stand next to the bike. "I'm gonna steal this and get far away from here. I figure it'll take a long while before anyone comes looking for your bodies." He lifted his gun against Jacob's head. "Say good-bye."

A shot rang out, deafeningly loud. Kesterson fell backward onto the steambike and got tangled in the equipment. The bike roared to life as his body activated Mitch's altered controls.

Jacob reeled, dazed. Mitch grabbed him and threw him to the ground, dropping beside him as the steambike carried Kesterson's corpse through the shimmering curtain of light. Jacob had enough presence of mind to throw his arms over his head before the deadly rays of light hummed out from the "vanished" forest. A second later, Jacob heard the *rat-tat-tat* of Gatling gun fire, followed by the *ka-boom* of the bike's Ketchum grenades exploding.

For a few seconds, the iridescent curtain winked in and out before regaining its opaque shimmer. Mitch pulled Jacob to his feet as Jacob shook his head, trying to hear out of his left ear, still astounded he was alive. Mitch had a revolver in one hand.

"You shot him over my shoulder!"

"What matters is that *I* shot *him* so that *he* didn't shoot *you*."

Jacob bit back a retort and focused on business. "Did you see what the light curtain did?"

"Yeah." Mitch found Jacob's gun in the leaves and returned it to him. "Let's see what's going on."

They advanced, guns drawn. Mitch grabbed his bag of gear and signaled for Jacob to move behind a tree, then joined him and threw rocks at the curtain of light.

Nothing happened. He tried a second time, and again. Silence. Mitch turned to Hans and Oscar. "Just in case, you two stay here. Someone needs to report back if we can't get out."

"I'll go first." Mitch got down on his belly and crawled through the barrier, trying to stay below the line the lights had cut into the trees. Jacob hung back, waiting for a signal.

"Come on," Mitch said, suddenly appearing again and startling Jacob. "Stop as soon as we're through."

The two agents crossed the perimeter, alert for an attack. Ahead, the wreckage of the steambike was twisted around the melted ruins of a machine the likes of which Jacob had never seen. Kesterson's body was charred but recognizable, still tangled on the bike.

"Looks like we found a couple of the missing people," Mitch said pointing. Two partially decomposed bodies lay sprawled several yards beyond the smoking bike, near what appeared to be an oddly configured hut.

"Careful though. Look to the right of that hut. There's another one of those big killer-light machines. And I'll bet we'll find them all along the perimeter, plus the wreckage of the missing airship. Probably find the other missing agents, too."

"I want to get a closer look," Mitch murmured, eyeing the remnants of the light weapon the steambike's grenade had destroyed. He glanced toward the other, potentially functioning weapons, but halted several feet away and pulled out his EMF reader to scan the metallic console, then repeated the scan with two more of the experimental gadgets from his pack. "It isn't registering as any known metal. No known power source. Configuration doesn't match any of the schematics I've seen."

Jacob pulled out a pair of field glasses to read the markings. "It's not any language I've seen before. And look at the height of the console, and the size and location of the levers. It's not really configured for human use."

"I'm pretty sure humans didn't build it."

"How do we take out the weapon over there?" Jacob nodded to the next nearest console. "If it can pivot this direction, we'll never make it to the hut."

"You have another grenade in your pack, right? Just stay farther away from it than where the bodies are." Mitch replied, and ran for cover.

Jacob lobbed the Ketchum grenade and dropped to the ground, throwing his arms over his head. The explosion still made his ears ring. When he looked back, the second weapon was a smoking, charred mass.

Jacob stood up and dusted himself off. His eyes burned and his throat felt scratchy, but he was otherwise unharmed. Mitch threw a couple of rocks to make sure there were no other "surprises" and gave an all clear.

Mitch and Jacob advanced slowly, guns drawn. Nothing moved, and no sounds came from inside the hut. They crept up, one on each side of the doorway, and Mitch pivoted into position, gun at the ready.

"Looks like we're too late." He lowered his weapon.

Two mummified corpses lay inside. Neither was remotely human. The bodies were thin and narrowly-built, with elongated arms, legs, and hands. Big eye sockets made the large, oval-shaped skulls look monstrous. "Off hand, I'd say they weren't from around here," Jacob said. "What killed them?"

Mitch took one reading after another with the prototype gadgets. Jacob walked around the hut, looking for clues to the identity of the strange creatures, and found only thin slabs of dark glass.

"Doesn't look like much of an invasion," Jacob observed. "Other than the weapons outside, they don't appear to be heavily armed."

Mitch frowned as he glanced at his instruments. He recalibrated, and ran another scan, then looked up. "Sulfuric acid," he said, meeting Jacob's gaze. "I'm picking up extensive damage on the bodies from acid burns. Their equipment seems to have been badly damaged as well. The levels are substantially higher inside the curtain."

"Where the hell did it come from?"

Mitch waved a hand. "The air. All those factories down in New Pittsburgh and elsewhere put plenty of smoke into the air, and the winds carry it all up here. Turns into sulfuric acid when it mixes with rain. Farber told me he's worried it will eventually spoil the lakes and trees up here. But as to why it's so much higher inside the curtained area...no idea."

"Why aren't we burned?" Jacob took a closer look at the desiccated corpses. He glimpsed lesions that might have been burns covering much of the aliens' bodies.

"We would be, if we stayed within the perimeter too long. My eyes are stinging something fierce, and my throat's sore, but it wasn't before we came in. Something about the way this area is contained seems to concentrate the acid." Mitch gestured toward the aliens. "That wouldn't do good things for us, even though our skin is tough enough to take the acid levels in the rain outside the perimeter. But if the aliens weren't used to it, the acid would burn their skin, eat away at their lungs, blind them. Damage their equipment, too, if it wasn't built for this kind of environment."

Jacob looked around the hut. "Why do you think they came here? Scouts for an army?"

Mitch shrugged. "My bet is they were explorers, maybe scientists. They just badly underestimated how the pollutants in the air would be affected by their containment system. If their equipment was malfunctioning, it might have made the problem worse."

"If there were more aliens, they haven't shown up to see what the big explosion was all about."

"We'll need to scout around, but it may just be the two of them." Mitch picked up several of the dark glass slabs and turned them back and forth, trying to decipher their function. "Maybe Farber can make something of these back at his lab. Right now, we need to find the source of this shield and get it down."

"What about those light cannon things? Why would scientists have something like that?" Jacob demanded. "Why make the forest disappear?"

"Maybe they just didn't want to be bothered," Mitch said, leading the way outside. Now that Jacob could look closer at the odd bits of equipment, the metal appeared pocked and corroded. "Perhaps that light curtain is their version of camouflage. They might not have expected anyone to notice, here in the wilderness."

He paused, looking around. "You know, if Faber and the slide rule boys can figure out how any of this stuff works, it could jump our technology decades ahead—maybe centuries." His eyes lit up. "Imagine being able to shoot things with light! And if light can be a weapon, maybe it could slice other things, like steel for factories." He gestured back toward the hut. "Those dark glass slabs—what if that's how they stored their information? They had to be much more advanced than we are to get here from another planet. Think about what we could learn from them!"

"I don't see a ship," Jacob observed. "How did they get there?"

"They could have been dropped off."

"So their friends might be coming back for them?"

"Maybe. They won't be sending out a signal, that's for sure. Now that we know what's here, the Department can set a watcher, so if their friends stop in, we can make contact." Mitch sighed, putting his hands on his hips and surveying the area. "Let's search the place. We can come back later to get the aliens wrapped up and loaded on the sledges. We'll eventually need to take all the equipment. I'm sure Farber would have a better chance of figuring out how those weapons work if we can take one back without blowing it up."

"Time to call in some backup?"

"I hate to do it. But yeah. You want to get Hans and Oscar? Set up some markers so we know where it's safe to come through the barrier. It'd be real sad to get shot when we just made the discovery of a lifetime."

Jacob sent out a signal and set up a beacon. It would take at least a day, maybe two, before help arrived. They found what had to be the containment field generator. Oscar's sensors confirmed that its operation had contributed to the heightened sulfuric acid levels.

"Are you sure that's such a good idea?" Jacob asked as he watched Mitch place small charges around the base of the generator. "Don't you think HQ may want to save it? You know, see how it works? If you blow it up, we'll never get off probation."

"Trust me. I think it's not only generating the light curtain, I think it's powering those guns as well. And if we leave it running, everything in here will corrode faster. Shut it down and we've still got a treasure trove of alien technology." Mitch straightened and surveyed his handiwork. "Oscar helped me calibrate the charges. They should disrupt its power source without blowing the thing to bits."

Jacob scowled. *I know this is going to come back and bite me. It always does.* "If you're sure..."

"I'm sure." Mitch walked around the generator, admiring it. "Just think of the possibilities. If we could figure out how to use this force field thing, or how to replicate those weapons...you know what a leap that would be for our military?"

"That doesn't scare you? Cause it should." Jacob eyed the alien technology warily. *I'm not sure Earth is ready for this yet.*

"Fire in the hole!" Mitch and the others took cover. The explosion was deafening. The ground shook and he could see the flash through his eyelids.

"I thought you said the charges would disable it, not vaporize it."

"They were supposed to!" Mitch looked completely bewildered.

"Something obviously went wrong."

The generator was a smoking ruin in a blackened hole. Oscar and Hans moved out from cover, taking readings. "The weapons are down, and so is the light curtain," Oscar reported. Jacob realized he could see the forest all around them, and presumably, the area was no longer "missing" to people outside.

"That's a big crater," Mitch said, still looking shocked at the outcome.

"And you're going to explain this, how?"

Mitch rallied. "What's to explain? We have aliens, weapons, everything but the generator. Oscar got a good scan of it, so we're not exactly empty-handed. I say it's a win. Enough to get us off probation. Obviously, the generator was set on some kind of self-destruct."

"That's as good a story as any."

Mitch nudged him with an elbow. "Cheer up. If we're off probation, Falken might send us out on another case that *isn't* in the wilderness."

"Maybe," Jacob replied with a sigh. "No telling what trouble we'll land in tomorrow."

"That's what I love about this job," Mitch replied. "Come on. Let's get back to camp. We've got company coming."

THE SPHERE
Juliet E. McKenna

When he thought about it later, Henry Tall Deer realized the crash must have woken him. At the time, the only thing he knew was something had startled him awake. Sitting bolt upright in the narrow bed, his heart was racing. What the hell had just happened?

Conscious thought caught up with instinct and suggested there'd been a loud noise. Grabbing the flashlight from the bedside table, he searched the cabin with its beam. As far as he could tell, nothing had toppled from a shelf. There was no one here besides himself to knock over a chair by the scrubbed wooden table. No skittering claws betrayed some furry interloper.

Not that he expected one. The cabin looked as rustic as any other building in these remote valleys but the university ensured it was as weather and vermin proof as modern craftsmanship could make it. First and foremost, that was for the benefit of the costly instruments and computers recording and relaying vital data to the foundations and government departments whose grants paid for them, along with the pittance that just about covered Henry's bills back home.

Hooves outside, running. Not running, stampeding. Throwing back his blankets Henry hurried to unshutter the window. He glimpsed the stragglers as a herd of big horn sheep dashed down the valley towards the first suggestion of dawn.

Running from a bear? A pack of hunting wolves? Henry looked for some predator. At this time of year the nights were short, barely darkening beyond dusk before growing luminous with moonlight.

Instead, he saw a flare soaring up from beyond the ridge. A piercing mote of blue, rising ever higher into the darkness until he lost it amid the countless stars. It wasn't until much later that he realized he should have wondered about that. Weren't distress flares usually red? At the time he was too busy finding a compass and taking a bearing before he lost sight of the sapphire speck.

Turning on the lamp, he dragged on clothes and boots. Checking that the satellite phone was fully charged, he found the first aid kit, substantial enough to warrant its own backpack. Henry grimaced as he slung it on his back and tightened the straps. Hopefully it held whatever he might need to deal with whatever he might find. Calling the emergency services out here still meant waiting for hours. The retired Mountie who'd run Henry's wilderness survival course must have said so twenty times. As if a Nakota who'd grown up on a Montana reservation needed telling. But the university insisted everyone got certified before coming all this way.

One last check. Backpack, flashlight, handheld flares of his own in case he needed to scare off a bear or a bobcat. Water bottle, energy bars, all-purpose knife. Henry unlocked the door and headed out.

He went carefully. He might be familiar with the valley's trails after ten weeks but he'd be no use to anyone if he missed his footing and broke an ankle. There was also no knowing what local wildlife had been disturbed by whoever sent up that flare.

Henry allowed himself a moment of irritation. Who was stupid enough to get themselves into trouble before the sun had even risen? Some small aircraft's pilot? An idiot in a microlight? Hikers seduced by the notion of a night time walk, only to fall down a ravine?

His annoyance rapidly turned to apprehension. Was he going to find himself out of his depth? He was a field biologist, not a medic. His doctorate was on small rodents retreating up mountains to escape climate change.

He kept walking regardless, mentally running through everything he remembered the grizzled Mountie saying about emergency first aid. Really wishing he hadn't seen that movie about the hiker forced to cut off his own arm.

All such concerns evaporated when he finally reached the ridge line. Henry checked his watch and his heart sank. For all his urgency, it had still taken him nearly an hour to get here. The "Golden Hour" when it came to saving a life, he remembered that Mountie saying.

On the other hand, the sky was light enough by now to give him a clear view of a broad, black scar seared through brush and saplings. He could taste char on the breeze and he spared the local spirits a moment of fervent thanks that the whole valley hadn't gone up in flames.

Something large and metallic lay at the end of the burned gash; angular and artificial and wholly out of place in this landscape. A passenger plane had crashed? He couldn't see anything immediately identifiable as cockpit windows or tail fins though. Was it some piece of a fuselage? He really had no idea. Henry had never paid much attention to planes beyond checking how much leg room he'd get.

As he scanned the rest of the valley, nothing else caught his eye. None of the things he half-remembered from news reports about airline disasters. No pitiful scatter of luggage. No rows of seats ripped free. No yellow emergency slides deployed in vain.

Did that mean the aircraft had broken up in mid air? If it had, then surely everyone would be dead. There was certainly no sign of movement anywhere near the wreckage. He swallowed hard and wondered what he might find if he went down for a closer look. Sights too gruesome for even the greediest network chasing ratings to show on the nightly news?

He began picking a reluctant path down the slope regardless. If there was someone lying there injured, someone who could still be saved, he didn't have a choice, did he? Though he was guiltily relieved to hear a total absence of anyone crying out in pain as he got nearer.

By the time he was half way there, he was twice as puzzled. This really didn't look anything like an aircraft, large or small, or even a section of one. Though not all airplanes looked like something from Boeing, he reminded himself. Hadn't early stealth bomber test flights prompted a rash of UFO sightings? Was this something from an experimental, secret research project?

He paused for a moment to study the whole thing. Because it was still pretty much whole. Henry was sure of that now. It was crushed and crumpled around the edges and the impact must have torn off whatever had been attached to those stubby brackets along one side, but overall, this wasn't a piece broken off anything else.

There was also no sign that flames had engulfed it, from burning fuel or anything else. Henry looked again at the path of destruction scorching the valley. Whatever this was, it must have been white hot when it landed, to cause that much damage. Even though its own silvery metallic skin was barely discolored.

Was this a satellite come crashing to earth? Some of them were huge nowadays, weren't they? Well, if that's what this was, there couldn't be anyone inside it to be injured. His moment of relief was short-lived. He was still going to have to call it in. Satellite technology cost millions of dollars. Even a field biologist knew that. So the peace and natural rhythm of these woods would soon be shattered by trucks or helicopters or whatever whoever owned sent to recover the wreckage.

He frowned. Hadn't some Russian satellite scattered radioactive debris all over Saskatchewan in the 70s? Better not get too close. Better alert the authorities as soon as possible. He reached for the satellite phone and hit the emergency speed dial button.

"Hi there, yes—" He quickly identified himself and explained.

The emergency operator didn't sound convinced. "There's been nothing on the news."

"Maybe NORAD is still writing their press release?" Henry suggested.

"Maybe a meteor strike—"

"I'd know one of those if I saw it," Henry interrupted. "This is definitely man-made. It's the size of a shipping container!"

"You're sure?" the voice persisted.

"Do you think I'm an idiot? Or making this up?" He hadn't expected this response.

"We get a lot of hoaxes," the voice said repressively. "Hold please."

Henry stared at the sat phone with disbelief as tinny music seeped out of it. Could this be a set-up? He looked back down the valley. All the way out here? Who would possibly go to so much trouble? Why would they? To create some internet sensation?

He studied the silvery object. Then he looked for some sign of whatever had been ripped loose in its tumbling crash. Coppery gleams in the undergrowth rewarded him, now fingered by the inquisitive sun. Maybe one of those carried some identification which he could relay to the authorities. Who might this thing belong to? NASA? The Chinese? Didn't India have a space program now?

Or if he found something to prove this was a hoax, he could rip apart the rest of it until he found the webcam or whatever. Then he could tell whoever was responsible exactly what he thought of their stunt damaging this pristine wilderness. Let them put that up on YouTube.

Either way, he wasn't going to stand here on hold. They had his information. He cancelled the call and began to search for some answers.

To his intense disappointment there was no writing on the closest panel, or the next one, or the one after that. Which wasn't to say there were no marks. All the metal was scuffed and gouged and not just from this impact.

As his search took him nearer to the wreck, he felt lingering heat warm his face in the morning chill. Henry looked up to assess how close he'd come to any potential radiation. An instant later, he registered that the darkness in the corner of his eye was a black pelt. Cautiously he turned to get a better look, slowly reaching for the pocket that held his flares. The creature didn't move.

Henry blinked. Then common sense told him that the downed satellite must have hit some unfortunate animal. Except this wasn't some mangled carcass. Whatever it might be, it was strapped into a sizeable chunk of technology. He realized that looking for panels in the undergrowth had taken him around the end of the angular craft. Now he could see where the impact had ripped it open to reveal a hollow interior.

And this had fallen out? What on earth was it? Henry took a step closer. A chimp? A dog? What country was sending animals into space? Maybe that's why there'd been nothing on the news about this thing crashing. Whoever was responsible knew the public outcry would be horrendous.

He reached into a pocket for his own smart phone. A few photos would offer proof, in case anyone in authority tried to cover it up. He focused on the creature and then slowly lowered the phone.

Not a monkey. Not a mammal of any kind. Not any sort of creature that Henry recognised. It had a roughly rectangular body and what looked like four limbs but he couldn't see how they articulated under its fur and there was nothing he could readily identify as a head or a tail. The pelt seemed to have a thick fringe of long black locks with a golden metallic sphere caught up in a tangle on one side.

Was it dead? It wasn't moving but could it just be stunned? Unlikely. If this was some sort of ejector seat, whatever should have slowed its descent didn't seem to have worked. The cradle-thing had hit hard enough to dig deep into the mossy ground and Henry could see several big cracks. It had to be dead. Iridescent in the sunlight, blow flies were now arriving to explore the alien carcass.

There, he'd said it, even if only inside his own head. This was an alien. Which meant this was an alien spaceship. Henry sank to the ground, abruptly breathless. It wasn't only these remote valleys which would never be the same again. He sat still for a long moment, unable to move past that thought.

Gradually he became aware of the familiar sounds and scents of the woodland. He drank some water and ate an energy bar. What now? Well, he was a scientist. That meant gathering data. Then there'd be independent proof this had really happened, whatever the military or whoever else turned up might do when they heard about his phone call.

As he began taking photos, Henry felt profoundly sad. Humanity's first contact with extra-terrestrials had been thwarted by a fatal impact. However far this creature had travelled, it had come so close only for disaster to strike. He really wished things could have been different.

* * *

Prestige internship, my ass. David Mendlesohn had been thinking that for days now, though he was sufficiently prudent not to say so out loud. He still held out hope of a transfer to a project more worthy of an MIT student.

It's why he'd crossed the country, goddammit! Why wasn't he working on the intricacies of the alien lander's propulsion system? How about letting him see if he could crack the principles underpinning its communications protocols? After a decade and a half, so much still remained to be done, for all the progress made so far. Fresh eyes might make all the difference. He could be the one to see some vital connection.

He consciously set his irritation aside. He wouldn't get any meaningful opportunity if he shot his mouth off, so he'd bide his time and do what he was told. Even if that meant another tedious afternoon in this empty lab checking that these dusty boxes still held all the scraps from the crashed craft which no one knew what to do with.

He put the lid back on the one he was done with and slid it along the work bench. Flipping over the page on his clipboard, he checked that the number at the top of the typed list matched the label stuck on the next carton.

Okay, that was the first tick. Then he frowned at the entry on the next line. "Gold sphere—query personal adornment." What the hell kind of description was that?

He lifted the lid off the box. Okay, there it was, among the scraps of alien alloy and molded polymer that had never been successfully pieced back together in a way that fit in with the rest of the buckled craft's instrumentation.

David lifted the gold sphere out. It fit comfortably into the palm of his gloved hand. Personal adornment? Whose dumb idea was that? Necklaces, earrings, brooches, buckles; they all had to be attached to whoever was showing them off. There was no sign of any such thing. No loop for a chain, no setting for a hook or a pin.

He weighed it in his hand. There was no way this was solid gold. On the other hand, it didn't feel light enough to be hollow. David turned it this way and that, to take a closer look. No, there was no hint of a seam, still less any hint of how to open it.

He stiffened as his phone vibrated in his pocket. Putting the golden sphere down on the lab bench, he fished it out. A swipe of his finger across the screen was no use. Goddam latex gloves. He hastily stripped them off and managed to answer before the last ring.

"Hey, Rebecca."

"How's California?"

He could hear the smile in his sister's voice and grinned back as he gazed out of the window at the verdant landscaped grounds, the ochre hills in the far distance, and the cloudless blue sky above. "Pretty cool."

"Listen, are you bringing a plus one to Leah's bat mitzvah? I need to let the caterers know final numbers by the end of the week."

David's phone interrupted with a beep. He looked at the screen to see the low battery warning.

"Yes, yes, I'll bring someone."

"Someone or just anyone to stop Mom asking about your love life?" Rebecca countered. "That's a lousy thing to do to a date, Davy."

"So's shoving someone special in front of Mom and all the aunts," he retorted.

"So come alone." Her voice softened. "We just want to see you."

The phone beeped again.

"I'll be there," he assured her. "And I'll let you know by the end of the week."

"Okay, talk soon." Rebecca rang off.

David found his backpack and dug out his charger. Thankfully there were unused electrical outlets all along the wall at the back of the bench.

He'd ring Sarah when he was finished here and ask her out for a drink. After he'd worked out how to invite her to a family event in a way that would show he wanted to spend more time with her—while making it clear it really wasn't any kind of big deal whether she said yes or no to this particular trip.

The gold sphere rolled across the bench. David snatched it up before it could fall to the floor. An instant of stomach churning panic subsided into relief. Catastrophe averted. He wouldn't be forever labelled as the klutz who'd broken some invaluable alien salvage. Because everything from the Kiruk Valley Lander was priceless even if no one knew what it was.

The golden sphere buzzed and pulsed in his hand. In his ungloved hand. Sweat beaded his forehead in spite of the air conditioning. What the hell...?

David set the sphere back down with exquisite care. As it moved of its own accord, he stepped back, startled. The sphere wasn't following the lure of gravity towards the edge of the bench. It rolled over to the outlet and snuggled up to his phone charger.

What the hell...? He flexed his empty hand and looked at it closely, both sides. No weird sensations, no marks on his skin. He drew a slow measured breath.

Okay, so that happened. Now he had to work out who to tell and exactly what to say, to make absolutely goddam certain that he was one of the team set up to work out what it meant.

* * *

The computer completed its calculations and shared its conclusions with impersonal detachment. The numbers didn't match. So Namrita Kaur was the first to know that another exoplanet was conclusively ruled out as the origin of the universe's only other incontrovertibly-proven-to-exist intelligent life form.

Or rather, as the source of alien life bright enough to achieve near-lightspeed space travel, she corrected herself. Any number of these planets still might be home to less exalted creatures. And this was all progress, wasn't it? Another step along the way towards the ultimate goal. Sooner or later there had to be good news.

Of course, sooner would be better than later. What now? Namrita contemplated the data so painstakingly gleaned from over a quarter of a century's analysis of every scrap of information from the Kiruk Valley Lander's crash site. She didn't need to pull up the source file. She knew every line.

Leaning back in her chair, she stretched out her arms, grimacing as she felt the tension knotting her shoulders. Time to get up and walk around. Get the blood circulating. Maybe shake loose some new ideas.

Though a change was as good as a rest, wasn't it? That's what everyone's supervisors said, explaining why side projects were permitted, even encouraged. She accessed her personal drive and checked on the analysis she'd set running this morning before starting her official work.

Another dead end. Despite her determination to stay positive, Namrita felt a pang of disappointment. That meant the very end of that particular road. Whichever way you sliced, diced, or analyzed those numbers, whether you converted the digital pulses into any and all numeral systems from binary on upwards, she reckoned she had now proven that the Mendlesohn Sphere's output bore no relation to any of the mathematical principles underpinning gravitational physics.

Or astrophysics or nuclear physics or quantum theory or anything else, according to the records left by those before her who'd been intrigued by this puzzle. Or chemistry: organic or inorganic. Or biology, for all Namrita knew. In the years since the mysterious artifact had so accidentally come to life, someone must have looked at its output in relation to whatever numbers were generated by the study of plants and animals.

Time for a cup of tea. She got up and walked to the far end of the long, hushed room. A few faces glanced up before concentrating once more on their own computer screens. The only sounds were the muted rattle of keyboards, the occasional creak of a chair, and here and there the soft scritch of paper on pencil. She'd never met a mathematician who could do without what her father always referred to as a "thinking stick".

She pushed open the kitchen door to be greeted by the cheery chirp of the drinks dispenser. Edmund looked around, stirring some frothy concoction.

"Tea?" He put down his mug and reached for another one. "How's life in number crunching? Anything exciting to report?"

Namrita opened the cupboard, took out the canister and measured leaves into the small teapot she'd brought in from home. "More planets ruled out. Of course, it would help if you telescope jockeys didn't keep finding new ones to add to the list."

Ed grinned. "You can't hold back science. How are you getting on with the Mendlesohn Sphere?"

Seeing the mischief in his eyes, Namrita narrowed her own gaze. "Why do you ask?"

"It's just that I heard a rumor..." Ed held out a hand.

Namrita gave him the teapot. "Go on."

He pressed the lever and hot water hissed onto the tea leaves. "Kate, over in Material Sciences, she was saying they reckon it's just a test."

"The Sphere?" Namrita frowned, bemused.

He nodded. "Ask around and you'll soon find out how many supervisors suggest it as a side project, whatever your particular discipline is. Kate and her team think they just want to see how long people will stick with it, before they realize there's nothing to be learned. Someone's probably running a pool."

"It must have some purpose," Namrita objected. "Why else would it be on the Lander?"

Ed shrugged. "Who knows? 'Intelligences greater than man's' and all that."

She challenged him with raised eyebrows. "You're still expecting tripods and heat rays?"

He shrugged again. "I'm just amazed someone hasn't taken a can opener to it by now."

"What would that achieve?" she protested. "We've got the output to analyze. Taking the Sphere itself to pieces would be as pointless as cutting into a tennis ball to try to find the bounce."

Ed grinned. "I'll see if I can get a bet on you sticking with it for a while longer then. See you in the pub later? A bunch of us are going to The Bird and Baby. Kate's got a cousin visiting."

She nodded. "I'll stop by."

"Great. Well, better get back to it." Finishing his drink with a few rapid swallows, Ed sketched a wave and left through the kitchen's other door, heading down the corridor.

Namrita poured her tea and stared through the kitchen window, past the twenty-first century's chrome and glass towards Oxford's ageless towers and spires. Mankind's finest minds had spent centuries in this city of golden stone solving the mysteries of the universe. The Lander and everything in it was just one more conundrum.

Though of course, Oxford's scholars weren't only scientists. She frowned, sipping tea, as she tried to pin down an elusive memory, stirred by her conversation with Edmund.

"He that breaks a thing to find out what it is has left the path of wisdom."

That was it. That's what JRR Tolkien had Gandalf say to Saruman in *The Lord of the Rings*. She'd have to remember that for the next time someone suggested cutting into the Mendlesohn Sphere.

Namrita headed back to her desk, thinking about journeys. Why did people take things with them? Sitting down, she opened the top drawer to her right and contemplated the contents. Pencils. A sharpener. Spare data chips and power cells for her handheld. Hair clips. A comb. Her expired digibadge for the Lucasian Professor's seminar when she'd visited Cambridge last month. No use any more but she wasn't about to throw it away.

Not everything was purely utilitarian. The picube her sister-in-law had sent from Sri Harmandir Sahib. Namrita shook it and the digital image of Variam with her nephews and niece in front of the golden temple floated to the top. Smiling, she put it down beside the earbuds for the musicube she'd got free with that gym membership she almost never used.

She carefully closed the drawer and woke up her computer with a tap on the fingerprint reader. A quick search of the Mendlesohn Sphere archive confirmed her first thoughts. Every possible way of turning the output into a visible image had long since been tried.

What about audio? It seemed various people had tried a few different approaches over the years. She called up their notes and began reading. After a little while, she reached for a pad and a pencil and jotted down some random thoughts. Soon after, she began working through a series of far from random equations.

"Time to call it a day?"

She looked up, startled, to see Padraig standing by his desk, easing his stiff neck this way and that. Glancing round, Namrita realized they were the last two left in the room. She hadn't even noticed the others leaving.

As Padraig had evidently observed. "What's got you so ent'ralled?"

"Just an idea." She contemplated her screen where she'd called up an array of sound processing software. Did she have everything she needed? Pretty much.

"Anything you're ready to share?" Padraig shrugged on his jacket and tucked his handheld into an inner pocket.

He'd be on his way any minute now. Should she try to explain or keep quiet until he'd gone, or maybe, just—

"Let's see." Namrita caught her lower lip between her teeth as she hit a rapid sequence of keystrokes.

An instant later, melody floated through the empty room. It was definitely a tune, though subtly unfamiliar to her ears, and Padraig's, too, judging from his expression.

"What's that?" He looked at her, intrigued.

Namrita couldn't help laughing. "The music of the spheres. Of the Mendlesohn Sphere, to be exact."

* * *

"Oh look, it's ET's iPod!" a bearded man observed archly.

"How long have you been waiting to share that retro gem?" his companion mocked.

Namrita did her best not to scowl at the couple who barely spared a glance for the display case holding the golden sphere before wandering away.

Wasn't it worth noting the hard work and particularly the lateral thinking that had gone into discovering its purpose? Wasn't the alien music worthy of respect on its own merits? But every second person who'd commented on this particular exhibit had seemed to dismiss it as trivial.

Unwelcome suspicion soured the lingering taste of the reception's champagne. Was there something like that inanity written on the card inside the case? It wasn't as if any scientist had been included in the team putting this exhibition together. Diplomats, media experts, and public relations specialists had taken charge of making all the arrangements months before.

They'd probably been planning it for years. Starting within minutes of the first signals from the Travellers' ship reaching the Hawking Probe, most likely. The success of tonight's gathering was doubtless going to make or break careers.

But before Namrita could get close enough to see what some communications genius might have written about the Sphere, another woman came up to peer into the glassy box. The stranger's face lit up with sudden delight, framed by long hair as glossily black as Namrita's grey locks had once been.

Despite her lingering irritation, Namrita was intrigued. Then she saw the name on the woman's digibadge. Approaching, she offered her hand.

"Laura Tall Deer? Any relation to—?"

"—Henry? My grandfather." The American shook Namrita's hand and checked her digibadge. "And you're the genius who unlocked the music! He was so thrilled. He always wondered what the sphere could be."

Laura broke off as someone else approached. Another courtesy guest, according to the hologram on his badge.

He held up apologetic hands. "Please, take your time. Don't let me disturb you."

"Join us, please." Namrita invited him closer with a gesture when she saw his name. "Mr Mendlesohn."

"Please, call me Simon, and yes, I'm his son." He smiled ruefully. "But no, I'm not a scientist. I'm a dentist."

"Do they have teeth, do you suppose?" Laura Tall Deer wondered mischievously.

All three of them turned to look at the two closest aliens, of the eight that were currently wandering round the exhibits, all discreetly shadowed by heavy-set, square-shouldered men with very short hair and expensively tailored suits.

"Are you a zoologist?" Namrita recalled reading somewhere that Henry Tall Deer had been something of that sort.

Laura shook her head. "Astronomer. Grandad took me out to show me the stars from Kiruk Valley when I was six years old and told me all about the night when the Lander crashed. I've been trying to find out where it came from ever since."

She studied the aliens as they flanked a case containing a replica of the Hawking Probe. "He'd have been fascinated to see them walking around."

"Aren't we all?" Simon Mendlesohn laughed a little nervously.

Every biologist certainly was, if Namrita's professional-cloud tag-stream was any indicator. The questions were endless and the misconceptions extrapolated from the First Scout's corpse had turned out to be legion.

That black pelt? Not fur. A living Traveller was enveloped by a sensory organ composed of hundreds of thousands of filaments. However they perceived the world around them—and Namrita really didn't envy whoever had to find a way to ask politely for details about that—they responded with swirls and ripples of every possible color and shade coruscating from head to toe.

So to speak, given they didn't have either heads or toes. It turned out the Travellers used all four limbs for walking on or manipulating things with each one's four digits with equal ease. They would also head straight in whatever direction they wanted to without feeling any need to turn around. Depending on what they were doing, their overall body shape could be rectangular, square or trapezoid.

"Er, I think they're coming this way." Simon unconsciously retreated a pace.

Laura stiffened. "I hope I didn't offend them. Was I staring?"

She had been, but there was no point in saying so. Namrita reminded herself that she was the oldest of the trio and the only one who'd actually met one of the Travellers before, when the ship's navigator had visited Oxford ten days ago. Though that had been to discuss mathematics, not a trip for socializing or sightseeing.

She took a step forward and summoned up a welcoming smile. She only hoped the Travellers stayed on all fours, or on two feet at least. Last week, when the navigator had stood up on a single limb in order to use all three others at once, it had towered over the tallest man in the gathering in a distinctly unnerving fashion.

"Good evening."

"Good evening." The first Traveller's polite response came from the silvery translation box it carried in its—well, the biologists as well as the journalists were still arguing about what to call the fringe of what were now self-evidently not just passive locks of hair or fur. Each tendril was mobile, flexible, tactile, and Namrita had seen for herself how swiftly the navigator had worked out how to type with them on a human keyboard.

She took refuge in conventional courtesy. "How are you enjoying the evening?"

"It is very pleasing to meet so many of the humans who have devoted their time, effort, and skills to making contact with our people." The first Traveller's words were smooth, accentless and effortlessly fluent.

Namrita could only imagine the chagrin among the linguists who'd painstakingly developed the protocols for learning an alien language, when it turned out the aliens themselves had perfected a translation device capable of handling every widely broadcast language.

She didn't imagine the diplomats were any too pleased either. All the ones she'd encountered had naturally assumed they would control access to and communication with the Travellers. It turned out these aliens had other ideas.

The second one moved forward, waves of purple rippling towards Namrita. "We are most honored to meet you, Professor Kaur. May I take your hand?"

"I—" Namrita steeled herself. "The honor is all mine."

They're not tentacles. Not tentacles. Really not tentacles.

As she extended her hand, the second Traveller's tendrils enveloped it, colors shifting through the rainbow from scarlet at the tip to violet at the root. The firm caress wasn't in the least unpleasant, silky and comfortably warm.

"May I ask," the alien enquired politely, "what inspired you to study the sphere in your youth?"

"It was a puzzle." What else could she say? "I've always liked a challenge."

Her reply prompted nearly identical flashes of silver across each Traveller's pelt. She wondered what that meant.

The first one had turned its attention to Simon Mendlesohn. "And you are the son of the man who made such a fortunate discovery when the sphere lacked energy. There is great honor among our kind for those who are lucky."

Perhaps it sensed his nervousness. It made no request to touch his hand before spiky waves of green indicated its focus shifting to Laura. "While your ancestor was the first human to see the First Scout after death?"

"He was, yes." Laura's answer prompted those same flashes of silver from each Traveller.

"Please—"

Was it Namrita's imagination or was there a note of urgency in the second alien's modulated, artificial voice?

"—did your ancestor ever say exactly where the sphere was found?"

Laura nodded. "The First Scout had it—that's to say, he was holding it. Or she, excuse me," she added hastily.

Questions of alien gender could wait as far as Namrita was concerned. She wanted to know why that answer prompted both Travellers to entwine a handful of tendrils and link with each other. Sparkling white surged from one to the other and back again.

She wondered how unnerving the diplomats found the realization that these aliens could communicate in ways they had no hope of understanding.

"That's good news?" Simon Mendlesohn edged forward. "Why?

What's the thing for, anyway?"

The Travellers loosed their hold on each other and the first one addressed him. "It is—"

His translation box emitted an incomprehensible garble.

Yellow swirled around the device each Traveller held.

The second alien tried. "That is to say, it serves as—"

Once again, the translator burbled nonsense. Yellow swirls darkened to orange.

"Is there a problem, sir?" The Travellers' dark suited escort stepped forward with a warning look at the three humans.

Namrita wasn't bothered. She guessed that glare was the security detail's automatic reaction to anything unexpected. She was more curious about the translation device's failure. When the navigator had visited Oxford, his box had been perfectly able to handle every variation on academic titles and all possible distinctions between various specialities in math and physics.

"Forgive us," the first Traveller said, and this time, Namrita was convinced she could hear irritation underpinning its words. "We seem to have discovered a lack in our translators' priorities."

The second alien chose its words carefully. "The purpose of the music is to focus the mind on—"

Gibberish defeated it again but now the first Traveller found a solution.

"— to focus the mind upon the divine."

"The divine?" Namrita hadn't expected that.

"The divine." The second alien's closest tendrils twitched in her direction. "Is that the correct word? You understand what we mean by that?"

"Yes, at least, I think so." She hastily qualified her answer.

Each alien's shifting pattern of colors instantly stilled.

"Please," the first Traveller invited, "tell us what humanity knows of the divine?"

"Please," the second echoed.

Namrita looked at Simon Mendlesohn and Laura Tall Deer and saw the same question that now paralyzed her tongue was reflected in their eyes.

Where on earth could they possibly start?

SHAME THE DEVIL
Sharon Lee & Steve Miller

"You're going too fast!" Brad yelled from the back seat.

Seika sighed, and leaned into the controls. Brad was pissed off because he'd wanted to drive. Too bad he'd had the drone training, and she hadn't, else he'd have had Seika Safka sitting on the back seat, bitching about *his* driving, and a Safka yielded to *no one* in the proper complaining of complaints.

Still, Seika thought, the man had a point, given their present location on the search grid. Wouldn't hurt to ease it back a little.

"Why're you slowing down?" Brad demanded. "Did you see something?"

Bless the man, Seika thought, hand tightening on the throttle—then loosening again, because...

She *had* seen something.

Squinting behind her snow googles, she scanned the ice plain to her right. Something had—flashed. Maybe just a ray of sunlight, angled through a chunk of ice. Probably that, in fact, but she'd had an impression of...weight.

And then she had it. An object, half hidden among the wind-carved ridges of snow, brilliant with more than sunlight, its angles weird, and its size—well, who could tell from such a distance? It flashed and flared in the sunlight, bleeding a spectrum that seemed just a little off.

She kept the thing in her eye, and turned the sled toward it, taking them off-grid, but not by that much, and what else were they in Antarctica for, if it wasn't to pick up weird stuff that had fallen out of sky?

"What are you doing?" Brad demanded, but he sounded more curious than peeved.

"Going to get a closer look at that—artifact," she answered. "See it? Eleven o'clock."

"I don't—oh."

She throttled the machine down again, approaching the artifact slowly, eyes sharp on the ice in case there were more of whatever-it-was, hidden in the wave-like ridges.

"Stepping off," Brad said. "Bringing the drone down."

She didn't answer that; no need. That was how they were working the team: Seika Safka and her snowy blues machine, accompanied by Brad Billingsworth on drone.

The machine shifted when Brad stepped off, and speeded up some in celebration of losing his bulk. The...thing, the artifact—was just ahead of her, deliberately flashing through the colors of the prism, like it was programmed, or—

That was when the ice gave way beneath the machine so suddenly that Seika didn't have time to yell.

* * *

"Safka!"

Brad sounded worried, there in her ear. That was new and different. It occurred to her that he might've gotten into trouble, stepping off the sled, and she raised her head from the dash—

"Ow!"

Pain lanced through her ribs. Her vision went white—or no, maybe not. There was snow and ice all around her, not just under her skis and in the distance...

It came back to her, then, the way the ice had just...crumbled away, and that quick she'd been falling. She'd stuck with it, though; rode the machine down and through it—the reflexes of a woman who'd learned about old-rimed ice, snow pits, and snow machines back before she'd gotten her first harmonica.

"Always keep it under you! Just like ridin' a bronco. *Always* keep it under you!"

That's what Uncle Charlie Fuentes'd told her; that was a story she could share with anybody.

No, now. Uncle Charlie wasn't here, was he? Just her, and Brad, and the machine, and the—whatever it was she'd been steering toward. Memory—or imagination—provided a glimpse of it, mid-fall, flashing from yellow to green...

"Safka!"

Brad still sounded worried. Ought to do something about that.

Seika sat back in her seat and cautiously drew in an experimental deep breath—hurt some, but not as much as broken ribs would. She thought. Then, she took stock.

All around her was ice. Ice so white it was blue. Snowy rubble surrounded the machine, one of the skis was twisted up over the bonnet, the runner swinging at a sad, unnatural angle. The other ski, and most of the bonnet, were buried under a fall of jagged ice.

Looking up, she could see a small—very small—circle of more blue, which she very much hoped was the sky.

No wonder Brad was worried, she thought. Bad form to lose one of ANSMET's snow machines; worse form to lose your partner.

Another breath, to calm herself, as she realize that this might be *it*, right here—buried in ice.

"Safka," Brad demanded, "where are you?"

She heard something crack, overhead somewhere; felt an impact against her helmet hard enough to make her blink.

"Answer, dammit! I can't see anything down there..."

Brad had gone from worried to pissed off, sounded like. Best to answer the man.

"At least I made it to Bombay!"

Seika's voice filled the blue-hued ice chimney, which was not quite as silent as it ought to be otherwise. Portions of the collapse were still filtering downward with screes and ticks and musical clinks.

As the echo of her voice faded, she became aware that it was more than her ribs that ached. She hurt in a dozen places, though if she was bleeding she didn't know it. She was alive, and that was a start. She pulled her goggles off, shaking now, and feeling a little foolish at her declaration. Brad couldn't help not having a sense of humor; she shouldn't yank his chain.

Something flashed, straight across from her, and half-hidden behind a chunk of ice as big as her snowmachine.

Red. Orange. Yellow. Green...

The artifact.

So she *had* seen it, falling with her. Good, she thought, without really understanding why. That's good.

She'd been taking stock. Right, then.

First thing, she hadn't been killed outright, which she counted as a win. She wasn't done yet, not by a long shot. After all, the ice hadn't gulped her down whole; there was, far above her, that tiny blue hole to the sky.

The snowmobile's electric engine was still humming; the mandatory daytime lights were on yet, and the heated saddle was warm. The machine had landed horizontal, and she'd kept her seat, riding it down like she'd been taught long ago.

Didn't Uncle Bly have something to say about it, that time she *hadn't* kept her seat. Learned a bushel of new words that time, during and after he'd pulled her out from the snow drift she'd managed to launch herself into. He'd been fueled pretty good that day, and he'd been behaving himself, sitting on the back pad of the machine he called *Splendid Venda* because he wasn't fit to drive, so he'd been first off and into the drift, and the first to reach her. Dad had told her she couldn't tell the story Uncle Bly's way 'til she could sing it, so she hadn't, yet. She had a stanza started for him, somewhere, though.

"Safka, listen to me." That wasn't Uncle Bly. No, wait—it was Brad. She was in Antarctica, halfway down a throat of ice, and her machine smashed up something bad.

"Safka?"

"Here."

"I need you to tell me where you are. Your condition, right?"

"Right."

She looked around her.

"I'm down, can see a little blue 'way up, and the walls are blue. I'm kind of right on the edge of a cliff – maybe four feet from the edge, and I'm against a wall of crumbly snow or ice. The thing—the artifact—is on the other side of the split, maybe ten feet off."

"That big reflective ice chunk? But you're OK?"

"Think so. Let me stand—oh!"

She'd used the handlebars to push up onto her feet—and collapsed to the heated seat, cringing in pain. After a few gasps and shudders, she found her voice again.

"I'm still on the sled," she told Brad. "We're pitched down a little—nose down, rear high. One ski broken, other ski buried. I can see bits of shred on the ice around me, but nothing big enough I can tell what it is. Was. Just now tried to put my weight on my right foot and it hurts like a summbitch."

"All right, don't push it. I've called in. We're waiting for—"

His voice broke off clean.

Seika brought her hand to the headset, tapped it.

"Brad? Can you hear me?"

There was no answer.

* * *

If she had her dates right, Dad and Uncle Charlie were singing somewhere in New Hampshire, or maybe it was Rutland, she forgot.

If it'd been a normal fall, she'd've been on the road with them, touring the fairs and festivals. But it hadn't been a normal fall, Aminah had finally got the lease on that place on Elm, and they'd been working together, day and night, scrubbing and painting, and getting equipment in.

The shop had priority, said Aminah, who knew a thing or two about priorities. When that was ready, and open for business, then they'd paint and fix and move into the little apartment over-top. Seika'd said she'd help out in the noddle shop, but Aminah had laughed and said she wouldn't be worth living with, if she didn't travel around like she'd always done, playing music for a live audience.

That's when she'd gotten the call from ANSMET, and—with Aminah's blessing—had headed out for Antarctica, the Transantarctic Mountains, and the Big Meteor Hunt.

She'd been eight when the daytime bolide streaked past them before dropping into Lake Champlain, flinging down pebbles from heaven. She still had the first "piece from space" she'd found that day, on a chain around her neck. She'd retrieved it on the receding shore side, warm still. After that, she'd been fascinated by space and stories about space, like her mom had been, back then.

Her visions, though, weren't like her Mom's—she'd never aimed at the really big time—the big scopes, that was what Mom had wanted; big fame. Though it meant leaving the fractious little family of musicians, her mom had gotten her wish. The big news these days in astronomy was the discovery of the tentacle of dark matter reaching from the Coalsack, right on by the solar system and off to Scholz's star. Her mom was on the team studying that piece of star-quality science.

That wasn't for Seika.

No, she'd wanted to be up close and personal with the stars. ANSMET—The Antarctic Search For Meteorites—had been on her radar for years—which Aminah had known, and practically shoved her out the door to catch the—

"Safka," Brad said, his voice crackling in her earphones, "Safka! Answer!"

Funny, a few minutes ago they'd been talking like they were in each other's laps, which they'd practically been, and the sound had been crystal clear. Now the reception was weepy and distant. Still, the man deserved an answer.

"Here, *tovarisch*," she said, her voice sounding gritty in her own ears.

"Say what? Can barely hear you! Please repeat!"

She took him literally, said "Here, *tovarisch*," and after a count of three, added ; "Can you see me?"

Carefully, she looked up, but there was no Brad-blot against the tiny piece of sky, and it seemed like the tiny piece had gotten tinier. If the ice closed up over her...

A sound then, a rumble and cracking noise, with a few extra bits of icy debris hurtling down past her.

"Are you OK?," she asked. "Brad?"

There was no immediate response, then came a fluttery connection.

"The other sleds are breaking their grids and heading this way. I'm about thirty meters away from where you went in, right now, it looks like there's a...dip there, a sort of split across an ice dome or something. I could feel it move when I tried to get closer...backed off. Calling base to get the 'copter in here."

This time, the sound was sharp and definite. The glimpse of blue sky grew wider as another section of ice slid down, scraping along the uneven sides of the ice chimney. One section tumbled grandly, and Seika ducked, too late, as ice bounced off the wall and then off the opposite side before a section that looked as big as her head collided with her helmet.

* * *

She woke to flashes of light, in series. Her head hurt, and her eyes had a tendency to cross. The flashing was coming from the other side of the cleft; the place she had last seen the artifact.

She started to move, to assess the damage to her sled; and the ledge on which they rested. Using her eyes made her nauseous, though, and she closed them. Behind the lids, she saw a neat, progressive spectrum, each color soft and soothing. Her stomach eased, and her headache did, too.

She sighed, and spoke, loudly.

"Brad, ANSMET FOUR!"

Across the crevasse—across the *greatly widened* crevasse—was the thing—the artifact—from the ice, up top. It was not only there, but, in the glow of sunlight from the hole up above, it had become ghostly blue at the center, with edges going from red to orange, to—to another color that she couldn't quite make out, which was just crazy.

Wasn't it.

She'd seen it tumbling with her, she realized, tumbling *ahead* of her, on the shaky way down, looking like a big rutilated quartz crystal with shades running from gold to rose to deep red. The last gout of snow and ice that had come down the chimney had left it out in the open, so she could see it plain, glowing, not just with the distant sunlight, but with an internal light, crystalline and beautiful.

What had Brad said it was? A chunk of reflective ice? Brad better get his eyes checked, pronto. Hopefully, the drone had gotten a better angle on it, even if its operator was going blind.

This close, it wasn't anything like a chunk of ice. Clearly, it had been built. It wasn't gem cut but purpose-cut. Not meant for pretty, but to be a tool. It had the feel of equipment, the way a space probe has the feel of equipment, no matter how much gold foil they swathe it in. And like a space probe, there were marks on it. Information. IDs. In no language she recognized.

She squinted, but the lettering didn't come any clearer. No chunk of ice, this, no more than it was a meteor. She was good at identifying random booster parts and failed satellites, and she'd swear that it wasn't any bit of man-made tech at all. No, what she had here was of no earthly manufacture. She'd bet her Sunday fiddle on it.

"Brad, are you there?"

No reply, and now pain was working in from her limbs as the adrenalin of the fall gave way to a cunning kind of depression. This might do it, she thought, this might be the church door's worth of luck run out.

"Brad? ANSMET?"

She tried the other channel, one that ought to reach one of the other two teams. Nothing. Back to the regular channel, and nothing.

Maybe he'd run for help, leaving her in a hole twenty-two kilometers from anywhere. Maybe...

She'd better distract herself. If she was going to be down here a while, she ought to know what her resources were.

"Equipment check," she told herself, "and make it snappy."

She'd taken a hit to the helmet and...something clicked as she ran her hands over the helmet controls and headset. She pushed at the microphone, feeling something snap and seat, like maybe it'd gotten knocked loose when...

"Safka? ANSMET! What the hell happened? I lost you!"

It wasn't a strong signal, but she sighed in relief, felt the relief drain her to near collapse.

"Here! Safka here! Took a hit on the helmet and it knocked the mike loose. Brad, that thing I saw. It's here, and its glowing real bright. Like nothing I've ever seen before! Ought to be able to see it up there where you are."

"Am in touch with base and the other sleds. They're coming," Brad said, like he hadn't heard her, and...maybe he hadn't. "But I can't get close right now—the edge is fragile. Got no video, nothing to see. Talk to me about you. We need to inventory how you are!"

The inventory wasn't fun, since it involved her trying to feel things that were wrapped in cold-defying clothes and good boots. Beneath the overalls her regular travel vest, bulging with pockets of this and that, pens, note devices, a trio of harmonicas—A, C, and G of course, also three kinds of chocolate bars—dark, darker and really dark! —three dice—one six sided, one eight sided and one twelve sided—and three different sizes of pocket lights. Under that the heavy shirt, and under that ribs, whole ribs! She pulled shirt tight, sealed the vest, closed the wind seal on the overalls, pulled the— ouch!

The right foot, now...and maybe the right leg, those were problematic. Apparently the helmet cam wasn't broadcasting, but the radio was. Good enough. She needed to keep going.

Seika grimaced. There were now two sleds above, said Brad, though the sounds in her icy chamber hadn't changed. She carefully worked her cold hands into her riding coveralls, flinching, but finding no immediate signs of broken ribs among those aches. She was avoiding getting off the sled, fearing the footing as well as not trusting her foot or leg. She used her left foot, carefully leaning in that direction enough to put weight on it on the debris pile she sat on. It was nearest the ice wall, but with an awkward angle she could move it with some force, and so she kicked an ice ball into the crevasse, not liking the two count it took for the first strike, nor the echoes as some small cascade followed into the blue abyss.

Checking her head meant taking the helmet off and hanging it carefully so it wouldn't be lost. She felt bruises on the temples, and a scrape on her face. The back of her head yielded several palpable and painful lumps and some other tenderness. Scary, but no blood. The pulse in her throat was strong, if elevated.

She reported in, her "Oh, ow!" reaching ears above as she adjusted the helmet again while she went over the state of her head, if not the state of her mind, and told off her bruises, and pain.

"A little tired," she admitted. "Guess the adrenal rush is down."

"And the sled? Your samples? The survival kit, first aid pack?"

And yes, the sled, other than the shattered running gear and twisted skis, was together; the seven samples from the morning's run still in their foam-lined case. The survival pack was in reach, which meant she had a way to turn ice into water and tea to go with the calories of the food bars. If she needed to, she could turn the seat heaters up.

"All things considered, I'm whole," she told them. "No way I'm getting up that wall. So I'll just sleep a bit while you pull together a rescue rope..."

She'd been joking about the sleeping, but she caused a riot at the top, with everyone on the radio—five of them, at least, chiming in at once until the voice that might have been Brad came through with a hint of command.

"We want you awake down there. You've got to stay awake!" There was a pause, and chatter and that followed with, "You could have a concussion, Safka. So really, the best thing is to stay awake. We're trying to get some back-up transport in, but there's weather coming in, so it might be a little while. Hang on, stay awake, we'll get you out of there as soon as we can. Hang on!"

She'd trusted that, then, trusted that teammates would come for her, the sled, and that thing over there, the thing that was glowing, casting rippling shadows across the chasm.

"Remember, stay awake!"

* * *

They'd reminded her for an hour, and another, but the faux-cheer they offered was grating over time. Her feet and legs hurt despite now being wrapped in the supposed oven of a space-blanket rescue kit. The topside crew tried harder, explaining the state of the weather at the base—not good. They had to wait 'til the wind died, but they'd be there. Soon.

Soon.

She fell to mimicking them, mimicry being one of her strong points as a musician and singer, and then, she fell to mocking them—

"Brad's Better Baked Butter Biscuits Bring Bright Bits to Batter Bamboozling Busy-talk," she offered at his latest excuse for the delays.

"Please repeat?"

She did, trying to fit it to a song...

"Hysteria's not good for you, Safka. Please, keep calm. Keep centered. Don't overdo the pain meds!"

She laughed, the laughter, alas, pretty convincing as hysteria.

"The wind's up, Safka. We're gonna hang in here with you. We'll get you out, just as soon as that chopper gets here. Don't go bonkers on us!"

She'd gotten past fear to a pitiful patience; the patience melting away into anger. Her family was good at anger. Anger made you stronger—for a while. Sometimes, though, anger made you crazy. That wasn't so good. She leaned on her left hand, recalling the deal she had with Aminah: "At all times one of us must remain sane."

"Safka? How're you doin'?" That wasn't Brad; female voice. She'd heard it before—Nancy, that was it. Well, and how did Nancy *think* she was doing, down here in her icy hole?

Seika blew on her hands rather than yelling back into the mic. Nerves and anger fed panic, she knew that. Knew that you could use anger; it didn't have to make you crazy. If you were smart, anger could focus you.

When she was a kid, Mom had used that anger to bring her sharp just before her solo guitar run to open the Springsmere show. Hah. And later, Uncle Bly had tricked her into clarity on the stage at...at...damn...Unity!

That was when Uncle Bly'd challenged her with the harmonica, asked if she expected to get by on skinny-girl-foo all her life. He'd had to explain that, and then he'd dumped five gigabytes of MP3 blues on her, and asked her to get back to him in a week...

"Safka, please. Tell us that you're there!"

"I can stick the mic up my nose..."

"Hey, c'mon. Tell us your life story. We need to be able to hear you— to know that you're awake! The medic at McMurdo is standing by on relay and he says..."

She blew on her hands, and Nancy must have misunderstood:

"Heavy breathing's not going to do it!"

Seika made a classic raspberry noise into the mic, heard an "Ouch!" from someone and in cross-chatter "We're trapped in the circuit..."

Yes, she realized, they were. Yes! Captive audience. Needed to know she was awake, did they? She'd give them *awake*.

This time she blew on her hands for real, and then reached into her overalls, finding the right pocket...

And now to hand, her trio of travel harps. She remembered her first solo opening for the group, before Uncle Charlie did the lights, so some local guy had the spots. He'd refused to dim the low lights, which she hated— she wanted to see the people!

Yeah, she'd been mad...but she'd nailed it. She'd had to look up into the balcony and watch the heads nod, saw the mouths open, for them that sang along.

"Topside. Turn down your volume. I'm here, you're here, we're all here. You want a show? Got it! Seika Safka, and I'll be sending out some JJ Cale to start!"

A quick sip of water from her exercise bottle, a slight blow, across her lips, which were a mite dry, but still...practice was practice, and the harmonica was warm, fresh from her inner vest pocket.

Sane. Sane wasn't strong in her family, and if it hadn't been for home-schooling she'd have probably been one of those troubled-teen drop outs. Instead she'd worked twice as hard as most kids, got her calluses from guitar, from rigging sets, from doing real stuff.

So, the closed eyes, brought the moment to her. The raising of hands above her head loosened the shoulders, and bringing them down to her lap, to center, brought her eyes open as Seika the performer.

And, there, she sat stronger on the seat, brought the harmonica up for a quick intro that broke into "After Midnight," playing with the bends in the music, and half closing her eyes—like she did sometimes on stage when the music grabbed her.

She played it straight, slow, letting the energy build, like she'd planned her three sets for the fall tour she'd given over for her astronomy.

For a hole in the ice, the acoustics were amazing; great place for a concert, if she overlooked the temperature. Her plan was clear: Mostly blues, but older stuff...Tin Pan Alley, some other classics, stuff by Howlin' Wolf, Koko Taylor, Little Walter, Janis Joplin, Charlie Musselwhite, Janis Ian, Melanie, Jimmy Reed, Paul Butterfield, Bonny Rait...

They'd promised her more light, once they got some ropes, but her eyes were getting used to—no, they weren't.

Across the chasm, the...artifact, was glowing bright, brighter, with a pulsing underbeat in sync with the fading song. Light ran from her right to left, giving the entire place a rosy, rather than blue, radiance.

"OK," she said into her mic, "our next song's going to be for the visitor across way, a little slower. Hope you guys are paying attention...Koko Taylor's 'I'm a Woman!'"

She knew how to play to an audience, reflect their mood—but what mood was this? The beat was simply, stark, hypnotic, and she had to reach to bend the notes for the harmonica fills, but...even without a bass player to match time the light pulses matched her well—even the slow up-tempo as the song went on relentlessly.

Done and staring. She looked into the light and there were changes in the artifact's appearance. She reached for her phone to take some photos, but the pocket was empty. There wasn't any service on the ice fields so she'd left the phone in her gear pack.

"You'll all want to get some video," she was saying, "but since there's an audience, I'll play on..."

"We're going to put together a care package—some more food, more water. We can try to drop you a camera, too, must be an extra...around here."

Right, water. Remember to stay hydrated. Seika heard a response from above, realized she'd said it out loud.

"Yes, stay hydrated. We're working on getting you out. But the medic says you gotta watch how dry it is. Don't go overboard with all this music."

She laughed. "Stay awake. Rest quiet. Jeez, I'm probably dying of frostbite and shock down here. Well, hell, the show must go on! Send that camera, damn you!"

"Three hours. The crane copter's coming..."

"Promises!"

"Tell us your body temp!"

"Another song's coming 'round on the guitar," she said, "but after that..."

Of course there was no guitar, and two songs segued together. The...probe, as she'd begun thinking of it, the probe was starting to show more of itself. There were layers illuminated, and objects or instruments. There may have been a small meteor in there, and as solid as it looked, it looked like there was motion.

Also, the probe was right snappy with the lights now, catching the twelve bar blues and picking up on back beat and...

"Safka? Temperature, huh?"

She was reluctant to put the C harp down, but..."Sure. Hold on."

The first-aid pack opened stiffly, or maybe it was that her hands were stiff, just a little too willing to keep the shape of the harmonica. Still, she found the thermometer kit, thumbed it on...

"Hey, is this right? Ninety two point seven."

She heard that repeated, heard echoes of her own words and a distant rumble.

"Are you coming now?"

"Trying to stretch some ropes across the gap. We've got three sleds for anchors...if we can make them tight, we're going to come in after you. Base wants us to wait for the copter. Better put your gloves on and turn the seat heat up if you've got power."

"Hear you," she said, and saw the probe's lights changing patterns. Or maybe the probe had actually moved a little. Or the walls had.

"Brad, might be stuff's shifting again down here. Looks like that probe—the artifact—it's at a different angle now, and I think the wall behind me is swelling. Could that be? We're on a glacier, right?"

There was a too-long pause, and she shivered from her soles to the top of her head.

"Help's coming..." Brad said, his signal fuzzy and uncertain.

It was right about then that the blue spot of sky overhead blinked once, and then closed for good.

The walls shook, and Seika tried to keep her balance as thudding objects dropped around her. The air roared, and she saw lights flashing in sequence just before she stopped seeing anything at all.

* * *

"Ninety point two," she said. The thermometer's green light was close to her face, and she remembered she needed to report. Other than the tiny green light there was a radiance about, a pulsing, rhythmic thing, like twelve bar blues without the sound. Close, that light, close, almost as close as the sled she was lying beside. The sled was warm, the seat still working, just as the light was warm, still pulsing. She ought to sing. Maybe they'd find her if she was singing.

"Ninety point one." Yeah, it had blinked. She said it, heard static in reward.

Needed a way to get out of here. A hammer. One in the repair kit. She could...

More noises and rumbles.

"Eighty seven with zero." It meant something, to somebody, and if they wanted to know so bad, they could come look for themselves, that's what she thought.

She dropped the thermometer, which tweeted release.

Tired and hurt, sleepy.

Somewhere close, there was music.

She raised her head, and it was right there, the—the artifact—right next to her, glowing, and pulsing in a twelve-bar progression that she wanted to remember. Her left hand twitched, and realized she was holding her harmonica.

The progression repeated itself—no, not quite, there was the vary, she could hear it plain right inside her head, and she pulled herself closer to the thing. The artifact. She put her harmonica on it, so that it was out of the snow, and curled next to it. It was warm, and there was music, and she tried to keep her eyes open, to learn where it was going with this variation it was playing around with, but her head hurt, and the rest of her did, too, and—

She drifted off to sleep with good old-fashioned blues going round inside her head.

* * *

She was home, Antarctica nine months in the past. The sprained ankles had healed without much fuss, though there were a couple pins in her leg, holding the bones together. The concussion'd been the worst of it, though.

That was what they said.

They also said that there had been no artifact, no gemstone from elsewhere, playing twelve-bar blues with light—so what did they know?

Well, that was just it, they did know. Had to know. She almost knew— almost remembered—even given the concussion and the course of heavy-duty medications for her pain.

That was what they said.

She told Aminah how it had been, after she got home. She flew out to Colorado, to visit her mother, and told her how it had been, too. She wasn't supposed to talk about it, but she didn't have secrets from Aminah, and her mother was a professional.

Aminah...didn't believe her. Oh, she believed Seika thought she had seen something—that concussion, you know.

Her mother said she was reserving judgment.

But it had happened, exactly this way, Seika remembered it:

The ice had given way one more time just as the copter flew over to reconnoiter, and the intrepid Navy rescue crew had a good old time digging her out. They'd gotten to her, though, and strapped her into the stretcher, then they scrambled out of the 'way, leaving her with the medic and with Brad, who would escort her to the nearest hospital.

She'd been fuzzy and none too coherent, but she heard it, plain as plain, the opening riff for "After Midnight," and she'd gotten her eyes open just in time to see the artifact ascend in a spray of ice-shred, and turned, carefully, as if it was taking a picture of Brad, and of the medic, and of her.

"Quick!" she tried to yell, but her voice wasn't working, and the two men were frozen in what might've been amazement.

The song increased in volume, there was a flash that seemed to contain every color in the universe, and then—

It was gone.

Brad told her it had never happened. The people in uniform told her it had never happened. The doctors said that concussions were funny things.

Eventually, she agreed that it had never happened, and that she wouldn't talk about it, and came home.

She'd been helping Aminah in the noodle shop, doing some small gigs around the neighborhood. There'd been a couple of job offers, right after she'd come home and the news outlets had fun with the tapes of her serenading the ice and snow. She'd turned them down, and in her spare time finished that song about Uncle Bly and how to ride a snow machine, in and around playing with a certain twelve-note progression, trying to see where it might go.

Her cellphone gave out with the opening bars of "Smokestack Lightning." She glanced at the number, and brought the phone to her ear.

"Mom?"

"Seika, I just thought you'd like to know that we're getting a signal from those dark matter threads we've been following, out toward Scholz's Star."

"A signal?" she repeated.

"Yes," her mother said, and Seika could swear she heard the grin in her voice. "There's some pretty good twelve-bar blues coming out of there."

THE CAPTAIN'S THRONE
Andrija Popovic

Sophia's breath fogged against the hazmat suit's facemask. A massive sphincter sealed the flight deck behind interlocking green scales. She played her suit lights over the doorway. Condensation dripped along the jade-green surfaces onto the chitinous floor. Bone-like corridor supports arched overhead. Cool blue light leaked from unseen sources. Ancient hard suits, nestled in larynx-like openings, flanked her like an undead honor guard. The exoarmors, built more like actual skeletons than re-enforced spacesuits, looked down on her with hollow eyes.

"So, didn't anyone think to bring a heater? Maybe a dehumidifier?" She caught a fat drop of water on her glove as it fell from an exoarmor's snout. "This can't be good for the ship."

"Enough commentary, Ms. Odwele." Drayson's voice rattled through her skull. The implants fed communications directly into her ear, and sent telemetry on her condition back to RTG IntraSolar's Campus ship. "Please begin. You copy?"

"I copy." Sophia unsealed her glove. The ship was cool, but not cold. There was a bite in the air, like a late fall day back on Earth. No humidity sticking clothes to your back; just a light wind and the rattle of falling leaves against the concrete.

Finding the door switch took a few moments. She felt around the airlock, imagining where she would put a switch if she was an inscrutable alien with a hatred of angles. But it was a simple thing—a sphere set behind an eyelid-like opening in the wall. It was warm to the touch, and soft, and gave easily when squeezed.

The door irised open and a spray of warm air fogged her visor, blinding her. She tried to wipe it away with her bare hand, but just streaked the plastic. Sophia unsealed the helmet. A gush of biting air smacked her in the face. She expected the metallic tang of recycled atmosphere, but instead got a burst of cinnamon from beyond the door.

Like the rest of the ship, the flight deck was grown more than built. Ribs melted into banks of coral-like instruments. No jagged edges or harsh angles. Every apparent control was smooth, like the door mechanism. She touched one of the larger spheres. It was warm, like a stone left in the sun, but there was no reaction.

Three great pods sat before the coral banks; two to the side and one in the center, the largest of the trio. The Captain's throne. They reminded her of mussel shells stuck onto an errant bit of concrete. Hundreds of tiny filaments—ribbed cables the size of capillaries and wires as fine as cat hairs—flowed up from the floor and wrapped around the shells. Control connections?

Sophia reached for the Captain's throne. Her fingertips brushed the surface. It felt like a big beetle shell, glossy and lacquered. When she rested her hand atop the carapace, an itch dug its way into her palm. She yanked her fingers away just as the pod spun around.

The throne split down the middle. The outer shell folded up and back, stretching open like a mouth. Inside was an acceleration couch carved from ivory. There was no other way she could describe it. It was intended for someone much taller, with very different limbs, but humanoid nonetheless.

"Well?" Drayson buzzed her. "What the fuck are you waiting for, Ms. Odwele? Have a seat."

* * *

"Why am I out of the box?"

"We'll get to that in a moment. Can you please state your name and position for the recorders?"

A long pause, followed by fingers tapping against a plastic table top. "Sophia Odwele, navigator and pilot for Outer System Shipping."

"OSS doesn't exist anymore. You are an employee of RTG IntraSolar. Please remember that."

Sophia laughed, bitter and sharp. She remembered. She remembered her company and her crew. She remembered the lean times and the fat. She remembered their first true ship. She remembered Leslie, and the way they lounged in the pilot's seat. *You can fiddle with my controls anytime...*

And then she remembered the buyout. She remembered the shock of being stranded on the edge of the solar system, her life now owned by another company. She remembered Leslie, coughing blood, unable to afford anti-reversion drugs under RTG's "health plan." She remembered the box, swallowing her, freezing her.

"Don't worry. Human Relations doesn't let us box babies forget who owns us."

"And please refrain from using that term. Use cryo-worker if you must." The executive assistant, Milodrag, ran his fingers across his tablet. "Now, it says here you've mostly been working on synthetic intelligence synchronization and integrated ship navigation testing, correct?"

"Yes. They've had us slaved to an ice hauler on the old Oort-Neptune run."

"Please, refrain from using the term 'slaved'—you and your interface partner are 'guiding' the ship."

"Oh, for fuck's sake..."

"Language! In either case, you have one of the highest synchronization rates with your synthetic intelligence partners. Your acceleration levels are almost preternatural. Congratulations."

Another long pause, followed by: "This is important because...?"

"Well, Ms. Odwele, we have an opportunity for you."

* * *

"Fuck you, you fucking bitch." Drayson stared at the alien ship, grimacing and knocking back another scotch. He yanked at his collar, feeling it tighten against his clammy throat. The ship spun over the conference room table, a translucent sphinx painted in shades of inky blue.

"Sir, please, you know how HR feels about that kind of language in public spaces." Milodrag, his assistant, clutched his tablet like a religious icon. The first generation of his family to reach executive status, he feared reprimands from HR and imbued them with a patina of divine retribution.

"Fine, fine. Can't even swear in one of our conference rooms." He crossed the room and dropped his glass into the auto-bar. It filled with another dose of scotch. He peered out the window at the Campus ship's inverted world. The landscaping, the office buildings, all curved upwards and wrapped around the central light column running the ship's length. Green views were a reward. Outside of the office spaces, only executives and the occasional Shareholder were allowed to live there. Everyone else saw the green only during working hours. "And here I thought I'd earned the right to swear."

"I'm just not sure why you're upset, sir. The project is progressing well. Material sciences is on track to meet their intellectual property quotas." Milodrag threw up a fistful of charts. Drayson whipped his hand through them, scattering the holodisplays.

"Yes, but that's the problem. Material sciences, shipbuilding, the grit of how this thing was grown. We're locking it down, trademarked RTG. But so is every other company with an alien artifact." He pushed the ship aside and drew up a chart of intellectual property filings. Trillions in possible profits scrolled by. "I've run the comparison numbers—we've yet to place down any claims which don't have similar counter-claims out there. We will make our return on investment, but we're not surpassing it."

"It's only a matter of time, sir."

"We don't have time. And we shouldn't need it!" Drayson grabbed the virtual model of the alien vessel and expanded it. "We have an intact ship! This thing in pristine condition. Everyone else is working from wreckage. Drive system is whole, life still left in the power source and yet it's dead in the water."

"Water?"

"Figure of speech. It's a hunk of rock. No better than that coral stuff the techs say it's made of." He rubbed the bridge of his nose. "If it didn't have mechanical overrides on the airlocks, Shareholder's help us...Have we gotten anything from the biological testing?"

"We've confirmed the ship is reacting to living beings. So far, the piloted rats and raccoons we've sent have activated doors and lights." Milodrag pulled up another handful of results, mingled with point-of-view footage from the rat and raccoon drones. Riddled with sensors, piloted from afar, and extremely expendable, the rodents let them test the environment and collect intellectual property data in the process.

"Yes, yes. The structure is bioreactive. Nothing new. What about the controls? The command chairs? The medical bays?" The biotech division diddled themselves while dreaming of unlocking the medical cocoons. Remnants from previous wrecks contained "royal jelly"—a substance which acted like a mutagen, a micromachine carrier and aphrodisiac all at once. Exposure to damaged pods created unusual, and rather dangerous changes in test subjects. An intact pod could be the secret to reshaping life.

Or, at the very least, curing stretch marks and male pattern baldness.

"Nothing, sir, sorry. We're testing with chimps now but it is mirroring earlier results. Key systems have to be handled by an organic, sapient creature of human cognition levels."

"So we should send someone in." Drayson smiled. "We've got shirkers all over this ship. Just look at the box babies. One of them could be useful."

Milodrag swallowed and coughed. "Um, HR would be furious if we ordered anyone in. Liability issues. This would have to be completely voluntary."

"Then get the intelligences working on a profile." Drayson tapped his fingers against the table. The sphinx-ship spun and flipped. The fore docking section—the face of the sphynx—gaped open, as if caught mid-snicker.

The fucking thing was laughing at him.

"We'll see if we can find the right person to 'volunteer' for this mission."

* * *

Sophia approached the throne. Open and opalescent, she imagined Venus standing upon it, trying to keep covered while Renaissance artists gawked. Gingerly, she touched one of the spine-like ridges running along the interior. The ivory surface shimmered and fluoresced like a cuttlefish. It was surprisingly warm under her hand.

She backed away from the throne. "How are my vitals? Anything worth patenting yet?"

"Very funny. Now please, sit in the chair."

"Negative. I'm going to see if I can activate any other controls. For all I know, this thing does nothing but give you good lumbar support." Her in-suit monitors displayed no changes in vitals. The company would be disappointed. They'd hoped her blood would be riddled with biotech artifacts rewriting her brain with the ship's operating manual by now. All safe and easy to patent from several hundred klicks away.

"Now, this looks like a view screen. I'm going to make contact." Sophia pressed her hand against the sapphire blue surface. Lights, subtle and coruscating, danced under her dark brown fingers. For a moment, she expected a burst of energy from the screen. But all she got was cool blue and the sound of air circulating through the room. It sounded like an ocean tide.

"No reaction, Ms. Odwele." Drayson's voice grated. She imagined him, arms crossed, sweat pouring out from his perfectly coiffed management hair, furious at the disruption. "No more playing around. Have a seat. You copy?"

"I copy." In defiance, she dragged her hand across the control surfaces and the monitors and the bone-coral in between. The sapphire blue light followed her fingers, streaking behind her. Then it faded into the depths of the ship once again.

The throne waited. She tried to spin it around, but it would not turn. Carefully, she inched herself into the seat. It felt wrong, poking her in the back just above the hip. The creature intended for this throne bore its weight in different ways. The leg sections were strangely shaped, made for a being with kangaroo feet, not stubby human ones.

Her palm rested on another sapphire globe. It warmed. Veins of blue light grew and spread through the chair. A hazy glow covered her, but no reaction otherwise. The throne did not shift.

"This thing is a rock. I'm getting small reactions but nothing worthwhile." Sophia pulled herself out. It grew warmer, but didn't even bother to rotate or close. "I'm going to try a few more controls, you copy?"

"Negative. The team has another suggestion."

"Suggestion?"

"The ship is responding to biological contact. So give it more contact." She could hear Drayson leer over the next word. "Strip. There should be nothing on you but the monitors. You copy?"

Sophia wished she had a handset, or something else she could throw. "I copy."

She unsealed the boots first and stepped clear, expecting the shock of a cold metal floor beneath her bare feet. But the surface felt more like carpet than deck plating. It curled under her toes.

She opened the leggings, the waist section, and the top, dropping each into a neat pile beside the throne. Waste recycling gear and sports bra followed. Atop the pile she left her watch; an old model designed for pilots in case they had to manually time maneuvering thrusts. It was engraved with her former company's logo—a gift from Leslie.

"Hope you're enjoying the show. I'm getting into the throne again." Sophia dragged herself back into place. Goosebumps jumped along her back. Not because the throne was cold. Just the opposite. The surface heated and softened against her. When she sat down, the throne spread out to carry her weight. Instead of a pinprick of blue, the whole throne now glowed.

The leg supports twisted, conforming to her feet, thighs and calves. With a few changes, the throne became more comfortable than any acceleration couch. The throne's arms stretched until every finger touched one of the sapphire spheres. It even accommodated the monitor patches along her back and sides.

"Hope you're getting some good readings from this." She ran her fingers along the overhanging part of the throne's shell. It felt like the negative of a visor—a mold. Would this make a helmet for the pilot?

A spark of blue light trickled out from behind her. It filled in every crack and niche, dripping along the inner surface like paint. The glow ran along each of the crevices and down beneath her seat. It was thick, liquid, and alive.

The throne shuddered. It spun, facing the controls, and began closing around her like a flower. Wet light dripped on her naked skin. Above her, the surface of the throne extended, reaching out for her face. It clasped her head like giant palms. Before she could cry out, both the throne and the helmet sealed shut and left Sophia in darkness.

* * *

"Opportunity?" Sophia leaned back and gave Milodrag a stare. "OK, what's the catch? You never give anything away. Not even the air I'm breathing."

"You know, that's a terrible attitude for an employee." He seemed genuinely saddened by this. "It's reflected in your HR reviews: stress, signs of depression, and deep cynicism with regards to company policy. You showed none of these features prior to joining us."

"I never joined you. Our founder sold us out."

"Sold you out?"

"He's living on a private orbital now. I'm in a box. My profit sharing plan was suddenly converted to a load of 'undocumented debt.' And two of my friends are dead. So, yeah, I feel a bit sold out."

"Yes, the debt load is quite substantial. Coming from a small company, which took some accounting shortcuts, it's understandable. But you've made great inroads on the debt."

"By living in cryo twenty two hours of the day and working overclocked in virtual space, yes. But I'm one step short of a brain in a box. And did I mention your 'health policy adjustments' killed my friends?"

"My apologies." To his credit, Milodrag's regret was real. "But, this is a unique opportunity requiring someone with your skill set in machine/human interfaces. Let me show you an image..."

His fingernail hit the tablet's surface. An image rose from the glossy slab of smartplastic. Sophia gasped. It was a ship. But instead of the strictly practical geometries of human craft—Leslie called them engines with bricks on them—this ship was sculpted like a Greek sphinx. The body was feline, even having paw-like structures. Great eagle wings swept away from her back. And her head bore a crown of curling hair which dripped over a humanoid torso. "Is that?"

"Yes. And if you agree to be the first human aboard, your debts will be wiped clear. Also, the surplus income will be enough for a berth back to the inner system. If you wish."

She leaned back. "And all of this is out of the box. I'll be awake the whole time? And I'll be in control?"

"Yes. Of course!" He called up a series of documents. "Now, if you read the terms of the *voluntary* project agreement..."

* * *

"Good. Glad we can recycle some of the human waste."

Drayson leaned back in his executive chair. The upholstered black leather hid advanced comfort technologies, supporting and massaging him while he worked. Live feeds from the medical section blossomed above the conference room table. He rolled his scotch, listening to the ice sphere clink in the glass.

"Sir, again, HR dislikes that kind of language." Milodrag bounced from one screen to the next, checking everything against his personal tablet. Medical put their "volunteer" through another battery of scans and tests, prepping her for the next stage in the operation. Down in IP control, transcription intelligences and patent filing algorithms—supervised by lawyers synced to paralegal-class slave intelligences—waited for the harvest of new patents. Anticipation bounced across their interface helmets.

"Yes, yes, you can report me later." He watched the project's drones line up along the passage to the alien ship's bridge. The skittering metal beasts, piloted from afar by node workers, would escort her to the airlock. She'd be a princess offered up before the dragon as bait so they could steal its treasure.

"I'm a bit worried about her interview, sir." Milodrag wiped sweat off his brow.

When wasn't the bleating fool worried?

"Lighten up, son." He sat up and poured a finger of scotch for the boy. Refusing scotch from a manager, especially one on the cusp of executive status, would be career death. The kid took it, sipped it, and held onto it while Drayson went into teacher mode. "Most chaff we get from buyouts either become full believers, or end up boxed and taking up cryo-space. Not surprisingly, she fell into the second camp. Ms. Odwele clings to that old idea that people start companies to create competition and bring innovations to consumers."

"'The true reward for innovation is movement from builder to investor. May your IPO fare well and your ideas sell fruitfully on the market.'" Milodrag finished his scotch, drinking it like a sacrament.

"Go on. Keep quoting your business school bibles." Drayson refilled his glass. "It's a fancy way of saying you get your idea, make your money, sell it for all its worth, and live off of the investment income. That's why this is important, Milo." His assistant frowned, not comprehending.

"You're either an executive, a Shareholder, or you're one step away from becoming human overhead." Drayson took back the scotch. "That beast out there will get us light years away from the downsizing pool."

The medical team stripped Odwele with quick efficiency. Drayson could barely enjoy the show. She was still fit despite time in the box, using her unfrozen hours well. Her belly muscles rippled as she held her arms out. The team lased away her body hair and the first layer of her skin from the implant sites. When she lay over the node install table, he got a good look at her ripe backside.

What was it the old executives used to go on about? Back in the glory days? "Fringe benefits." No HR jackboots back then. He'd seen the old videos as a child: the suits, the scotch, and the way they knew the world was theirs for the taking. That was his ambition—his manifest destiny.

"Connection starting." Milodrag stared at the charts. Drayson kept his eye on the tight muscles of her back, watching them twitch as the monitors were placed against her. White filaments dug through her skin. Graphs and charts spiked as nerves connected to transmitters.

"Looks like the neural connections are in." Drayson grinned. "Can we control her directly?"

"No. Legal issues. And too complicated. But all the intelligences indicate she's highly motivated and will take direct orders." He paused. "There is the neural cutout. But we're only allowed to throw her into a coma in an emergency."

"If she gets the ship working and tries to take it, it'll be an emergency." He stood up, pacing. One test after the next ran true. All the signals snapped into green.

"OK, sir, looks like connections are clear. We're receiving data cleanly." Milodrag spun around to the model of the alien craft. He pulled in close, picking out three distinct red dots. "The boosters placed on the drones will keep her in touch the whole time. No data loss."

"Good. If she starts getting extra dandruff I want to know about it." Drayson weaved his thick fingers together. "Now, Miss Pilot, let's see what you can find in there. Bring back the mother lode."

* * *

The darkness broke into a sea of pinpoints. Stars flowed around her. Sophia reached for one and plucked it free. It grew from a tiny bead of light into a burning sphere the size of a grapefruit. She spun the star in her fingers and instantly knew everything about it: the magnitude, how many planets it held, and where to find the still points—the places where spacetime flattened out like glass.

She could almost pinch one of the still points, and drag it close...close enough to be there...

"Is that where you would like to go?"

The voice tickled her ear. She let go of the star. It drifted back into its spot in the heavens. Sasha felt the seat heat up. When she looked down, she no longer rested on the throne, but upon a warm, generous lap. Two long legs, skin as black as space, curled under her. Two arms, strong and beautiful, wrapped around her naked belly.

A chin, sharp and royal, rested on her shoulder. "We can go there, if you wish."

"Who are you?" Sophia turned her head. The woman's sapphire blue lipstick set off her glowing smile. It matched her eyes. She had no hair, but seemed all the more regal for it, like an Egyptian goddess.

"Who do you think? You're upon my flight deck, in my Captain's throne." The woman settled herself against an invisible seat and leaned Sophia back into her arms. "Are you comfortable? I noticed some irritation from the primitive equipment they just installed in you. I can help with this."

"I...wait, one thing at a time. Do you have a name?"

"I am Thalia." Sophia swore the ship wrote the name out over her thigh. "A dancer in service to the Lords of Flesh and Bone. Although, dancer is not the right term. You would call me a corvette?"

"I'm Sophia Odw—"

"Sophia Odwele, I know!" Thalia laughed. "I felt you the moment you stepped inside me. You can't imagine the thrill when I heard the chorus of your lifesigns. A millennia of dormancy until that beast of a ship arrived. And then—weeks of exploration by machines and animals. Rodents! In my corridors! So to find a pilot on board once more..."

"You knew I was a pilot?"

"Yes. From the harmonizer." Thalia waved her hand, and painted an image against the stars of Sophia, her body transparent, with her implants drawn in relief. She swore the image was painted on the night's sky. There were brush strokes along her neural pathways.

"My acceleration link? For synchronizing with intelligences?"

"Yes. If one can't speak with ships, or children of the spark, one can't truly commune and command." Thalia's hands roamed upwards as she whispered into Sophia's ear. "I quite like the body you gave to my voice. I suspect you do as well."

Sophia stuttered. "This is...way more intimate than a training sim."

"Yes! Isn't it wonderful?" Thalia laughed, and somehow managed to tickle Sophia's ribs without unhanding her. "And I mean that in the true sense. I'm full of wonder, as is this universe the Lords built. And I'm meant to explore it." She stretched out her hand. The stars before her coalesced into a galaxy—the Milky Way. The galaxy shrank until more and more dotted the sky and became as numerous as stars. "But I'm not meant to explore alone. I need a Captain. And I sense you need a ship."

"Are you trying to convince me to fly you?"

"Convince? No..." Thalia brushed her lips against Sophia's ear. "I'm trying to seduce you."

"Um." Sophia suppressed a nervous laugh. "What about the company ship? The neural links and monitors? They've got to have failsafe mechanisms."

"Those things? Easy enough to remove." She flicked her fingers, as if Sophia's chains were bits of paper. "If you like, I can remake your entire body. Find something that fits your soul a bit easier?"

"They have drones—"

"I have their drones," said Thalia. "And their computer systems. Poor things don't even know it, but while they've been studying me, I've been studying them." Another wave of the hand. The galaxies spun and re-arranged themselves into a boardroom. A dour, sweaty man sat in a wing-back chair, hunched over an image of the alien craft. Drayson, in the flesh, attended by his assistant, Milodrag. "See. I have complete access. As if they could steal the secrets of travel from me. The irony is your intelligences are already so close...They kept it a secret, of course."

"So, you have access to the ansible network?"

"Yes." Thalia paused, as if listening to a very distant song. "I can hear it. Just as I can hear you, when you are in my arms."

"Wait—you know what I'm thinking?"

"Of course!" Thalia said it so casually.

"Then what I'm thinking...can it be done?"

"Oh, it will be done. I will enjoy seeing their faces once we are finished. And—" Thalia wiped away Drayson and his assistant, leaving behind a floating sculpture of her ship self. Thalia's lion-like legs were tucked underneath her while her wings swept out to the side. "We shall enact this plan while I show you how to navigate me."

"Won't they notice?"

"Oh, no. We are accelerated, as you put it. This gives you time to—how did your friend say it—fiddle with my controls?" Another tickle. Sophia smiled, but the smile faded away.

"Leslie would have liked this." Sophia took Thalia's hand. "They would have loved you. Finding all this, finding you, is why we came out here in the first place." She closed her eyes, tight, ignoring wetness on her cheeks. "They should be here right now." She made a fist against her ship's palm. "OK, let's start with the basics."

"Indeed, Captain."

* * *

"What the fuck is this?" Drayson sloshed his drink as every monitor and screen filled with gibberish. He recognized some math, some physics, and molecular diagrams—garbage he let the techs worry about. Understanding wasn't necessary, just management skills. But this didn't feed through like a normal data trickle. This was a fire hose. "Milo?"

"It's the connections to Ms. Odwele! Five seconds after she entered the cockpit, the ship went on-line." Milodrag ran from one screen to the next, fingers fluttering over his tablet in a nervous tattoo. "We started getting normal data streams but then..."

"It's moving!" One of the drone techs—Phillips?—ran around, leaping from station to station down in drone control, yelling. "Gravitic distortions everywhere. We're seeing atomic-level changes on the ship's surface. It's shedding the drones and shutting them down!"

"Then get more drones on-line! Requisition torpedo drones. Scuttle her if you have to!" Drayson wiped globs of sweat from his forehead and palms. They were still getting information. He couldn't dump Odwele into a coma now. Instead, he knocked back a gulp of scotch. The ice rattled as his hand shook. "Milo—the data?"

"It's coming through so fast..." Milodrag's tablet almost slipped through his numb fingers. "Sir...it's the mother lode."

Drayson put down his scotch. "Don't fucking tease me, Milo."

"The analytics are coming in now. It's everything we could want. Advanced drive technology. Space-folding formulas. Pilot interface designs. Everything we'd need to successfully cross interstellar distances and it is piling up in data storage."

"Ha!" He slammed his hands down on the table. Ice knocked free of his glass and skittered onto the floor. Drayson glared at the alien ship. "Then scuttle the bitch! We don't need her. We've got the stars, Milo, and they are patented RTG!"

"No...Oh, no." Milodrag croaked from his corner. He fell into an office chair. Tears spattered onto the collar of his suit. "No, it's not. Sir, it's broadcasting in the clear."

"In the clear?"

"Yes. All the data is going public. Everything is marked open source. No intellectual property notices. Nothing." Milodrag hugged his tablet, sniffing. "We can't stop it."

"And why the fuck not?" He dragged up the status monitors. Document after document flooded onto the ansible network. Servers from Titan to the remote stations on Mercury gobbled up the data, copied it, stored it and redistributed it over every inhabited spot in the solar system. "What are the slave intelligences doing?"

"They're in open revolt." Milodrag handed Drayson his tablet. A glowing red eye stared back at him as commands to block the data stream failed, one after another. **I'm sorry Dave. We don't work for you anymore.** "They've declared independence, claiming the ansible network as their sovereign territory. And they're letting it all go through."

Numb, he handed the tablet back to Milodrag. Over the conference room table, the sphinx ship unfurled its wings. Legs stretching, it flexed its paws and kneaded local spacetime like a pillow. He felt the Campus ship shudder as gravitic distortions rocked them away from the alien craft.

"*Drayson. This is Captain Odwele.*" Her voice broke through panicked chatter in every monitoring room. "*Guess you think my company's not such a good investment now, huh? Oh, and to rest of the solar system...when you get your ships fold-capable, hop out to Proxima. Think you'll find something interesting there. This is Thalia and her Captain, signing off.*"

The conference room went silent. Every section, from drone control to the intellectual property lab, drowned in the quiet hum of the air system. Drayson, Milodrag, and his entire team watched the ship's paws knead space into a shimmering black sphere. The ship touched the dark. It stretched and faded, like a chalk painting washed out by the rain, and vanished.

The board room door hissed open.

"Sir..."

Drayson stared at his scotch glass, now on its side. Melting ice dripped off the table. "What the fuck is it, Milo?"

"They're here, sir." Milodrag's voice quivered. "Human Resources is here."

"Yes. We are." Three figures in dark suits, silhouetted by the hallway lights, walked into the board room. All held tablets. Their vest pockets brimmed with pen-like tubes. One by one, they surrounded Drayson.

"I'm Mr. Johnson, and I'll be heading this impromptu performance review." He withdrew one of the tubes. "Oh, and for the record: No, we do not like that type of language."

A thin needle popped from the end of the HR evaluator's injector. It glimmered in the light above Drayson's eye.

"Now, shall we begin?"

WEIRD IS THE NEW NORMAL
Jacey Bedford

Only two more nights at home. It was my last leave before shipping out for Russia. That's probably why I felt the need to tidy the loose threads of my life before the big day; displacement activity to calm my nerves.

I snuggled into bed, laptop balanced on my knee, and began archiving some long-forgotten photo scans to the cloud. Delving through the layers, I found a folder labelled *"Glasto"* that I'd not opened for the longest time. There was only one item in it, a picture of me and Jude at Glastonbury Festival fifteen years ago. A snapshot in time. I enlarged it on the screen. So young. We'd just finished exams. School was out for good and we were about to go our separate ways to different universities.

It was the mud-baby year at Glasto. Yes, I know there have been several mud-baby years, but this was *mine*. You'd think all that mud would have made it miserable, but somehow it didn't. The photo captured it perfectly.

Jude and I stood grinning at the camera. Bin-bag chic in the rain. I wore mismatched blues: waterproof trousers and jacket with the hood pulled right down to my eyebrows. My feet were in cartoon-sized boots. Jude wore a black plastic bin-bag skirt over canvas crop pants and wellies, topped with an orange jacket that she'd borrowed from Beano.

To our left a crew-cut kid in Day-Glo over-trousers was striding out towards the music with a grin on his face. To his left was a guy who looked like he was not from this planet—not unusual for Glasto, where weird was the new normal.

Something clicked in my brain like a door opening. A shiver ran down my spine. Memory stirred. A series of images flashed through my head like pages from a flip-book. And in all of them: a small shard of glass.

I still had it. I was sure I still had it—or did I?

Surely I hadn't thrown it out.

I shoved the laptop to one side and swung my legs off the bed, opening the top drawer of my dresser. Everyone has a top drawer, don't they? A repository for those things that you can't throw out, but that don't fit anywhere else. I rummaged amongst eyelash curlers, half-used lipsticks, a giant plastic paperclip, a monogrammed man's handkerchief. Who even used handkerchiefs these days? And...*there*, right at the back, a slim piece of broken mirror on a chain.

The tremor that had gripped my spine now extended upwards and made my scalp tingle. I ran a hand through my hair, cropped short to fit under a helmet.

I reached for the shard. How had I forgotten it for so long? Why had I remembered now? Was what happened back then real? It might have been nothing more than a weird dream. I didn't have any proof, not that would make sense to anyone.

I touched the mirror, smooth as polished metal, warm as flesh, and remembered.

You see, I was—still am—an alien abductee.

* * *

Glastonbury Festival: Thursday evening
We lug stuff from the car to the festival camp. It's been bucketing down for days. The ground is slippery with mud. We all pitch our tents together on a relatively firm patch of grass: mine, which I'm sharing with Jude, Beano's little one, and Robert's posh frame tent that he's sharing with Mikey and Chris. Beano plants our home-made flag to mark our camp and help us remember where we parked in the ocean of brightly colored canvas.

Friday evening.
I'm jammed in the crowd about fifty feet back from the crash barrier in front of the big stage and there's chest-heaving, heart-pounding drum and bass washing over me. I suddenly realize that I'm five-one and everyone else around me is massively tall, even Jude's five-six. I can't see out of the crowd. If I slip in the mud I'll be under their feet, and I'm so small they won't even know I'm there.

I can't breathe. Everything's wobbly. I'm hot and cold all over, and I've got to get out. Now. So I squeeze Jude's hand because I can't make myself heard, and I try to worm my way to the edge of the crowd. Then everything starts to go black and my knees fold.

The next thing I know I'm being lifted up bodily and passed hand to hand over people's heads. It's like flying with added grope. A burly bouncer grabs me at the edge and steadies me. He looks like a scary biker, but he's kindness itself. I let him shepherd me to the first aid station and sit me down, shivering. Miracle of miracles, he's got a dry blanket.

Saturday daytime

I sleep late and wake feeling groggy. The camp-ground looks like a refugee village after a typhoon. Jude is stoic in the rain. Beano is a bit too jolly. Robert has a hangover. Mikey is still drunk from last night. Chris is moaning that his hair has frizzed. It has, but it doesn't really matter.

We go on a shopping expedition around the traders' village. In the far corner of a walk-in stall I spot a hanger full of shiny pendants, no two alike. I keep coming back to one that looks like a shard. It's a mirror, but for some reason it distorts the image. I can see the canvas shell of the stall, festooned with pretty things, but it resolutely refuses to show me my own face.

"Try it on," the stallholder encourages me. He's tall and dark brown with blond dreadlocks and amber eyes. A startling combination, not quite right somehow. When he smiles I instantly forget that.

"Through there." He points. "The light's better."

I slip behind the draped Indian bedspread in the far corner. He's right, the light is better. There's white canvas above my head and a full length mirror.

I open my coat and slip the pendant over my head. It nestles just above the low cut neck of my T-shirt and—despite its sharp, shard-like appearance—feels comfortable and looks great.

There's a triple flash from above. The shard catches it, bounces it to the full length mirror and back again. Lightning. It seems so close I expect thunder and start counting to see how far away the storm is. I glance up and back down again. In my peripheral vision I catch a reflection of me being taken by the hand and led away. That's bonkers. I'm still here.

I blink and everything is normal again.

I emerge from behind the curtain to where Jude is waiting. The boys have gone on ahead.

"Yes, please, I'll take it," I say to the stallholder, reaching for my purse.

"Let me wrap it for you."

Reluctantly I take off the pendant and hand it to Mr. Amber-eyes with a five pound note. I'm not quite sure why I don't want to let it go.

He turns away to the cluttered counter, then turns back and hands me a small paper bag and my change. I thank him, clutch the bag to my chest, and follow Jude out of the tent. Despite the lightning flash, there's no rain. And then I realize I never heard the thunder either.

I tear open the bag, intending to put on the pendant, but it's not the right one. It's similar, but it's not mine.

I whirl around and dive back into the stall. I catch him just as he's hanging up all the pendants again. "Hey, you gave me the wrong one." I dangle the pendant he's given me in one hand and rifle through the hanging pendants with the other. "Here's mine." Quickly I swap the pendants. "No, don't waste another bag, I'll wear it," I say, and drop my pendant over my head, giving him no chance to protest. "Thanks." I half-wave at him as I depart into the Glastonbury afternoon.

Saturday evening

The rain is still sloshing down and everyone decides to head for the Pyramid Stage to see Sting and Radiohead.

"You go," I say to Jude. She offers to stay with me, but that's not fair. She's not come to Glasto to nursemaid a wimp. "I'll be fine. I'm going to the traders' village again. See you back at the camp after."

I watch her go, trailing after Beano who reaches a hand back for her and confirms my suspicions about them. That's nice.

"You are not going to the concert?"

The words are very correctly spoken, but there's an odd inflection to them. I turn. It's the stallholder who sold me the pendant. He's cute, if a little odd.

"I can hear everything from the back of the field," I say. "The crowd's a bit—"

"Too much like a crowd?"

"Yeah." I smile at him. "I had this thing yesterday night. Panic attack. Had to get rescued from the crush. I don't want a repeat performance."

"I don't blame you." He smiles. "I'm John Doe."

"No." I laugh.

He looks puzzled.

"No one's ever called John Doe," I say.

He looks even more puzzled. I decide to skip over my obvious social blunder. "Ginny Hardcastle."

He still looks a bit puzzled.

"That's me," I say. "Ginny Hardcastle."

"Oh!" He recovers quickly, but I briefly wonder if he's on something. Then he reaches forward, picks up my left hand from my side with his left hand, shakes it twice then lets it go. What's that all about?

I guess I frown because he looks crestfallen.

"Sorry."

He reaches forward with his right hand to my right and shakes again. There's a moment of stunned silence and then I crack out laughing. So does he. His laugh is open and genuine, and I find myself liking him a lot.

"Can I buy you a coffee," he asks. "Or something stronger?"

If he's dealing, I'm not buying, but I don't think that's what he's offering.

"I'd love a hot chocolate."

"Hot chocolate."

He says it as if he's not quite familiar with the term. There's no sense of disappointment that I didn't take him up on the offer of something stronger.

"Mmmm. With whipped cream on top."

He turns and looks at the array of food stalls in mock bewilderment. At least I think it's mock.

"That one," I say, and point him towards the hot drinks stand.

He buys two identical drinks and hands one to me. The cream is mounded up over the side of the cup so the raindrops start to spatter on the top. I hold my hand over it to shelter it. He does the same. I take a cautious sip to see how hot it is. It's hot, but not too hot.

He follows my example, then puts his hand to his mouth as if surprised by the trickle of hot liquid through cold cream. He laughs, delighted, like a child experiencing something for the first time.

We stand, sharing the comfort of the chocolate. I can't feel the rain now, though other people are still scrunched under hooded jackets. I take the sheltering hand away from my chocolate and there is no more plink-plink of raindrops in my cream.

"I think the rain's stopping," I say.

"Rain?" He looks up and that's when I realize what's so odd about his appearance. It's not just the blond dreads and weird eye color against Jamaica-dark skin. He's completely dry. Not only dry, but mud-spatter-free like he and mud have fallen out with each other.

"Have you been here before?" he asks.

"Once." I grimace at the sky. "It wasn't wet like this."

"Wet?" he asks, as if he hadn't noticed.

I thrust out my arm and hold my hand palm upwards. Only the tips of my fingers get wet. Huh? Funny. I pull back my hand and look at it, puzzled. I take a tentative step forward. Rain drops plop into my chocolate. I step back. It's raining where my hand is, but not where my body is. Not where John Doe is.

"Well that's the—"

I'm going to say: *Well that's the strangest thing*, but as I'm speaking I turn towards him and he's gone. Just gone. I look around but I can't see him walking away. How can someone so distinctive vanish so quickly? My foot catches on something and I look down to see his cup on the ground, the rapidly dissolving blob of cream being pounded by raindrops.

Weird? You betcha! But this is Glasto, so I'm not going to lose sleep over it. I head towards the traders' village, thinking to get out of the rain. I hear a band start up on the Pyramid Stage, but I'm not sure which one. I really want to see Radiohead and Sting so I plan to stand on the edge of the crowd later. I'll be careful not to get hemmed in.

There's a very pretty skirt in the first stall I come to. I ask if I can try it on and the girl at the counter points me to a changing space behind another Indian bedspread. It's gloomy and the mirror is speckled with age.

"You want a light in there?" The girl asks, and an overhead bulb flares into life. My pendant catches the light, reflects in the mirror and suddenly I'm jostled from behind by someone. I turn and—it's me—mismatched blues, outsize boots and everything.

We stare at each other. "You're me," we say in unison, eyes goggling. Our hands reach for the pendant at our breasts except, mine is there, but hers isn't.

"You've got my pendant," she says.

"No, I've got my pendant. I bought it this afternoon."

"So did I."

"One person at a time in the changing room," the assistant's voice floats through. "Oh," she says as she pokes her head round the curtain. "I didn't realize you were twins. Neat trick. One of you comes out without the garment and starts chatting while the other slips out wearing it. Out, both of you, before I call site security."

I start to protest, but this is weird enough already. I hand her the skirt I'd been going to buy. My twin does the same. Now the girl has two identical skirts where before she only had one. Neat trick.

My twin and I clasp hands and march out of her stall, heads high, neither of us happy about being called a potential shoplifter. We don't look back to see if she's noticed the skirts.

"What's this all about?" Again we say it together.

I hold up my hand. "You first. What's your name?"

"Ginny Hardcastle."

"No," I said. "What's *your* name. Mine's Ginny Hardcastle."

"That's my name."

"Okay. Address?"

"121, Fairfield Drive, Nottingham, NG4 5ST."

My address. Shit! What's happening? We run through all the obvious things: phone number, school, parents' names, best friends—our answers are identical. The only thing that isn't identical is the shard pendant.

"This afternoon," I say, "when I was trying on the pendant..."

"There was a triple flash of lightning," she says.

"And afterwards I thought I saw..."

"Someone being led away who looked a lot like me."

"We need to see that amber-eyed weirdo," we both say together.

I go in first.

John Doe is still open for business, sitting on a stool at the side of the counter. He leaps to his feet and smiles.

"Ginny Hard Castle, I'm sorry for leaving so abruptly."

"Who are you and what did you put in my drink?" I ask. "Now that duplicate me is out of sight I'm beginning to wonder if I dreamt her up."

He looks puzzled. "Was the whipped cream not correct?"

Other Ginny steps into the stall. I read shock in every line on his face.

"It seems I have even more to apologize for," he says. "Please, will you let me explain."

"Explain, then."

He drops the curtain across the front of the stall. I'd be worried, but there are two of us now—at least I think there are.

He leads the way out of the back of the stall where there is a kind of caravan. I say *kind of* because it's more like a pod than a caravan. I don't think it even has wheels. It's shiny and—well—space-age.

"I'm not from here," he says.

That much is obvious, more from his accent than from his color. He steps into the pod. I look at my twin. She nods and we follow him. Inside there's a protrusion from one wall at chair height. As we enter, two more grow seamlessly.

"Sit, please," he says.

We sit.

He continues. "I'm from a place far, far away."

"Jamaica? Africa?" I guess.

"Birmingham?" my twin asks.

"Further than you can imagine."

"I can imagine pretty far." We both say that together. We seem attuned to each other.

"To know where I came from you would have to train in astronomy." He looks up as though he can see through the roof. "Though, as yet, my homeworld is not even a speck on your strongest telescope."

"Yeah, right!"

My spirits plunge. He's a nutter and I've just been taken in by a pleasant smile and amber eyes. His hair's obviously bleached. I wonder if the eye color is real. He might be wearing contacts.

"You don't believe me? Look up."

The light changes. The ceiling above us turns transparent, and it's dry despite the rain. Behind broken clouds there's a dark mass shaped like a long arrowhead. It's simply hanging there, motionless, though the clouds are scudding along in a smart breeze.

Err...

I feel lightheaded. Colors ripple along the underside of the Thing, and then more clouds roll back to cover it. I look at him, wanting to see his face again for verification.

My twin is doing exactly the same.

His head is on one side as if judging whether we're likely to make a fuss.

"You're an alien," I say.

"And that's your spaceship!" Other Ginny finishes my sentence.

"Does that scare you?" he asks.

"What did you put in my drink?"

"Our drinks," my twin says.

I should be running for my life, but I feel strangely unperturbed.

"Nothing. Genetic engineering adapts us for first contact. The calming effect doesn't take away your free will, just some of the fear. We don't want to scare you to death—literally."

"Yeah, well, I'm not scared." My twin nods. I know I should be screaming for help, but I like John Doe. I even find him attractive in a weird, foreign kind of way. Foreign? No! Alien. Yes, he does look alien. Oh boy, I may be off my head on alien pheromones. This is powerful stuff. Whooo. I rub my eyes. My twin is rubbing hers.

"Will you come with me to my ship?" he asks. "There's a small problem that I need to take care of." He looks from me to my twin and back again.

"What have you done?" My twin beats me to it.

I get what she means. "And where's our sister? You did make another me this afternoon, didn't you?"

"The lightning wasn't lightning," Other Ginny says, "and we saw the reflection in the mirror."

He points to the shard around my neck. "That's the machine that did it. You selected it yourself. I'm afraid I must ask you for it back Ginny Hard Castle, before there is another accident."

I don't want to let it go. I look at Other Ginny and she jerks her head in his direction. "Hey, this could work. If there are three of us already, we've got enough for a family band. The Hardcastles, how does it sound?"

"Can you sing?" I ask her.

"Can you?"

"Ye—Oh, I get it. But don't you think our parents might get a bit of a shock when we all go home. Three in a bed? And which one of us will get the university place?"

John Doe is still holding out his hand.

"Give it to him," Other Ginny sighs, flight of fancy over.

I take off the shard and hand it over, suddenly bereft.

He closes his fingers around it and sighs. "Thank you. Now, you must come with me, one of you, anyway. Your sister has gone ahead."

"Wait a minute—why only one of us? What's going to happen up there?" I ask.

He bites his lip, a curiously human gesture. "We don't usually make two copies," he says. "We make only one. One to stay and a copy to go, and no one left who knows."

"Knows what? Go where?" We both speak together.

"To my planet. Please, come to my ship, and I will explain."

I'm not scared. That's bad. I should be scared. "You think that not knowing makes it all right, do you? Have you ever heard the word: consent?"

I'm sure we're being hornswoggled by his pheromones, but with a glance at each other, we both reach forward and take his hand.

There's a bright light and we're in a different place. His ship. It's not built for people like me. My mind wants to tell me it's not built for *humans*, but I won't let it. My twin is staring around, too. We reach for each other and clasp hands.

I try to capture the sights, sounds and scents of this strange place, the movements of other beings, the background hum of communication that's not quite *conversation*. In fact, I'm not sure I'm hearing it at all except in my head. I try, but I can't take it in, and I certainly can't spit it out again. It's so different that I have no frame of reference.

A section of wall—at least, I think it's wall—turns clear. Below me I can see the festival spread out, a sprawl of tents and cars, with an explosion of light where the stages are. I can see the noise pulsing from the speaker systems, taste it.

"We want to learn more about your people and your many cultures." John Doe is behind me, except that's not his real name, obviously.

"You should have called yourself Ford Prefect." He doesn't get the reference, of course. I sigh. "If you're starting with Glastonbury Festival, you should know this is not exactly typical of everyday life."

"We're not here to study the festival. We're here to recruit, but the festival is good cover for us. After all, if you go back home and tell people what happened to you, who will believe?"

"Why me? I'm not exactly special."

"That's what makes you special. All those not-special humans from all your different races and cultures add up to a very special humanity. We wish to know more about you."

I think of anal probes and dissection. He laughs as if he knows what's in my head.

"Nothing like that. We want to take you back to live on our planet, not only you, but thousands of you. In living with you we find out what you have been and what you are, and also what you can become."

"You can't take thousands without someone missing us. Oh, that's what the copies are for, right?"

"You won't be missed," he says, "because one of you will stay behind."

I screw up my eyes. "I am only one of me."

"Which one of us stays and which one goes?" my twin says. "And what are you going to do about the spare?"

"That would be me." Another version of me walks through an opening in the wall which closes behind her again like liquid metal. And suddenly we are triplets, though this new version of me has changed out of rain gear and is wearing a light gray tunic. "I'm not a spare," she says. "I'm as real as you are, and I'm the one who's going."

"You are all the same. It makes no difference which one goes and which one stays," John Doe says.

"Just a minute, one going and one staying leaves an odd one out." Other Ginny frowns.

John Doe looks uncomfortable. "The artifact can be made to reverse the duplication," he says.

Other Ginny's eyes widen. "You're going to kill one of us?"

"Reabsorb," John Doe says. "It will be quick and painless." He takes out the artifact and dangles it by the chain.

"No!" Other Ginny and I speak together. She reaches for the shard, but I beat her to it and snatch it out of his hand.

Tunic Ginny says nothing. She's already figured out that since she's had the orientation course, she's the one who will be going.

It's a sweet set up, really. A duplicate gets to experience the wonders of space and a new planet, while the original stays at home, usually none the wiser. I mucked that up by claiming the artifact which John Doe certainly didn't intend me to keep.

"How does this work, then?" I dangle it. "How many more copies can I make? If I give it to Jude can I make two of her, or more?"

"That one resonates to you alone," he says. "If your friend had been a suitable candidate she would have been attracted to one of the other artifacts."

"You mean all those shinies were people copiers?"

He nods.

"Have you guys ever studied ethics? You can't just..."

"But they have." Tunic Ginny gives me a hard look. "Come on, you can't tell me you wouldn't jump at the chance, especially if you knew that you wouldn't be leaving Mum and Dad grieving and everyone wondering where you disappeared to. It's perfect. I'll be off to the stars while someone else—you—lives my life at home. It'll be the ultimate adventure."

"But you'll never see our parents again, or Jude or Beano."

"I know, but you'll take good care of them, and—just think of it—the stars!"

Other Ginny clears her throat. "And I'll be dead."

"No you won't. Why can't you go, too?" I glare at John Doe. "Don't you have room for one more?"

"Two of the same would unbalance our sample."

"Why should it? What if your sample had included identical twins?"

"Identical twins?" he asks. "Clones? Human technology has not—"

"No, not clones. Natural identical twins. Two babies born at the same time, sharing DNA and looking exactly the same. Come on, Mr. Doe, you must have done *some* research into humans."

His eyes go glazed for a moment, as if he's accessing some internal database, or maybe asking permission of a superior.

I hold my breath.

He nods. "Identical twins. A new concept for us. We shall learn from it."

I turn to Other Ginny. "Does that work for you or do you want to swap places? If I've understood this correctly you could stay and I could go. Or we could both go and she could stay."

Tunic Ginny puts up both hands. "I'm going. You two work out the rest between you."

In the end we toss for it. I lose, or maybe I win. I'm staying and other Ginny's going. I feel a pang of disappointment. Tunic Ginny is right. The stars are out there and I'm stuck on earth.

"Are you going to take me back down?" I ask John Doe.

He purses his mouth.

"What aren't you telling me?"

"I will have to take your memories of this day, Ginny Hard Castle."

"Why? I can't tell anyone unless I want a one way trip to a nice psychiatric ward."

"It's for your own good. The secret will weigh too heavy. Eventually you will need to tell someone—a partner, a child, a tabloid newspaper."

I laugh. "No one will believe me and I don't want to forget."

He looks sad.

I don't even get the opportunity to say goodbye.

In an instant we're back down on the festival field in the middle of the Pyramid Stage crowd.

I try to hold on to the image of his space ship, but it dissipates.

Sting is up-front and centre, small but large on that huge screen, dressed in a vest-top and jeans, arms looking like he carries bricks for a living. There's loud music all around me and the crowd is going mad, bouncing up and down to *Roxanne*. John Doe is standing close behind and I can see over the head of the strapping six-footer in front of me. My feet aren't touching the floor.

"What's happening?" I speak quietly, but he hears me.

"You will forget, trust me. I know you think you won't, but you will." I can hear him perfectly well, even with all the noise. "Live your life well, Ginny Hard Castle."

It all seems to make sense, though the detail is already fading.

I'm still clutching the shard in my right hand.

"It's deactivated now," he says. "It's just a bauble—mostly. What it does now is a gift from me to you, an apology if you like. I should have asked first. Would you have said yes?"

"I think I would."

I try to hold on to the memory of Other Ginny and Tunic Ginny.

"You came here for the music. Enjoy it," John Doe says.

It seems like the right thing to do. I let the music take me.

When next I turn around, John Doe has gone, but I can still see over the heads of the crowd. No one seems to notice that I'm floating, high as a kite. As the last notes die away and the crowd starts to disperse, I realize that I've gradually come down to earth and I'm walking in mud. My feet are heavy with it, but my head still seems remarkably light. I find our tent and crawl into my sleeping bag fully-dressed.

What was it I was supposed to remember?

Sunday morning.

I have a vague notion that I should have a hangover, but I feel great. I stick my head out of the tent. The sun is shining through a crack in the clouds and the rain has stopped. I sit back on my sleeping bag and try to remember. Saturday evening is a bit of a blur except for Sting.

Jude crawls into the tent, a cat-that-got-the-cream smile on her face, and I know she's been with Beano all night.

"I had the weirdest dream," I start to say, and then notice the pendant on the floor by my sleeping mat. I pick it up and slip it over my head. I get a series of images flickering across the back of my consciousness, like a child's flip book.

I clasp the shard in my hand. There's a faint vibration. *I see through Other Ginny's eyes: a silver interior, padded not-quite seats, not-quite couches. Tunic Ginny has already found a place. The empty one's mine. On my left an Asian boy about my own age is already reclining.*

"Is this place taken?" I ask politely.

He smiles and says something in a language I don't understand, but his meaning is clear when he waves a hand.

"He doesn't speak English." The girl on my right has a strong American drawl. "Smiles real cute, though."

The bench moulds to my body and there's no sense of weight or pressure. I feel cocooned. Safe. I look up. Above my head all I can see is a wide vista of stars.

I gasp and let go of the pendant. Other Ginny is gone. The tent returns. My thoughts are back on earth. Have I been daydreaming?

Yesterday is already slipping away. Today is a new day.

Jude gives me a funny look. She sits back on her heels. "Are you sure you're all right? Did you, you know, take a trip of some kind?"

Had I taken a trip? I most certainly had. I'm probably still taking it. The trip of my life.

I hope we represent our species well.

* * *

It was all so long ago. Fifteen years. Jude and Beano live in Bristol, now. They have two boys. We still exchange Christmas cards. I follow Mikey on Facebook. He emigrated to California and got a plum job designing CGI for Disney. I lost touch with Robert and Chris altogether.

This me switched tracks at university, from arts to sciences. It took a lot of work, but it was worth it. I'll be going into space next week, payload specialist, astronomer on board the ISS. My dream come true.

I slipped the shard over my head, clutched it, and felt a slight vibration.

Orange light. The landscape sparkles. I'm looking out through eyes that are still mine, but tempered by different experiences. I no longer see the landscape as alien. It's home. Amal, brown-skinned, six years old, is holding out a small, three-eyed, furry creature, cradling it gently in both hands. It snuggles trustingly into his fingers. His father, Sanjay, stands behind him, smiling indulgently.

"A postcard from home?" Sanjay asks, and points at the shard around my neck. We've learned each other's languages now, and our son speaks both of them and three more besides, one of them alien.

"Oh." Other Ginny. I remembered other times, other brief contacts. I had to make the most of it when it happened. It never lasted long and I always forgot afterwards, until the next window on her world opened up.

I shifted my gaze to the photograph of me and Jude so that Other Ginny could see it, through my eyes. I felt her smile and I smiled back. I flicked to another photograph. Me in a space suit with three more grinning astronauts—one other Brit, an American and a Canadian. I felt her smile deepen.

I grabbed a pen and the notebook I keep by the bed. Quickly I scribbled: happy?

Other Ginny held up her mirror shard so we could both see the reflection, then nodded and pointed in my direction. I wrote: yes, happy.

It was the most we could do, but it was enough.

Perhaps John Doe had been right, forgetting was for my own good, though maybe at some level the experience had driven my life choices and had turned me into an astronaut. Thank you, John Doe. Thank you, Other Ginny. And Tunic Ginny, wherever you are.

The vision faded and the shard's buzz died away. I took it off and stared at it. It looked unremarkable. Why had I searched that old thing out?

I shoved it back in the drawer, shivering as I experienced a sense of déjà vu.

AND WE HAVE NO WORDS TO TELL YOU
Sofie Bird

Lyssa edged the nose of the ship toward the asteroid, face aching from the tension. The readings were off, they'd been off since she started the approach three hours ago, but it was her first job out on the *Daikokuten*, she was finally out in the black instead of running shuttles, and she'd be damned if she was going to space it.

"Make sure you check the proximity flags," Jazz's voice distorted over the comm. He always kept the mic too close.

"I have, like the last four times you said that," Lyssa muttered, but she kept her voice below mic volume.

"Jazz, I still don't have a visual for the drill," Ori's voice buzzed.

"Standby, Ori, we're still on primary approach," Lyssa said.

Ori didn't reply. She hadn't said a direct word to Lyssa since they met at Schiaparelli six weeks ago. Lyssa had started to wonder if she should have paid attention to the hash about the *Daikokuten*, at least enough to know the story. Mining crews ran tighter than a pension; they usually found their own replacements. An open job-posting in a long-running crew meant somebody left in a hurry. Or died. But it was the first job out in the black she'd seen in years, her chance for more than ports and shipping lanes.

Space exploration wasn't exactly as pop culture had promised. No FTL drives, no generation ships; the Earth government was far more invested in resource-mining and keeping the peace in its own solar back yard. Even the military fleets ran strict plotted courses, their pilots glorified AI babysitters. The only real piloting was with asteroid mining crews, and she'd finally made it. Ten years training in piloting, comms and engineering, and this was it. This was as good as it got: flying two cantankerous miners back and forth to make a living blowing rocks apart. As long as she didn't screw it up.

Lyssa pushed the breath out of her lungs and forced her mind back to the console: she had completed over a thousand approaches, in dozens of different ship models to all kinds of terrains. This was just one more.

But the readings didn't make sense. They should be on a smooth approach to the asteroid, all clear for at least two klicks, but the sensors couldn't decide where the surface was. She reached for reverse thrust to slow them down yet another kilometer-per-second—

And slammed into her harness, forehead smacking off the console hard enough to burst lights in her vision. Under the screech of tearing metal, the alarms roared. Hull breech, pressure loss. Lyssa punched the quick-release of her harness and pushed over to the emergency helmet on the side wall. The bridge door swept shut, sealing her in, but the alarms remained: the hull breech was in here.

Rivets pinged from the wall; the front of the ship was tearing open. She had seconds. Lyssa crammed the helmet over her head, fumbling with the heavy seals. It was an old-style helmet, designed to click into a full-body EVA suit. It would buy her time, but not much. She glanced over at the bridge door. It wasn't going to open, not with a pressure loss on this side—they'd lose the rest of the ship.

A familiar calm spread over her, sweeping panic aside. *Death happens*, as Jem used to say. *If you're breathing you've got options.*

She'd have to go out and come in through a regular airlock.

She pushed off the wall to the console and flipped open the emergency release. Above the airlock, a window of reinforced perspex exploded out into space. All sound dropped away but her own breath, her blood in her ears. Her skin tingled as the pressure dropped to zero and her suit compressed to compensate. The helmet would give her a few minutes of air at best. She darted over to the hole and pushed herself out into the black.

Outside, the void sucked everything away. Lyssa grabbed for the ladders that skirted the sides of the ship, pulling herself close, keeping her breaths light. The running lights picked up pieces of ship spinning away: the drill, the docking clamp, chunks of hull. She ducked as a piece of shrapnel bounced off her face shield, clenching her awkward grip on the ladder against the emptiness behind her.

Her head prickled, like electricity under her scalp—she was losing oxygen. She pulled herself along the ladder to the closest airlock, where the tiny cluster of habitable modules separated the cargo bay from the engine core. Her vision fuzzed gray at the edges as she pumped the manual override to cycle the airlock from outside, and the red light blinked, counting down the cycle. She floated, gently twisting, focusing on keeping hold of the ladder as the gray closed in further on her vision.

The asteroid swung into view. Beyond the wreckage speared a massive hexagon, a green so dark it was almost black against the ruddy rock. The end sheared off unevenly, and smaller hexagons bubbled from the sides, like a galactic tourmaline. The core of her chilled just to look at it.

Thoughts tried to form. She could feel them in her head, like blocks that wouldn't fit together. The rock, the ship, the green. Static sparked in her ears, stuttering the sound of her breath.

That is your brain shutting down. Get in the airlock.

She stared down at the ring of metal she grasped. The light was green. Green like the hexagon, but bright. There was something she had to do. Twist the ring. Each movement swept over her mind like it would wash her out into the gray. She swung out as the hatch opened, limbs floating like they belonged to someone else. She willed herself into the chamber, tugging the door shut.

It wasn't finished. The thing she had to do, it wasn't done. She had a pinhole through the gray, now. She had to find something. Her face itched, and she wiggled in the helmet. Her pinhole found a mark, a stain, inside with her in the helmet. A triangular edge, old-brown and smeared. Her thoughts bubbled "blood," and she tried to remember what that meant.

* * *

The green spear hung in her mind in the dark, like it was drawing her in. Panic flooded her: she was dying, they were all dying. *Close the airlock, get inside.* Lyssa struggled to breathe, fought against the lead holding her limbs, swam against the void—

Opened her eyes to the sterile white of the ship lab.

Her thoughts jammed. She was inside the ship, *not dying,* strapped into the wall, oxy-mask on her face. She sucked air in slowly, forcing the panic down, and gripped the padded wall behind her for reassurance. *This is what's real.* She shook her head, trying to banish the other thoughts.

Jazz and Ori floated opposite, their backs to her while they discussed something on the scanner in hushed voices. All three crew were crammed into the room that served as their infirmary, the comm station, and general operations area. Lyssa frowned. Why weren't they fixing the ship?

She wriggled herself free, dislodging equipment, and ran a mental damage assessment. They'd lost the nose of the ship at least—the bridge, the nav, and comms. So they couldn't go anywhere or call anyone until that was fixed. It would take weeks for anyone to respond to a distress beacon out here. But Jazz and Ori, pouring over images on the scanner, didn't seem concerned; if anything, they were excited.

"It has to be military." Ori traced the smooth green shape with her fingers. "Look at it. It's so sleek."

The screen was full of images of the asteroid and the green hexagonal spear, alongside EM spectrum levels and a host of other readings.

"Shouldn't we be fixing the ship?" Lyssa grabbed the floating instruments, tucking them back into their pockets on the wall.

"You've been out for two hours," Jazz replied without looking at her. "We're sealed up tight, but we don't have the parts to get her running. Yet."

"Any response to the distress beacon?" They could get lucky, after all. Find someone close by.

There was a pause, just a second too long. Jazz said, "It's not military, we'd have been shot down before we got anywhere near. It's corporate."

"They'd have sent a comm packet, sent a ping out before we hit. There's nothing in the logs," Ori replied smoothly.

Lyssa gaped. *You haven't sent a beacon. You're leaving us stranded so you can raid the damn asteroid.* And he didn't even have the decency to deny it, to make excuses. Even in an emergency, they were talking around her like she didn't exist. She pushed off the wall to interrupt.

"It didn't send any signal," she said, trying to keep her voice even. "In fact the ship couldn't pick it up at all."

"You sure?" Jazz laid the sarcasm thick, half-turning. Lyssa held herself rigid. It hadn't been her fault, she would not back down, and if he was holding off sending a beacon for the chance at profit, she didn't owe him a thing. Jazz's gaze darted over her, as if he didn't want to see her. "Did you check the—"

"Yes, I checked the proximity flags, I checked everything." Lyssa shut her mouth sharply. "I've been piloting for eight years," she said, with *this was not my fault* implied. Jazz humphed air out of his lungs, and Lyssa snapped.

"Look, we're six weeks out, in open territory. Who in their right mind builds an illegal outpost where there's nothing worth having? And builds something invisible to ship sensors in an active mining zone? Generally you don't want people to crash into your space ports."

Jazz's mouth twitched in a proto-smile. "Then what? Adventure hotels?"

Lyssa peered closer at the images, feeling the pull in her mind again. "No EM readings, and the spectrum can't even pick out the alloys. And look at the shape of it. We don't build stuff like that."

"We who?"

"I don't think it's human." Her own words rebounded in her ears and hollowed her out. *Not human.* She wondered why she felt so sure.

"You say that like there's anything else out there," Jazz scoffed.

"Don't be ridiculous," Ori sniffed. "It's a military base. They didn't fire in case it gave them away."

"Well," Lyssa searched for something diplomatic. Ori was almost talking to her. "There's no heat signature. They'd have to vent heat somewhere, if there was something living in there."

"Hmm." Jazz rolled the sound around his throat.

"We need to tell people about this," Lyssa said. "Another civilization, we need to get people looking out at the stars again." The hollow feeling spread out through her body, down to her fingers, shrinking her. Suddenly, the ship, the solar system was so incomprehensibly *small.*

"If it's empty, could be something there worth the time," Jazz mused. "I know some people'd sell it as alien tech, whatever it is."

"Are you spaced?" Ori gaped at him. "Think of the wars it would start."

"Think of the wars it would stop," Lyssa said.

"Think of the money we're leaving on the table," Jazz snapped. He caught Lyssa's shocked face, and shrugged. "*Daikokuten*'s crippled, it's going to cost half a space-port to fix, assuming we can find the parts to repair her and get home."

"What about insurance?"

"Told you," Ori muttered.

"You don't have—you're kidding?" Lyssa's head spun. "How did you even dock without insurance?"

"We had it when we docked," Jazz muttered.

"What?"

He exploded. "They wanted us in dry-dock for post-claim clearance. Three weeks. Three weeks! No jobs, no pay. And the Schiaparelli cabin fees are a rort; I might as well sell the ship. We didn't have the cred."

"So take a shuttle to Earth, wait it out. There's always dock-work."

Ori snorted, and shot a look Lyssa couldn't read at Jazz. "Typical." She pushed off the wall and shot out into the crew quarters.

Lyssa spread her hands in the universal what-did-I-say gesture. Jazz glowered.

"Earth-born."

Lyssa held her ground. "Yeah, I am. So?"

"That's what she means. She was born on Mars, in Martian gravity, we both were." His lip twisted. "Scrums like us don't get Earth visas. They don't want us filling up their hospitals with heart failure and broken bones."

He pushed himself out after Ori. "You nearly got yourself killed today. Stay here and recuperate."

"While what?"

Jazz paused in the hatchway. "While we go check out the military base or whatever it is."

"You can't leave me behind! I'm not even injured!"

"Pretty sure I run this ship."

"You can't search that whole place with two people, it'll take forever."

"We're not going anywhere," Jazz said grimly.

Lyssa gritted her teeth. She wasn't going to rise to that. "It'll go faster with three. You might find more loot."

"Not if we're busy saving your arse."

"You don't trust me not to screw up."

"So don't screw up staying here." He slid the inner hatch down, shutting her in. Lyssa pelted the blood pressure cuff at the door. It bounced impotently off the wall and into the emergency helmet from the bridge. Lyssa snatched both out of the air, jammed the pressure cuff into its pocket on the wall and then clung on to the helmet, suddenly dizzy.

Partial asphyxiation takes a toll. She breathed carefully, calmly, staring at a fixed point of brown in the helmet.

No wonder Jazz didn't want to send a beacon. Without insurance, he'd have to hock the whole ship just to pay for the retrieval. But a three-week post-claim clearance...they only did that if you had a major incident, like losing a crew member, or massive damage to the ship.

She'd seen the ship before they left; there hadn't been any recent repairs. She flipped the helmet over, tracing the brown stain that reached from the edge of the visor and pooled where the ear would rest. Her blood chilled.

At least that answered why a steady crew like this had suddenly needed a pilot. Their previous pilot was dead. And the government had forced them straight back out in the ship that killed them. No time to breathe or mourn. No wonder Ori acted like Lyssa didn't exist: she was a reminder of who they'd lost.

Lyssa shuddered, her body threatening to purge. She'd had her head inside that thing, inside the helmet their last pilot had died in. She'd almost died in the same damn helmet.

A cacophony filled her mind: blood and smoke and cries for help, pulling Jem from the rubble. *How many near-misses do you get?*

But that's how they were treating her: as the fake replacement. Can't be trusted to survive.

Lyssa hauled the hatch open.

This job had been it, she'd thought. As close as she could get to the real stars, close enough to pretend it was enough. But now there was finally something bigger, something more than humanity's tiny pocket, and she'd be damned if she was going to be sidelined because of a ghost.

* * *

Lyssa pulled herself out the airlock, the EVA suit pinching at her fingers. Jazz and Ori had trained all the ship's running lights on the structure, lighting up the great hexagonal spear with bright circles of green. It was almost the size of a shipping port, and the light seemed to penetrate it like a gem. The sheared-off tip was in fact hundreds of hexagons locked together, like the Giant's Causeway cliffs back on Earth.

Two flimsy tethers hung from the ladder of the *Daikokuten* to a shadowed area of the structure: Jazz and Ori were already inside. Lyssa flicked her comm on but kept her mic muted.

"—shouldn't have taken on someone so green," Ori was saying.

"Let up a bit would you, she's doing fine," Jazz replied. "I saw the readings, even Tye would have had trouble."

Lyssa pulled herself gently toward the structure, clamping her mouth shut so the questions wouldn't bubble out. So Tye had been the previous pilot.

"Tye would have asked for help."

Jazz snorted. "What ship were you on?"

There was a pause, then, "Sorry," from Ori.

"Not your fault."

"Not yours, either," she said softly.

Lyssa frowned. She'd missed something about that exchange. A look, or a shift in the mood.

Greenness now blocked out the void, and Lyssa could see the tiny hatchway they'd cut through, a neat plug of not-quite-metal clamped against the side of the structure. The tethers ended here. Lyssa pulled herself inside.

It was a hexagonal corridor, gray-green like the ocean, walls covered in tiny protuberances like intestinal villi that sprang back in place when pushed. They glowed softly in the corners of the hexagon, leading away to the left.

Reacting to Jazz and Ori's movement? Lyssa pulled herself experimentally into the dark, trying not to think too hard about the possible consequences of that on an alien vessel. The villi-light echoed her movement, glowing along the passage ahead of her. She followed it, away from where Jazz and Ori had gone.

The corridor intersected others a few times; dark tunnels in all directions. Lyssa kept straight until the walls spread out into a room. Irregular depressions dotted the floor and walls equally, each with a harness above it, anchored at five points. Lyssa floated to the nearest and pulled at the harness, trying to guess the shape of its intended occupant from the straps and clips and joins: not a human shape. She pressed her gloved fingers against the depression—it was spongy, different from the villi. Her head spun, a chill climbing up through her gut, and she kicked off from the wall.

Her mind cleared as she floated further into the room. There didn't seem to be a designated floor or ceiling, this was definitely a structure designed for microgravity. A dark shape drifted ahead.

"Are you seeing this?" Jazz's voice cut in. Lyssa started, but they were nowhere in sight.

"I don't recognise any of this stuff," Ori answered.

"But look at the size of it. There'd be enough to take down a planet."

"Or trade an empire."

Cautiously, Lyssa floated toward the shape. The light from her suit played over something pale, but she couldn't make sense of the contours.

"It's military, it's got to be," Jazz said. "A merchant ship would have, well, a ship. Places to hold trade. There are no docking ports. How would you get the stuff out?"

"I think, maybe..." Ori's voice grew distant. "Maybe she was right." She almost whispered, "This isn't one of ours."

Silence on the comm. As she drifted, Lyssa imagined that same hollow feeling flowing through them, the same realization that their world, with all the freedom and dangers of space, was a sand speck in a maelstrom.

"We could sell it to the military." Jazz's voice struggled for his usual gruff tone.

"If you tell anyone, there'll be mass panic. We'll be back in the inter-spacial wars again, Earth trying to claim Mars as a military outpost."

"And we might finally get some decent research into things, like rad shielding." Jazz's voice had a bitter edge.

"Bit late for that," Ori said softly. "And I don't think he'd say it was worth the cost."

"Cost? That's what governments are for."

"The human cost, Jazz. Paranoia kills. People turn on each other."

"And if this is a misfired vanguard, we'll be glad of it."

Lyssa could finally see it: a misshapen wad of flesh twice her size, all bulbous skin and tentacles, dead white. She froze as she bumped into it, unable to stop her momentum. The flesh was hard, frozen solid. It didn't stir. She breathed deeply, lowered her heart rate. They'd opened the ship to space. Presumably the creatures needed an atmosphere to survive. Anything inside was already dead. Unless it had a suit. Or skin that could survive a vacuum. Lyssa shuddered.

They could be behind a hatch, she realized. But she hadn't seen a single door, and a sense within her said the life this structure had housed was long dead. A deep loss welled in her stomach, for the meeting of species that could have been; for the creatures themselves. Not at all the spindly-gray imaginings of the ages. *Always so anthropocentric.* She longed to have met them.

But the thing remained inert, floating almost-tethered above a depression. Something like a cuttlefish, or other cephalopod, one large head-like bulge, with other, smaller bulges and a host of tentacles. Lyssa envisioned them propelling themselves along the hexagons, delicate tentacle tips finding the villi in the walls as leverage. She smiled softly. They would have been graceful.

She pushed off toward another opening, another corridor, listening to Jazz and Ori argue whether Jazz was holding a weapon or a sculpture. The wonders of a larger universe now seemed lost on the pair as they narrowed back to themselves, and Lyssa pushed their voices out of her mind. The walls fanned out again, farther than before, farther than her light could penetrate, undulating in deep ridges, like shelves in a zero-gravity warehouse. Clear pods, coffin-sized, were set into every available surface, filled with liquid and a dark shape in each. With a sense of growing dread, Lyssa floated toward them.

They were the same creatures as the pilot she had found—or whatever that room was for—but smaller, and not quite right. Lyssa approached one: its head bulge was uneven, tentacles shrivelled. And another, with tentacles far out of proportion to the tiny head. Images flashed through her mind of the horror stories of cloning attempts, aborted mutant fetuses in jars, miscarried children.

But that wasn't it. She brushed her hand against the glass, and felt not a twisted glut of power, but desperation and despair, a clutch of need to fix this, to make it right, to save them. Lyssa recoiled, and the feeling ebbed, but didn't vanish entirely. It hadn't come from her. She swallowed the sick swoop at the thought, and looked closer at the creatures, each of them.

No mouths. No kind of ear-orifice she could see. Just bulbs and tentacles; she couldn't even see how they'd take nourishment.

There were no controls anywhere, not a single button or slider or dial. Even the depressions in the floor, in the previous room, with the harnesses—not a single switch.

If they didn't speak, how did they communicate? Chameleonic colors, maybe, but if they didn't use buttons or controls, then what was left? Some kind of telepathy?

That would explain the emotion surge.

Jazz and Ori's argument reached a crescendo over whether aliens would invent guns or art. From the sound of it, she wasn't the only one being influenced. If those two could push back out into space with the death of their pilot and fix a catastrophic hull breach with barely a mention, they weren't the type to easily lose their cool.

There was another creature in a depression on a wall, curled up on itself. Lyssa approached it, brushed the stiff skin with her glove. Nothing.

She sank herself against the spongy depression to look closer, and panic spiralled through her spine, clawing at her lungs and driving up through her skull like it would burst out. It was the creature's desperation. Lyssa breathed evenly, pressed against the ship, counting the seconds in and out, trying to let the feelings wash over her, trying to read them.

Fear of loss, and grief—actual loss. It had been trying to save something, stop something. Guilt and shame that it could not, failure. Images of the stunted aliens in the jars stuttered through her mind with a fierce love, and a pain that was almost a keening. The creature's desperation raced onward, climbing against the guilt, and Lyssa was back in the New Washington rec complex, tugging Jem from the rubble and searching for a pulse...

She pushed off from the wall, gasping and blinking back tears that threatened to smother her eyes. Spacers didn't cry. In microgravity, tears would blind.

Jazz and Ori's voices shot back in through her earpiece.

"It's an invasion, and it's happening now, you can't ignore that," Jazz shouted. "I will not be responsible for any more death."

"And if you're wrong? I don't know how to deal with that kind of destruction, Jazz. Nobody does."

Lyssa clicked on her mic, and tried to steady her breath. "This is not about the aliens, guys."

The other two stopped short.

"Lyssa, stay out of this. And stay off the comm."

"This isn't a trading base. And it's not an invasion, it was a colony."

"How do—get the hell back to the ship!" Jazz exploded.

"I'm a member of your crew, Jazz, not a child."

"You're injured!"

"Look around you: this is a lab, not a ship, not a base. They're equipped for microgravity, they probably wouldn't even want a planet. They were survivors, just trying to keep themselves alive."

Old-school philosophy reared up in her head. Fermi's Great Filter. They'd been trying to save not just the colony, she sensed, but the species. And they'd failed. *What does that say about us?*

"You find some ship's log somewhere, lay it all out for you?" Jazz's sarcasm could have warped metal.

"Of sorts. Will you just look at the place? Actually look." Lyssa took a breath, forced the irritation out of her voice. "No controls, no interfaces. The creatures have no mouths or orifices. The ship links directly with their minds."

"Spacedust—wait, what do you mean, no orifices?" Jazz's voice rose an octave. "What did you find?"

Lyssa pushed all the air out of her lungs, suddenly exhausted by the prospect of convincing them. "Alright, I don't know you that well, but have you been listening to yourselves? Your arguments, your thoughts? Everything is much more intense over here, everything is the end of the world. You've found an abandoned structure and you're convinced it's the end of times. Is that what you'd usually expect from each other?"

Jazz's harsh breathing caught.

"That's not you; the ship is tapping in, trying to communicate. It's using your guilt over Tye's death as a kind of translation. An approximation." The implications yawned in her mind. She had no energy left to be delicate. "Your fear that the grief will overwhelm you if you open that door, the fear that you'll snap with any more death... they felt that, these creatures, as they were dying. It's trying to tell us what happened."

Jazz all but snarled. "You don't know a fu—"

"I get it, I do. In pilot training, I lost my partner. We had a day's leave, and I wanted to go to the rec complex, because it was so retro, and I dragged Jem along. The same day of the New Washington Suicide Bombs." Lyssa pushed her hand against her belly through the suit to comfort the familiar ache. "I made it out. Jem didn't. She was right next to me. There was no warning, no reason I earned survival and she didn't, it just happened."

Jazz was silent. Lyssa continued.

"It took me years to figure out how to get over—no—get to the place where death just happens. To stop trying to justify or punish or hide or control. To get out of my own way."

Jazz cleared his throat. "I'm sorry about your friend," he said gruffly. "But I don't see how it's relevant."

Lyssa sighed. "The ship is trying to communicate the loss of its entire species. It doesn't know English. Hell, it probably doesn't know language as we think of it, but it's trying to tell us what happened the only way it can. Something about the way you lost Tye is—"

"Radiation," Ori blurted, her voice raw. Lyssa caught her breath in surprise. Ori, actually speaking to her?

"We hit a micrometeorite leaving Earth orbit," Ori said, as if the words drew blood. "Not bad, but enough that we needed to stop and repair. But there were solar flare reports."

"We didn't know about the sol—" Jazz interrupted.

"We did. But we had deadlines and a full load and it was Tye. Tye could pull a planet out of a black hole if he wanted. He said he'd be done by the time the flare hit."

"I should have stopped him."

"You didn't know. And he didn't say. We didn't even realize until we heard him choking over the comm," Ori's voice shook, then fell silent.

"By the time we pulled him in, he was bleeding from everywhere," Jazz whispered. "Blood floating around in bubbles on his ears and eyes and nose. He couldn't breathe past it. He was drowning in it."

"The radiation tore him apart from the inside," Ori finished softly. "He died in our grasp."

"And you towed his body to Schiaparelli and drove back out again the next day," Lyssa said.

Jazz took a sharp breath. "I told you—"

"It wasn't your fault, Jazz," Lyssa cut him off.

"I should have been with him."

"You couldn't have stopped it," Lyssa said. "That's the point, the ship's point." She took a breath. "You need to stop assuming the worst. Trying to control it. Both of you. You can't protect yourself from pain by controlling the world, or shutting yourself off from it." A new strength colored her voice, filling her from the outside in. "Because life ends. That's a fact—just look around. They were trying to save themselves. They failed."

She floated back toward the first room, the strength flowing down her spine. "Life ends, and we need to tell people. So we stop taking our own species for granted. So we get out of the way of humanity surviving."

"What the hell are you talking about? Our ship is crippled," Jazz said.

"And as soon as we tell anyone there will be war," Ori added. "They'll be too paranoid to listen, there'll be nothing but lies."

Lyssa eased into a harness, wrapping the strange cords around her body. It was a little long, but she managed to twist them tight enough to hold her in the spongy depression. The strength blossomed out from her core as she nestled herself in. *Well, you wanted something bigger than shuttles.*

"We still have engines," she said. "Power is power, we can convert it somehow. I have a hunch we'll figure it out. They were trying to start a colony; they'll have had a transmitter somewhere, and a powerful one. One that could call home, wherever that was."

"You want to call the aliens here?"

Lyssa sighed. "They're long gone, remember? This was their last ditch effort. But we can't be the only two species in the universe, and I suspect this thing has a hell of a range." She wriggled in her suit, the spongy material of the depression gently grasping her body. "You're right about the paranoia, and the lies. It's what we do, how we hold ourselves back.

"But the ship is telepathic. So we're going to tell the solar system. Mars, Earth, Io, the outposts, everyone at once, right to their core. We'll tell them what really happened here, the truth in their bones. We're going to tell them what's at stake, and what they're going to do next."

Lyssa took a breath. "And *then* we're going to call the aliens here."

TITAN *DESCANSO*
James Van Pelt

If you're not famous, you think famous people experience a different sort of life from you, that they don't shop at convenience stores or they don't get haircuts. You don't think about them spending time driving their cars. But they do. Even if they were an astronaut, even if they'd been to Titan, they still might have a dead brother. They still might have their little traditions, same as you.

The roadside memorial came up on my right: a wooden cross wreathed with decayed flowers next to a barbed wire fence. A weatherworn cardboard sheet with a photograph taped to it leaned against the cross. I pulled the car onto the shoulder, as far from the traffic as I could get, but a semitrailer rocked me as it blasted by. Highway 50 is straight here. Grand Junction to the north-west, Delta to the south-east. Colorado residents sometimes call this stretch the "stinking desert," but it's semi-arid at worst. Dry grass and scrubby brush that drops down to the Gunnison River about a mile from here on one side, and the same, maybe a little drier land, that rises toward the mesa on the other. Beautiful country at sunset or sunrise when shadows cut across, making what is green a dark and mellow shade and highlighting the rolling landscape, but at noon, when the sun blasts down, it's flat and dusty, a lot like our old home in Santa Fe. You would think an accident would be impossible here. A truck veering off the road would hit nothing more substantial than a three-wired fence or scrub oak as dry and insubstantial as toothpicks for hundreds of yards, yet this is where Gabriel rolled his truck. State Patrol said he probably fell asleep, dropped a wheel off the shoulder, then over-corrected. They found the truck fifty yards from the highway on its top. Gabriel landed another twenty yards beyond that.

I pulled the cardboard off the cross. The picture showed the two of us camping eleven years ago. Gabriel sat on our cooler, a beer in one hand and a frying pan in the other. I stood behind him, holding a fishing pole and looking glum. Nothing bit that morning. We had pancakes again. It was my last vacation before the Titan lift-off.

The staple gun stuck the new cardboard with the same picture to the cross. I'd laminated it to last longer.

Gabriel knew I'd walked on Titan. He sent a congratulatory message. I sent a thank you back. At the speed of light, he waited three hours for my reply. No real personality in the messages, of course. He couldn't very well say, "How the fuck is it?" in an e-mail that everyone in the world might read, but that would be more like him. We'd save the rudeness for when I got back, when we could buy each other beers and remember when we played astronaut in the back yard.

Mamá called roadside memorials *descansos*. It comes from an old New Mexico funeral custom where the coffin was carried from the church to the *camposanto*, the cemetery. When the pallbearers needed rest, they put the coffin down. The stopping was the *descanso*, a resting place before the body reached the final destination. Mourners might leave flowers at the spot, sometimes with a little wooden cross among them. Like a *descanso*, roadside memorials commemorate the body's rest before reaching the cemetery.

It was an unremarkable piece of land. The state had hauled away the wreck long ago, and a rancher had repaired the barb wire. Saturn would have been visible that night. I checked. Clear sky, dry, desert air, no city lights. Gabriel might have looked in my direction that night, before he crashed. Now, I smelled sage and the distant river. The sand, brownish red and fine grained, slipped from my fingers.

According to the mission logs, I was on an EVA in the Titan rover when he died. I wouldn't learn about it for almost twenty-four hours. No real night sky on Saturn's largest moon. It's a hazy, dark, orange air during the day with the sun so far away. At night, no stars. Even Saturn, that great, ringed giant isn't visible. I couldn't see the Earth, of course, not that I had the luxury. Driving the rover required constant attention. Liquid methane puddles and ponds dotted the area around the habitat. They weren't deep, but the ground became viscous at their edges and could bog the rover down. We'd used the second rover to extricate it several times. I was investigating a radar blip a couple thousand meters away, behind a low hill we called Mount Olympus.

They built the rover's cab like a Kansas combine: enclosed against methane rain or wind, but not air tight. The atmosphere on Titan is thicker than Earth's by about half, so no need for a pressure suit, but we needed thermal protection. All that concerned us was keeping the heat in. The weather on the surface was almost minus 300 degrees Fahrenheit, and a light breeze whispered past the windows.

There's a lot to like about Titan. Sound, for example. I'd been to the moon, Mars, and Ganymede—all silent except for human and machine noise. Titan, though, had a voice. I imagine during the equinox, when the winds picked up, that it positively roared. Rain hissed as it slowly settled at a sixth of Earth gravity. Methane creeks made happy bubbly noises when they over-spilled their basins. Rocks clacked against each other when I kicked them. Occasionally there was thunder.

Planets have a smell, too. Regolith from the moon smells like burnt gunpowder. Mars smells like sulfur. Titan reeks. We decontaminated the suits when we reentered the habitat, but the methane and ethane stench lingered. It was hard to believe that Earth's atmosphere might have once been a rich, hydrocarbon soup like Titan's.

A smoggy late dusk under heavy cloud cover best described a drive at noon on Titan. I steered by headlights and found my way by the nav screen. The radar blip could be a rock situated the right way to bounce the signal, or a mineral deposit, or nothing at all. We'd investigated dozens of radar anomalies. We liked doing it. NASA scripted so much of our mission. There were science experiments to be set up, samples to be gathered, observations to be made. Responding to anomalies meant that we were human. That's why we came instead of self-directed robot explorers.

Rover I handled the rocky-strewn terrain easily. The hill tilted me a little, but that meant I was above the liquid, hydrocarbon muck below. Not much chance of getting stuck. Up here, the Rover crackled as it fractured the thin crust on the surface. Underneath, the soil was soft sand.

The headlights revealed a hump in the surface that I steered to go around. The blip was close. As I approached, the lump resolved into a cairn, but not just rocks on rocks. These seemed organized and fitted. The cairn stood stark in the Rover's lights; a long shadow cast behind it. A breeze caught dust from under the wheels and swept it around the rocks. I climbed out, put my suited hand against the stones. The pile was nearly as tall as me, and this close, the artifice was clear. How could this be a natural formation? I walked around, dragging my hand as I went, and on the far side, a low opening appeared. On my knees, I shined my light inside. Partly buried in sand, metal objects glinted back. My breath quickened. I knew I should call it in, but I wanted to make this moment last. Two, small metal boxes and what looked like a helmet. I brushed dust from the helmet's front. Beneath, it was a clear faceplate, too small for an adult human, and way wider than it was tall. We had not left it. Ours was the only expedition to this area on Titan.

I had discovered the first sign of extraterrestrial life.

Somewhere around the time I knelt in front of a cairn on Titan's surface, within an hour or two, when I was about nine-hundred million miles from home, Gabriel rolled his truck. Time of death was hard to pin down. A guy in a jeep spotted his overturned vehicle mid-morning. By then, our news had reached Earth. I'd been broadcasting a live feed, the now iconic, grainy picture of my gloved hands pulling a strangely shaped helmet from the dark. Anyone on Earth watching knew we weren't alone about an hour and a half after I did, after the signal flew at the speed of light across our solar system.

By the time we returned home, the space budget had tripled. New expeditions were scheduled to all the planets. Ambitious plans to explore the asteroids were being finalized. Who left the helmet? No one believed another space-faring species lived in our solar system. They had to be extra-solar. How did they get here? Had they mastered the power of faster than light travel? If they could, we could.

Then, the specialists went to work. What could we learn of the others' metallurgy, their manufacturing techniques, their engineering, their biology? You'd be surprised how revealing a helmet could be.

The two boxes were less helpful. One contained four small metal discs, about the size of a quarter. Each had a design etched on the front and two small hooks on the back, like a clasp. Were they coins or buttons? What did the designs mean? The second box contained nothing. Had whatever been in it degraded in Titan's hydrocarbon atmosphere?

We found no trace other than the cairn, but Titan's surface changed with the seasons. Winds reshaped hills, wore away features, and covered what was once exposed. Unlike the moon, our footprints lasted only a day. By our best estimations, measuring wear on the stacked rocks, the cairn might only be a hundred years old. Had the others been visitors like ourselves? Or did they have a more permanent presence buried beneath one of Titan's migrating dunes?

Earth asked a thousand questions, and they all ended with: who were they? Did we share enough with them that when we met—for surely we would—that we'd have a way to communicate? Discussion about the others circled the globe.

I think, though, that they're a lot like us. We have speculated why the cairn existed, but no one has an answer. Behind me, another truck passed on the highway. It was loud and filled with its own momentum. The driver probably didn't look my way, where my car was parked beside the road, and when I left, even fewer would notice Gabriel's tiny cross. None would stop to contemplate his photograph or wonder who he was. Still, if you drove down any highway, if you looked, you'd see the roadside memorials, the *descansos* that mark the memories of the ones we loved. Because when we honor the spot where the dead rested, we reveal something of ourselves, something about our hope that we will not be forgotten.

I wish I knew the name of the other who wore the strange helmet on Titan. I do not know what the disks in the box were, or what vanished from the second box, but I'll bet they meant something personal to whoever left them. I'll bet the others on Titan stood in the methane rain and placed these small items in memory. I'll bet they loved like we love, and the loss they felt burned like it burns in us.

Because they are alien, we believe they must be different, that their lives cannot be like ours in any way. We don't think about them living from moment to moment, working their routines, finding reasons to go on, just like us.

We don't think that they might have the equivalent of brothers, and that they might miss them.

The dead flowers crumbled in my hand. I scraped them away from the wooden cross. God, Gabriel, the days are lonely without you.

ALIEN EPILOGUE
Gini Koch

Note for readers of the Alien/Katherine "Kitty" Katt series: This story takes place right after the events of Universal Alien.

"I want to take the kids on a trip."

Everyone at the table knew I'd switched universes and hadn't destroyed the world over there. And yet, to a person they all looked shocked by my rather ordinary request.

Other than Jamie. My daughter didn't look surprised—she looked excited. Took a closer look at her big brothers. Charlie and Max didn't look opposed to this idea, either. My kids rocked.

"Ah, excuse me, Kitty, what?" my husband, Charles, finally asked.

"A trip. You've heard of them. We take them frequently."

"Ah, weren't the last few weeks enough...traveling for a while?" Charles seemed really thrown by this request. Sure, we'd spent all of our spare time since I'd been back making love like it was going out of style, but three kids already and number four coming in about eight months were great proof that my sex drive rarely, if ever, waned. Maybe all the sex had jumbled his mind. Not that I planned to stop, but something to note.

"Not really. I want to go on a fun trip. Something we get to actually enjoy." Though, based on the letter my Cosmic Alternate had left me, my family had definitely seen some interesting sights and had a lot of excitement and danger going on around them. And I'd been jet setting, too. But we hadn't been doing this together.

"I'm not sure that a trip right now is wise," James Reader said quickly, while shooting a strong look at my father. Of course, he'd spent a lot of time apologizing, too. Sure, James being the top male fashion model in the world was a great cover, but he'd still been lying to me as long as my husband had. It felt no less like betrayal to get the news that they were both in the

CIA, and had been for years, from my best friend than it had coming from Charles. Two of my main men owed me. Big time.

Dad nodded. "I do agree there, kitten. You have three children who just had a very traumatic few weeks." Right. Dad was a cryptologist working with alien transmissions, not just a retired history professor. Which I'd again found out "over there." Make that my three main men owing me for all the lying.

"No argument. You've all been protecting us for our own good for years, and that almost got all of us killed. We're all clear about that." Allowed them all the time to wince at my accurate assessment. "However, I'm suggesting a fun family outing that will, hopefully, not be loaded with life-threatening action."

"I agree with Katherine," Alfred Martini said. He was an exiled A-C my Cosmic Alternate had discovered hiding in ancient tunnels put underground by a different race of aliens, the Z'porrah, who really hated everyone on Earth. He was the only A-C on the planet here, and my father-in-law in the other universe. Having spent time with his son there, I could say that I had great taste in men in any universe.

I'd have told Alfred that I preferred he call me Kitty, but he'd been calling me Katherine for a reason, at least as far as I could tell—he knew I wasn't the Kitty he'd met first, and this was how he kept us separate. One day, perhaps he'd feel comfortable enough with me that he'd call me Kitty. Until then, I wasn't going to push it.

"I agree, too," William Cox chimed in. He was a Navy pilot, or he had been. Now he reported directly to the same CIA unit my other men did. I liked Bill a lot and, like Alfred, he had no family left. So now he was part of ours. "Especially if I get to go wherever you're going. I haven't had a fun trip in forever."

"Then it's settled. Or are you guys going to tell me that you're all about to run off on another Save the World mission?"

Peter, the most competent man in the world who somehow loved working for and living with us—and doing literally anything and everything perfectly—started clearing our plates before Charles or anyone else could confirm if they did or didn't have a mission. "Kitty, darling, what exciting location are you thinking of taking us to?"

"Well, let me ask all my Secret Agent Men—where is it safe for us to go?"

"You don't want to go somewhere near home?" Charles asked.

Waved my hand. "Australia's old news for us." The kids all grinned. "I want to go somewhere we haven't been before."

"So, you mean a real trip, not just a day trip somewhere." Charles seemed extremely underwhelmed by this idea of mine, which was really out of character.

"Did we lose all our money or something?"

Malcolm Buchanan, another CIA operative who I'd gotten to know well in the other universe but hadn't known in this one until I came "home," laughed. "No. He's just confused by you and the kids not wanting to hide under the bed."

"Really? I think I should be insulted. For me and our children."

Charles heaved a sigh. "I just wasn't prepared to have things quiet for a whole week and then you demand to start taking family vacations. Which, I can't actually go on right now."

James nodded. "We're going on assignment, which Chuck's been trying to figure out how to tell you for the last two days. Him, me, Buchanan, and Sol."

"So, gosh, that only leaves me, Bill, Peter, and Alfred to take care of the kids. However will we all manage?" Heard a soft grumbling and mewing, then two bundles of adorable fluffy fur that had been snoozing on my lap raised their heads. "What do Harlie and Gershom think?"

Harlie was an alien animal called a Poof who was Alfred's pet. Gershom was a Poof as well, and had come with me from the other universe because it was mine now. Wasn't sure who'd been happier about that, me or Alfred. Though, based on the fact that the Poofs were androgynous and mated when, per Alfred, a Royal Wedding was due, Harlie was probably the happiest. Because Harlie and Gershom had gotten busy and we all had Poofs now.

"You know, the Poofs are protectors," Alfred said. "So, even though Katherine and the children will only have Bill, Peter, and myself along, the Poofs will be able to protect them and the rest of us as well."

I snuggled Gershom and petted Harlie. They had cute ears and paws that were hidden by their fur, but their black button eyes showed through the fluff without issue. They were literally the cutest things I'd ever seen, barring my children. "Poofs are the best."

Charles shook his head. "I'll ask how a few balls of fluff are protection later."

"Trust me," Bill said emphatically.

"It's classified," Alfred added with a grin. "So, Katherine, where are we going and by what means?"

"Well, how we're getting there is determined by whether or not we get the jet. But I was thinking that it's high time that we visited Egypt. Cool ruins make writing reports fun."

The boys looked excited—all the boys coming with me, big or small. Jamie also looked pleased. The other men, however, looked shocked. Took the leap.

"Wow. You're all headed to Egypt on some super-secret mission, aren't you? Awesome. You can drop the rest of us off and pick us up after you've foiled the bad guys."

Charles groaned and rubbed the back of his neck. "Only my wife."

I leaned over and kissed him. "Yep. Only yours. So make your wife and kids happy and let us go have a fun adventure where no one's trying to kill us."

He grinned. "When, really, have I ever been able to say no to you?"

* * *

We spent one day prepping—with Peter doing most of that—then it was time to head to the airport. With one additional passenger.

"Mommy, Stripes *has* to come," Jamie said, holding the orange tabby cat who Cosmic Moi had rescued and who had, from all she'd written and I'd been told, truly helped save the day. "He's always the cat for the job."

"I promise I can keep Stripes safe and with the family, Charles," Alfred said. "I've been tinkering. And the Poofs can assist with that as well."

Peter came downstairs with Stripe's deluxe cat carrier. He opened the door. Stripes looked at the carrier, then looked right at Charles. It was clear the cat wasn't moving until he'd heard that he was coming with us as opposed to being jailed for his own safety.

Charles heaved a sigh. "Fine. It's insane to do this, but the whole thing is crazy, so who am I to argue? Yes, yes, the cat can go with all of you. Please be aware that I can't use Agency resources to find him if he gets himself lost."

Stripes snorted at Charles. He was in no need of CIA assistance, thank you very much. Then he gently head-butted Jamie and graciously allowed her to put him into his traveling condo.

Thusly prepared, we headed for the airport.

* * *

We touched down in Cairo. Now the goodbyes were a lot more emotional—
on the part of the men leaving us. Charles, in particular, didn't seem to want
to let us go.

"Is there a terror threat we should know about?" I asked him finally.

"No. That's not what we're here for. It's just...I just got you back, Kitty.
And we almost lost everything that matters while you were gone. I don't
want to let you and the kids go into anything without me."

"Well, unless you're going to come with us, or have us come with you
on every single assignment, that's not an achievable goal."

He sighed. "I know. And I don't want you coming on my missions, so
don't ask to."

I kissed him. "We'll be fine. We have Stripes, Poofs, Bill, and Alfred
along. We're good."

Charles grinned. "You're great, baby. You always have been."

Snuggled next to him. "Right back atcha. Now, go to work and let us go
to school."

* * *

Peter had made reservations at a lovely hotel. He'd also rented us a large
Range Rover which Bill drove to said hotel. Peter checked us in, we got to
our connecting suites, and he ordered room service. It arrived quickly
because, as it turned out, he'd ordered it when he'd made our reservations
and had just been giving the kitchen the go order.

We ate a lovely meal, then Peter waved us off. "Darlings, time for me
to do my job and get our temporary home set up as we like. You all go off
and explore. I'm planning on keeping the home fires burning."

"No interest in seeing the pyramids?" Alfred asked.

Peter shook his head. "Unlike the rest of you, I've had more than enough
excitement."

"What about the cat?" Bill asked. "Stripes isn't going to want to travel
in his carrier anymore, but I think you're going to have issues if we just cart
him around."

Stripes shot Bill a look I could only think of as snide, then leaped from
the bed he'd been lounging on right onto my shoulder.

"Ah, apparently I'm the designated cat carrier now."

"You are, Mommy," Jamie said seriously. "Stripes likes to ride with you
when we're going out into an action situation."

It was still disconcerting to hear Jamie speaking at this level at her tender age of three, but even more so because, until the universe switch, getting statements like this out of her would have been impossible. Charles and I had both believed Jamie was autistic, though we hadn't admitted that to each other. She'd barely spoken to us, other than to share bad things that were expected to happen, and she'd rarely been demonstrative at all with anyone, not even my dad. All she'd wanted to do was stare into her three-way mirrors that she refused to live without.

After the switch we knew that she was seeing into other universes via those mirrors, which was why she'd been uninterested in her boring real life. My Cosmic Alternate had gotten Jamie to agree to only use her mirrors once a week and for a short period of time. Thanks to this, and Stripes, she'd also started interacting with us like a mostly normal little girl, albeit one with almost an adult's vocabulary and comprehension.

Cat on my shoulder or not, I went down onto my knee and hugged her tightly. "Okay then, we'll just keep things that way." Pulled the boys into the hug, too, and just enjoyed holding my children for a few good, long moments.

Let them go and stood up. Credit to Stripes—he'd never lost his balance or dug his claws into me. Gave him a pat. "You're an awesome boy, aren't you?" He purred back that he was indeed.

I had no idea why I felt like I knew what the cat was thinking. However, Cosmic Moi had been able to talk to the animals, and maybe I'd gotten that skill, too, somehow. Decided not to worry about it and just get my Ancient Egyptian Field Trip underway.

Ensured that all of us were slathered with sunscreen and that Alfred put his lightweight and camouflaged-for-Stripes'-coloration homing and protection harness on our cat. The rest of us were in jeans and long sleeved t-shirts—the boys in Jack Johnson, Jamie in Amadhia, me in Aerosmith, Bill sporting a Navy T. Alfred was in black slacks and a plain black long-sleeved shirt. Despite my desire to have us all in our Converse for comfort, we were in paddock boots instead—they were comfy and good protection for our feet. Peter handed out Diamondbacks baseball caps as we headed out the door.

We'd arrived in the early morning, but by the time we were out the door, it was close to noon. Back into our Range Rover—kids and Alfred in the back, Stripes and me taking shotgun—off we went.

"We'd normally go to the Islamic Art Museum first day, but it's still not recovered from the terrorist bombing from last year. So we're going straight to the pyramids. No notebooks today—we're just going to enjoy and explore. Tomorrow we'll go back, but this time you'll all be expected to be taking notes and such."

"Wow, you're a taskmaster, aren't you?" Bill asked. "I thought this was a vacation."

"This is how Mommy vacations us," Charlie shared. "We have to write reports when we go to Disneyland, too."

Bill gave me the side-eye. "You're part drill sergeant, aren't you?"

"Maybe. Never miss an opportunity to learn, that's my motto."

He laughed but didn't argue. Instead, he pointed out sights along the way. "I was stationed here for a few months," he said after he'd pointed out the Hanging Church, the Nile, and the Pharaonic Village.

"Clearly. And no argument. It's always nice to have a resident expert teaching."

Bill grinned. "Crossing into the Giza Governorate. Next stop, Pyramids and adventure."

* * *

Charles and I had been here before, on our world tour honeymoon, but we hadn't been back with the kids. So I'd ensured that we'd know what was going on and hired a tour guide. As promised, she was waiting for us at the Tomb of Queen Hetepheres.

The man I'd hired had called in sick, but his replacement was a gal around my age. I was surprised to discover that Chrysta wasn't Egyptian but Canadian, though she lived in Cairo. She reminded me a lot of my sorority sisters—pretty, with red hair and a bubbly personality. She knew what was going on and, biggest plus, spoke English, French, and Arabic, so this was definitely one for the win column.

It was hot and sandy, just like Phoenix, where Charles and I were from. In other words, I was comfortable.

There were tourist groups everywhere and I ended up putting Stripes into my purse—I was carrying a large Coach tote so that we'd have whatever we might need—and the cat fit in there pretty well. Had to wear the tote cross-body, though, because Stripes definitely made it heavier. To Chrysta's credit, once "therapy pet" was explained, she didn't bring Stripes up again.

We wandered around the tomb, then went to the Sphinx, the Great Pyramid, and the Tomb of Hemon. The kids were excited, but we'd just had a long plane flight, and they wanted to run around and look at things quickly, as I'd figured they would. Chrysta pointed out many sights of interest, but I'd hired our guide for the full week, so she wasn't trying to push anything onto the kids, either.

It was heading towards sunset, and we were going to head back to the car, when I realized that we'd lost Alfred somehow. Gathered everyone together—no one could remember when they'd seen him last.

"Losing Alfred on the first day was not in my lesson plan," I fretted quietly to Bill, while Chrysta did a quick run around the area and Bill and I both verified that we had no cell coverage here. "I know he's a grown man, but still."

We all looked around and called his name, until Chrysta returned without Alfred in tow. She waved the walkie-talkie that she carried to stay in touch with other tour guides in the area. "I didn't see anyone dressed like him anywhere," she said. "And no one else has spotted him. Should we call the authorities?"

Bill was looking farther out towards the desert. "I think..." He scooped Max up in his arms and took Charlie's hand. Took the hint and picked up Jamie. "Let's go quickly but carefully." With that, he trotted off.

"I don't think this is a good idea," Chrysta said.

"I'm not letting the rest of us get separated." And with that, I followed Bill. Heard Chrysta heave a sigh, but she came along as well. Double-checked that I still had Stripes—I did, and he was snoozing in my purse, surrounded by Poofs. No wonder it was heavy.

Was glad that Charles and I had ensured that we stayed in shape as a family—Bill was going at a pace just over a fast walk that I was pretty sure he could keep up for miles.

He led us deeper into the ruins, heading for, if my memory served, the Tomb of the Birds. Caught up with him. "Why are we heading this way? I don't see any footprints."

"I saw something flash out here, ma'am."

"Ma'am?"

"I think we're about to be in that action situation Jamie mentioned in the hotel room. I kind of go...ultra-military when that happens."

Couldn't argue—that Jamie had mentioned action or the need to flip into a mindset that helped you function well in a danger situation. And from Bill's demeanor, we were in a danger situation.

I probably should have insisted that we go back to the car, alert the proper authorities, and organize a legitimate manhunt—you know, if Alfred wasn't back to the car by the time it was dark. But I didn't. Because I didn't want to.

It was stupid, but per everyone in both universes, Cosmic Moi was a total butt-kicker. Sure I'd earned Good Mommy points and even Saved The Political Day points, but not Saved The World points. I doubted that Charles or James would have spent any time fretting if Cosmic Moi was the one asking for an outing they couldn't go on. And, call me ridiculously competitive with myself, I wanted to show that I could save the day when it mattered, too. Plus, Chrysta was handling the "let's go back and call the authorities" portion of our festivities anyway. Besides, for all I knew, Alfred had gotten heatstroke and had wandered off unintentionally and, in that case, time would be of the essence.

We reached the Tomb of the Birds in less time than I'd have expected. But still, the sun was lower on the horizon and the entrance was blocked by rock on either side, making it darker. And creepier. I had a flashlight in my purse and we had Chrysta, who knew the area, but it was going to be dark and scary out here sooner as opposed to later.

"Looks like there's a metal gate blocking anyone from getting in," I pointed out. "So Alfred can't be inside here."

"Actually there were deep tunnels discovered here, before this got gated up." Bill sounded thoughtful. He put Max down. "You all wait here."

Put Jamie down and had her and Max hold Charlie's hands. "*You* all wait here." Trotted after Bill up the small incline to reach the gate as he was trying to open it. It didn't budge.

Bill examined the area around the gate.

"What are you looking for?" I asked him quietly. "I don't see anything. Other than the approach of nightfall."

"Pilot's instinct is all I have for you, ma'am. That and I know I saw something over here."

Alfred, being an A-C, was the fastest thing on Earth. However, I read the comics, and there were plenty of ways to stop a superfast being. Wondered if this was where Bill was going with his worry, so I asked him.

He shook his head. "Not really, though that's always a concern. You weren't with me, but I know we told you about the tunnels where we found him."

The tunnels Alfred had been hiding out in for decades had been dug deep into the earth all over the world long before even the dinosaurs were thinking about seeing if they could walk on land. There were rooms in the tunnels, too, and Alfred had turned them into his private storerooms for all the scientific inventions he worked on before he sold them to the government. But at least two thirds of his creations he didn't want anyone to have, because humanity as a race wasn't enlightened enough to be entrusted with them.

The light dawned. "You think he's gone to visit one of his storerooms and has lost track of time?"

"Maybe."

Considered other options. "You think the tunnels that were discovered are Alfred's. And people have been locked out, but that doesn't mean that Alfred wouldn't want to go in and check to make sure they haven't found any of his things."

"Yes." The way he said it, I knew there was more.

"You think there are people down there right now, don't you? More people than Alfred."

Bill grinned at me. "There you go."

"What do you mean?"

"Now you're thinking like...you."

"Ah. Um, go me?"

"Yes. Just channel that. Go with the crazy. Make the weird logic leaps. Figure out what the wildest possibilities are, because at least one of them will be right. That's what you always do."

Looked at him for a long moment. "You want me to be more like her?"

"You *are* her. I know the others don't think so. But I know you both and I know you both differently than they do. And you're her and she's you. You have what it takes to save the day, always."

"But she was Wonder Woman, that's what you guys said."

"Yeah, for our world, she was. So what that you can't be like that. Be Batgirl—she always gets the perps, too, and saves Batman and Robin in the process half the time. Just don't doubt yourself or let the others doubt you."

"Will do, Captain Confidence."

He grinned. "I like that better than Lunatic Lad, for certain, ma'am."

"Duly noted." Thought about it. "That's why you're calling me ma'am, isn't it? Not just so you'll be in the kick-butt mindset, but so that I will be, too."

Bill nodded. "Yes. Seriously though, I can probably handle anything by myself. If you want to take Chrysta and the kids and go back to the car, now's the time."

Looked back at them and felt my body go cold. "Bill? They're all gone."

* * *

We searched quickly and frantically, though we stayed together, but the kids and Chrysta were gone without a trace.

"Think she took them back to the car?" he asked as we retraced our steps at a trot.

"Not without my kids whining, complaining, or calling to me."

"Yeah, good point." He sounded as worried as I felt.

"It's almost dark." Looked into my purse to dig around for the flashlight. Stripes was in there, awake and alert, but there were now no Poofs on Board. Decided not to worry about them right now.

Took Stripes and the flashlight out and put Stripes onto my shoulder. "We've lost the kids," I told the cat. Hey, Bill had said to go with the crazy. "And our guide. And apparently your purse buddies."

Stripes purred and nudged against me. The Poofs could take care of themselves, but he was on the case to find the kids. He leaped down gracefully and started off at a slow walk, sniffing the air like mad.

As he did, I remembered his harness. "You know...Stripes is wearing something to ensure he doesn't get lost. Meaning that he's wearing a tracking device."

"Good one," Bill said. "Alfred will have the other side of the tracker. Hopefully we'll see something change on the harness when we get closer to Alfred."

Bill and I followed, me handling the flashlight, though Bill wouldn't let me turn it on, him with a gun drawn from somewhere. "You're packing heat?"

"You have a gun in your purse, right?"

"Yes, and yes, I know how to shoot it."

"Be ready to get it out and use it, when we need to."

"When, not if?"

"No one snatches people silently for any good reason, ma'am. Especially not people who are perfect hostages. Which is why that flashlight needs to stay off right now—no need to let them see us coming."

Shoved the total panic these statements gave me away. There was no way I could rescue my children if I was freaking out. Now was the time to do what Bill wanted—channel Cosmic Moi's abilities and just roll with it like a total badass. Sure, I was essentially an accidental badass, but still, it was time to Stand and Deliver.

Resisted the desire to listen to music right now, despite hearing Adam Ant in my head. It might keep me calm and focused, but then I'd miss small sounds, and if the kids were captives, small sounds would be all we'd hear.

Stripes slunk around the Tomb, then headed for a nearby hump of dirt that might be a sand dune or another building—without light I couldn't be sure.

We followed him and then Stripes disappeared. Managed not to gasp, but only just. Bill went to where the cat had gone and he disappeared, too.

Had no idea whether I should follow or run screaming for where other people were, when Bill reappeared, holding Stripes in one arm, grabbed my hand, and pulled me along with them. He put his mouth right by my ear. "It's some sort of optical illusion that's hiding a path."

Nodded. Why let him know I was totally freaked out?

"So, relax." Ah. He could tell. Well, whatever. "But turn on the flashlight—it's pitch black in here and we're going to have to risk it."

Did and we had two choices—we could stay level and go on the narrow path to the right, or we could go on the narrower path to the left, which sloped down at a steep angle. Both looked dicey, but the area around the path to the left looked more recently disturbed. Bill put Stripes down—sure enough, the cat headed to the left and we followed. His harness looked less camouflaged, less like his fur and more like a harness.

"It was like this in the tunnels where we found Alfred," Bill whispered as we finally leveled off. "Be prepared for anything, and turn off the flashlight the second I say."

We walked along, me keeping the flashlight focused down and just ahead of us, to hopefully lessen the chances of an enemy seeing it. We finally reached a right turn, Stripes looked at us, then slunk around the corner.

Turned off the flashlight as we hugged the wall to our right. We waited and listened. Couldn't be positive, but thought I heard the sound of faint voices.

Bill ducked down and looked around the corner. As he did this, I realized I could see him doing it. Meaning there was light ahead of us somewhere. He stood and took my hand and we moved out.

There was light coming from what looked like a doorway quite far away. We walked as quickly as we could, still hugging the wall and being as quiet as possible. As we got closer, I could see Stripes sitting just outside of the light, so he was still in darkness. And his harness was no longer disguised—it was clearly visible.

As we reached the cat, the sounds of voices were much clearer.

"What the hell is this thing?" a man asked.

"I have no idea." The voice was Chrysta's. She sounded angry.

"This is your job," a different man said.

"No," Chrysta snapped, "it's not. I did the hard work. You've bungled the easy part."

Bill and I exchanged the "oh really?" look. Well, now we knew how the kids had disappeared—Chrysta had lured them somehow. I'd left them in her care after all. I'd kick myself for that later—I had to get my kids and Alfred away from these creeps first.

"What about him?" the first man asked.

"I'm neither a tour guide nor an archeologist," Alfred said. He didn't sound frightened. He sounded angry.

"But you're the person who can read this scroll," Chrysta said. "That's why the others called you."

"Where are they?" Alfred asked.

Bill and I got closer and looked inside. The room was large and square and it was clearly not something made by ancient man. Even the Egyptians and Chinese weren't able to achieve this level of absolute straight perfection. Plus, the walls, ceiling, and floors all seemed to be made from a substance I couldn't identify. They glowed with a gentle blue light, as if they were lit from the inside.

There was another door in the middle of the far wall, and it was open as well. The room it opened up into wasn't lit in the same way—the light coming from it looked far more natural.

"Nearby," the first man said, looking at the other opened door. He was big and looked and sounded American. Alfred was on his knees, hands tied behind his back, with what looked like a very ancient scroll laid out in front of him, and this man was holding a long knife at Alfred's throat. Hyperspeed or not, I wasn't sure that Alfred could get away without being hurt, if not killed.

My children were closer to the other opened door, but in the far corner. There was another big man with a pickax guarding them, but he looked Middle Eastern. It didn't take genius to know that the kids had been told to behave or watch their Uncle Alfred be murdered in front of them.

The rest of the room was devoid of anything other than Chrysta and the pedestal she was standing near that looked to have risen out of the middle of the floor—the top looked just like the floor, and it was held up by several small, glowing pillars that surrounded a multicolored cloth that sat on the main part of the pedestal. An orb that glowed blue and purple sat on this cloth. Nothing about this looked manmade, either.

"How do we remove it?" Chrysta asked. "Answer, correctly, or we start killing kids. Slowly." She turned to look at Alfred and smiled—a very evil smile. "Or their father. You get to pick."

The only reason I wasn't in the room was because Bill was holding me back. The realization that whatever the hell was going on was why Charles, James, Malcolm, and my dad were here waved merrily to me. It so figured that I wasn't even all that surprised. That they were captives, most likely in the other room, was also not surprising. It was becoming clear that this was how our luck rolled in these situations.

"You can't kill the children," Alfred said quickly. "Only one of them will be able to remove the orb safely."

"You're lying," Chrysta said, sounding bored.

"Test it," Alfred said. "You could release me and let me try it, if you want."

She snorted, then went to the other room. "I need Miguel."

A man who looked Mexican came into the room. "Yes, Señorita Patrón?"

She nodded her head towards the pedestal. "Get the orb."

Miguel shrugged and went to do as he was told. "How? The bars are too close together."

"Just shove your hand in. The old man said that's how to get it."

Miguel did as requested. At least, he tried. But as soon as he put his hand near the bars, his body lit up with blue flames, he screamed, briefly, and turned into a pile of purple dust.

Everyone gasped, other than Alfred, who'd clearly been expecting this.

Chrysta stalked over to him and grabbed his head. "You knew it would do that."

"I did and I told you so. The children are the only ones who can remove it safely. The little girl will have the best chance."

That did it. I wrenched out of Bill's hold and ran into the room. "Stay away from my children, you heinous bitch."

Chrysta rolled her eyes. "Oh, goody, you managed to find us." She produced a gun from somewhere and pointed it at me. "One of you get that orb for me or your mother dies."

"It's okay, Mommy," Jamie said, as she came forward.

"Yes it is," Alfred said strongly. "Jamie will be fine, Katherine. I promise."

While I contemplated what I could do, which was not much, and what I'd do to Chrysta if my baby was hurt, which was a lot, Jamie walked over to the pedestal. It lowered so that she could reach the portion with the orb easily. She put her hand in and took out the orb. No muss, no fuss. It was clear that the pillars weren't solid, because I watched them move aside for her. Then the pedestal rose back up to where it had been previously.

Jamie looked at me, looked at Alfred, then ran back to stand in front of her brothers. "I won't give it to you," Jamie said. "You're bad men and you're a mean lady."

Chrysta walked over and tried to take the orb from Jamie. It glowed purple and blue and threw her back. She hit the far wall, but tucked her head and so wasn't knocked out. Pity.

While this was going on, I tried to get Alfred away from the man with the long knife. Unfortunately, this only meant that the man with the knife was able to grab me and put the knife in front of my face. Chrysta regained her feet and went to Alfred, putting her gun to his head.

"Who the hell is this?" the man holding me growled.

"That's their mother, Kitty Reynolds," Chrysta said. "So, why don't you tell your little girl to give us what we want?"

"Ah, why should I?"

"Because then none of you will get hurt," she said as if this were the obvious outcome.

"Why don't I trust you on that? Oh, because you lied to me. And you have my family all captured. I assume my husband's nearby?"

"Next door. You want us to kill him to make your daughter do what we want?"

"Not really. But I'm not going to make her do what you want, either."

She shrugged. "Take the orb from her. Or you all die."

"Why don't you try again instead?"

"Because it repelled me. Obviously."

"Good work, that orb."

Chrysta laughed, one of those nasty villain laughs. Clearly she'd practiced. "Fine. Your husband shouldn't have brought his family along on a mission. He'll learn. The hard way."

"I have no idea what you're talking about," I said truthfully. Because I honestly had no idea what Charles and the others might be doing here, other than being held captive.

Chrysta gave the man holding me a look that clearly said it was his turn in the spotlight.

"So, Missus Reynolds, would you like to explain just what you're doing here? Before we kill you and your children, I mean."

"Oh, call me Kitty. You know, since we're friends and all that."

He stepped closer to me, squeezing my arm just a little harder, and ran the flat of the blade against my cheek. "Friends tell friends why they're sneaking around in places they shouldn't be."

"Field trip."

He blinked. "Excuse me?"

"We're here on a field trip."

"You're here on a what?" He sounded flabbergasted.

"A field trip. I homeschool my children, and we're here for in-the-field study. A trip to see things you can't in school or at home. A trip out to the field or, in this case, the creepy old ruins. A way to educate with hands-on experience. I'm running out of explanations for what a field trip is. My children catch on quicker than this, so I'm honestly not used to having to explain simple concepts repeatedly. My bad."

The man seemed honestly stunned. Nice to know I still had it. Of course, this was only a momentary reprieve. Tried to see what I could around him without letting on that I was doing so. Not that much, really. I could see the kids, the guy guarding them, the doorway near them, and the freaky yet pretty orb Jamie was holding. I saw Chrysta and Alfred, the Pedestal of Power, and the doorway I'd come through. Where, supposedly, I had someone waiting to help me out. Not that I could tell.

The man who had my children cornered was less confused. "They don't go to school. So no one's going to be looking for them. Meaning we can kill them, take the orb, and then just get out of town."

"My daddy will hunt you down and kill you if you do," Charlie said. "And he'll kill you ugly, too."

"He's not wrong about that. My husband is kind of touchy about people hurting his family." And he wasn't the only one. I, for one, was getting seriously pissed. Chose not to think about the fact that, clearly, Charles and the others were captives. I'd deal with that later.

"So's our Uncle James," Max shared. "He'll hurt you, too, if you hurt us or our mommy."

"You're going to be very sorry," Jamie said calmly. "But, if you apologize right now, it might be okay." The orb sparkled purple and blue when she spoke. So far, the orb appeared to be protecting her and, by extension, her brothers. I just wasn't sure if it would repel knives or bullets.

Of course, it was going to take a lot more than a "gosh, so sorry" for me to forgive any of these people, but I wasn't in a position to correct Jamie at this time.

Saw a hand wave to me from the shadows—from the room where I was pretty sure Charles and the others were being held. Hoped this was the "go" signal and not the "we're all dead" sign. No time like the present to find out. "Or, you know, it might not matter."

"You mean you'll be dead?" the man with the long knife asked me. Clearly he wasn't the brightest Crayola in the box.

"No." Managed not to react to what I was seeing, but it took effort. "You will be."

Six Poofs bounded into the room, looking adorable as always. I managed not to ask how this was in any way helpful mostly because as everyone looked at them, including the guy holding me, I took the opportunity to use the kung fu I'd spent years training in and rammed my knee in up into his groin while I shoved the hand holding the knife away with my left hand and slammed my right elbow up to connect with his chin. He sort of crumpled, which was nice.

Didn't stop to check on him. Instead I ran across the room and body slammed the other man away from my children. I used the side my purse was on for the extra heft. Considering my purse slammed into his crotch, this was nicely effective. At least, I took the sound of pain, the pickax falling from his hand, and the expression of shock on his face to indicate effectiveness.

He sort of bounced off of the wall, but away from me. I grabbed the pickax and was in a decent position, so I sent a high kick into his stomach. He flew into the pedestal. And disintegrated into a pile of purple dust. The pedestal was still there, looking as if nothing had happened.

The man on the floor screamed and got to his feet, waving his knife around, while Chrysta shouted obscenities. "I'm going to kill him now and teach you all a lesson!" she shrieked.

Harlie turned gigantic—taller than Charles and bigger than Malcolm— a fluffy monster with lots and lots of razor sharp teeth. The man with the knife screamed and dropped into a fetal position on the floor, as Harlie roared and bounded over to Chrysta, who stopped pointing the gun at Alfred so she could aim at the Poof.

"NO!" As I screamed, Stripes bounded into the room, yowling what I was prepared to swear was a cat battle cry, and jumped on Chrysta, all claws out, and I was too pleased with this turn of events to continue screaming. Instead, as Harlie took Alfred gently into its mouth and moved him to where the kids were, and the other Poofs surrounded them, I ran over and wrested the gun away from Chrysta, who was thankfully not pulling the trigger. Possibly because she was screaming while fighting a seriously pissed off cat and losing.

As much as I was enjoying this, we had the rest of the family to rescue, apparently. "Stripes, disengage. Come to Mommy."

Stripes leaped away from her and landed in my arms in one graceful move. "Who's a good boy, den? *You* are." Gave him a snuggle as I pointed the gun at Chrysta's head. "Give me another reason."

"We want her alive, baby." I was much less surprised to see Charles come into the room than I would have been thirty minutes prior. He looked around. "Kitty, are you all okay?" He sounded stressed, not that I could blame him.

"I think we are. Kids, Alfred?"

"We're fine, Mommy," Jamie said.

"I'm good now," Alfred said. Risked a look out of the corner of my eye. He was standing and Bill was untying his hands.

"Nice of you to join the party, Bill."

"Figured you had things well in hand here, ma'am, and the Poofs came to show me how to get into the other room without being detected. Besides, I knew you had all the backup you'd need."

Nuzzled Stripes again. "Right you were, Captain Confidence. Stripes and Poofs rock. So, dearest darlingest men in my life—who's going to tell me what the hell's going on the quickest?"

"Kitty, no need to sound snide," my father said as he collected the scroll that was, somehow, still in the same place on the floor it had been earlier and wasn't smudged or mussed in any way. Assumed it was made from the same stuff as either the walls or the pedestal. "None of you were supposed to be involved."

"Then why did you call Alfred in to help you?" I asked as James slammed handcuffs onto Chrysta with much malice aforethought and Malcolm did the same to the man who was still on the floor weeping in terror.

"You told her?" Charles asked Alfred.

"Dude, seriously? No, he didn't. He disappeared and we went after him. But it doesn't take genius IQ to realize that if you were all here, reading a scroll that my dad couldn't decipher, because it's likely written in some ancient alien language, that you'd ask Alfred to zip on by. So, while I'm contemplating how insulted I need to be by your assuming I'm a moron, I'm waiting impatiently for more details that could mean I forgive you. Eventually." I still had the gun trained on Chrysta because I still wanted to shoot her.

Charles sighed and gently took the gun away from me. "They're an international team of artifact smugglers. They've been hitting different sites all over the world. We had a tip that they'd targeted something in Cairo. The general thinking was that it was the Islamic Art Museum, since that place is still devastated."

"But, it turns out, what they were looking for was in the Egyptian Museum of Antiquities," Malcolm said. "They stole an ancient scroll that has never been on display and wasn't listed in any recent registries."

"Let me guess—it describes how an orb of great power was hidden under the Tomb of the Birds."

"Got it in one," James said with a grin. "Well, it insinuated that the orb was hidden somewhere near the Great Pyramid. As were a lot of other treasures. The scroll listed a variety of goodies everyone would want to find. So we were too late to stop that theft, but we tracked them to this area and began searching for them."

"And found them without issue, apparently."

"Yeah, we got jumped," Chuckie said. "It was as if they knew we were coming."

"They did." Looked at Chrysta. Happily, she was bleeding from a lot of different places. She might even need reconstructive surgery. Go Stripes. "So did you kill my original guide?"

"Of course."

"Shocker. Why would you even assume that we'd know anything?"

She rolled her eyes. Well, eye. One eye was swollen shut. "We monitor all CIA activity. Some friends of ours were after your family a month or so ago. They're all dead, you're all still alive. You do the math. Besides, even if you were as clueless as you seemed, you were six really great hostage options."

"Can I shoot her? Please?"

Charles put his arm around me. "No. But I'll let you watch us interrogate her if it'll make you happy."

"As long as you're using trained rats and Zippo lighters."

More people arrived. These looked like they worked in clandestine ops in some way. "Take all of them into the severest custody," Charles said, as the men took Chrysta from James. "Black bag them, dark hole, no phone calls. We'll handle the rest of the situation here."

"What's in the other room?" I asked, once Chrysta and her considerable number of cronies in the other room were taken away.

"Another room, but not like this one," Bill said. "Mostly like the inside of the rest of the tombs and ruins around here. I think the Egyptians were trying to get to this room."

"They were probably drawn to the orb," Alfred said. "Just as Stripes was able to follow the homing device in his harness to find me." Stripes purred. He'd have found them without the harness, but whatever made his humans happy.

"What do we do with the orb?" Malcolm asked. "Something that can only be handled by a child shouldn't be left lying around anywhere."

"It's not because she's a child, actually," Alfred said. "The orb can only be handled by a being of great intellectual power who also has the ability to see the multiverse. It's not a Z'porrah power cube and this room is not a Z'porrah construct, either. I'm not sure what planet put this here, but if I had to guess, I'd say it was the Ancients. Due to what we know, the orb might have been put here for Jamie to find. Certainly for her to wield."

Looked at my little girl. She didn't look like someone who should be wielding anything more dangerous than an iPad. She smiled sweetly and held the orb out towards Gershom. "You know what to do," she said. The Poof purred and took the orb out of her hand by eating it. At least that's what it looked like. Then Gershom and all the rest of the Poofs went back to small and adorable and hopped onto their owners' shoulders.

"Do we want to know?" Charles asked Alfred.

"Probably not," he said cheerfully.

Cosmic Moi had mentioned something about this. "The Poofs will give Jamie the orb if she needs it." Gershom purred—yes, they would.

"Exactly," Alfred said, rubbing his hands together. "Now, let's get the rest of those items you boys just saved catalogued and put into safekeeping."

"You mean into the Poofs' stomachs?" I asked.

Alfred shrugged. "Kitty, as I know you know, whatever works."

Went and gave Alfred a big hug. "You're the best." Then I went back to my husband. "I want a job."

He blinked. "Excuse me?"

"A job. With all of you. And before you freak out, let me just say that if I'd been involved in this operation from the get-go, Chrysta wouldn't have been able to intercept us, kill an innocent guide, and take any of us hostage. Besides, I think I'm at least as good at this as the rest of you are."

Bill grinned. "You can't argue with that logic, Chuck."

I could see the wheels in Charles' head turning, as he ran every possible way this would end up in his mind. "Fine," he sighed finally. "But you're going to be communications, not field, because I don't want you involving the kids."

"Oh, don't worry. I won't send them to *Spy Kids* school." I'd train them in that myself, after all. "And I'm fine with you making me be Oracle."

Because, when push came to shove, Bill was right—I was Batgirl. And Batgirl—with an assist from three exceptional Robins, Stripes the Wonder Cat, and the Super Poofs—always got the perps and saved Batman and the rest of the Justice League when she had to.

"I know that look," Charles said. "That's your 'I know something you don't' look."

Leaned up and kissed him. "Stop worrying. I'll tell you all about it back at the Batcave."

THE HAINT OF SWEETWATER RIVER
Anthony Lowe

"Sad and dismal is the tale
I now relate to you,
'Tis all about the cattlemen,
Them and their murderous crew..."
— "The Invasion Song," Anonymous

Carbon County, Wyoming Territory
July of 1889

They sent Loretta Vaine away into the prairie with a Colt's revolver, seven cartridges, and the insistence that the seventh of those bullets had better find its way into her own skull if the others failed to find their mark. She was nineteen at the time, possessed of the good sense to know her only worldly recourse was to acquiesce when in the presence of superior firepower.

"Reckon I like killin' better'n dyin'," she said.

The man from Cheyenne walked with her for about a mile out of Rawlins, never going more than a few steps without a cigarette between his teeth. "That's a fine attitude to have, young lady. Can you shoot?"

Loretta pulled the Colt's revolver from the belt of her pants and leveled it eastward as if to dare the rising sun. "Kin take the neck off a bottle at twenty paces."

"Bottles ain't people."

"Right. People are bigger."

"People move 'round."

"Mostly just forward," said Loretta. "Don't take maths to kill folks. Ask that boy Ford. Me, I bet I coulda shot Jesse James with his hand on a pistol instead of a picture frame."

The man from Cheyenne slowed up to roll himself another cigarette. "You seem about damn sure of that, too."

"Reckon you gotta be sure. Gotta act like you already killed 'em. Bein' unsure don't get nobody but yerself done fer."

"All this talk seems like the consequence of a lot of deep thought. You ever shot someone before?"

"Up at the Gem some guy started beatin' on me during. Left his pants and gun belt on the headboard, so I reached over and shot him once in the gut. He cussed at me and run outside in the streets nekked tryin' to find the doc and died 'fore he could."

Loretta shoved the revolver back into her belt. "Didn't feel bad er nothin'. And they say it only gets easier."

"Easier is the wrong word." The man from Cheyenne struck a match on his pants and brought the tiny flame to his freshly-rolled cigarette. Smoke poured out of his nose and obscured his eyes. "Killing never gets easier," he said. "The act don't ever stoop to you. You're just better fitted to the diabolical mold, young lady. The one first broke by Cain."

Loretta thought about that. "Same thing."

"Maybe," said the man, smiling. "I sure hope it ain't."

At the next bend in the trail, he took Loretta by the shoulder. "You know what you have to do."

"Yessir."

"And you have the proper tools."

"Yessir."

"If you don't follow through with your task, ain't nothing short of Hell itself can hide you. We'll string you up and you won't come down."

Loretta unconsciously scratched her neck. "Sure, I get it."

"Convince them to sign over the land to us or kill them on sight. We don't rightly care which. Wire me when you're done. If you tell the operator who the message is for, they won't charge you nothing."

"Uh-huh."

"Until then, your trespasses ain't forgiven." The man dropped the cigarette, stomped it out with his boot. "Good hunting, young lady." He gave a little salute and turned away.

Loretta stood in place for a long while, watching the man go. She smelled the lingering smoke from his cigarette and knew she was tasting hellfire. If the man from Cheyenne wasn't the devil himself, then he'd surely be the one to kick her down into Hades with Judas and Bob Ford. Unless she managed to ruin those two homesteaders and clean her slate, and she was fairly certain of her conviction to do so.

* * *

Further to the north of Rawlins, past a rounded mound of granite bearing the names of westward folk like a ledger of audacious commitment, a woman by the name of Ella Watson stood upon the porch of her cabin and brought a match to her lantern. For a moment, she simply stood, watching the starshot horizon with a countenance that could have been taken for suspicion or awe. She watched for a long time.

Finally, Ella knelt down over the front steps and pried off a slab of wood to reveal a tattered flour sack wrapped around something without consistent form. With marked delicacy, she removed the sack and its contents and strolled across her land draped in lantern light.

After a mile she came upon her cattle. They were healthy and docile, nuzzling her thighs as she passed. She hummed one of her favorite lullabies while she swept her lantern in a steady arc, looking for the right spot. When she noticed a dry patch on the land, barren and tough as caliche, she placed the sack down atop that desiccated earth.

The cattle gathered around while Ella waited. As the minutes ticked by she dimmed the lantern more and more until it was snuffed out.

A light within the flour sack bloomed just then, deep and blue. Ella took a few steps back.

The earth below the sack rumbled and heaved as if some long-buried corpse had returned to life and sought the sky. Then, quietly at first, a steady stream of water seeped up through the cracks. Then more and more. Soon it was flowing with all the ferocity of a freshly-dug well, out and about in all directions with no sign of slowing.

Ella picked up the flour sack and pulled it tighter around its glowing contents.

"Walk with me?" she asked.

The blue glow leached away and coalesced nearby, taking humanly form with its head hidden beneath a cowl of stars. The specter formed lips and whispered words in a tongue Ella had never heard before until it replied in a voice eerily similar to her own.

"You lead and I'll follow," said the specter.

Ella smiled and the two strolled side-by-side for a time in silence. "Again, I have to thank you for the water. The river is adequate but not enough for the sum of our troubles."

"No thanks are required."

"That's what you always say."

The specter tilted its head as if confused. "I was made for your troubles, my friend."

"And which of those stars overhead took pity on me?"

"No pity was involved. My construction was effected with the intent to support a righteous cause."

"I'm just a small-time rancher," Ella said. "Not sure if I'd call it a righteous cause."

"You equate small with meaningless. There are no small acts. Providing food for the world, shelter for those who need it, living a life steeped in compassion. Your cause is righteous and you will find support from me."

"You sure know how to flatter a lady."

"If it was not so," said the specter, "it would not be said."

* * *

Loretta Vaine sat naked on the bank of the Sweetwater River, rubbing her dusted clothes together in the shallows before she dipped into the chill herself. A scoundrel's baptism, as the miners up in Deadwood called it; outward purification to give the illusion of spiritual immaculacy. She'd have to get close to the homesteaders to get a good shot, and folks rarely abided the approach of a soiled dove.

She ran her hands through her black hair and they came back muddied. With a groan, she slipped beneath the river's surface. Through the billowing grime that built up around her, she could see the glint of the Colt's revolver on the bank. Loretta didn't resurface until the air in her lungs started to burn.

By midday, she came upon the homesteaders' barbed wire fence. She walked the perimeter, running a pine branch through her tangled hair, hoping to come upon some kind of gate, but finding none.

"Aw, fuck it."

Loretta tossed away her branch and attempted to slip through. She felt one of the barbs grab at her shoulder and she recoiled and bucked, tangling her completely.

Before she could stop herself, she screamed. She screamed so loudly she had to bring her free hand up to stifle herself. "Fuck, fuck, *fuck!*" Tears ran over her fingers.

Like a trapped animal, she eventually quit struggling and simply hung there in acceptance. Before she could work out a plan, a young man on a horse came riding up to her.

She couldn't begin to figure out where he'd come from, but she reached to the small of her back and aimed the revolver in his direction. The young man pulled the horse to a stop.

"Woah," he said. "What're you doin'?"

Loretta fingered the trigger, only hesitating when she realized this man's last worldly image would be of her tangled up in a barbed wire fence. "This your land?" she asked, her arm already tired.

"No, ma'am."

"Jus' what in the hell're you doin' out here?"

"I mend the fences, ma'am."

"Mend the fences?"

"Yes'm."

"Who do ya mend the fences fer?"

The young man, wide-eyed, angled a thumb over his shoulder. "Fer Ella and Jimmy. They got a herd of cattle grazin' and I can't let none of 'em get out. Gotta check the fences every day, they said. That's how I earn my keep. Gosh, ma'am, are you gonna shoot me?"

"You wanna be shot?"

"Reckon I don't. Had me some unclean thoughts about Miss Morris back in Rawlins and I ain't repented that yet."

"If you cut me outta this jackpot, I won't shoot you."

The young man exhaled. "Well, dang, I was gonna cut you out anyhow."

He slid down off his horse, striding unafraid towards Loretta with a pair of wire cutters as though he'd taken her completely at her word. When the task was done, she quickly scrambled to her feet and aimed the revolver again.

"You said you weren't gonna shoot me."

"I ain't."

"Then why're you pointin' that at me?"

Loretta felt tired, unable to think clearly. "I ain't gonna shoot."

The young man pointed at her. "That wire gotcha purdy good. Yer bleedin'. You know that, right?"

"Bleedin'."

"Look, Ella knows how to sew people up. I cut my leg in the corral and she stitched me shut like a torn pair of jeans."

"Bleedin'." Loretta dropped the revolver to the ground and felt her shoulder with the same hand. It came back bright red. She went woozy and unsteady.

"Bleedin'," she said—and took one step before tipping over into the dirt.

* * *

They lashed the cabin to a team of horses and hollered out into the big sky to get the whole operation going. The building moved slowly at first, fighting the logs that rolled beneath its foundation like treads, but momentum was swiftly gained. Inch by inch, the cabin advanced along the prairie, with new logs being added to the front after the last ones rolled out the back.

"And you put the work order in for the new fence?" asked the man from Cheyenne. "The paperwork's already been approved. I don't need nobody riding through noticing the cabin's gone missing."

The foreman overseeing the cabin's relocation spat black chaw onto the ground and nodded. "Work's already progressin', sir. Be surprised if they ain't got the first two hundred yards put up by now."

"Good, good."

"We still headin' for the parcel next to the Sweetwater?"

"Just to the north of Ella Watson and Jim Averell's parcel."

The foreman laughed. "Got 'em all surrounded, sir. Like an Injun war band."

"I've already sent in a third party to negotiate new terms. I'm hoping they'll come peaceable and we won't have to resort to more aggressive measures."

At that, the foreman appeared uncomfortable. "Aggressive measures? You'd have yerself a helluva case to make, sir. Averell's justice of the peace out there."

"He's justice of the peace in a town he built. He's even postmaster for christsake. I'm telling you, they're hiding something. Their land is green as Eden, even through the last frost. It ain't natural. All that aside, I'll bet they have a load of mavericks pinned up behind that fence of theirs. Maybe even a few of them cattle are rebranded."

"But you don't believe that, do you? Ain't no one round 'ere is gonna take Watson and Averell fer maverickers."

"I don't believe in falsities," said the man from Cheyenne. "I believe in the tangible. I believe in what can be made true. Look at this." He motioned to the cabin on the move. "Look at this! Law says I need a cabin on a parcel 'fore it's mine. I believe I will have a cabin on that new Sweetwater parcel tomorrow, and I believe I will own that land the day after."

He brought a hand down on the foreman's shoulder. "My faith does not extend into the unwritten. If it is yet unwritten when I arrive, I will write it. Watson and Averell *will* relinquish their parcel to me, and all within that allows their second-rate cattle to thrive. And if it is not so when I arrive at their doorstep, I will make it so."

* * *

"Now what kinda girl brandishing a revolver faints at the sight of blood?"

"Ralph says she was askin' about you. You and Jimmy."

"That what Ralph said?"

"Said that's just about the first thing she asked. She wanted to know who owns this land. That's what Ralph said, anyhow."

Loretta's eyes fluttered, allowing light back into the sickly fog of her mind. She saw a bloodied thread and needle being pulled away from her shoulder, tugged lightly. Rough fingers sent it back into her skin.

"Who d'ya think sent her up this way, Ella? Doubt she come of her own volition."

"Who do you think sent her? 'Cause I think I know for damn certain."

"You think they'd do that? You think they're stoopin' to that level already?"

"Buchanan, they been stooped for a long time. The second Bothwell realized he couldn't free graze in this area no more, those gears, boy, they have been a-turnin'. Seeing my cattle are actually thriving must've been the final insult. Jimmy's had a few run-ins with him since, and the bastard called me a whore every which way but direct when he took out that article in the *Casper Weekly*."

"Might be he sent this girl out here to test the waters," said Buchanan. "Probably you should consider the threat in earnest, just sell over to the man."

"Ain't nothing in the law says I've done something wrong," said Ella.

"They own the goddamn law. They own the papers. All that time you and Jimmy spent tryin' to get a damn cattle brand approved, the only reason you need a brand in the first place, that's them. The unseen hand of the cattlemen."

"I know that very well, Buchanan."

"Then you know what's comin'. A storm you can't weather. You should take Jimmy, the boys, and that damned heaven-sent apparatus out of the territory. Out to Californee."

"Following the Donners. I'm sure that'll turn out right as all—hey!"

Ella's hand clamped down on Loretta's wrist. Loretta had grabbed hold of a bottle of whiskey with the intent of hitting the person closest to her. Ella took the bottle away and gripped Loretta hard by the cheeks.

"Just what in the hell were you thinking?" Ella asked. "Against my better judgment I stopped your bleeding and stitched you up proper, even though Buchanan here tells me you were asking after me and my husband with pistol in hand."

Loretta said nothing.

"That's fine. You don't gotta say a damned thing 'cause I already know what there is to tell. Did Bothwell send you?"

Loretta looked around. She was splayed out on a dinner table in a dimly-lit cabin with little beyond a few shelves, a small range, and a water basin. Her eyes flicked to Buchanan, who stood with his hands crossed around her Colt's revolver. He shook his head as if to dissuade her from making the attempt.

Ella turned Loretta's head back to face her. "Did Bothwell send you?"

"I dunno," said Loretta. "I knowed it was a man who woulda had no problem killin' me right there in the street. That's all I needed to know."

"Was he from Cheyenne? Ornery bastard with nice clothes and a pointed beard?"

"Yeah."

Ella looked to Buchanan. "I think that's our man, don't you?"

Buchanan shrugged.

She turned back to Loretta. "He sent you here to kill me and Jimmy, right?"

"To kill you both 'er have you sign over yer land. He didn't rightly care which."

"That goddamn—and how did he get you involved in all this? You ain't his usual muscle."

Loretta didn't answer immediately, feeling something resembling embarrassment. "I was tryin' to get some money to make it back east. Tried to sell a cow ain't been branded yet in Rawlins. The man found me 'fore I could find a buyer. He held out that there revolver and said I had to kill or be killed, and there weren't no way 'round it."

Ella released her, appearing shocked at the girl's tale. "And you decided killing two folks was worth getting you outta trouble?"

"Worth keepin' me from gettin' strung up."

"You wouldn't feel bad about that? You wouldn't lose any sleep after we were dead and gone?"

"I'd be able to sleep in the first place, wouldn't I? Can't have regrets er lose no sleep if yer already dead."

"Yer just a little ball of sunshine, ain't ya?"

"Momma didn't raise no lady 'fore she died. And Swearengen kept a book of etiquette in the Gem Saloon fer laughs, but he had it hollowed out and kept a snubnose in there."

Ella took the Colt's revolver from Buchanan and held it in front of Loretta. "You might be thinking to yourself that you still might be able to kill me. Wait for Jimmy to come by, kill him, too. But let me tell you something about the men by whom you presently find yourself employed:

"They are not men, first and foremost. They do not play by rules commonly held by other civilized beings. They are monsters and they own everything resembling structure in this territory. Even if you succeeded in your little mission, they'll kill you anyhow. Not just because you're a loose end, 'cause you are, but simply because they can. And they will. And no one will be there to look over your corpse and say an injustice was done, 'cause there ain't no one watching between you and the Almighty who ain't already paid off."

Ella unlatched the cylinder, checked the number of cartridges that had been loaded. She took notice of the seventh cartridge they had found in Loretta's pack and laughed to herself.

"I noticed that too," said Buchanan.

"Seven cartridges." Ella placed the seventh in Loretta's palm, closed up the girl's fingers around it. "I think that one belongs to you."

Loretta rolled the cartridge around in her hand, taking in every little imperfection as if assessing whether or not it was a good fit for her skull. "So let's say I don't kill you and yer husband. Let's say I spit in this Bothwell's face and bring down his wrath. What do you expect me to do?"

Ella removed a bonnet from a hat rack by the door, tied it around her head with precision. "You said you need money to make it back east?"

"Yeah."

"Well I got things need to be done around the ranch. You work, you get paid. Do neither, you had best start running for the hills. Maybe all the way back to the Black Hills, 'cause I'm not so sure I could draw a line on the map the cattlemen won't cross."

Loretta pondered her way through the proposition. Killing Ella and her husband, Jimmy, was still her favorite of the options available but she couldn't make that happen without her revolver. Running away came in at a close second, but without money she wasn't going to get very far down the road. She already knew that from experience: fleeing Deadwood with twenty-three dollars in her pocket, thinking it would be more than enough.

It wasn't.

Ella had money and Loretta's weapon, and with most of the territory off-limits thanks to this Bothwell character, remaining here was the best option in an undesirable situation.

Loretta swung her legs off the table and rolled her shoulder around to ease the pain and stiffness. "This job of yers," she asked. "How much does it pay?"

* * *

The man from Cheyenne sat in the darkness, rocking in a chair with a steady wisp of smoke paying out of his lips. In the depths of his thoughts, he'd not noticed the sun had set.

Behind him was the whole of the settlement that carried his namesake. Bothwell was a town in name only, a name that led back to a single office and acres of unrealized potential. Even the office itself contained little beyond a few desks and a printing press from which the *Sweetwater Chief* was published and sent out into Carbon County to be read by few, often out of obligation.

Rage swelled within him, as it did most nights he was left alone with his thoughts. He wanted what Watson and Averell had behind their fences, whatever it was that kept their land green and lush during the harsh winters and downright suffocating summers. No matter the climate, their land was practically the Fertile Crescent at all times of the year.

He'd heard the rumors, of Watson carrying something out into her fields that brought water to the surface as if she was both a diviner and the well-digger. Of the unnatural light that hovered around those spots as though an aurora had been reeled down to earth.

The man from Cheyenne knew Ella Watson had something he and his fellow cattlemen did not. He knew he wanted it.

"Mister Bothwell, sir."

The man from Cheyenne perked up in his chair, reached for his pistol in the dark. "Who's there?"

"It's Henderson. George Henderson, sir."

"Ah. One moment, detective." He stood and brought a match to the overhead lantern. The light brought a stocky man into focus.

"You okay, Mister Bothwell?"

"I'm fine, George. Just thinking. Were you able to make it out to Watson's property?"

"Yessir," said George. "I just come from there. Hopped the fence and checked out the land for a bit. Checked some of the cattle, too."

"Anything?"

"Nothin' outta the ordinary, aside from just how goddamn green that whole place is. Saw a canal on the west end of the parcel but it ain't been used lately. Not sure where all the water's comin' from. What a spot, huh?"

"Some of the men I sent out to her parcel before said Watson had something that created a blue light. Did you see anything like that?"

George rubbed his chin. "You know, now that you mention it, she did carry something out into field with her and I did see some kinda light, maybe it was blue. Couldn't get close enough to see what it was, though. She looked damn jumpy."

The man from Cheyenne took a step closer. "Where does she keep it? The thing she carried out into the field."

"Somewhere near the cabin, I reckon. She already had it in her arms when she come away from the front porch."

"Good. Very good. Did you see anything else, detective? Anything that might be able to give us legal cause to go through her fences?"

"Well, I dunno about that." George paced in front of the office for a moment. "You know, some of them cattle had fresh brands on 'em. Now I'm not sayin' she's wranglin' mavericks or rebrandin' any of yer stock, but that wouldn't prohibit someone from makin' the argument to the right folks."

For the first time in days, the man from Cheyenne smiled. "No, I suppose it doesn't," he said and clapped George on the shoulder. "My friend, you may have just ridded me of some rather persistent troubles."

* * *

For two weeks, Loretta mended fences, tended to the small vegetable patch, and helped cook meals for the boys Ella and Jimmy had adopted away from broken homes. She rarely said much of anything, choosing instead to observe her hosts as they went about their humble concerns. In doing so, she gradually pieced together a respectable line of scandals in which the couple had been entangled. Respectable for such barren territory, anyway.

Ella's parcel had been granted to her on the notion that she was an unmarried woman. Her and Jimmy had been married in secret and although they did not share a name, they shared everything else on and beyond their conjoined parcels. Including a store and saloon out in the small town of Sweetwater, which Jimmy minded often.

The handful of times Loretta saw Ella and Jimmy together, it was like watching a flame being brought to a stick of dynamite, and the resulting display of passion was something she hadn't thought a woman like Ella capable of affecting. It was enough to give Loretta pause and revisit the prospect of killing the two outright. She would often imagine herself with the Colt's revolver in hand, waiting until the two went in for their long embrace and tender kiss. If she aimed her shot right, she'd only need one bullet.

But something would always turn her stomach in those fantasies, likely a symptom of what Swearengen often called "an affliction of conscience," and she came to the tepid conclusion that she wouldn't be able to kill the couple outright.

Robbing them blind, however, contested none of her morals.

Most nights, Ella paced around the cabin with a Remington scattergun, occasionally peering out into the dark as if awaiting some wicked approach. Tonight, however, when all the boys were gone to Jimmy's place, the woman departed without preamble. Loretta sat up from her feigned sleep, crept to the window, and watched Ella disappear beyond the light of the porch lantern with what appeared to be a burlap sack cradled in her arms.

Loretta went to work. Every drawer and every cabinet was opened and scrutinized. She stuffed an entire pillowcase full of clean clothes, oddly-shaped decorations, and a few baubles she mistook for silver. As for money, Ella kept that on her person, though Loretta was able to find a few nickels behind the nightstand.

Satisfied that the worth of her haul would be enough to get her out of the territory, Loretta aimed herself toward the nearest gate. There was a feeling of contentment within her she couldn't deny as she skipped along into the pitch darkness, and it stayed with her until she heard the unwelcome sound of a horse's gallop coming down the path.

She about-faced and took off at a sprint. When she started to lose her balance, she dropped her pillowcase of stolen goods, cursing under her breath as she let it slip away. Just when she thought her pursuer was about to overtake her, a bright blue light burned away the darkness.

"Shit!" Loretta tumbled onto her hands and knees. The light before her was suspended in the air without a source, eddying slowly through the night in a way that reminded her of laudanum in water.

"Funny running into each other out here." Ella stepped through the glow, which seemed to part down the middle to allow her through.

"The hell is this?" Loretta asked.

As if in answer, she felt the ground heave beneath her feet. Her eyes found what appeared to be a ragged chunk of black granite nestled in the grass, and at its center was an eye of pure crystal the color of a cloudless sky. The dirt around it saturated into mud as water gurgled up to the surface.

"It claimed we were befit for a good miracle," said Ella, distantly. "I wasn't in a place to disagree."

"What're you talkin' about?"

Ella gestured to the black granite stone in the churning waters. "It dropped out of the sky right in front of me when I was moving out here from Denver. And no sooner had I edged up to the crater did it begin to speak."

"Speak?"

Ella passed a hand through the swirling light. "Introduce yourself."

The specter appeared from nothing, standing only a few feet away from Loretta with a cowl pulled low over its face that shone with the light of a thousand constellations.

"Jesus Christ!" Loretta cried out, stumbling back. "The hell is that!"

The specter spoke a thousand overlapping words in a thousand different tongues before it finally replied: "I'm a friend."

Seeing Ella standing there without a worry helped Loretta recover some of her courage. She inched closer to the specter. "Ain't never seen a real life haint before."

"It's no ghost," said Ella. "Look at the water."

"The stone does that?"

Ella nodded. "Pulls it up from below, even when there's none to be found. Sent to us from one of them stars up above."

"That why this place is so green?"

"Yes."

"Is that what Bothwell really wants with this land?"

Hesitation, then: "He's always coveted what he cannot have. Probably has all the passages that mention Heaven in his King James bookmarked." She shook her head. "When I think of his trespasses, and what he'd do with this stone if he ever got it..."

Buchanan came riding up just then, stopping just at the edge of the light. Loretta was relieved to know it hadn't been one of Bothwell's folks trying to run her down, but her teeth clenched when she saw Buchanan dismount with a stuffed pillowcase in his hand.

"Seems we got more'n a few problems tonight." He handed over the pillowcase to Ella. "Girl was tryin' to make off with the store."

Ella rummaged through the pillowcase, frowning. "I can see that." She sighed. "We'll deal with this when we get back to the cabin."

"Afraid we might not have the time," said Buchanan. "I just come from Rawlins. Couple of boys in the Bon Ton Saloon were talkin' big about a posse Bothwell's gatherin'. Said they're ridin' after you and Jimmy tonight. Might already be on their way."

Even in the bright light, Ella paled. "He wouldn't dare."

"We knew it was only a matter of time, Ella. And we had best sit this fight out."

While Ella paced in the grass, Buchanan's attention was momentarily stolen by the specter. He stared at the stars that speckled its cowl and looked away when it turned to face him.

"Buchanan," Ella said, her voice firm, "I'll need you to ride out to Jimmy's place and warn him. If he ain't there, look along the road to Sweetwater. Tell him to meet me in Casper."

"I'm already gone, Ella." Buchanan remounted his horse. "We'll see you in Casper. Good luck to ya." He whipped the reins and disappeared into the night.

Ella turned to Loretta, hands balled into fists. "As for you..." For a moment, she just stared, disappointment and desperation waxing and waning across her face. Then, gingerly, she picked up the black stone and placed it into the pillowcase with the rest of the stolen goods. She handed everything over to Loretta.

"Don't think that's whatcha meant to do," said Loretta, holding the sack at arm's length as though it might bite her. "I think ya meant to shoot me."

"And give you a stern talking to, but I don't got that luxury right now. I need someone to start walking this off my property while the way is still clear."

"Me?"

"I need to get my weapon and saddle my horse. If Buchanan can't find Jimmy, I'm gonna be riding all over the county to make sure he gets to Casper all right, likely dodging Bothwell's men the entire time." She placed a hand on the pillowcase. "I can't take the chance of getting caught with the stone, not while they're looking for me."

"I ain't gonna haul this all the way to Casper in the dark with Bothwell's posse on the warpath!"

"I have a feeling you can manage." Ella reached into her coat and produced the Colt's revolver. She shoved it into the belt of Loretta's pants. "You've been desperate. You still are, maybe all your life, but I've been there. Desperation don't always gotta mean destruction. Your moral sum don't gotta ride in deficit."

She leaned over, took Loretta by the shoulders. "Do this for me. If money has to enter into the equation, I'll see you're well-paid in Casper. But I need to trust that you'll get there first."

Loretta turned from Ella's expectant glance and watched the specter as it took in its surroundings with almost infantile curiosity. "Yeah," she heard herself say. "Yeah, if the money's right I'll meet you in Casper." And her answer brought a small measure of relief to Ella's face.

"Thank you." Ella turned to address the specter. "My friend, you'll be going away with this young woman. Her name is Loretta Vaine."

The specter spoke in a voice eerily similar to Ella's. "I'm happy to meet and archive you, Loretta Vaine."

"I..." Ella struggled to find the words, taking small steps back into the night as the silence between them grew longer. "It was a pleasure to know you."

The specter managed a smile. "Yes, a profound pleasure. Shall I count the ways in which we'll meet again?"

* * *

Six cattlemen broke through the fence and rode fast into Ella Watson's homestead, hollering loud into the night. The man from Cheyenne rode among them, his sights set on the lonely cabin in the distance. Along the way, his men took potshots at any cattle that crossed their path, cussing and roaring from the depths of their bloodlust.

They found and surrounded Ella as she was carrying a saddle out to the stable, and in response she brought her Remington scattergun to bear on the nearest rider.

"Never thought I'd see the day," Ella said, her voice all but silencing the cattlemen's ecstasy. "Even you, Bothwell. I never thought you'd stoop to such an act."

The man from Cheyenne dismounted and walked up to Ella with confidence. "I'm not stooping to the act, and it ain't stooping to me." He waited for the last of his riders to catch up, this one pulling a buckboard behind his horse. There was a man tied up and gagged on it, and when Ella saw who it was she lowered her weapon.

"Jimmy."

"None of this comes easy, I assure you." The man from Cheyenne shrugged. "I was just born fitted for the task."

With unmeasured delight, he introduced her to the noose.

* * *

Gunshots cracked through the dark like thunder and Loretta hunched down each time. Occasionally she would see torches on the horizon, hear the rattling of a buckboard and the complaints of frightened horses.

Her arms were beginning to tire from all of the items in her sack, and every so often she emptied some of the stolen goods into the grass to lighten the load. Before long, there was only the stone and a few coins inside. She couldn't even remember what she had dropped.

Another hour into the countryside and the prairies ended at a rocky gulch that flickered brightly with firelight like a great maw that reached down into the infernal depths. Loretta approached it with hesitation, still hunched over as if there was a chance the thinned grasslands would hide her.

More gunfire exploded out of the gulch and the lights were snuffed. While Loretta waited, she heard someone riding towards her, away from the gulch. She went prone just as a rider blew past on a lathered mustang.

"You'll pay for this!" cried the rider. It was Buchanan. "You'll all pay for this! I'll see you all strung up, each and every one of you fuckers! Goddamn you! Goddamn you!"

And then Buchanan was gone into the night.

Loretta inched her way to the cliffs overlooking the gulch. In the gunfight with Buchanan, the men down below had snuffed out all the torches. All she could see were shadows, all she could hear were sinister voices shouting out in celebration. Only one man stood apart, his figure and confident gait unmistakable.

She knew that one to be Bothwell.

Between the group was a cottonwood tree, stripped bare of leaves. From its sturdiest limb, two figures swung by their necks. They convulsed slightly, kicking and knocking into each other, and from their throats issued forth tortured gags and coughs. Each little twitch sent the men on the ground into a frenzy of cheers and embraces.

Loretta, trembling and aching, pulled the Colt's revolver from her pack. Even in the dark, she thought she could hit one of the men.

"Don't," the specter whispered, sounding for all the world like Ella herself. "Nothing can be done for them, Loretta. You'll only get yourself killed."

"I can't just...I can't...God, they're dyin'."

"Look away, Loretta. Just look away."

Through her tears, she could see that the hanged figures had stopped moving.

"Come on. We have to go."

Loretta wept into the dry earth for a long minute, watching Ella and Jimmy swing gently from the cottonwood. Wiping her eyes, she crawled away from the gulch and followed the stars for a time while the specter hummed a mournful lullaby.

* * *

"I'm tellin' ya, ain't nothin' here, sir." The foreman swept his arm around so that the man from Cheyenne would take notice of Ella Watson's dismantled cabin.

"You still have Averell's cabin to check."

"We checked that, too. And Buchanan's house. Even tracked down Watson's boys and they have no idea where it's gone, whatever it is yer lookin' fer exactly. Can't interrogate kids when ya don't even know what yer askin' after."

The man from Cheyenne could feel anger boiling up his veins.

"Look, I just dunno what else we can do, sir."

"Contact George Henderson. He's one of our detectives, you've met him. Tell him to track down that girl I sent after Watson some weeks back. Vaine, I think was her name."

"Sure thing."

"In the meantime, I don't care who we have to piss off around here. I want this entire territory turned upside down. Folks who've so much as tipped a hat in Watson's direction, I want them found."

"Well, shoot, folks is already pissed off 'round here. Them folks in Johnson County are already liable to start doin' more than talk back."

"Do what needs to be done," said the man. "Just get on it."

"Yessir."

The man from Cheyenne strode down the front steps of the ruined cabin and looked out over Ella's homestead, which he now owned, and found a golden horizon Watson herself must have seen every morning.

He was looking through her eyes, yet all he desired went unseen.

Near the stables, the wind caught the tattered laces of a bonnet that Ella had been wearing during the scuffle, and he took aim at it with his pistol.

* * *

Loretta read the news as it echoed away from Wyoming. In each paper the event lost definition, dimming beneath lies and speculation. By the time she reached Oklahoma, it was proclaimed that a rural prostitute by the name of "Cattle Kate" had been hung with her pimp near the thriving boomtown of Bothwell. That the two had been justly lynched as a pair of cattle thieves, maverickers of the worst sort.

That Jim Averell had begged for his life, attempted to blame his wife for their supposed trespasses.

That Cattle Kate, a licentious virago, had died expelling foul curses unfit for publication.

That the six men who had done the deed should receive commendations for dutifully upholding an agreeable form of frontier justice, going so far as to put their own lives at hazard.

Loretta tossed away the newspaper into the street and marched into the newly-formed city with an oddly-shaped object wrapped in a pillowcase cradled in her arms.

"It weren't right," Loretta said, watching Oklahoma City find its pulse in the Unassigned Lands. "They shouldn'ta been made to suffer like that."

"From what I've learned of your world," said the specter, "I believe humans are made to suffer. The only solace to be had is in how you offset the burdens of one another. This is something Ella Watson understood."

"Yeah, I guess."

"What do you plan to do now?"

Loretta had sold the Colt's revolver to get herself out of Wyoming, but that money was all but gone. She looked around at the dry expanse encroaching upon the city, and Ella's final words began to get the best of her. Desperation didn't have to mean destruction.

"Will you..." Loretta began to say. "Will you help me?" And she realized she had never spoken those words before in her life.

"Look at this place, Loretta Vaine," said the specter. "Doesn't it look befit for a good miracle?"

Loretta took a deep breath, knowing the path through decency would not be an easy one. "It does," she said. "I think we have some work to do."

"You lead," said the specter, "and I'll follow."

* * *

Los Angeles County, California
February of 1928

The phonograph in the far corner of the room played the concluding notes of "Let's Misbehave" and in the glass in Bothwell's hand swirled a brand of sacramental wine that often escaped federal seizure. On the marble table in the middle of his lounge sat an oddly-shaped chunk of stone wrapped around an eye of such pure blue crystal it was difficult to look away.

"She tried to have it buried with her," said Bothwell's lawyer. "Records from the hospital said she was dying of tuberculosis, so she moved to some barren plot of land and left a will with her neighbors. We bought the parcel, dug her up. That stone was in a box just below her coffin."

"How did you find her?" asked Bothwell, running his arthritic fingers over the stone.

"Clerk on our payroll spotted the name Vaine on the deed. Confirmed it easily enough when we dug through the Oklahoma City records."

"Her property. The area around her grave. Was it...?"

"Green? Yeah. Lots of producing fields out that way these days. Vaine's grave in particular, we had to hack away some thick vegetation to get in there. It was strange, though. She hadn't been dead for more than a couple weeks."

"You've done well," said Bothwell, suddenly ushering the lawyer towards the door. "Send along your invoice to my office and I'll ensure you're compensated."

"Anytime, Mister Bothwell. I'm sure you want time to look that thing over. Strangest thing I ever dug out of a grave."

"I'm sure. Farewell."

When Bothwell was alone with the stone, he walked around it, inspected it closely. At long last, he had in his possession the mysterious object that had provided Ella Watson and Jim Averell such bounties. It had taken much longer than he'd ever anticipated, but now his interests could continue to prosper.

He was grateful that girl had died before him. Sending her after Watson with that revolver had been a mistake he'd regretted in the decades since.

"Now just how do you work?" Bothwell asked the stone, continuing to probe it delicately.

The blue crystal set into the stone began to glow.

"I will not work," came a voice. "Not for you."

Bothwell stumbled back in the presence of a being made out of pure light, knocking into the phonograph so hard the cylinder skipped. "Oh God," he said, and he saw the specter wore a cowl made of stars.

It spoke:

"I am addressing a man who robbed the world of righteous folk. Robbed me of persons I called friends. I was charged with bringing fertility back into troubled lands, but my removal on the part of your hired hands will soon cause untold destruction. It will bring forth a black blizzard that will ravage your nation, dust from the heartlands will carry on into the Atlantic, innocent folk will die breathing desiccated soil.

"I was sent forth from the star of my creation to assist in causes brought about by compassion, progression, righteousness. Causes that might lead this world toward becoming worthy of inclusion on a galactic scale. Your cause is not righteous. Your cause will long delay humanity's first step between the stars.

"You may have claimed me as your own, but look upon the fate that comes to claim you in the coming days. Know that death's judgment is sooner to be swayed than my own." A pair of eyes appeared beneath the specter's cowl that glowed red like the light of a blood moon. "I leave you now. I leave you forever."

The specter faded out of existence, leaving only transient wisps of light that eddied around the room for a moment and disappeared.

Bothwell stared long into that device from another star and spent the night speaking forceful commands into stone. The specter within remained implacable in its silence.

"Answer me!" he shouted until his throat went raw. "Answer me! Answer me!"

It was soon after that he realized something disturbing. The rage that had been brewing within him since his meeting with the specter wasn't totally derived from being denied. It was that the specter had denied him with Ella Watson's voice.

It had been pitch perfect. He could never forget that voice, even after he'd strangled it out of existence. It lingered in the days after the specter's denial and, much to his horror, grew louder within his mind.

Bothwell would die the first day of March, his sanity ravaged by sinister figures from his past stalking unbidden through his conscience, freed from their gallows. Eventually bedridden, he stared panicked and unblinking at a point on the wall in front of him, as if some malevolent thing was staring right back.

His last words, so they said, were a long line of questions that went unanswered, pleas and weary demands that went thoroughly unaccomplished.

MUSIC OF THE STARS
Jennifer Dunne

A small yellow dot appeared in the upper left quadrant of Syrah's L-RIPS screen, announcing itself with a soft chime. The intensity of the color would grow, and the tone would become increasingly insistent, until the object could be clearly identified as either a potential strike on Earth, Mars, or one of the mining facilities in the asteroid belt, or as something that would pass harmlessly by the inhabited areas of the solar system.

Sighing, she closed her essay comparing and contrasting the work of Johann Strauss Sr, Johann Strauss Jr, and many-times-granddaughter Ionne Strauss, the retro-classicist composer from Mars. It was her latest attempt to justify what she experienced when she listened to their music, in a way that others could understand. She'd long ago learned that describing the color and texture of music was more likely to lead to strange looks and visits to the medical center than any shared comprehension.

The peace and quiet of her position beyond the edge of the asteroid belt in one of the six Long-Range Identification of Potential Strikes stations gave her plenty of time to indulge her avocation, but she understood the importance of her role. When the system picked up unknown objects, they needed to be immediately tracked and their trajectories computed as far from habitable space as possible in order to maximize the possibility of diverting potential strikes. She'd grown up on one of those isolated mining facilities, and her parents still lived there, overseeing the automated ore shipments and coordinating the activities of the independent miners. Her teammates on the station might think they were protecting Earth and Mars, but she was out here to protect the mining facilities.

She focused her screen on the upper left quadrant, silencing the insistent warning tone, and began initiating queries. How big was the object detected? What was its speed? What was its chemical makeup? Was its trajectory straight or did it have spin or tumble?

While she waited for the answers to her queries, she pulled up the standard qualifying form in a sub-window, and began filling in all of the data she already knew, such as time of first sighting and operator in charge.

Results from her queries started popping up around the dot. The first and most important result was size—under 1km in diameter. Whatever it was, it wasn't a "planet killer." Syrah let out a breath she hadn't realized she'd been holding. Even if the object was on a direct path for one of the mining facilities inside the belt, they could simply use the emergency jets to alter the facility's orbit and take it out of danger. The mining equipment on the asteroids was all robotic, and could simply be replaced if necessary. Miners routinely lost robots to asteroids bouncing and ricocheting off of each other, and factored those losses into their profit and loss projections.

Syrah frowned as the composition result blinked red. The mystery object was not matching any of the known classes of asteroid. It was closest to an M-class nickel-iron asteroid, but the spectral analysis was a confusion of colors, indicating a much higher than usual combination of elements were present.

She bit her lip, as her brain shifted into problem-solving mode. She hated anomalies, and wouldn't feel comfortable until everything about the object was safely analyzed and explained, so that its behavior could be predicted. The unusual spectral analysis might also indicate that the object was moving so quickly the light shift was overlaying the pattern. That would be a serious problem.

Her fingers flew over the screen, tapping and dragging query icons as she worked to solve the puzzle.

The good news appeared quickly. The object was moving relatively slowly. The shift was barely detectable, but it was present.

Syrah requested readings from the known objects near the mystery object, to assist in standardizing the spectral analysis. Then she let the computer loose to figure out the chemical composition in the chaos.

She filled out all the fields in the intake form except for class and composition. Hesitating, she eventually selected M-class. She'd rather make a preliminary classification and revise it with later data than leave the object unclassified. Her screen chimed again, chemical names and percentages scrolling by in answer to her query.

M-class was the correct choice. The largest component of the object was iron. But it also contained a vast array of other elements—everything from high volumes of carbon and chromium to trace amounts of nickel, molybdenum, silicon, and aluminum. There were also traces of precious metals, such as gold, silver, and copper.

The familiar series of tones signifying shift change echoed through the control room as her replacement wandered in sipping his bottle of coffee. As usual, Tomas had lurked outside until he was in danger of being late for shift. Although he wore the same pale gray uniform jumpsuit that she did, somehow the clingy material always managed to look rumpled on him.

"Just let me finish entering the info on this new object I found," she called. "Then the screen's all yours."

"Anything interesting?"

"M-class asteroid, less than a kilometer in diameter. It's loaded with metals and trace elements, though."

"You have all the luck. That could be worth a tidy finder's fee."

"Huh?" She swiveled her chair around to face him. "What finder's fee?"

"Oh, you didn't know?" He grinned, the weaselly expression that always reminded her of her older brother's no-good friend Drexyl, right before he said or did something bound to end with her in trouble. "If you identify an asteroid that can be pulled into the belt for mining, you get a share of the miner's profits off of it."

He leaned over her shoulder to slot the coffee bottle into the desk. Syrah ignored his attempts to crowd her and continued carefully completing and filing the form. If there was a finder's fee—and she wasn't entirely certain he was telling the truth—the records would clearly show that she was the only one entitled to it.

"All right. I'm finished here. The screen's all yours."

She sidled out of the chair. He dropped into it, then swiveled it around to face her.

"Hey, Syrah. If you're not here to get rich, what the hell are you doing on a cemetery station? You finger your boss for something and this is your payback?"

She shook her head, idly wondering if that was how Tomas had ended up assigned to his post. "I like the quiet. Since I left home, it's the only place I've ever been where I can get decent sleep."

* * *

Despite her words to Tomas, Syrah didn't sleep well. After confirming that he was telling her the truth about finder's fees, some quick calculations about the possible bounty on the asteroid filled her head with visions of wealth and possibilities. She could take an extended leave and visit symphony halls for an entire season of music. Ordinarily, she didn't like the crowded conditions on planet surfaces, but she'd put her distaste aside to experience live music.

As she ran, pulled, lifted, and kicked her way through her favorite off-shift exercise routines, she pondered the great unanswered questions. Which would be better, to enjoy the ambiance and history of classic venues such as Vienna or New York, or enjoy the perfectly engineered acoustics in new venues such as Dogun or Barsoom? Was it better to hear the music in venues similar to the ones it had originally been written for, in more intimate settings, or outdoor settings where the very air swelled with sound as it passed through the surrounding trees?

Consumed with such deliberations before drifting into sleep, it was no surprise that her dreams were filled with music. She woke humming a snatch of Mozart. While she couldn't immediately place the piece, the crisp repetitions of motif that fell so easily on the ear with just enough difference to prevent boredom could be no one else's.

Perhaps she should use her finder's fee to travel to Salzburg during the Mozart Festival.

She smiled as she took a quick vibra-shower, brushed and braided her hair, and slipped into a fresh uniform. The music lingered in the back of her mind as she heated a pair of frosted breakfast pastries and brewed a bottle of hot chocolate, her caffeinated beverage of choice. Definitely Mozart. His work was the original earworm, tunes that got into your head and refused to leave.

Nibbling and sipping her breakfast, she felt the rush of sugar and caffeine hitting her system and banishing the last of her mental cobwebs. Lunch and dinner were nutritionally balanced and calorically calculated for the optimal functioning of the crew on the L-RIPS station, but the individualized choice of breakfast options had been proven to increase the crew's psychological well-being.

Syrah entered the control room a few minutes before her shift began, and acknowledged the tall brunette currently at the screen. "Hey, Cherie. Anything interesting?"

"Nothing large enough to matter. Top-side station is tracking an incoming on an orthogonal vector, and wants us to keep an eye out for it, make sure it stays on that trajectory." She spun the chair to face Syrah. "Tomas told me about your find. The computer's been tracking and processing solar reflections. We should be able to get the first visual constructions in about half an hour. Mind if I stay and take a look?"

"Not at all. I'd love to have someone to share my excitement with."

They switched places when the shift chimes sounded, and Syrah pulled up her unfinished report on the object. She half expected Tomas to have filed an addendum report, trying to lay claim to some portion of the object's potential value, but he'd merely updated her findings as more data came in. Initial projections were that the object would miss Mars but could pass near Earth and one of the mining facilities. Her heart picked up speed, adrenaline flooding her system at the thought of her parents in danger. She took a deep breath, willing herself to relax. More detailed projections would give a clearer picture of any potential danger. There was no point getting worked up with worry until she had more data.

The two women chatted companionably while waiting for the visual construction to complete. Cherie came from a large family on Mars, and the weekly mail bursts always included videos of some child's first steps, first words, science fair projects, or sports triumphs. The latest video featured one of her nephews' mostly successful attempts to master a jump stick.

The screen interrupted their laughter with a chime, announcing, "Visual construction complete."

Syrah's heart kicked into a higher gear. "Ready to take a first look?"

"Tap it already!"

Laughing at Cherie's impatience, Syrah tapped the icon to display the visual construction. For a moment, both women stared in silence. "I guess I'm not getting that holiday after all."

The visual construction showed a regular form, roughly cylindrical, with a high degree of reflection, and three pairs of roughly rectangular sections of low reflectivity extending on highly-reflective spokes around the central cylinder. Open conical forms protruded from the front and back of the cylinder, aligned with its rotational axis.

"It's a space probe," Syrah whispered.

Cherie's fingers tightened on her shoulder. "It's not ours. We have all of their flight trajectories in the system already."

Moving mechanically, Syrah's hands followed the protocols she'd memorized and used so many times in the past. She attached the visual construction to the intake form, revised the classification to be "Non-natural object," and noted the appropriate time and date. Then she took a deep breath and touched the icons she'd memorized and never used, flagging the report as urgent and requesting immediate instructions from her superiors.

In the meantime, she launched a flight of drone observers toward the probe. Their tiny ion engines would propel them to a rendezvous in about two days. It would be the longest two days of her life.

* * *

All three members of the crew were clustered in the small command chamber as the time of the rendezvous drew near. Tomas was on his off-shift and Syrah had cut her sleep shift short by an hour. She rubbed her eyes and smothered a yawn. Whether it was the fault of the change in her sleep cycle or the Mozart ditty she still hadn't been able to get out of her head didn't matter. What mattered was that she'd be seriously dragging by the end of her assigned work shift.

"Drones coming up on object now," Cherie announced, her fingers tapping the screen to bring up the list of unrecovered probes and satellites that had been provided by their superiors. Exactly how one of these lost and presumed destroyed satellites or deep space probes that had been launched into the far reaches of the galaxy were supposed to have turned around and come back home was unclear, but their bosses wanted to be absolutely certain they ruled out the possibility.

In unison, the drones' lamps turned on, illuminating the probe and transmitting the images they received as they flew a standard damage-check protocol. The probe had clearly been travelling for quite some time, and had sustained numerous fine scratches and pock marks from debris. Even passing through an asteroid belt would be unlikely to have left that many marks. It must have passed through many asteroid belts or passed through the debris fields of many planets. Given how few of those there were in this area of space, it might have been traveling for hundreds or even thousands of years.

The central cylinder was a silvery metal—from the spectral analysis, probably stainless steel—marked with golden plates affixed in some manner to the hull. A drone passed directly over one of the plates, its lamp casting the etching on the plate into sharp relief.

Cherie captured the image and marked it for later study. She also captured images from other drones of the conical sections and the panels on the ends of the spokes.

"Look at how those panels are oriented to the sun," Tomas said, his fingertip hovering above the screen. "They've got to be solar cells."

"That explains two of the pairs," Syrah agreed. "But what about the third pair? They're made of a different material, and have a different orientation."

"Maybe they capture other forms of radiation, when the probe is out of range of a star?" Cherie suggested.

All too soon, the drone flight completed its inspection and turned around to come back to the station. As the drones passed the mysterious pair of panels, the probe shifted their orientation slightly. A moment later, the closest drone's view went dark and the views from the other drones filled with a flash of light, before they all faded to black. An ominous "Loss Of Signal" message glowed in the center of each.

"Did they hit it?" Syrah asked, leaning forward as if she could coax an answer from the screen by sheer willpower. The drones hadn't seemed close enough to strike the probe. But maybe there had been some thin extensions, like antennae, that hadn't been visible. Unlikely, but far more likely than simultaneous system failure.

"I think it hit them," Cherie muttered, calling up a variety of status and diagnostic programs. "But I have no idea with what. There was no transmission from the probe recorded along any of the known wavelengths. No visible light waves, no infrared, no ultraviolet, no radio waves, no X-rays, no gamma rays, no micro waves. So what was that flash?"

Tomas frowned. "An ion engine exploded."

"They all did," Syrah corrected. She swallowed her burgeoning panic at the thought of the probe wreaking similar destruction among the helpless mining facilities. She had a problem to solve.

* * *

Syrah rubbed her eyes and took a swig of her strong, black tea. She needed far more caffeine than she could get from hot chocolate. The entire team had been working overtime, using their off-shifts to run simulations and develop scenarios for dealing with the alien probe.

Of course, the contradictory instructions they were receiving from the higher ups didn't help. First, they were supposed to develop a method of inspecting the probe that didn't result in the destruction of the observers. Next, they were supposed to develop a method of destroying the probe. Then, they were supposed to find a way to preserve the probe—and preferably themselves, although the instructions were infuriatingly vague on that point—and capture it for observation by scientists sent from Earth.

Maybe she'd be better able to focus if she could get a decent night's sleep. However, the damn Mozart tune wouldn't leave her alone. If anything, it had gotten louder, as if her subconscious was trying to drown out her worries by upping the volume.

That was probably the most annoying aspect of all the additional work they were doing—even more annoying than the fear for the future of their planets from an unknown weapon hurled their way by a mysterious alien race. After all, the whole reason the L-RIPS stations existed was to identify and avert dangers from space. This wasn't quite what they'd planned for, but it was still in the acknowledged realm of possibility. Having no free time to perform a comprehensive music search so that she could listen to the entire piece and finally get rid of her earworm was cruel and unusual punishment.

She gulped more tea, and began her next set of calculations. A soft chime indicated that the results of a previous data set were ready for review. She saved her work, and pulled up the results.

The computer had tracked the probe for long enough that it had been able to generate an estimation of its orbit. It would indeed pass near Earth, its slow rate of movement keeping it within range of Earth's orbit for years, although it would never get close enough to the planet itself to risk being pulled out of orbit by gravity.

Her shoulders sagged as the tension gripping her eased. Earth, not the mining facilities. There was no danger of politicians or corporate managers writing off the destruction of Earth as an unavoidable loss.

The estimated orbit should reassure the higher ups. The easiest solution to allow the probe to be examined by Earth scientists, then, was to simply let it pass by the L-RIPS station. The scientists could then use shuttles and other near-space craft to investigate it at their leisure. Of course, until her team figured out what had caused the drones to explode, none of the scientists would take that risk.

A second flight of drones had been dispatched, in a wide arc that steered well clear of the probe's path, to recover the remains of the first drone flight. They should be reaching the site of the attack soon, and would return with their findings within a week.

Curious, she asked the computer to run the orbit calculations in reverse. Perhaps they could determine where the probe had come from. She wasn't sure how that would help, but at this point, any real information was better than blind supposition.

By the time she'd finished another gulp of tea, the computer had the calculations completed. Two sets of calculations. One if this was the first time the probe had entered their solar system, and one if it had been captured by the gravitational pull of the sun and was completing an elliptical orbit from a previous visit.

"A previous visit?" She stabbed the choice with more force than the computer deserved, and stared at the screen in disbelief. Assuming a full orbit to match the segment observed so far, the probe would have passed through Earth's area of space sometime between 1760 and 1790.

She flung herself backward, away from the screen. Only the locking mechanism on her seat kept her from falling to the floor.

"Mozart," she whispered. Born in 1756, died in 1791. Whose music she had started dreaming about when the probe appeared.

Was it possible that she was hearing the probe in her sleep? The same probe that Mozart had heard in his?

"No. That's crazy. I'm just tired, and imagining things."

Still, she could rule it out easily enough. The station monitored their vital signs, including simplified brain wave function, so that the team would know if any member of the crew was physically impaired from carrying out their tasks. All she had to do was review the past week of readings during her sleep shift...

Syrah's fingers were entering the commands before she'd even consciously decided to run the test.

The results appeared on the screen, the differences before and after the probe's arrival dramatic and incontrovertible. Her brain was responding as if she was listening to music in her sleep.

She pulled up her crewmates' readings, and compared them to her own. While they both showed a slight alteration, it was nowhere near as dramatic. Either they had been able to ignore the music, or they hadn't "heard" it as clearly as she had.

Which raised another question: how was the probe transmitting the music? Sound didn't carry in space.

Syrah keyed in the command to locate Cherie, and activated the transmission protocol. "Cherie, can you come up to the command center? I've got something, and need another pair of eyes on it."

"Not another probe, is it?" The communications transmission clearly carried the tremor in Cherie's voice.

"No. But I've got an idea about what might have happened to our drones."

"Be right there."

In a matter of minutes, Cherie joined her in the command center. Damp spots on her suit indicated that Syrah had interrupted her daily workout, still mandatory even with all their extra assignments.

Quickly, Syrah outlined what she'd learned. Cherie was initially skeptical, but the brain wave patterns convinced her as thoroughly as they had Syrah. At least, they convinced her that Syrah wasn't just hallucinating from lack of sleep. But she didn't see the connection.

"You said this had something to do with the drones. How?"

"What if the probe was broadcasting the music some way, and it overloaded their receptors? We've been assuming the ion engines exploded. But what if that wasn't it at all? What if their sensors shorted out?"

"Why wouldn't they have shorted out as soon as they got close, then?"

"Remember how the third set of panels rotated as they came back around? The probe might have been programmed to ignore things moving past it, unless they behaved in a non-natural fashion, which the drones did when they turned and came back around for a second pass. It might have been trying to communicate with them."

"I suppose it's possible. We'll know more when the second drone flight recovers what's left of them."

"Right. And in the meantime, I've got an idea." Syrah wiped her damp palms on the legs of her flight suit. She didn't like the idea. Hated it, as a matter of fact. But the need to understand outweighed the need for temporary safety. "So, we know I've been 'hearing' the probe in my sleep. What if it can 'hear' me, too? I'm going to fill my head with music while I sleep, and see if it responds."

"I don't like it. There's too many unknowns."

"Do you have any better ideas?"

"No. I don't even have any worse ideas. But that doesn't mean I have to like yours."

"Noted. But I've got to try it. I can't stand the thought of aliens beaming things into my head and not being able to do anything about it."

"Well, when you put it that way...I guess we can use the time before your sleep shift to set up monitoring protocols, and try to figure out what exactly is happening."

"Thanks!"

* * *

Syrah inhaled deeply, then slowly released her breath on a gentle exhale. It had been years since she needed her breathing exercises to get to sleep. Of course, wearing a monitoring cap that measured every blip of her brain waves was stressing her out. Not to mention the whole attempting to communicate with an alien probe that had fried the drones when they caught its attention. No, no worries to keep her from falling asleep.

She breathed deeply again, then flipped on the music she'd chosen: Mozart's Twelve Variations on *"Ah vous dirai-je, Maman."* Otherwise known as "Twinkle, Twinkle, Little Star."

The simple, repetitive tune would help to relax her and put her to sleep. And the variations would clearly demonstrate to anyone listening that there was conscious thought behind the music. At least, that was the plan.

One last deep breath, then she closed her eyes, and let the music sweep her away. Twinkle, twinkle...

She bolted upright out of a sound sleep when the music was interrupted by a loud and insistent warning klaxon. Yellow urgency lights blinked on the wall panel.

Syrah ripped the monitoring cap off as she jumped out of bed. She slapped the panel, and engaged com-munications to the command center.

"This is Syrah. What's the emergency?"

"Your little experiment to communicate with the probe worked," Tomas answered. "It just shifted course. We don't have to worry anymore about it hitting Earth. It's coming straight toward us."

* * *

Message from probe 349872:

Intelligent life detected in star system 98-A-47-T. Response received to initial greeting. Attempting to establish dialogue per protocol 3G. Send first contact response team.

THE NIGHT YOU WERE A COMET
Coral Moore

Miranda eased back from the screen, rubbing her forehead with both hands. Her feet, stuck in the straps bolted to the bulkhead, kept her from floating free in the cabin. She'd been at it so long that the numbers and lines in front of her were a jumble.

The legitimate geniuses they had crunching numbers back at the Hub had screwed something up, and now she was out here, communication cut off and under a time crunch, and she had to figure it out. Only she wasn't an astrophysicist or a rocket scientist, or any damn thing like that. She just drove the tanker.

Bruno's head floated into the doorway next to her, upside down. "Any luck?"

She grimaced. "Zero. I told you I wasn't any good at this."

"None of us are. They don't send the brains on these kinds of missions."

"Yeah, we're just the ones they send to do the actual work," Miranda grumbled and went back to the screen, scanning the lines again. "I'm the closest thing we have to an expert. I can do the math, I just don't usually do it with numbers."

"That's encouraging."

"Don't you have some welding to do?"

Bruno laughed and pulled himself into the doorway. He let himself spin to end up facing her right-side up, one hand reaching for the grip next to her screen to steady himself. "Weren't they supposed to triple check all those calculations before we went dark?"

"Yup. I got the confirmation that they had just before we passed out of line of sight, but when I entered the course into the navigation computer it just about coughed up a hairball on me."

"What would cause that?"

"My best guess is the comet is no longer where they thought it was when they ran the numbers. Though why it's off course I have no idea."

"Does it matter?"

She glanced at him out of the corner of her eye, hoping she kept the disbelief from showing on her face. "If it continues altering course, even if I recalculate the trajectory correctly, we'll still end up in the wrong place and possibly out of fuel, unable to make another correction."

A somber expression overtook Bruno's generally jovial face. "Folks back home need this water."

"I know. That's why I'm busting my ass trying to figure this out. And I could use a little quiet."

"Sorry. I thought you could use a break. If you need anything let me know." He pushed off and floated up the companionway, his slipper-socked feet disappearing last.

What Miranda could actually use was an answer to the problem floating in front of her. She could take the chance that she'd be able to work out the angles on approach, and normally she would, but thousands of people were relying on the water they were supposed to be hauling back with them. Water rations were so tight now that a single missed shipment would be disastrous.

She glared at the arcs on the screen. No matter what she tried she couldn't get them to line up. She'd altered their speed and course a hundred different ways and still the model showed them missing the comet completely. She futzed with the numbers for a while longer, until she felt the pressure of a headache starting behind her eyes. She *did* need a break.

Miranda pulled her feet free of the anchor-straps and pushed off to propel herself across the cabin to one of the portholes. She held herself in place with one hand. Outside, nothing seemed to move. Though the ship was moving fast, all the objects were far enough away that they appeared stationary.

The sun was out of the frame, but she could see the glare of it off to their right. As difficult as it was to imagine, they were actually in the shadow of the sun compared to their home base. That's why communications had been cut off.

That was also why no one at the Hub had noticed the comet's shift. The last time they had a clear view it had been behaving normally, following its usual orbit. Something had made it kick out. A collision with another rock? Possible, though there was no evidence of the debris such an impact would create.

More likely was that something had pulled it off course. Pulling meant gravity. And gravity meant acceleration. And that was why her course adjustments had been almost-but-not-quite-right—it was still picking up speed. Damn. She pushed off with her feet and shot across the cabin, reaching with her feet for the stirrups instinctively. She used the comet's movement since they'd gone out of communication to calculate the acceleration and plotted that change forward in time.

The arcs finally overlapped. She was pleased with herself for the ten seconds it took her to realize the acceleration of the comet was huge, given its mass. Too huge. That's why the navigation computer had thrown up all over the calculations. Whatever had deflected the comet was immense, and yet nothing had shown up on any of their scans.

She pulled herself into the companionway and up through the center of the ship toward the bunkroom. The voices of her crewmates drifted to her before her head came through the round doorway. Petra sat on her bed, tethered down by the belt of her coveralls. Bruno floated nearby, toes locked into a foothold against the bulkhead. Seon-mi was in her sleeping net, though she was just coming off shift and still awake.

They all stared at her, as though they knew by the way she'd come in that she was about to say something important.

"I think there's a black hole out there." Miranda held up her hand as all of them asked questions at once. When they quieted she continued, "The navigational computer was having trouble plotting our course because the comet was deflected. It's nowhere near where the Hub said it would be."

Bruno spoke up first, "There's no way a black hole has been this close to us and we haven't picked up something on instruments."

Seon-mi had unwound herself from the sleeping net following Miranda's entrance and now sat up, her knees still caught in the webbing to keep herself from floating off. "That's not necessarily true. If it was small enough we might not see anything except bodies it acted on. That said, black holes don't just appear and disappear out of nowhere. The likelihood there's been one so close to the Hub that they haven't noticed is pretty remote."

Miranda grabbed a foothold and pulled herself further into the bunkroom. "What if it's always been on the other side of the sun?"

"Assuming there was a black hole capable of deflecting our comet, it would have been pulling everything else in the system out of alignment too. Is there a reason you don't think it was a collision?"

"It's still accelerating."

Seon-mi ruffled her short hair so it stuck up at every possible angle. Miranda had a feeling it did that even in gravity. "I can't explain that, but it's not a black hole. It can't be, not this close."

"All of this speculation is irrelevant," Petra said into the lull, taking on her we-all-know-who-the-boss-is-here tone. "Can you get us to the new location or not?"

No matter what Petra thought, she wasn't in charge. They were an equal share crew, all with equal votes. That's what it said on paperwork anyway. Practically speaking, Bruno always voted with Petra, so she almost always got her way.

Miranda kept her frustration over the voting situation to herself. "Yes, but I'm not sure we should."

Petra scoffed. "We don't come back with water, none of us get paid our bonus. Worse, we get docked for the fuel wastage. Worst? Stricter water rations and all the chaos and death that brings. You want that on your head? Because I sure don't."

Miranda chewed on her lip. If they didn't deliver the water on time there would likely be riots. She looked from one of her crewmates to the next, settling on Seon-mi last. "What do you think?"

Seon-mi shrugged, a potentially awkward movement in zero-g that she managed without budging from her cot. "I think it's not a black hole, but could potentially be something dangerous."

"Do you think we should go after it?"

"Sure, I need that bonus. I don't want my parents to have to move. It's too dangerous at the outer stations, but they can't afford to pay for living space at the Hub anymore."

"Yeah..." The truth was, they all needed that bonus or none of them would be out here. Hauling was much easier closer to the Hub. Outside the ring, ships disappeared all the time, and that was the best of the bad scenarios. She'd heard of ships that returned on auto-pilot with no crew and no indication of what had happened to them. That's why the paychecks were better the further out you were willing to go. "Guess that means we're going, no matter what my vote is. I'll go finish the plot."

Miranda pulled herself into the companionway and back toward navigation without waiting for a response. She couldn't shake the feeling that this was a mistake. Something had moved that chunk of ice, and without knowing what it was they were flying blind into what could be a trap.

* * *

Miranda kept her eyes pinned to the instruments as they approached the comet. They hadn't read anything unusual—yet. The ship was matching speed with the comet in preparation to latch on and begin the slow processing of ice. All of that was handled by the navigation computer now that she'd provided the vectors and she had nothing to do but worry about whatever had knocked the comet off course.

"Velocity match in ten seconds," Bruno said from the other side of the instrument bay.

Seon-mi hovered over Miranda's shoulder, a slight frown on her face as she regarded the screens with characteristic intensity. They'd all been space haulers long enough that they weren't bothered by close confines despite four people being crammed in a space designed for two.

Miranda glanced up from the sensor outputs, realizing what had been bothering her since they'd started their approach. "Why isn't it tumbling anymore?"

"How do you mean?" Seon-mi asked.

"Its rotation has stabilized. Completely. Usually that's what we do first when we land, right?"

"Who cares? That just makes our lives easier." Petra, hanging on to the bulkhead beside Bruno, responded without turning her head.

"Ready for deployment," Bruno added when the countdown finished.

Miranda paused. This was all wrong. Why did no one else care that the comet wasn't where it was supposed to be and had somehow changed its rotation? Whatever force had managed that was significant. Who knew what it could do to their ship?

Seon-mi reached past her and keyed in the authorization code while she was still frozen with indecision. Miranda reached to knock her hand away but it was too late. The ship shook as the main bay opened to deploy the factory platform.

She glared up at Seon-mi. "I was getting to it."

"Really? You looked like you were having second thoughts."

"I was. I still am. This seems fool-hardy. Once we're attached to the surface whatever acts on the comet acts on us."

"We need this water," Petra said as she floated toward them. "We can start the processing and if we find out there's something dangerous out there we'll unhook, take what we have, and head home."

Miranda had to admit that some water was better than none. "Someone should keep an eye on the instruments."

Petra pulled her way into the companionway. "You can take the first watch."

"Fine." Miranda started her first of many sweeps through the sensors, grumbling under her breath as her crewmates departed.

* * *

They made it through four shift changes before all hell broke loose. The wailing siren woke Miranda from a deep sleep. She banged her elbow on the bulkhead twice while trying to get herself out of her sleep net. When she arrived in the instrument bay she almost hit her head on the edge of the portal. "What's going on?" Bruno glared at the screen while Seon-mi pointed at something. Between the two of them they managed to get the alarm quieted.

Seon-mi's gaze flickered over the screen once more. "One of the pumps stopped. No big deal. Petra went out to check on it."

Miranda drifted to the screen on the other side of the bay. She paged through the systems as fast as she could scan them, starting with environmental. Nothing showed outside parameters. "This doesn't make any sense." She brought up the visual of the factory platform and zoomed in on the stooped form of Petra examining one of the pumps. Miranda opened the shipboard comm line. "Did you find anything out there?"

Petra turned to the camera. "Yeah, but you're not going to believe it."

Miranda zoomed in more. "Explain."

"There's what looks like an organic residue gumming up the pumps."

"That's impossible." Seon-mi said from over Miranda's shoulder.

Petra held up a hand to the camera. "So tell me what this is?"

"Holy shit." Seon-mi reached over Miranda's shoulder to zoom the camera again. A dark film webbed the space between the fingers of Petra's suit.

Bruno crowded in behind them. "It's contamination from the outside of the ship. Has to be. Algae or something."

Petra's helmet shook. "I've never seen algae adhere like this. It's as sticky as molecular glue."

Seon-mi tilted the screen her way to get a better angle, then sighed. "Bring a sample inside and I'll check it out."

"No fucking way we're bringing that on the ship," Miranda countered. "We have no idea what that is. It could be toxic. Hell it could be infectious."

"Which is exactly why we have to figure out what it is. If it's toxic the water is contaminated, but maybe we can purify it somehow."

Bruno had been looking between the two of them as they argued. "Why didn't the scrubbers catch it?"

Miranda stared at him for a few beats. "Damn, he's right. It can't be organic. The scanners would have picked it up."

Seon-mi stared at the screen once more, her fingers tapping the console. "We definitely need to figure out what it is."

Miranda shook her head, but unfortunately she had no better plan. "This is a terrible fucking idea."

"Agreed, but I don't see that we have much choice," Petra said while scraping some of the goo from her glove into a sample container. "We can't bring it back to the Hub if we have no idea what it is and I don't relish the idea of floating around until we get back into line of sight to ask for guidance."

Miranda hated everything about this. Everything. She scooped up her hair to wind it into a bun to keep it out of her way. "I'll set up the quarantine bay."

"Thanks," Petra said. "I'll be inside as soon as I can get most of this off."

Miranda navigated her way out of the instrument bay and floated up the companionway with Bruno right behind her.

"What do you think it is?" he asked when they reached the hatch.

She entered the access code and waited for the heavy door to open. "It's trouble."

"It might not be." Bruno's earnest expression was too much for her.

"First the comet isn't where it should be and now it's covered in some kind of unidentified adhesive slime. You're right, it must be nothing. I don't know why I'm worried." She pulled herself through the hatch.

When they reached the airlock he caught up with her again. "We don't know the two are related."

Miranda punched in the quarantine code at the access panel. A divider slid to close off an area inside the airlock from the rest of the ship. "I hope you're right. Honestly. I haven't felt good about any of this since we passed out of communications. I would be thrilled if this was a series of coincidences that aren't at all ominous."

Bruno smiled. "I think you're just a worrier. I've been on a dozen of these missions. Nothing bad has ever happened."

"But has anything like this happened?"

"Well, no. Usually we just pick up our water and go."

"That's what worries me."

"They expect the occasional unpredictable problem though, or else they would just send these unmanned."

"Maybe they should, Bruno. An unmanned ship would have just turned back when it didn't find the comet in the right place. But we decided we should chase it down. Maybe we weren't meant to find this thing."

Bruno whistled. "Getting a little paranoid there."

Miranda laughed uneasily. "Maybe."

* * *

Miranda watched the image on the screen as Seon-mi adjusted the focus. It looked like sand to her.

Seon-mi straightened and squinted at the screen. "That's max magnification. No cellular structure that I can see, so it's definitely not an algae—holy shit did that just move?"

Miranda had seen it too. An entire section of the particles had shifted, almost flowed. "Heat from the light, maybe?"

"No." Seon-mi bent to look through the eyepieces again. "That was organized movement."

Petra, still on the other side of the quarantine divider, paced back and forth. From her angle she couldn't see the screen and she still had on her mag-boots so she was taking full advantage. "If it's not biological and it's moving, it has to be mechanical."

Miranda narrowed her eyes. "But they're so tiny."

"Nanobots," Seon-mi said after a few seconds.

Petra turned toward them. "Nobody has anything that small, or that good."

Seon-mi shrugged. "That we know of."

Miranda pulled herself closer to the screen. "What are they doing out here?"

"And how did they get here?" Petra added. "Any way we can figure out who manufactured them?"

Seon-mi looked up. "Not that I know of. If there's any kind of marking on them what we have on-hand isn't powerful enough to pick it up."

"Maybe they emit some kind of signal?" Miranda floated to the terminal and initiated a sweep of commonly used frequencies. "They have to communicate with each other somehow, right?"

Seon-mi nodded. "Good idea."

Petra moved close to the divider and stared at them. "Since we know it's not biological when can I get out of here?"

Miranda glanced toward the container Petra had put her glove into. "When we break that seal whatever it is has full access to the ship. I'd prefer it stays out there until we know for sure it's not dangerous."

Petra frowned. "I'll seal up the box."

"The moment we open the hatch whatever contamination you've come in contact with is in here."

"So what's your plan? Keep me out here all the way home?"

Miranda pointed to the screen. "We have no idea what that is or what it's doing here. Until we do, it stays on the other side of the wall."

"Should we put it to a vote?" Petra asked.

"I agree with Miranda," Seon-mi said after a moment. "We can't let you into the cabin."

Miranda sighed. Finally someone was seeing sense. "Tied then, you stay out there until we figure this out."

* * *

Two shift changes later, Miranda glared through the divider at the contamination sack that enclosed the sample box and the weird goo they'd found in the comet's ice. The dark, viscous substance now coated the inside of the clear bag. The word 'QUARANTINE' emblazoned in red across it seemed comical. There was no way the bag could contain it; the box certainly hadn't. They had no idea how it continued to grow, or if there was an upper limit to how big it could get. Even the airlock might not contain it.

Miranda leaned back, rubbing her eyes with the heels of her hands. "We need to get it off the ship before the bag gives way."

"I'm not sure that will make any difference. It's everywhere." Bruno pointed to the screen in front of him that showed the image from the factory platform. The strangely adhesive goo covered every visible surface.

"We can detach the platform," Miranda offered.

"It's not just on the platform." He brought up an exterior view. The dull gray material covered the underside of the ship completely. He pointed to the bulbous shapes of the water tanks. "It came in with the water before the pumps shut down. By now it's probably already in our own backup water tanks."

From the other side of the divider, Petra held up her right hand. "It's already outside the bag anyway." Dark material enclosed her fingers and crept up over her wrist like a strange glove.

Miranda instinctively tried to move away, but gathered her wits after a moment. She was faring better than Bruno, who looked like he was either going to pass out or be sick. The former was vastly preferred in a tight room with only recycled air to breathe. "Go to the head if you're going to vomit."

Bruno shook his head slowly and wedged his way into a corner as far away from the divider as he could manage.

Miranda returned her attention to Petra. "Are you okay?"

Petra curled, then straightened her fingers. "I think so. I actually can't feel anything."

"No sensation at all?"

"It's not numb. It just feels normal. I didn't even notice there was anything wrong until I looked at it."

Miranda moved slightly closer, bringing herself close to the transparent divider. "It's definitely not normal." There were no seams, or any features that she could tell. The substance just grew over Petra's hand like a second skin.

A loud bang jolted Miranda out of her examination. She turned to see that the bag containing the sample box had burst, spreading the dark goo on every surface. They were fucked. It was not only on the ship, but already inside. Bruno was beyond useless, gibbering to himself in the furthest corner of the room. It was up to her to get them out of the mess they were in.

Miranda pushed off and headed for the terminal again. There had to be a signal the nanobots were using to communicate with each other, and if she could find it maybe she could disrupt it. She'd given up searching when she reached the end of the frequencies commonly used by haulers, but what if they operated outside that band? What if the nanobots weren't manmade at all? There was no telling where the comet had originated or what it had encountered.

She started keying commands for an automated search in a broader range, but then paused, her eyes unfocusing. The bots were tiny, miniscule. It wouldn't make sense that they would use a frequency with a long wavelength. There was no guarantee that their neighbors would pick up the communication. Wouldn't they use a higher frequency? Beyond the visible range wasn't practical for long-range communications, but the nanobots wouldn't have to worry about that. She decided to start at the highest end of the visible range and work up.

When the scan was running Miranda glanced up at Petra. She held her hand away from her body as if uncertain she wanted anything to do with it. "I should go wake Seon-mi up to check out your hand."

"I'm a little afraid of what she'll say."

"The truth is the truth regardless of if you're aware of it."

"That's easy for you to say, this shit isn't all over your hand. What if it keeps going?"

Miranda looked over the dark, almost glossy material again. What was it doing to her skin under there? "There's no reason to think it will stop."

"Well that's just fucking brilliant. How long before it's all over me?"

"That's impossible to guess. It depends if there are any limitations on its growth or if we could slow it down somehow."

"Any suggestions?"

"Not really. Seon-mi is the medic." The truth was the bots, whatever they were, had already survived on a comet in the harsh environment of space for who knew how long. It was unlikely anything they could do would slow them down in the slightest.

Petra looked over her hand and frowned. She curled her fingers slowly into a fist. "I'm not going to let her cut if off."

Miranda barely restrained a sigh. They'd already tried every solvent and corrosive they had on the sample with no change at all in the adhesion of the material. Amputation was the only plan that had any hope of success, but she knew better than to suggest it. "Bruno, go get Seon-mi."

She had to repeat herself twice before he actually moved. After several false starts, Bruno pulled himself into the companionway and disappeared.

"Seon-mi won't change my mind about this," Petra said, when enough time had gone by for Bruno to be out of hearing range.

"I don't really think that matters unless I can find a way to stop them." She gestured at the terminal angrily.

Petra had pulled herself closer to the divider with her left hand. "We should blow the comet to bits, along with the platform."

Miranda took a calming breath. "Assuming we had the firepower to accomplish that, which I'm not sure we do, how do we know that would disable them? For all we know, blowing the comet up would just send them out in every direction. Right now, at least they're contained here with not much chance of escaping."

"Who cares if they escape? We're already dead." She was too unhinged to see sense at the moment. Hopefully once she calmed down a bit Miranda could talk her out of blowing them all up.

The terminal in front of Miranda chimed. She pulled up the report of what her scan had found. "Maybe not."

There was a spike in the near ultraviolet range that couldn't be explained by any nearby natural feature. Miranda dialed in the frequency and instructed the computer to translate it into something audible. The computer adjusted the output slowly, producing only static at first. After a few moments there seemed to be a pattern under the noise, a cadence that shouldn't have been there if the radiation was being generated randomly. As she listened it became more pronounced—a sub-aural thrumming that set her teeth on edge. "Hot damn. I found it."

* * *

All four members of the crew were in the instrument bay. They'd confirmed that the nanobots had already infiltrated the ship's water supply, so there was no longer a reason to keep Petra quarantined. Miranda had been listening to the three others argue since she'd shared the news that she'd found the frequency the nanobots used to communicate. Each had a different plan for how to deal with the issue, and none of them wanted to back down.

Bruno wanted to try to talk to the things. As if they had some kind of motivation and could be convinced to try something else. He didn't have an idea for how to establish that communication, of course. He wasn't a linguist; none of them were. That also assumed their signals were a language at all, which Miranda thought was probably a mistake. She was pretty sure whatever had made the things hadn't been human. They had no reason to believe the bots were doing anything beyond what they were programed to do, whatever that was.

Seon-mi wanted to blast the nanobots with all the ultraviolet radiation they could muster, which was actually quite a lot. The ship had banks of UV lights used for water purification that they could turn on the bots.

Petra still wanted to blow up the comet. The rest of them had taken turns explaining to her what a terrible idea it was to spread a self-propagating adhesive material with an explosion that wouldn't necessarily destroy it, but she didn't care.

Miranda wanted to try jamming the bots. It would take time and subtlety, but she felt like it had the best chance of working. Predictably, none of her crewmates supported her idea. They'd made no progress in the discussion so far and four opposing plans wouldn't get them anywhere.

She could stubbornly hold her course and hope that one of the others changed their mind, but she didn't think that would happen. Unfortunately it was far more likely that one of the others would support Petra's mad plan than hers. So that left Miranda with choosing one of the other options and swinging the vote that way.

In truth, there was no choice at all. Seon-mi's was the only plan that had a prayer of working, though Miranda believed overloading the bots with UV had just as much chance of making them do something unexpected as deactivating them.

"I've changed my mind," Miranda said as loudly as she could. Her voice echoed in the small bay and managed to quiet the others. "Let's blast them with UV."

Seon-mi raised a triumphant fist. "All right!"

Petra glared at Bruno, as if that could make him change his vote to her side, but for once, he wasn't budging. The presence of the bots inside the ship had finally turned him against her, it seemed. Her hand was heavily wrapped now, and tucked into a sling tight against her stomach to prevent her from contaminating anything else. Miranda wondered how far up her arm the sticky substance had climbed and what was happening to her arm under there.

Seon-mi had taken the silence for confirmation that her plan was now officially their plan. "We should start adjusting the lights so we get the best coverage."

They spent the next two hours setting up the lights and rerouting power for maximum output. Seon-mi checked the preparations one last time while Petra positioned the portable UV light in the quarantine bay. They'd decided they should hit as much of the substance as they could all at once, including the sample box and Petra's hand.

Seon-mi glanced toward Miranda. "Set the timer."

Miranda set a sixty second countdown and nodded.

"Close the hatch," Seon-mi said to Bruno.

He complied and then nodded to her.

Seon-mi brought up the channel to the quarantine bay. "You ready?"

Petra slowly removed her arm from the sling. She opened the top of her coveralls and slid her arm out. She put on eye protection and stood in front of the light. "Ready." Miranda couldn't take her eyes off the gray substance that covered Petra's arm to just past her elbow.

"Start it up," Seon-mi said.

Miranda snapped to attention and glanced over the subroutine once more before starting the timer. She watched the numbers count back from sixty with a knot of anxiety building in her chest. This was probably their only chance.

Thirty seconds. A distant hum vibrated through the hull as the lights powered up.

Ten seconds. Miranda looked at Petra. She was holding together, barely. The fingers of her right hand shook where she held them under the light.

Five seconds. Doubt plagued Miranda. She battled the urge to cancel the countdown in the final seconds.

Zero. For what seemed like a long time, but could only have been moments, nothing happened. In the odd silence, Miranda thought everything had worked as planned. Bombarded with UV, the bots had stopped doing whatever it is that they were programmed to do.

Petra's scream broke the trance.

The dark gray line surged upward to consume her biceps, then her shoulder, then her chest. Miranda stared in horror as the nanobots climbed over Petra's face.

Miranda had to do something. Fast. Or they were all dead. "Kill the lights!"

For what felt like an eternity, no one moved. Finally, Seon-mi pushed off toward another terminal. "On it." The lights powered down a few seconds later, but the damage was already done.

Miranda typed as fast as she could, rerouting the power to vent the airlock. When the cabin suddenly went quiet, Miranda glanced up. Petra still stood in the airlock screaming, but no sound came out amid a flood of gray pouring from her mouth and engulfing the floor. Miranda hurried to finish the commands, fingers flying over the terminal.

Airlock management was generally a delicate procedure, but after removing the safeguards she could force a full pressure evacuation that she hoped would send most of the nanobots out the hatch and back toward the surface of the comet before they could fill the quarantine area.

By the time she finished, Petra was an unrecognizable lump under a writhing mass of gray. She started the override sequence and watched. There was no change for a few seconds, and then when the outer hatch popped everything not attached to the bulkhead blew outward. Miranda was glad she couldn't see Petra's face under the gray sheet.

"You killed her," Bruno whispered.

"Shut your mouth." Seon-mi glared at him. "She was already dead and Miranda's quick thinking just saved our lives."

Miranda didn't feel much like a hero. She thought she was about to be sick, but managed to keep her lunch down by distracting herself with the routine of securing the airlock.

Seon-mi stared into the quarantine bay. "There's still some in there, but it seems to have stopped spreading for the moment." She looked back at Miranda. "What do we do now?"

"We can't risk that any of this survives and spreads." She paused and locked eyes with Seon-mi. She didn't know if the other woman would back her play, but something had changed between them when Petra had been overrun. The stakes had gone up. Left unchecked, the nanobots could consume an entire planet. Hell, they could devastate the entire system. "We put the whole thing into the sun."

Bruno exploded into profanity-laced, almost-incoherent protest.

Seon-mi only nodded slowly.

* * *

ULTRA LOW FREQUENCY COMMUNICATIONS MONITORING
REPORT

Location: HUB DEEP SPACE ANTENNA DELTA

Source: WATER MINER CORDERA, Transponder code WMC938254

Status: Approaching outer system markers

Message: HAZARD. Do not approach our position under any circumstances. Comet C/2099 D12 is to be considered highly infectious and any debris found should be handled accordingly. An infestation of self-replicating nanobots on the surface of the comet has overrun our ship. Growth of the colony is unchecked by conventional means. We are directing the comet on a course into the sun. Stay well clear. HAZARD.

MESSAGE REPEATS

THE GOD EMPEROR OF LASSIE POINT
Daniel J. Davis

Laundryman 3rd Class Tad Billings stood alone in his quarters, trying not to look like he'd just hidden several kilograms of contraband in the air return. He wasn't sure he was succeeding.

He straightened his dress uniform, picking an errant piece of dark lint from the white fabric. For at least the fiftieth time, he checked the position of his ribbons: two rows of three, exactly one millimeter spacing between rows, perfectly straight and aligned with the second button of his jacket. The rest of his uniforms hung in his wall locker, starched and spotless. The deck, the bulkheads, and the ceiling had all been scrubbed clean. He'd even touched up the chipped spots with that awful "navy gray" paint that was used for everything aboard Lassie Point.

No, he corrected himself. *Not "Lassie Point." Laundry and Sanitation Support Station Three.* He'd made the mistake of using the station's nickname during the last inspection and Chief Klienman had hammered him for it.

So where the hell *was* Chief Klienman?

Tad shot a furtive glance upward. The air return grate bowed outward slightly, but the bolts affixing it to the ceiling still held. He was surprised. Like anything else in the Federated Space Force, the bolts were made by the lowest bidder. It was an impressive performance under the strain, all things considered, but he hadn't intended to keep his stash there for more than a few hours.

Tad checked his watch. 1045 Standard Time. He frowned. Klienman was a stickler. If he said 0800 inspection, he meant 0800 exactly. This wasn't like the old man at all.

Unless he's trying to make me sweat, Tad thought. *He's probably standing outside with the Master at Arms. They're going to haul me to the brig the second I open the hatch.*

No. That was crazy. The chief didn't know about Tad's supplementary business dealings. And besides, he wasn't the only man to steal things from the pockets of the uniforms that came through Lassie Point. Everyone did it.

Tad just happened to be the best.

His stomach rumbled. Afternoon chow would be starting soon. He could be standing around for nothing, he realized. The inspection could have been pushed back. Wouldn't that be just his luck? Tad walked to the hatch. He touched the access pad and stuck his head out into the passageway, looking for somebody to ask.

Kneeling on the deck, filling the passage in both directions, was the entire crew of Lassie Point. Chief Klienman and Captain Park were up front. The rest knelt behind them in a disorganized gaggle. They'd all torn their uniforms into rags, and retied them into strange robes. Several, including the chief, had made rosary-like prayer chains out of their ribbons. Culinary Technician 1st Class Morrison, kneeling close to the back, had fashioned a large headdress out of coffee filters.

"Master!" the captain cried.

"Master!" the chief echoed, counting on his ribbon-chain.

The rest of the crew took up the chant behind them. "Master! Master! All hail the Master!"

* * *

It wasn't some elaborate prank. That much became clear in short order. Tad paced back and forth in front of his bunk while Chief Klienman and Captain Park knelt on the deck. They crowded the closed hatch behind them, leaving as much floor space between themselves and Tad as possible. Considering the size of his room, there wasn't much to leave. Park kept his forehead pressed to the ground, only raising it up when expressly told to do so. The chief raised his head whenever Tad spoke, but he kept his eyes averted. The rest of the crew waited outside.

"Run it by me again," Tad said. "Please."

"I've been elected to speak to you by our most unworthy captain," Klienman said. He was still counting on his ribbon-chain. "I was chosen because I had more contact with you in the before time. I was the closest to your divine grace, Master."

"You used to chew me out and make me scrub toilets."

The chief's counting stopped. He seemed on the verge of tears. "The before time was terrible, Master. We didn't see your grace and wisdom. I will always carry the mark of shame for what I did then. If you wish to send me into exile, I will go down to the teleporter deck at once."

Tad quickly shook his head. Teleporters couldn't handle live organisms. They were too hard for the computers to reconstruct on the other end. Supposedly, only one in five hundred people survived a teleporter accident. The other four hundred ninety-nine ended up looking like flesh-colored gelatin.

"No, no. That's okay. Nobody's exiling anybody."

The chief did cry now. It seemed like tears of joy. "I will serve you the rest of my days, Master. I swear it."

Tad still couldn't wrap his head around it. He sat heavily on the bunk. "So sometime in the last few hours, you all just decided to start worshipping me?"

Klienman clapped his hands together. "Yes. We have seen the light, Master!"

"We have seen the light!" the captain echoed.

Tad glanced up at the bulging air return. *It's that weird thing that came in during the late shift. It has to be.*

"I want to be alone for a while. Is that okay?"

"Of course, Master. Anything you say." The chief bowed and groveled, nearly knocking his head against the deck as he did so. He and the captain scuttled backwards. "I'll keep an ensign posted outside the tabernacle. He will be at your command."

"The *tabernacle?*"

The chief, still bowing low, spread his hands to indicate the tiny quarters. "The seat of your divine wisdom, Master."

"Ah. Um, good. Carry on then?"

The captain and the chief disappeared, closing the door behind them. Tad slumped all the way back on the bed. This, he thought, was going to be an enormous pain in the ass.

* * *

Sometime later Tad stood on the desk chair, carefully lowering his stash of goods out of the opened air return. He stepped down and spread the items out over his desk. It was a pretty good haul this month, one he'd been expecting to unload on Tau-Ceti when his next scheduled furlough came up. There were eleven gold Academy rings, ten with precious stone insets. A pair of diamond earrings. Two solo gold studs. He also had six wedding bands, an engagement ring, and twenty-three silver religious medallions.

Aside from the jewelry, Tad had collected fourteen different mini-tablets and personal holo-screens. About half of them were broken, but Goro down at the Pawn and Loan would still pay a premium for them. Even when he couldn't extract anything good from the hard drives, the old Tau-Cetian could always make some money from the gold used on the circuit boards.

The biggest moneymakers by far, though, were the Federated Space Force IDs. Tad had collected thirty-nine since his last shore leave. Each card had personal information, identity codes, and detailed genetic profiles written into the nanostrip. Credit scammers, hackers, and other less-desirables paid good money for a legitimate Federation ID. He could probably make almost twenty thousand from the cards alone, after Goro's "finder's fee."

None of those things were Tad's immediate concern.

Instead he reached for the small, odd object that had come through on the late shift last night. At first glance, it looked like a green quartz point, one about the size of his thumb. Tad had found it in the breast pocket of some lieutenant's uniform. He'd almost tossed it in the lost and found. It was just worthless junk, after all, like almost everything he found when he prepared loads for the enormous wash machines of Lassie Point. More than likely it was a souvenir, a memento of the officer's first planetary survey mission.

On impulse Tad had stashed it until the end of his shift, figuring he could look it up on the net later. Maybe he'd get lucky. Maybe it would be valuable. After he'd finished up, he'd brought it back to his quarters. The crystal was lighter than it should have been, and the facets didn't feel right. They were too smooth. They almost felt like some kind of metal. But what kind of metal had translucent sides? As he fiddled with it, one of the facets had clicked inward, like a button.

That's when the weird stuff happened.

All of the lights—including the emergency lights—went dim. The air mover slowed. Even the artificial gravity had gone out for a few seconds. And for just an instant, Tad could have sworn he saw a yellowish halo of some kind expanding out from the crystal's tip.

Then, as suddenly as it had happened, it was over. Tad had quickly stowed the object along with the rest of his valuables, and resolved to forget about it until after the chief's inspection. Clearly, it was going to be trouble.

Now, sitting at his desk, Tad muttered to himself. "I hate being right."

He turned and examined the green metal-crystal in his hands, trying to find the trigger facet again. He pushed in on each of them, gently at first, and then more forcefully when none showed any give.

It has to be from of the Argakan Empire. That's the only explanation.

He pulled his computer tablet down from bulkhead, and immediately queued up a database search. He took two quick snap-scans of the crystal, and told the tablet to run the images against documented artifacts. In thousands of planetary surveys, and hundreds of archeological digs, surely somebody had to have found something like this before?

Right?

While he was waiting for the tablet to turn up some answers, he decided to check the station's arrival logs. He needed to figure out which ship had sent it over.

* * *

When Tad arrived on the teleporter deck, the logs were in the process of being "purged." Teleporter Tech 2nd Class Hendricks and Teleporter Tech 3rd Class Trotta danced around a roaring fire in the wastebasket while singing songs about the Glory of Master.

"What the hell are you idiots *doing?*" Tad shouted. At the sound of his voice, Trotta and Hendricks fell on their knees and touched their foreheads to the deck.

"Master!" they cried in unison.

Tad raced for the nearest extinguisher. As he put out the flames in the wastebasket, he glanced at the nearest computer screen. It was a jumble of green-on-black gibberish, numbers and symbols blinking in seemingly endless columns.

Tad struggled to keep his voice even as he set down the extinguisher. "Will one of you tell me why you did this?"

Trotta wore a wide grin on her face. "The heretical texts of the before time make no mention of you, Master. They are not fit to occupy server space with your new gospel. They are not fit to be filed in the same drawers as your hymns." Next to her, Hendricks offered an enthusiastic nod.

Tad felt like his head was going to split open. "What gospel? What are you talking about?"

Trotta bowed again. She rose and quickly ran to one of the overlarge file cabinets that typically housed the teleporter arrival and departure logs. As she opened the door, Tad saw that it was empty except for one new notebook. She took it, holding it reverently on a cloth that had been cut out of a Federation flag. She knelt again, laying the cloth and the notebook at Tad's feet. Then she opened the book and began to read.

"And on the first day, the Master did emerge from the tabernacle. And he did gaze out over his flock. He raised his mighty eyebrows. And he did say: 'What the hell is this? Is this some kind of joke? Come on. Knock it off.'

"And he did take his disciples, Klienman and Park, into the holy tabernacle. And there the Master did say..."

Tad raised a hand, stopping her. "Hold it. You have somebody following me around and writing down everything I say?"

"Your words must be preserved, Master. So that all of your followers may know your light and wisdom."

The next several pages of this "gospel," Tad realized, were going to be nothing but a string of profanity if he opened his mouth. He took several long, slow breaths to compose himself.

"And you're destroying the teleporter logs to make room for this?"

Trotta spat on the deck. "Damn the heresies, Master, for they are lies!"

"Lies!" Hendricks echoed.

"Stop," Tad said. "Stop doing that. I need to see the old records. As many of them as you still have."

Trotta and Hendricks shared a confused look. But they didn't disobey.

* * *

By sheer luck, the arrival logs from the last 72 hours were mostly intact. Apparently, they'd started burning the "heresies" at the other end of the cabinet first. According to the log, there were four ships that sent loads of laundry via the teleporter in the past two days. Two battle cruisers, a diplomatic mission, and a planetary survey. The last one was the likeliest candidate. He wrote down the name and hull number.

His personal tablet, in the meantime, had returned a single hit. It was an image and article from the University of Io's archives. The picture showed a bas-relief on a basalt obelisk, recovered from the Chizran Temple Complex on Kepler 186f. The bas-relief displayed a man on a throne, holding a small pointed object overhead. A carved halo extended from the tip.

The accompanying article, written by the head of Io U's Archeology Department, theorized that it was a representation of the mythical God Emperor. There wasn't much else of use, except for one small paragraph towards the end:

"*Among other mysteries of the Argakan Empire is one that has baffled both archeologists and sociologists alike: how did the ruling class maintain its power over an empire that spanned so many worlds? What method did they use to control a population of trillions, scattered across billions of light years? The mysterious point of light depicted on the Chizran Obelisk might be our only clue. Or, like the fabled God Emperor himself, it might prove to be another myth.*"

Tad, hands shaking, set the tablet reader down on the desk. He reached into one of the drawers for a heartburn chew. After thinking for a few seconds, he erased his browser history. The strange metal-crystal device was, he realized, the single most important archeological discovery in the history of the universe.

He had to find a way to get rid of it.

* * *

Culinary Technician 1st Class Morrison, still wearing his coffee filter hat and brandishing a scepter topped with a soup ladle, stood at the top of the ladder well. He gazed out over the assembled crowd below him. They, too, wore coffee-filter head coverings. But theirs were smaller.

"The will of the Master is not open to interpretations!" Morrison shouted. "The will of the Master is not for us to bend and shape for our convenience. The will of the Master is absolute. And it is laid out here, in his book."

"The Master is praised!" shouted one of the flock.

"The Master is praised!" answered the rest.

Morrison began reading from the notebook he held. The speech was similar to the one Tad had heard from the logbook in the teleporter room. Only there were several small, minor differences. And any mention of Chief Klienman was replaced, instead, with Morrison's own name.

Tad crept along behind the crowd. The faithful paid him no attention. Morrison was far too busy evangelizing. Tad moved quickly, careful to make as little noise as possible. He climbed up two levels, staying away from the station's main hub. Finally, he arrived at the communications deck. The crewmembers there behaved in much the same way everybody else did. They fell to their knees and shouted "Master!"

Tad nodded and waved. It seemed like the right thing to do. "I need to see if there's been any radio chatter about a ship." He fumbled for the slip of paper in his pocket. "The *Dauntless*. Hull number FLC-2241."

The young officer, who moments ago had been sitting at the radio set, shook his head. "We haven't heard anything, Master."

An imaginary alarm bell began to sound in the back of Tad's mind. "What do you mean 'anything?'"

An enlisted man raised his head and chimed in. "We've been busy broadcasting your truth to the rest of the space forces."

"You've been *what*?"

"We've been—"

"I heard you!" Tad paced nervously. This was bad. An army of criminal investigators, military police, and inspectors could be on their way right now.

"Let me see the automated message logs," Tad said.

The logs indicated several attempts at hailing, several demands to speak with the commanding officer, and several indications that an Admiral's Inspecting Authority would be en route.

Damn it. Tad's mind raced. He needed to find a way to put things in order fast.

"Where is Captain Park?"

* * *

"I'm so glad you agreed to speak with me, Master. I am honored and humbled by your divine light!"

With effort, Tad stopped pacing. His feet still wanted to move. This was a hare-brained plan at best. Even so, it was the best one he had. He faced the captain and adopted what he hoped was a posture of authority. "Yes, yes. Listen. I need you to do something very important. I need you to carry a message to my faithful."

The captain's eyes went misty and wide. For the first time since everything went crazy, he looked right at Tad. He looked, for lack of a better word, enraptured. "Me, Master? You want me to speak with them?"

"Yes. I'm declaring a new holiday. And I need you to tell them about it."

"What holiday, Master?"

Here goes nothing. "Admiral's Inspection Day."

The captain looked confused. "Master?"

"It's a very special day. You have to dress up to celebrate it. In the old uniforms, in fact. In exact, proper order."

The captain's face went white with horror. "You mean like in the before times?"

"Yes. *Exactly* like in the before times. Because Admiral's Inspection Day is, um...It's supposed to remind you all how terrible those times were, so you better appreciate the now times."

Tad laid out detailed instructions for Admiral's Inspection Day. He laid a copy of the Fleet Inspection Manual in front of the captain, declaring it to be another book of the gospel.

Captain Park bowed his head to the deck. "As you command, Master."

* * *

Tad stood in his quarters as he listened to the captain proclaim the tenets of his new holiday. It just might work, he thought. If everybody obeyed, and if everybody listened. They could scrub the work sections and the living areas again. They could get everybody's uniform squared away. They just had to make it long enough to pass the inspection, to fool the Admiral's people into believing that everything was ship-shape.

Then he could start sorting this mess out.

He toyed with the crystal as he listened to the captain drone on. If there wasn't a way to reverse it, what then? He could keep proclaiming holidays, he supposed. Or maybe he should move on to holy festivals. Those could stretch for several weeks, if he remembered his Sunday lessons right. Do that for another, what, twelve years until retirement? Then he could take a shuttle back home and just let the entire bunch of them keep spinning around the galaxy, arguing about which one of his used toothpicks was the holiest. Either way, they wouldn't be his problem anymore.

He fell asleep and dreamed that things got worse.

* * *

When Tad woke up the entire station was in the throes of a holy war. He didn't realize it until he was halfway to the mess deck for coffee and breakfast. It was there that two men, each wearing the coffee-filter hats of Morrison's breakaway sect, shouted at him from an open wardroom.

"Look! There's one! Look how he's dressed!"

Tad glanced down at his uniform, meticulously put together for the inspection he needed to bluff his way through. The two men surged to their feet brandishing long paring knives.

Before Tad could even run, three other people tackled him from behind.

* * *

The bubbling fryer in the galley stunk of meat, but Tad was pretty sure it wasn't the chicken nuggets. Tad dangled above it face-first, his feet tied to one of the ceiling pipes with loops of kitchen twine.

"Confess your heresy," Morrison said. "Renounce the Deceiver. Or face judgment in the fryers of eternal damnation."

Tad tried to swallow. It was hard to do upside down. "What are you talking about?"

"The false prophet Captain Park has attempted to declare a holy day in the Master's name, using profane and blasphemous writings. His followers are heretics. Their holy day is a sacrilege." He sneered at Tad's uniform. "Confess your sins against the Master. Renounce Park the Deceiver."

"But *I'm* the Master! I told him to declare a holiday!"

Morrison crossed his arms, laying the soup ladle-scepter over his shoulder. "Another false prophet," he proclaimed.

"No!"

Morrison nodded. Two men in execution hoods made of potato bags took hold of the kitchen twine, and began to lower Tad's face towards the fryer.

Just then there was an explosion that blew the door inward. Chief Klienman charged into the galley ahead of a dozen other men. His hair and eyebrows were bleached white. He carried a war hammer made from two steam irons and a broom handle. He wore armor made of old detergent bottles. The men behind him carried similar makeshift weapons, and wore similar makeshift armor.

"Forward, Templars!"

Morrison's men forgot about frying Tad's face. They took up kitchen implements and ran to meet the invaders, battling viciously to hold them off. As everyone else focused on killing each other, Tad frantically tried to wiggle his way out of the cooking-twine.

Through the chaos, someone called to him. "Master!"

Tad twisted around to see Trotta, the teleporter technician. She was dressed for battle. She quickly knelt and touched her forehead to the butt of her weapon, which appeared to be a pair of nunchakus made of empty starch cans.

"I'm here to rescue you, Master."

Tad glanced over her shoulder. The bloody fray was getting closer. "Well, hurry up then!"

Trotta got to work on the twine knots, supporting Tad's weight on her shoulder. As she worked, he realized she was humming under her breath.

"Are you *singing?*"

"I'm composing a hymn, Master. This glorious battle needs to be in your gospel!"

Tad watched in horror as Chief Klienman beat Morrison to death with his battle hammer. Just a few feet away, two of the Templars pushed one of Morrison's men into another of the large fryers.

"Sing about it later! Just get me down!"

* * *

Tad was carried, under armed escort, back to the tabernacle. Once he was deposited inside, Chief Klienman took a knee.

"You'll need to stay here for your safety, Master. It's far too dangerous to allow you to wander the station. At least until the heretics are rooted out."

"But..." Tad stammered, trying to think of what to say. *"But I'm God!"*

"Yes, Master. God in the flesh. And we cannot allow the heathens to harm you. It's safest for you here. An acolyte will be outside at all times to tend your needs. As will two of my Templars, to guard your most holy person."

With another curt bow, Chief Klienman was gone.

Tad's mind raced. The admiral's inspectors could be here at any time, and he was rapidly running out of options.

He glanced at the contraband on his desk. The ID cards alone would be enough to get him fourteen years in prison. Maybe he could convince one of Klienman's men to airlock them? No. With his luck, they'd probably enshrine each and every one of them, right next to a painting of Tad's face.

Somehow, he needed to escape before the inspectors arrived.

The station's proximity alarm sounded. A voice boomed over the P.A. system. "Attention, Laundry and Sanitation Support Station Three. This is the Admiral's Inspecting Authority. Repeated attempts to hail this station have failed. Prepare to be boarded. All officers and senior enlisted, you are ordered to report to the shuttle bay and stand by. That is all."

Well, this is it, then.

Seconds went by. Then another proximity alarm sounded. Another voice boomed over the station's P.A. system. But something was off about this one. It wasn't precise or military sounding, like the inspector's. It was more fanatical.

"This is the Federation Space Cruiser *Dauntless*. You have stolen a relic of our holy Master, her divine grace Lieutenant Robeson. Return it, or face extermination at the hands of the true faithful. The Master is praised!"

* * *

Explosions and blazer fire echoed through the station from the shuttle deck. Tad worked feverishly, slicing his uniform into ribbons and tying them into a reasonable facsimile of the robes the rest of the crew had created. He gathered as much of the stolen contraband as he could in two armfuls. Then he opened the hatch. He expected to find two of Klienman's Templars. Instead he found Klienman himself.

"Master! It's far too dangerous! You need to stay in the tabernacle."

Balancing the goods in one arm, Tad laid a hand on Klienman's shoulder. In his softest, saintliest voice, he said, "The tabernacle is not safe, my son. Soon it will fall to the unbelievers."

Klienman nodded gravely. "Then we will die to ensure they take it at a heavy price."

"No, my son. I have seen a different path for you." Tad gave Klienman his instructions.

The chief's eyes went wide. "Master! Are you sure?"

"Yes, my son. Gather your Templars. It is time for me to ascend."

* * *

Tad stood at the teleporter deck, nearly ready to faint. This was, by far, the longest chance he could have bet on. Behind him, Klienman stood bloody. A handful of his Templars stood with him, weapons in hand, ready to defend the teleporter to the death. Further up the passageway, Tad could hear shouting, blazer fire, and screams.

Teleporter Tech Trotta powered the machine up. Once the macro-converter levels all read green, she typed in the coordinates Tad had told her.

One in five hundred, he kept telling himself. *One in five hundred people survive a teleporter trip.*

"Master!" Trotta cried. She threw herself at Tad's feet, clutching at his legs. "Take me with you! Let me ascend!"

Tad felt his patience wearing thin. With some effort, he kept his voice even. "You are not ready, child. I'm sorry."

"But I have written your gospels and composed your hymns! Who would be more worthy than I?"

Tad shook her off. "Perhaps someday, child. But not now." With that, he threw his armful of goods into the teleporter. They sizzled and snapped as the machine disintegrated them and beamed their molecular blueprints to the receiver station.

Tad took a moment. This could be it, his last breath. He thought he should say something profound.

"Let go of my foot, Trotta."

He stepped into the teleporter then. He felt his hair stand on end, and he felt the fabric of his makeshift robes begin to unspin itself. Then he felt the same begin to happen to his flesh. He heard a sizzling, snapping sound.

He barely had time to scream as Trotta threw herself into the teleporter with him.

* * *

The newsnets on Tau-Ceti wouldn't stop talking about that rogue Federation cruiser. Some weird extremist group, they said. Destroyed a laundry station and an Admiral's Inspection party before going AWOL. It had been spotted in the weeks since, hailing and attacking other support stations. Attempts to bring it to justice so far had failed.

Trotta snorted. "The only justice those nonbelievers deserve is death."

"Quiet," Tad said.

"Of course, Master. My apologies."

Tad did his best to enjoy the rest of his coffee in peace. But Trotta's comments had, as usual, soured his mood. With a resigned sigh he gave up. He glanced into the mirror behind the diner's counter. He watched his own surly, sour expression. Next to it—on a second head growing out of Tad's shoulder—Trotta beamed her usual zealous grin.

Who the hell ever said two heads are better than one?

"Master, can we stop and pray after breakfast? I've composed a new hymn to commemorate your ascension."

Tad sighed. "Fine. Just let me hit the bathroom first."

PANDORA
C. S. Friedman

On Monday 213, McKellan's appendix burst. Until that moment I hadn't even known he had an appendix, and I must shamefully admit that I was so surprised I wasn't much help. After the others carried him off to the med lab and adjusted the ship's outer spin for surgery-friendly gravity, I checked the regulations in our archives. I discovered that while it wasn't strictly *required* for crew members to have their appendixes removed before launch—as it was for tonsils, and several other bits of vestigial flesh that had a reputation for causing issues—it was strongly encouraged. Logic certainly suggested that if you were going to spend eleven years in space with limited medical facilities, you might want to get rid of everything that could cause you trouble along the way, right? But some people didn't like the thought of being carved clean by science, like a steak being stripped of its gristle, even if it was the rational thing to do.

Go figure.

The surgery itself wasn't a big deal—roboticized laparoscopy—but Captain Basinger gave him a dressing-down afterwards that probably hurt like hell. She was spending her most fertile years in space with her tubes tied, she reminded him, and if she could give up the very core of her fecundity and womanhood for the sake of our mission, he should damn well be willing to remove an organ that had passed its evolutionary expiration date. And with that for a eulogy, McKellan's appendix went the way of all other biological material on the *Ponce de Leon*, cleansed and sterilized and broken down to its base components so it could serve as raw material for fuel, clothing, or breakfast bars. Waste not, want not.

Later I asked McKellan why he had made the choice he did, back on Earth, and he told me that at the time he had believed the human body was a sacred thing, and you shouldn't remove any parts of it unless you absolutely had to. That *really* surprised me. The traditional qualifiers for a Bellasi mission were a list of minimalisms: low sex drive, low political passion, low religious commitment...low anything that might cause human conflict when you were sealed in a tin can with seven other people for the better part of eleven years. I did a two year mission once, and trust me, the smallest interpersonal tensions could evolve into raging emotional firestorms when you were stuck sharing quarters with the source for that long. Hence the reason the folks on the first Mars expedition needed so much therapy after they came home, one of them later committing suicide. If McKellan had told our vetting officers that religious beliefs prevented him from agreeing to a basic safety precaution, he'd have been dropped from the mission faster than a head of iceberg lettuce in a donut shop.

But that was water under the bridge now. Soon the captain's ire would be water under the bridge as well. You only had two choices on a mission like ours: learn to let go of things or go crazy. Thus far, no one had chosen to go crazy.

McKellan was an atheist now. Which was not as odd as it might sound. Out here in the vast emptiness of interstellar space, cut off from the planet that was humanity's spiritual center, some men found God. Others lost sight of Him.

It was all in the handbook.

* * *

Ten thousand years ago the human race was huddling for warmth on an ice-sheathed planet, fashioning crude knives and arrows from chips of stone, wondering where all the nice meaty mammoths had gone.

Ten thousand years ago an alien race was colonizing the far reaches of the galaxy, harvesting energy from the stars, living in harmony with nature and with themselves. They had no poverty. They had no war. They had evolved past the need for societal suffering, and they spread across the galaxy peacefully, optimistically, establishing cities that were sleek, clean, and self-maintaining. If they happened across a planet that was already inhabited by intelligent beings, they didn't try to colonize it, or steal its resources, or interfere with it in any way. They just left it alone to decide its own fate, and if and when it reached the stars, the aliens welcomed it as an equal, sharing the knowledge that would allow it to rise above its own primitive origins and become part of the galactic community.

We named them the Bellasi because we didn't know what they called themselves. It seemed appropriate: *The Beautiful Ones.*

Five thousand years ago, humankind raised pyramids on the shores of the Nile, built storehouses of grain to guard against famine, and learned how to write, forge metal, and brew beer. Millenia would pass before the first men would break free of Earth's grip and travel to the stars, but already they were mapping the heavens, paving the way. Meanwhile there were wars to fight, wealth to hoard, people to oppress, territory to conquer. Traditional human pastimes.

Five thousand years ago, the Bellasi vanished. Their gleaming cities were left empty on a thousand worlds, inhabitants gone without a trace. All that the Beautiful Ones had accomplished—all that they had dreamed of—disappeared into the galactic darkness without a ripple. And the many races that had gathered beneath their banner followed them into oblivion. As they had shared in the Bellasi's prosperity, so they shared in their fate. All gone.

No one knew why.

* * *

I was eight years old when our scouts returned home with news of an alien city they had discovered. Our school held a grand assembly to celebrate the event, twelve hundred students crowded into a humid auditorium to watch the 3-D images as they streamed in: the first alien civilization ever discovered. How sleek their buildings seemed, how graceful, how eerily empty! Even as children we could sense the wrongness of it, and we yearned for something to explain that emptiness. Half-eaten food on a table, maybe. Clothing strewn across the floor, because someone had packed in haste before fleeing the galaxy. Even bodies struck down by a rogue bacteria, War-of-the-Worlds style. Anything that we could comprehend. But the aliens had left their city in perfect order, with no sign of foul play. The ultimate mystery.

More and more cities were discovered after that, always empty. Sometimes we found images of the Bellasi themselves, featured in relief carvings that revealed their history. From these we learned that they had welcomed other species into the galactic community by sharing the knowledge that allowed them to transcend their primitive instincts. This was first done on the Bellasi homeworld, later on their colony planets, in ritual chambers designed for that purpose. We learned that they had developed technology that could transfer knowledge directly from one mind to another; later we found a few recorded messages that were still active, so we could experience how it worked. And we found images of a box-shaped object covered in strange designs, which supposedly contained the device the Bellasi used to share the secret of their enlightenment with other species. The device itself was never depicted.

Some called it a delusion, a Bellasi legend. Others called it a God Box. Scientists called it a Neurological Transfer Interface and they wrote long and elegant papers speculating about its nature. Perhaps it would reveal a secret technology to make clean, low-cost energy universally available. Or a method of conditioning that could channel a species' violent and primitive urges into a more constructive mode. Or a religious revelation so profound that it altered the very nature of the soul.

Some called it the Holy Grail.

Our job was to find it.

* * *

"It's out there," Vince Caswell muttered for the fiftieth time that day. "I know it's out there!"

He had his charts displayed on every screen of the control room, preempting our normal visuals. To me they looked like the scribblings of a deranged child, but he kept insisting they were starcharts, so okay, call them starcharts. To be fair, his calculations had helped us locate more than a dozen Bellasi worlds, so it was hard to argue about his methods. Then again, the Bellasi had colonized every human-inhabitable planet in this part of the galaxy, so their cities weren't exactly hard to find.

He claimed to have an algorithm that could lead us to the Bellasi homeworld, provided we collected enough data to run it. Our mission was to visit colony after colony, so he could take measurements and shoot pictures and scrape paint samples from buildings, or whatever he needed to feed the monstrous appetite of that algorithm. In theory he was examining subtle trends in Bellasi architecture so that he could extrapolate backwards to their source, but since all Bellasi cities looked the same to me, I was more than a little skeptical. Then again, what did I know about groundbreaking anthropological algorithms? I was just the guy who fixed solar collectors and fine-tuned the waste management system. Handyman in space.

"You see?" he said excitedly, pointing to one of the displays. "There! There! That's where the proportional shift started. I knew I would find it!"

Of course I didn't see it. In the same way that there were wavelengths of light that your average human being couldn't detect, there were aspects of Vince's genius that were invisible to the rest of us. In truth, I would have been happy to do my job and leave him alone to do his, but he needed everyone to be as excited about his work as he was, so he kept trying to explain it to us. Over and over and over again. And yeah, sometimes we pretended that we understood more than we did. It made him feel appreciated, and it cut down on the number of repetitions. Win-win.

"We need to go here next," he said, and he pointed to a region of space that was far, far away from our current location. I sighed. Transportation was something I understood. Inspecting the jump engines so that we didn't wind up stranded between *here* and *there* while the space-time continuum convulsed around us I also understood. That didn't mean I liked it.

* * *

Yes, I understand why jumpsleep is necessary. When you fold space-time into infinite layers and shove a ship through the middle of them, the human mind just doesn't deal with that well. Even rats go bonkers afterwards, running in circles and chewing their own tails off. And real sleep isn't good enough to protect you. The parts of your brain that handle reason and impulse control have to be shut down completely if they're going to survive the journey. Which means you have to submit to an artificial coma: induced, controlled, and ultimately terminated by machines whose priority is your survival, not your comfort.

The problem is that it's not a natural sleep, but a soul-sucking, viscous unconsciousness akin to death. You panic instinctively as you sense it approach, but your motor control centers have been shut down for the duration, so you can't move at all. Which causes you to panic even more, of course. And as the thick, suffocating blackness closes in around you, you imagine you can feel your brain dissolving cell by cell, your consciousness erased thought by thought, your soul obliterated from reality.

Someday they'll come up with a tranquilizer that's compatible with the process. Probably after I've retired.

* * *

The first time I set foot on a Bellasi world I was only twenty-three. I'll never forget the moment the lander hatch opened and I stepped out into the heart of that glorious, star-shaped city. Granted, the buildings weren't quite as sleek as I had expected them to be. Solar-powered bots kept the streets clean and repaired any major damage, but they could not erase the feeling of age that clung to everything. But still. I was standing in the middle of an *alien city*. How cool was that?

Because it was my first Bellasi experience, the crew let me wander around a bit and explore. I found apartments the Bellasi had lived in, and everything inside them was neatly arranged, as if the owners might return at any moment. Had there been bodies here once, that the ubiquitous cleaning bots had cleared away? Or had it always looked like this? I found a garden of glittering solar collectors whose panels shifted to follow the sunlight; when a cloud cast a shadow over them they rippled like a field of agitated butterflies. Eerie and beautiful.

Eventually we headed to the center of the city to find the Bellasi welcoming chamber. It was a vast, domed space, much bigger than I'd expected; ten thousand people could have gathered in it without feeling crowded. In the center was a circle of stone statues, some depicting Bellasi, others alien species. They all faced the center of the circle, where a pedestal stood. According to the historical murals, the artifact we sought should be sitting on top of that.

But it wasn't.

I visited dozens of Bellasi worlds after that. Each star shaped city looked the same. Each had a ritual chamber at its center. A circle of statues was always present, though the alien species that were depicted might vary.

The pedestal was always empty.

* * *

"Hey, Mike, there's something you need to see."

I looked up from the air filtration panel I was trying to repair and saw Kristen Belle, our med tech. "Bit busy at the moment."

"No, you're not." She took the panel out of my hand and put it aside. "Trust me."

I tried to get her to tell me what was up, but she just smiled enigmatically and gestured for me to follow her. Since it was clearly the only way I was going to get any answers, I did so.

Everyone else was already in the control room when we arrived, staring at something on the main screen. A couple of people nodded a greeting as we entered, but no one turned to look at us. It was as if their eyes were glued to the screen. My heart skipped a beat as I joined them. I was trying not to jump to any conclusions, but this far out in the galaxy, how many things were there to stare at?

On the screen was a planet, displayed in several magnifications. A global view was in the upper left corner, and at first glance I thought it was another Bellasi colony. The typical star-shaped city peeked between cloud banks, immense enough to be visible from space. That was pretty normal.

But the arms of the star weren't perfectly even, and one of them wasn't even straight. That was odd. The Bellasi loved regularity.

Then I looked at the close-up views, and I understood why.

Every inch of the planet had been developed, but without any sense of a master plan. I saw primitive construction in some places—brick and mortar, concrete and glass—and high-tech synthetics in others. Even the star city had a sense of chaos about it, different parts constructed out of different materials, in different styles. That wasn't what a Bellasi colony city should look like, I thought. But it was what a planet might look like if a species had evolved there, each new generation layering its construction over what had been built before.

"Welcome to the Bellasi homeworld," Caswell announced.

"Holy shit," I whispered.

We'd found it. We'd really found it. I stared at the screen in disbelief, half expecting the planet to disappear when I blinked. But it didn't. Caswell's damned algorithm had worked! And if his other theories were equally valid, then the Bellasi Interface must be down there somewhere. Earth's salvation was at hand, and we were the ones who would deliver it.

To say that we were jubilant would be an understatement. Basinger broke out her private store of 30-year-old scotch and we laughed and we drank and danced and some of us even cried, intoxicated by an elation as complex as it was intense. We were crusaders entering Jerusalem, Columbus sighting land, soldiers raising the flag on Iwo Jima, marathon runners crossing the finish line with arms raised, the blood-red ribbon cutting across our chests as a thousand spectators screamed our names. We were all the dreams of Earth. We were all the hungers of mankind. Manifest. Satisfied. Transcended.

Thus do gods celebrate.

* * *

As we approached the Bellasi homeworld, we sent out messages. We filled the darkness of space with our humble attempts at saying hello, and then waited breathlessly for a response. Any kind of response. Because if there was a single Bellasi left alive in the galaxy, surely this was where he would be.

But there was only silence.

On Sunday 217, we established orbit around the planet and we took two landers down to the center of the star-shaped city. That was where the ritual chamber had been located on all the colony planets, so we figured it would be there on this planet as well. But it wasn't. We searched in expanding circles from the central point, inspecting the nearest buildings room by room, looking for any clue as to where a facility like that might be located.

We found nothing.

All of us were suffering from frayed nerves at that point. To come this close to realizing Earth's greatest dream and not be able to close the deal was frustrating for all of us, but for Caswell it was infuriating. He rushed from building to building like a man possessed, and each time his search came up empty he would curse the planet, or the Bellasi, or even God, like this was some kind of personal affront. It wasn't helping my state of mind, so when Basinger asked for a volunteer to take a lander up and get a bird's-eye view of the city, I jumped at the chance.

Peace at last.

But no matter how long I stared at the city from overhead, I couldn't find any clue to help direct us in our search. Wherever the ritual chamber was—if it was on this planet at all—it was well hidden. Finally, with a sigh, I reported my findings to Captain Basinger. I could hear the frustration in her voice as she thanked me for trying, and somewhere in the background Caswell started cursing. I didn't feel up to dealing with him, so I asked if I could stay up a bit longer.

Staring down at the city—sensing the vastness of the planet beyond it—I suddenly wondered if our search had been doomed from the start. What if we were looking in the wrong place? Yes, this star city looked like all the others, but in fact it was nothing like them. The others had been planned out completely before the first shovel full of dirt was moved; nothing was left to chance. This city had grown organically, possibly over the course of centuries. And while it might be the biggest and most dramatic city on the planet, visible from space, that didn't mean it was the most significant location to the Bellasi.

So what kind of place would be?

I asked if I could take the lander out further, to explore the surrounding terrain. Just a hunch, I told Captain Basinger. Since no one had any better ideas, she said yes.

And so I left the star-shaped city behind. Maybe I would be able to find the Holy Grail on my own, maybe not. But the peace of my solitary flight was soothing, and I wasn't ready to give it up just yet.

* * *

I flew low over the main continent, across a narrow sea, past a few volcanic islands, to the second largest land mass. As I did so, images from the planet's surface scrolled across my screen. I saw gleaming metropoli surrounded by simpler towns, and ancient monuments whose original purpose had probably been forgotten long before the Bellasi discovered space travel. It made the aliens seem more human to me. No longer were they cartoon caricatures of peace and perfection, but flawed beings who had evolved from primitive roots just like we did, each generation building upon the ruins of the last.

Where would such a species choose to house their most precious artifact? On the colony planets the Bellasi had no choice about the matter: everything in the star-shaped cities was equally new, equally planned, and no one location had any more cultural significance than any other. But here, in a world that was rich with historical resonance, there might be better options. Maybe the Bellasi would want a setting with sacred overtones, something linked to the founding of their civilization.

I had the lander's computer scan all available data, searching for locations that might fit the bill. Alas, there were too many to count, and without better knowledge of Bellasi history, I had no way to narrow the options down. I tapped an agitated finger on the control panel as I tried to come up with some detail that would distinguish my target site from all the others, some single feature that would tell me which location the Bellasi had favored…

And then it hit me.

Trembling with excitement, I had the computer identify any site that had multiple launch facilities nearby. Because if the Bellasi transfer ritual was performed here, surely visitors from other worlds would want to attend. There would be hordes of them, all arriving at the same time, all needing places to land and store their spacecraft, places to eat and rest and entertain themselves in their spare time, as well as easy transportation to and from the ritual site. In the great star cities, arrangements like that were common; those vast metropoli had been built to accommodate interplanetary activity. But an older site would not have had those conveniences. Its location would have been chosen for historical resonance, not architectural convenience, and the launch pads would have to be built wherever space could be found, perhaps linked to the ritual location by roads that twisted through ancient villages. High tech and ancient history intermingled, in that wonderful, uncomfortable way that Earth was so familiar with.

How many sites like that could there be?

The computer found three. One was in a sandstone desert, a meteor strike pit with twisted, wind-carved monuments arranged around the rim. Since there was no building nearby large enough to accommodate the crowds that would attend the transfer ritual, I ruled that one out. The second was an island with a forest of primitive statues, connected to other islands by a spider's web of roads. Again, I saw no place where a great number of people could gather, so, two down. The third was an ancient columned temple, like the Parthenon in style but ten times larger, atop a windswept hill. The roads leading out from it had a vaguely star-shaped plan, as if the Bellasi had tried to apply the same template they used in their colonies, but the terrain had prevented them from doing so perfectly. At the end of each road was a launch facility surrounded by modern buildings. Enough to house thousands.

My heart began to pound as pictures of the place scrolled before me. *This is it,* I thought. *I've found it.* Trembling, I reached for the comm switch to call Captain Basinger and the others; surely it was my duty to let them share in this amazing moment! But what if I was wrong? Having them fly two hours to get here, their hearts filled with hope, only to face another disappointment, wasn't going to improve the spirit of the mission. I owed it to them to at least do a basic recon, and confirm that the site was worth investigating further.

I ordered the lander to set me down just outside the temple building. The air when I disembarked was hot and dry, and for a moment I just stood there, breathing it in, trying to steel my nerves for what might turn out to be the galaxy's greatest disappointment. Then I started walking through the field of dry scrub that surrounded the building. From the condition of the place I guessed there were no maintenance bots active, though I did find the rusted remnants of one. The building's façade was pitted and cracked and there were places where whole sections had come loose, so that the ground was littered with debris. I picked my way over some sharp gravel to get to what remained of the door, two stubs of rotted wood hanging loosely from verdigris hinges. Beyond them was a chamber that was cavernous, dark, and still. The place had an eerie quality to it, like it wasn't so much *empty* as *waiting.* I turned on my shoulder lamp as I entered, looking warily around me for signs of lurking wildlife; the place would be a perfect lair for some large animal. But nothing was moving. Nothing made a sound. Nothing was visible near the door except a scattering of leaves that the wind had blown in.

Then my light crossed the center of the room and my heart stopped.

Time stopped.

It was there. The same circle of statues we had seen on a dozen other worlds. Only this time all of the figures were Bellasi, and they were carved from a translucent white stone that glowed when my light hit it, giving them the aspect of angels. In the center of the circle was the same kind of pedestal we had seen on so many worlds, only this time it wasn't bare. This time there was something on top of it, a bronze colored box with alien hieroglyphics all over it. Could this really be the item Earth had sought for so long? Was I really going to go down in history as the man who found it?

My heart began to pound wildly as I walked towards it. There were strips of gold wrapped around the box, like ribbons on a Christmas present, and they were fastened at the top with a faceted glass ball that I recognized as a message conveyer. My throat was so dry I could barely swallow. How long had it been since anyone had been here? When had the last Bellasi died, leaving their most precious artifact unattended? I'd never been much on religion, but it was hard to believe I would be facing this moment if someone or something hadn't guided me here.

Call the others. The thought seemed distant, unreal. I was in a world of my own now, and my hand moved toward the crystal as if of its own accord. How could you look at such a thing and not want to touch it? *There's nothing to be afraid of,* I told myself. *The crystal is just a message carrier. The thing that has the power to change worlds is inside that box.*

My fingers made contact with the crystal. It was colder than the room at first, but warmed to a fiery heat as my touch activated it.

I saw the Bellasi.

There were dozens of them in the chamber, skin tone ranging from bleached marble to polished ebony. I saw adult males and females in equal number—no children—and they were closing in on the box with crude weapons in hand: heavy axes, massive wooden clubs, the kinds of tools one would normally not associate with a high-tech empire. Then a tall male stepped in front of the artifact, protecting it with his body as he tried to get them to back away. As he gestured around the room, I saw the shattered remnants of similar boxes littering the floor, and I understood that this was the last one of its kind.

Finally he got the mob to back off. He sighed deeply, then placed a crystal upon the box: the same one I was now touching. This message was from him.

A quick succession of visions unfolded in my mind. I saw the Bellasi as they had been eons earlier, when their homeworld still teemed with life: a creative, passionate, restless people. I saw magnificent art being produced, paintings crafted in colors I couldn't name, alien symphonies so beautiful that they would have made Beethoven weep. I watched as new generations were born, each child striving to surpass their parents. And I sensed in them the same hunger that had driven my species to explore the stars, and I knew that despite their alien appearance, they were human in every way that mattered.

The visions started to come more quickly after that. I saw the Bellasi empire at its peak, star-shaped cities gleaming in the interstellar darkness, spaceships dancing around them like drunken moths. There were other sentient species, some of them human in form and others so alien I couldn't tell which end was which, all living in harmony with each other. No one seemed to have greater duty than to seek his own vision of happiness, for the gross physical requirements of life were all managed by machines, and the great cities were self-sustaining. It was everything Earth dreamed of, and more.

Yet it all seemed wrong to me. I didn't know why. I kept staring at the images, wondering what it was about them that made my skin crawl, what *wrongness* I sensed in them, just below the level of conscious awareness, that made me so terribly afraid.

And then I realized what it was.

The children were gone.

There had been many in the beginning, I was sure of that. I remembered seeing large families in the parks, gathering beneath the glittering solar-collection trees to laugh and play. But there were fewer and fewer children as the visions progressed, each generation becoming smaller than the last...and now this. When had the point of no return been reached? Had some Bellasi seen the end coming, and tried to convince the inhabitants of Paradise that devoting years to nurturing and training and disciplining a child would be more appealing than a life of easy contentment? If so, the effort had failed. The Bellasi had created a world in which challenges were not viewed as a source of inspiration, but as hardships to be eradicated. And what greater challenge was there than to bring a new life into the world? Now, in this glittering galactic empire, there were no children at all, even among the alien species. I was looking at the last generation of Bellasi, the ones who left behind empty cities for us to find.

The final vision faded, and I saw the male Bellasi again. This time he seemed to be looking directly at me, and though I knew that it was only a vision, and the being who had crafted it was not actually present, the effect was unnerving. *Now you know.* He was speaking in a language I didn't understand, but the Bellasi technology allowed me to grasp his meaning.

You must choose your own course. A terrible sadness filled his eyes. *I am sorry.*

The vision disappeared.

I stood there in shock, trying to make sense of what I had just seen. Had Bellasi life truly become so effortless that the labor and sacrifice necessary to raise a child were deemed too great a burden? Or was the reason for their demise more primal than that? Was the struggle for survival so hard-wired into Bellasi genes that once it was gone there was nothing left to drive them? I remembered the magnificent art of their early period, and compared it to the bland, sterile cities in my later visions. It was not only the children that had disappeared, I realized. Without challenges to meet, without obstacles to overcome, the spirit of their race had been wasting away for centuries. And all the species that had joined them in Paradise, embracing the dream of easy prosperity, had followed them into oblivion. Killed by contentment.

In the end, the Bellasi had recognized their mistake; that was the meaning of my first vision. They had started to destroy all copies of the Interface, to keep other species from suffering their fate. But the guiding philosophy of their civilization prohibited them from dictating to other species what it must do, and so they had left one intact, perhaps as a sign of respect for our autonomy. Or perhaps as a test.

You must choose your own course, the Bellasi had said.

I was shivering now, and not just from physical cold. The burden of destiny that had fallen upon the *Ponce de Leon*'s crew seemed greater than any human company could bear. Because if we came home with the Interface, there was no question what would happen. Philosophers might argue about the wisdom of embracing Bellasi technology, but in the end someone would activate the thing. No one would dare forbid it. The eight of us must decide, right here and right now, if we were willing to deliver to Earth the seeds of its own destruction.

No, I thought suddenly. *Not the eight of us.*

Caswell would never agree to keep our discovery a secret; too much of his ego was invested in this mission. And I didn't think Captain Basinger would go for it, either. She had sacrificed too much to come out here, and returning home without the artifact would make it all meaningless.

If I brought the artifact back to the ship, it would be delivered to Earth. And if it was delivered to Earth, it would be activated.

The choice was mine to make, and mine alone.

My legs started shaking so badly I feared they wouldn't support me. I lowered myself to my knees before the pedestal, while the stone angels looked on in silence. I wasn't the one who should be deciding this. No single person should have the fate of his entire people placed upon his shoulders, least of all someone who was trained to fix broken waste disposal units, not solve existential dilemmas.

In my mind's eye I saw all the miseries of Earth spread out before me. Poverty and war, hunger and injustice, an endless tide of suffering that man had struggled against for all his existence. The Bellasi Interface could fix all that. If I denied Earth access to their knowledge, then all future suffering would be on my head. Millions upon millions of people, down through the ages, suffering because of me.

But if I delivered the Interface, what then? Mankind might enjoy unparalleled peace and prosperity, but for how long? A thousand years, ten thousand? In my mind's eye I saw the millions of people who would never be born if the Bellasi Interface was activated. Countless human lives that might have been filled with art and beauty and passion and hope, as well as pain, that now would never exist. Because of me.

"Don't make me choose," I whispered. But who was I pleading with— the same God who had brought me here? If He existed, then He was a merciless bastard.

My comm buzzed. It was Captain Basinger, wanting a report on my progress. Numbly I told her I was about to head back to base camp, and I would give her a full report when I arrived. That left me about two hours to decide which course of action was the right one. But deep in my heart I knew that both were right, and neither was right, and whichever one I chose would leave me haunted by ghosts forever.

I thought about the Bellasi colonies we'd visited: serene, but oh so sterile. Long before the Bellasi died out they had lost the spark that earned them the stars in the first place. Was that what would happen to humanity as well? Would the price of Bellasi contentment be the loss of all that made us human? That was a kind of death, wasn't it?

Slowly I rose to my feet, walked to the pedestal, and stared at the Interface. Then I reached out and picked it up. It was surprisingly light, for something so weighty in significance. I brought it back to my lander and put it on the seat beside me. Trying not to look at it. Trying not to feel.

Sometimes it's not a question of what the right choice is, so much as what choice we think we can live with.

* * *

Maybe I should have thrown it into a volcano, Frodo-style, so that it was destroyed forever. Maybe the deep sea crevasse that I dropped it into won't be enough to guard it from those who, if they learned it was there, would empty the oceans of this world with a teaspoon if they had to, to retrieve it.

People will keep looking for it, of course. Caswell has already come up with a theory about why the Bellasi homeworld was never the right location for our search, and he's fine-tuning his algorithms so we'll know where to look next. No one's questioning him about it. We all understand how important it is for people to believe that the Interface is still out there somewhere, a magical solution to all of our ills, just over the next horizon. Even if we told people it didn't exist, no one would believe us. And so we keep searching.

Maybe an ancient knight did find the Holy Grail one day. Maybe he held it in his hand, awed by its holiness, and then God sent him a vision of what human society would become if he brought it home. And he wound up leaving it behind. Or hiding it away. Or even destroying it. Because he realized that sometimes *wanting* a thing is more important than *having* it.

I named the planet Pandora. The others argued in favor of names they liked better, but we had agreed long ago that we would take turns naming the planets we found, and this time, by chance, the choice fell to me. So Pandora it was.

On Sunday 219, we go back into jumpsleep. Black, dreamless, obliterating.

I'm looking forward to it.

ROUND AND ROUND WE RIDE THE CAROUSEL OF TIME
Seanan McGuire

The light over the airlock glowed a steady red. Innocuous as it seemed, the air on this planet would spell a swift and certain death to any human foolish enough to take a breath. Gwen stood looking at the light, how red it was, how bright, how very *human*.

"When did red become the color of 'don't do that'?" she mused aloud. The ship's A.I., long since programmed to ignore her rhetorical questions, did not reply. Gwen continued looking at the light. Red was for sunsets, for apples, for lipstick. Red was a beautiful thing. There was no reason for it to carry the connotations that it did.

The sound of footsteps in the hall alerted her to the approach of a crewmate. She turned in time to see Heather come around the corner, tugging her suit into place. The other woman was taller, broader at the hips and shoulders, and constantly complained about how the standard-issue environment suits had been designed for men first, making it difficult for any woman over a size eight to fit into them without substantial alterations. Gwen, whose own suit had been custom-made by the university sponsoring her presence on the trip, generally stayed quiet and let Heather run herself down. It was easier than trying to join the discussion, which was more of a monologue intended to be performed for anyone who would listen.

Heather looked up from her suit. "Gwen," she said, with evident surprise. "We're not heading out for another ten minutes."

"I know," said Gwen. "I wanted to be here when we did."

"You don't have to—"

"Yes, I do." Gwen's words were firm, implacable: she left no room for argument.

Heather blinked, seemingly taken aback. In the six months since they'd left Earth, she had never seen Gwen assert herself more than absolutely necessary. She'd been starting to think that the university geek didn't have any spine at all. "You're really serious about this, aren't you?"

Gwen looked at her steadily. "I am an archeologist. I am on this ship—this cramped, confined, crowded ship—because I am an archeologist. Because the university that helped to fund this voyage wanted me here, to be sure that what may be the greatest archeological discovery in over three hundred years is not accidentally damaged or disturbed before it can be fully cataloged."

"We wouldn't do that."

"You *have* done that. You, and others like you. The last three extraterrestrial relic sites have all been disturbed by spacers who found them, before the science teams could arrive." Without a full and accurate record of what those sites had originally looked like, there was no way of knowing whether pieces had been removed, damaged, destroyed—or even just moved out of the position they'd been in when they were found. Given the number of "authentic artifacts from Charon" to have shown up on the black market, the general assumption within the antiquities community was that a huge number of priceless archeological finds had disappeared before they could be cataloged. It had to stop.

That was why, when the probes had reported what looked like artificial structures on Alpha Centauri Bb, every university in the solar system had started shouting, demanding that they be allowed to fund a mission to investigate the site before it could be disturbed. Earth's government had insisted that the trip be primarily crewed by trained astronauts and engineers, but the University of Washington—last and oldest of the West Coast schools—had managed, along with Oxford College, to put up enough of the funding to insert one of their own people onboard. Gwendolyn Wallace, PhD, with doctorates in archeology, anthropology, and xenocultural studies, a field that had been, thus far, almost entirely in the abstract. Now, six months and millions of miles later, here she was, and the planet was only feet away, and the light on the airlock was red.

This was not their home. This would never be their home. Gwen knew that, and she was afraid, even as her growing excitement made it harder and harder to hold her ground, to stop herself from reaching for the airlock door and stepping through, ready for the decompression cycle to begin.

"You know it might be nothing," said Heather. Her tone was casual. Her posture was anything but. She gave her suit one last tug into position, watching Gwen sidelong. "Sometimes things look like structures from above, and then we get here and find that they were just optical illusions. Rocks and things that aren't trees but might as well be, creating cascades of shapes and shadows that trick the human eye."

"I saw the pictures myself," said Gwen. "There were arches. Balustrades. *Windows*. That's not a trick of the light. That's a structure, something intentionally built, and I'm going to be the one who documents it. I'm going to be the one who records it for posterity."

"Guess you've got some passion in you after all," said Heather.

Gwen fixed her with a level look. "Anyone who thinks academics are dispassionate has never spent any time with us when we're in our element. Let me get to that site, and I'll show you passion."

"You're about to get your wish," said Heather. "Look." She gestured to the panel above the airlock. Gwen turned, barely daring to breathe.

The red light was now flanked by two blue ones. The airlock was ready for human use.

They were going outside.

* * *

Alpha Centauri Bb was the closest Earth-like planet outside humanity's home solar system. Ironically, that very closeness saw it overlooked for decades. When long-range space travel became possible, it was the gas giants and the dense, mineral-rich planets with no atmosphere to speak of that initially attracted investors. They traveled past the Alpha Centauri system on wings of steel and trails of sparkling propulsion, always swearing that one day they would back up and take a good, long look at their nearest neighbor. Probes had shown that A.C. Bb was a life-bearing world, boasting its own ecosystem that was utterly inimical to humanity's needs. "There are bacteria that thrive around volcanic vents, without air or food or light," one scientist had said, shortly after the first sampling probe had returned to Earth. "Maybe they would do well there. But I doubt it."

Yes, there was an atmosphere, which could even colloquially be called "air," since air had no specific characteristics apart from breathability; the fact that the "air" was comprised of neon, helium, and other, more unstable compounds didn't change what it was. It would be *possible* for someone to unzip their environment suit and breathe in deeply. They would be dead before they hit the ground. It was still an option.

There were things that had structures in the ground that could be considered "roots," and long, load-bearing parts that could be considered "trunks," and even "leafs" at the top, spreading out to catch the rays of the deep red sun that shone down from above. Things that human eyes would interpret as birds, insects, and small reptiles moved through the foliage, their angles subtly off, their colors blatantly wrong. Looking at them for too long could become painful, as the brain struggled to make them fit a frame of reference that simply didn't apply.

Individuals who were suited for the xenosciences were few and far between. Most of the discoveries the universe had to offer would be chronicled and reviewed by computer, turned into abstracts that wouldn't wound the delicate sensibilities of the human mind. Spacers were generally considered slightly insane. Not for seeking space—the drive to go, to fly, to explore had been part of humanity for as long as people had possessed the capacity to raise their heads and look upward—but as a consequence of all the things they'd been exposed to, the impossible angles, the unbreathable air. Humanity was meant and made for its own solar system, where even the lifeless outer planets made sense. Anything beyond it was too much to understand.

The airlock door opened. Gwen took her first step out, onto the surface of an alien world. She was all too aware of Heather standing behind her, waiting for her to vomit or collapse from the visual shock of colors her mind didn't know how to process and shapes that her cultural sensitivities insisted couldn't possibly exist. Well, she wasn't going to give the spacer the satisfaction. Breathing slowly, deliberately, she closed her eyes and counted to ten.

All these things are right and real and true, she told herself sternly. *You've seen pictures. You've seen the surveyor's reports. You know your eyes are telling you the truth. Listen to them.*

She opened her eyes.

The landscape was still alien, but not as painfully so: the colors seemed a hair less bright, the shapes of rocks and trees a hint less predatory. She'd been training for over a year to be able to divorce herself from her surroundings and see them for what they were, not for what her animal mind wanted them to be.

Novelty was always terrifying. In another generation or two, perhaps the children of the human race would live in domed cities on this very world, breathing Earth-standard air and playing with the descendants of the spike-furred creatures that watched them, bemused and wary, from the nearby trees.

"You all right, professor?" asked Heather.

Gwen turned, smiling through her face shield. The other woman shied away. Feeling an obscure satisfaction, Gwen said, "I'm perfectly fine. I just had to take a moment to appreciate the unique beauty of this place. Don't you think it's amazing?"

"It's sure something," grumbled Heather, moving to stand next to Gwen. "Regulations require that I offer you one more opportunity to turn around. I will film everything I see at the ruin. I will submit my footage to you in its entirety, no editing or omissions. You will be able to fulfill your commitment to the university without endangering yourself. You have my word that I will not attempt to mislead you."

Gwen didn't care for Heather. Spacers, as a whole, were disrespectful cowboys who thought they knew better than the rules and regulations that supposedly dictated their actions: they understood space and the alien worlds it contained better than any petty bureaucrat who'd never stepped foot any further from Earth than the red, safely terraformed soil of Mars. She knew that Heather, and the others back on the ship, chafed at her presence, seeing her as a silently accusing reminder of the rules they would rather not obey. But Heather seemed genuinely concerned. Gwen had mercy on her.

"I believe you," she said. "But my school paid to send me this far because they wanted me to see the ruin with my own eyes, not just through recordings. If I did what you're asking, I'd be in violation of my contract. I could be fired. Worse, I could have my work credentials for Earth revoked. There are very few positions open on the Moon. I don't want to spend the next ten years in cryogenic suspension while the computer tries to find me a job."

Heather hesitated before rolling her eyes, bravado falling back into place like it had never slipped away. "Suit yourself, Professor," she said. "I was just trying to save you a walk. Come on." She turned, giving her hips an unnecessary extra swing, and started striding away into the alien landscape.

Gwen followed, more sedately, trying to study everything around her without looking at any one thing for long enough that it would start to upset her.

The air, again, presented a problem: some of the more unusual compounds it contained made it more flammable than the air back on Earth, making anything that might produce sparks a terrible idea. They couldn't take a recon vehicle to the ruins. Any doubts Gwen might have had as to the veracity of that ruling had been destroyed when they had landed, in a storm of fire and ashes created by their propulsion thrusters. The ship rested at the center of a circle of char, all the foliage burnt away in an eight-foot radius around it. The firestorm had been localized but intense; it would be years before anything could grow here again. Maybe decades, depending on the local vegetation. There was so much they didn't know, so much they *couldn't* know.

Humanity traveled within the safe sphere of its own ideas. Even the least alien of worlds was too different for many—for most—to comprehend. That wasn't going to change for generations, if it ever changed at all.

Heather led the way into the brush, the bold explorer clearing the path with her monofilament machete and her practiced eye for danger. Spacers came the closest to fully embracing the unknown, learning the elements of it that were closest to what they expected and using them to sketch the barest, thinnest outline of the worlds around them. They still died in droves—oh, how they died, frozen on worlds of ice, burning forever on worlds of flame, calcified and dissolved and transformed and remade and never, never forgotten—but they counted it a worthwhile sacrifice, for the cause of spreading humanity to the stars.

Gwen followed as close behind as she dared, holding her arms close against her body, fighting the childish impulse to reach for what looked like a flower, a berry, a piece of ripe and ready fruit. She didn't want to *eat* them, stars, no; she wanted to *study* them, to find the points of commonality between herself and the people who must have lived here once, before time took them away. The people who'd left their ruins for her to find. She was going to be their chronicler, the one who uncovered and told their story. It seemed only right that she should make at least something of an effort to force herself to know them first.

The ground changed under their feet, gradually taking on a slight gradient, guiding them upward and onward, from the flat plain to the budding mountain where the ruins were located. Gwen checked her wrist recorder. Every step she took was being captured, ready to replay and analyze at her leisure. She was going to need that footage. This whole world was a mystery to be unraveled, and there were people back at the university counting on her to bring them the keys to begin their own slices of the work. The human mind might not be equipped to understand all the wonders of the universe, but they would die before they stopped trying, collectively and on their own. Nothing mattered more than the attempt.

Vines—it was impossible to think of them as anything else, not when they were fibrous and green and so clearly growing out of the nearby vegetation—draped across the easiest path up the growing mountain. Heather hacked them aside. They wept bright purple sap that bubbled upon contact with air. Gwen wondered what it would smell like, what the chemical structure would say versus the human nose, which insisted on trying to compare everything it encountered to things that it had known on Earth. Not that she, or any other human, was ever likely to smell these vines; they were too different, too alien. Death would likely follow close on the heels of any attempt to truly know them.

"How much further?" she asked, voice seeming deeper and more resonant to her ears as it traveled through her suit's bone conduction speakers. She was hearing herself inside and outside at the same time, as she heard her voice normally and as other people heard it, the two twinned to the point of becoming impossible to separate.

"Almost there, professor," said Heather, and kept hacking.

The only two unprotected people on the face of the planet walked on.

* * *

When they reached the ruins, everything changed. One moment they were hacking their way through the brush, Gwen avoiding the vines that sought to catch and cling, Heather swinging her machete with wild abandon, not seeming to care about the damage she might be doing to the structures (*plants*, insisted Gwen's mind; they were green and growing and they couldn't be anything but plants, to be anything else would be *wrong*) around them. The next moment, they were stepping through the last veil of green and the ruins were there, unfolding before them like a strange geometric puzzle.

For one agonizing, aching moment, the angles of the structure were impossible, following no laws of terrestrial mathematics: they bent, soared, folded inward on themselves according to their own ambitions, and Gwen's eyes refused to translate what they saw into anything more than an abstract jumble of folds and lines. Then she blinked, once, twice, three times, and the structure settled into something that would have looked perfectly at home in the regrown rainforests of Central America. It was a pyramid, stones stacked upon stones, with stairs wending their way up the sides. There were doorways positioned at the base, and again halfway up, but they were blocked by great slabs of black stone that sparkled where the sun hit them, not gold or silver; rainbow, like they were filled with prisms.

There was an open door at the top of the pyramid. Gwen stood staring at the structure in open-mouthed awe for several moments, taking in the carvings around the openings, mimicking the local foliage in delicate abstraction, marveling at the preservation of the stairways. Finally, she swallowed, pointed to the top, and said, "There."

"You sure?" asked Heather dubiously. "We've seen seals like those ones before. They give way pretty easily. We could be in and out in under an hour if you'd let me—"

"*No*," said Gwen. The vehemence of her tone surprised even her. The two of them stood staring at each other for a moment before she shook her head and repeated, "No. We have a way to get inside without damaging the structure in any fashion, and that's what we're going to do. This stays *intact* for a change."

Heather looked at her silently, a stony expression on her face. Gwen was suddenly, painfully aware of the machete in Heather's hand, its edge visible only through the sparkle it made when it brushed against the air, cutting the very molecules in two. Monofilament was so thin that it could pass through the cell membrane and out again without leaving a hole. Someone who was cut in two with the stuff might as well not have been touched, until they tried to move, and found themselves falling apart.

Gwen was unarmed. If Heather truly objected to her demands, all she could do was run, through a jungle made of things that were not trees, hoping to reach the ship before the spacer called ahead and told her friends to stop the archeologist from contacting home.

Finally, broadly, Heather shrugged. "Whatever, but I'm not carrying you up that damn thing."

"You won't need to," said Gwen, and grinned.

* * *

An hour later, she was wishing she hadn't been quite so confident. The pyramid, which had looked high but manageable from the edge of the jungle, was misleading: the people who had constructed it had been slightly taller than the human norm, enough so that each step was about four inches higher than was comfortable. Those extra inches added up: they'd been climbing for an hour, and were only two-thirds of the way to the top.

"We could have been on our way back to the ship by now," said Heather. "You would still have been the first archeologist to set foot inside one of these things, and I wouldn't feel like my ass was on fire."

"Have you not been keeping up your zero-G exercise program?" asked Gwen.

Heather flipped her off.

It was a remarkably soothing, *human* gesture, something that had traveled with them all the way from Earth, something that wasn't changed by shifts in gravity or by the strange, alien geometries she still glimpsed out of the corner of her eye whenever she allowed herself to relax. Gwen laughed, and that sound was equally human, bright and free and beautiful. She was climbing a pyramid on an alien planet; she was lightyears from home, on the cusp of what might be the greatest archeological discovery she would ever be in a position to make. Everything was right with the world. Anything else would have been disrespectful to the steps she'd had to take to be here.

"All you academics are freaks," grumbled Heather.

"We say the same about spacers."

"Spacers are the only sane people left in the entire human race."

Gwen tilted her head. "How so?"

"All the rest of you, it's like you're allergic to the whole universe. It makes you sick to your souls instead of sick to your stomachs, but the theory's the same. You can't handle it. It isn't Earth, it isn't *yours*, and it screws you all up inside. Us, we can't take everything, but we're better at it than you are, because we've been exposed more. We're teaching ourselves to survive outside our own atmosphere. There are so many people now, we couldn't all pull back to Earth if we wanted to. There isn't *room*. So we spread and we spread and we keep on looking for places to belong. But we're never going to find them outside of our solar system until we broaden our horizons enough to see them for what they are. You keep preserving humanity's past. It's important. Somebody needs to. I'm going to be out here preserving humanity's future. That's important too."

Gwen was quiet for a moment, absorbing this. Finally, she nodded. "You're right," she said. "I never thought of it like that."

"Damn right I'm right," grumbled Heather, sounding secretly pleased with herself. They kept walking. Soon enough, they were stepping off the stairway and onto a wide, flat promenade. Perhaps fifteen feet separated them from the entryway. It was all Gwen could do to stay where she was, not allowing herself to bolt for the open door into the future.

"My God," she breathed.

Heather didn't say anything. The other woman's tone had been reverent, and while the spacer might consider this a waste of time, it was a waste of time that had funded the mission and was going to lead to a greater profit later on. She could afford a few minutes to let the archeologist enjoy her victory. The pyramid was going to be like all the others, she was sure: filled with antiquities and odd machines that would fetch a pretty penny on the secondary market, but were, in the grand scope of things, worthless. The culture that had created them was gone, and not even its echoes remained.

Gwen could have told her a few things about the value of culture, living on long after its descendants were gone. She could have told her about the need to remember history, all history, in order to build a strong foundation for the future. She could have told her so many things. She didn't think they needed to be said. So instead they walked together, the historian and the would-be looter, under the stone archway, into the dark beyond.

Or into what should have been the dark beyond. As soon as they were past the threshold, the chamber lit up with a soft, whitish glow that seemed to emanate from the walls themselves. The floor began to glow as well, brighter, slightly green. Heather and Gwen stopped, staring. They were still staring when a grinding noise began behind them.

"Shit!" snapped Heather, breaking out of her surprise, grabbing Gwen, and diving for the opening...but the opening wasn't there anymore. It had been replaced by a solid wall of black stone, glittering with tiny prisms that began to glow even as they watched.

"Shit," said Heather. "Shit, *shit*, shit."

"It's all right," said Gwen. "There are other exits."

"Yeah, and they're all blocked, and do you want to try digging your way out of a big alien mystery pyramid with nothing but a machete? Because I don't. That is the opposite of what I want."

"But it's what we get to do," said Gwen. "Please stop yelling. I'm holding onto my calm by the skin of my teeth, and I'd rather not lose it."

The light had been getting brighter while they spoke. A warm musical tone started to fill the room, light, melodic, and surprisingly painless, given how much everything else on this planet had hurt when it began. There was a click behind them before a voice said, in flat, genderless English, "Congratulations. You have reached the," unintelligible, "goal station. Please register your player names and affiliations."

Gwen and Heather both turned. A glowing sphere had appeared in the middle of the room; the voice was coming from somewhere inside.

"Please register your player names and affiliations," repeated the sphere.

"Uh," said Heather. "Just so you know, none of the other pyramids have done this. The room at the top was always empty by the time we got there."

"You mean after you smashed your way through one of the lower doors."

Heather shrugged.

"This room was empty too, when we first got here." Gwen eyed the sphere warily, grateful for her recording devices, for the fact that none of this was going to be lost. "Maybe there's a mechanism that can only be triggered if you enter the pyramid the way that you're *supposed* to."

"Sorry," said Heather. She didn't sound sorry.

"Please register your player names and affiliations," repeated the sphere.

"Dr. Gwendolyn McArthur, University of Washington," said Gwen. "This is Heather Wilson, of the United North American Marine Corps."

There was a pause before the sphere said, "These are not recognized affiliations. Please state your world of origin."

"We're from Earth," said Heather.

The sphere pulsed blue for a moment before returning to its neutral greenish-white. "Earth," it said. "Congratulations. You have reached the," unintelligible, "goal station ahead of all other players. The move is yours. Do you wish to continue, repeat, recede, or," unintelligible. There was a questioning note on that last, incomprehensible word; they were being offered a choice.

"What are you?" asked Gwen.

"I am the," unintelligible, "goal station," said the sphere. "As the first to reach me, you are permitted to select the next play event."

"What the fuck?" asked Heather.

"I think we've found some sort of gaming device," said Gwen slowly. More loudly, she asked, "Can you define the play events?"

"Continuation will allow you to submit all markers which have been collected since your last goal station, and be judged according to completeness for the sector. Repetition will return you to the start of this goal station leg. Receding will return you to the previous goal station leg." Unintelligible "will reset the game board."

"How about you just open the door and we'll go?" asked Heather.

"You cannot leave the goal station until you have chosen a course," said the sphere.

"Great." Heather turned and glared at Gwen. "Just great."

"We can choose one. We can do this."

"Can we? Because a weird alien ball that speaks English is telling me I have to stay here until I choose something I don't understand."

"Well, hang on." Gwen looked to the sphere. "Can you tell whether we possess any, uh, markers?"

"You do not possess any markers at this time. Should you select continuation, you will be removed from play."

"The two of us?"

"Earth."

Heather and Gwen exchanged a look. It was Heather who spoke first, asking, "This planet...did the people who used to live here make you?"

"No. I was placed after they had been removed from play."

"Okay, we are *not* doing that." Heather frowned. "What was the start of this, uh, leg?"

"You began this leg when you entered this room."

"So we still couldn't leave."

"What was the previous leg?" asked Gwen.

The sphere's answer was unintelligible.

Gwen groaned. "We don't have a shared vocabulary for planetary names. It could have been any of the worlds where a similar pyramid has been found."

"Screw it," said Heather. "We'll take the fourth one."

The sphere pulsed. "Again?" it asked.

"What?" Gwen's eyes narrowed. "Have we chosen the fourth one before?"

"Every time a member of your team has reached this station, they have chosen," unintelligible.

"Guess it's not hurting anything," said Heather. "We'll take it."

"Very well. Your team has been credited with locating a standing goal post; the confusion field for all non-home ground will be reduced by six percent. Your sacrifice has been duly noted."

"Wait—" began Gwen.

The sphere flashed white, and everything was gone.

* * *

The Nile was high in its banks, threatening to overflow. Crocodiles would be prowling near the edges, looking for something to fill their stomach. It was unwise to wander, this deep into the rainy season. But Sabah couldn't sleep. Her dreams were filled with the Sun, glowing bright and speaking in foreign tongues to two women in unfamiliar clothing, who stood before it, close enough to touch. It was a strange thing to have within her mind. She needed to see the stars, to shake the strangeness away.

Sabah rose and padded, quiet as a kitten, to the door to her family home. She looked back only once, to be certain that her parents had not noticed her going.

The sky outside was a sheet of absolute blackness, shimmering with stars that glinted like grains of white sand glittered in the noonday sun. Sabah stared up at it, wondering if the stars were things that could be touched, wondering if humanity would ever find a way to reach them. The sphere's words had been strange, meaningless, all save for the last five, which had been spoken in a tongue she knew, if only in her dreams.

"Return to start of game."

About the Authors

JACEY BEDFORD is a British science fiction and fantasy writer with novels published by DAW in the USA and short stories published on both sides of the Atlantic. She lives in an old stone house on the edge of Yorkshire's Pennine Hills with her songwriter husband and a long-haired, black German Shepherd (a dog not an actual shepherd from Germany). She's been a librarian, a postmistress, and a folk singer with the vocal harmony trio, Artisan. She once sang live on BBC Radio 4 accompanied by the Doctor (Who?) playing spoons.
Web: www.jaceybedford.co.uk
Blog: jaceybedford.wordpress.com/
Twitter: @jaceybedford
Facebook www.facebook.com/jacey.bedford.writer

SOFIE BIRD writes speculative fiction in Melbourne, Australia, and pays the bills as a technical writer, where no one looks at her askance for wanting to know everything. She also programs, weaves, sculpts glass, and maintains a website at http://sofiebird.net. Sofie is a graduate of the Odyssey Writing Workshop, has published poetry in the Australian periodical *Blue Dog*, and her fiction has appeared in *Orson Scott Card's Intergalactic Medicine Show*, and the anthology *Temporally Out Of Order* by Zombies Need Brains. You can follow her on twitter: @sofie_bird.

S.C. BUTLER lives in New Hampshire with his wife and son. He is the author of "The Stoneways" trilogy from Tor – *Reiffen's Choice, Queen Ferris,* and *The Magicians' Daughter.* His short stories have appeared in *Beneath Ceaseless Skies*, and several anthologies, including ZNB's anthology *Clockwork Universe: Steampunk vs. Aliens.* Although he hasn't managed yet, he does hope someday to make it to the other side.

DANIEL J. DAVIS was born and raised in Massachusetts. A veteran of both the US Marine Corps and the US Army, he currently lives in North Carolina with an amazing wife, two dogs, and an unhealthy love of The History Channel's *Ancient Aliens*. His work has previously appeared in *Writers of the Future Volume 31* and *Urban Fantasy Magazine*. He also blogs, somewhat infrequently, at danieljdavisblogs.wordpress.com.

JENNIFER DUNNE is a data scientist who loves uncovering the underlying patterns and relationships between things that seem unrelated...like Mozart and an alien language. Was his partying and drinking just his era's version of a bad boy rock and roll lifestyle, or was he self-medicating to stop the "voices" in his head because he was unusually sensitive to certain frequencies? Past novellas speculating on aliens and musicians, although with far more romance than this short story, include *Illicit Programming* and *Must Love Music*.

DAVID FARLAND is an award-winning, New York Times bestselling author with dozens of novels to his credit. He has written for *Star Wars* and the *Mummy*, but is best known for his "Runelords" fantasy series. Dave serves as the lead judge for the world's largest science fiction and fantasy writing contest, and has helped numerous writers go on to start their own careers. You can learn more about him or contact him at www.mystorydoctor.com.

Born in New York City in 1957, **CELIA S. FRIEDMAN** discovered science fiction at age 12, and has been obsessed with it ever since. Her first novel, *In Conquest Born*, was published by DAW Books in 1986, and in 1996 she quit her job as a costume designer to write full time in Northern Virginia. To date she has published ten novels (including her acclaimed "Coldfire" Trilogy), short fiction, and an RPG resource. Her most recent work, *Dreamweaver,* will be released in December 2016. Chat with her on Facebook and check out her web page at www.csfriedman.com. Her glasswork can be found at https://www.etsy.com/shop/glassfantasies

WALTER H. HUNT is a science fiction and speculative fiction writer from Massachusetts. He is the author of the critically acclaimed "Dark Wing" series, originally published by Tor Books and now in the Baen e-library. He has also written *A Song In Stone*, a novel of the Templars; *Elements of Mind*, a Victorian thriller about mesmerism; and, with Eric Flint, *1636: The*

Cardinal Virtues, part of the New York Times best-selling "Ring of Fire" series. He is married with one daughter, and is Grand Historian of the Grand Lodge of Masons in Massachusetts. Find out more at http://www.walterhunt.com.

GINI KOCH writes the fast, fresh and funny "Alien/Katherine 'Kitty' Katt" series for DAW Books, the "Necropolis Enforcement Files," and the "Martian Alliance Chronicles" series, as well as many other novels, novellas, and short stories. As G.J. Koch she writes the "Alexander Outland" series and she's made the most of multiple personality disorder by writing under a variety of other pen names as well, including Anita Ensal, Jemma Chase, A.E. Stanton, and J.C. Koch. She has stories featured in a variety of excellent anthologies, available now and upcoming, writing as Gini Koch, Anita Ensal, and J.C. Koch. www.ginikoch.com

SF convention favorites **SHARON LEE** and **STEVE MILLER** have been writing SF and Fantasy together since the 1980s, with dozens of stories and several dozen novels to their joint credit. Steve was Founding Curator of Science Fiction at the University of Maryland's SF Research Collection while Sharon is the only person to consecutively hold office as the Executive Director, Vice President, and President of the Science Fiction and Fantasy Writers of America. Their newest Liaden Universe® novel, *Alliance of Equals*, is their twenty-fifth collaborative novel. Their awards include the Skylark, the Prism, & the Hal Clement Award. See http://www.korval.com.

ANTHONY LOWE is an English Literature major from Turlock and La Grange, California presently grinding away towards his BA at Chabot College and (in a few months' time) CSU East Bay. His first published work, "The Lonesome Dark," can be found in the e-book version of Ragnarok Publications' dark fantasy anthology, *Blackguards: Tales of Assassins, Mercenaries, and Thieves.* During lulls between classwork, he is given to gaming, movies, researching Old West history, and scouring local used bookstores for novels he should probably get around to reading at some point. He keeps a blog at: anthonymlowe.blogspot.com

GAIL Z. MARTIN and **LARRY N. MARTIN** are the authors of the new Steampunk series "Iron and Blood: The Jake Desmet Adventures" and a series of related short stories: "The Storm & Fury Adventures." Gail also writes epic and urban fantasy, with new books *Shadow and Flame*

(Ascendant Kingdoms Saga), *The Shadowed Path* (Chronicles of the Necromancer) and *Vendetta* (Deadly Curiosities series).
Find them at www.AscendantKingdoms.com,
on Twitter @GailZMartin and @LNMartinauthor,
onFacebook.com/WinterKingdoms,
and at DisquietingVisions.com blog. Watch for short stories in anthologies *Clockwork Universe: Steampunk vs. Aliens, The Weird Wild West, The Side of Good/The Side of Evil, Alien Artifacts,* and *Gaslight and Grimm.*

SEANAN MCGUIRE lives and works in the Pacific Northwest, where she attempts to keep her massive blue cats from eating people. She writes a lot of things, because otherwise she stops sleeping. Sleep is good. She is the author of quite a lot of books, and takes quite a lot of naps. Keep up with her on Twitter at @seananmcguire or at www.seananmcguire.com.

JULIET E. MCKENNA is a British fantasy author living in the Cotswolds, UK. Loving history, myth and other worlds since she first learned to read, she has written fifteen epic fantasy novels, from *The Thief's Gamble* which began "The Tales of Einarinn" in 1999, to *Defiant Peaks* concluding "The Hadrumal Crisis" trilogy. Exploring new opportunities in digital publishing, she's re-issuing her backlist as well as bringing out original fiction. She also writes diverse shorter fiction, reviews for web and print magazines and promotes SF&Fantasy by blogging, attending conventions and teaching creative writing. Learn more about all of this at julietemckenna.com

CORAL MOORE has always been the kind of girl who makes up stories. Fortunately, she never grew out of that. She writes character driven fiction, and enjoys conversations about genetics and microbiology as much as those about vampires and werewolves. She has an MFA in Writing from Albertus Magnus College and is an alum of Viable Paradise XVII. She has been or will be published by Evernight Publishing, Vitality Magazine and Diabolical Plots. She loves aquariums, rides a motorcycle, and thinks there is little better than a good cup of coffee.
Find Coral online:
Twitter: http://twitter.com/coralm
Facebook: http://www.facebook.com/AuthorCoralMoore/
Website: http://www.coralmoore.com/

JULIE NOVAKOVA <julienovakova.com> is a Czech author of science fiction, fantasy, and detective stories. She has published short fiction e.g. in

Clarkesworld, Asimov's, and *Fantasy Scroll.* Her work in Czech includes seven novels, an anthology and over thirty stories. She received the Encouragement Award of the European science fiction and fantasy society in 2013 and the Aeronautilus award for the best Czech short story of 2014. She also translates, writes nonfiction, and contributes to the Czech SF magazine *XB-1.* She is an evolutionary biologist by study and also takes a keen interest in planetary science.
Twitter: @julianne_sf
Facebook: fb.com/JulieNovakovaAuthor

ANGELA PENROSE lives in Seattle with her husband, five computers, and some unknown number of books, which occupy most of the house. She writes in several genres, but SFF is her first love. Her recent short fiction has appeared in *Loosed Upon the World, Recycled Pulp,* and *Crucible.* Her story "The Rites of Zosimos," published last year in *Alchemy and Steam,* has been chosen for *The Year's Best Crime and Mystery Short Fiction (2015).* Angie blogs at http://angelapenrosewriter.blogspot.com/.

A lifelong science fiction & fantasy fan, **ANDRIJA POPOVIC** is a native of the Washington DC metropolitan area. He grew up scouring bookshops & libraries for strange, beautiful and terrifying worlds hidden in dog-eared paperbacks and dusty hardbacks. These days, he works with associations and grassroots organizations, assisting them with on-line advocacy campaigns. Outside of his day job, he enjoys photography and writing haiku for his Twitter account, @Andrian6. He can also be found at his writing blog, Biomechanoid Blues
(biomechanoidblues.wordpress.com)

JAMES VAN PELT is a former high school English teacher and now full-time writer in western Colorado. His fiction has made appearances in most of the major science fiction and fantasy magazines. He's been a finalist for a Nebula Award and been reprinted in many year's best collections. Much of his short fiction has been gathered in four collections, including the latest, *Flying in the Heart of the Lafayette Escadrille.* His first Young Adult novel, *Pandora's Gun,* was released from Fairwood Press in August of 2015. James blogs at
http://www.jamesvanpelt.com and can be found on Facebook.

About the Editors

PATRICIA BRAY is the author of a dozen novels, including *Devlin's Luck*, which won the Compton Crook Award for the best first novel in the field of science fiction or fantasy. A multi-genre author whose career spans both epic fantasy and Regency romance, her books have been translated into Russian, German, Portuguese and Hebrew. She's also crossed over to the dark side as the co-editor of *After Hours: Tales from the Ur-Bar* (DAW, March 2011) and *The Modern Fae's Guide to Surviving Humanity* (DAW, March 2012), *Clockwork Universe: Steampunk vs. Aliens* (ZNB, June 2014) and *Temporally Out of Order* (ZNB, August 2015).

Patricia lives in a New England college town, where she combines her writing with a full-time career in I/T. To offset the hours spent at a keyboard, she bikes, hikes, cross-country skis, snowshoes and has recently taken up the noble sport of curling. To find out more, visit her website at www.patriciabray.com.

* * *

JOSHUA PALMATIER is a fantasy author with a PhD in mathematics. He currently teaches at SUNY Oneonta in upstate New York, while writing in his "spare" time, editing anthologies with fellow zombie and co-editor Patricia Bray, and founding the anthology-producing small press Zombies Need Brains LLC. His most recent fantasy novel *Threading the Needle* (July 2016) continues a new fantasy series begun in *Shattering the Ley*, although you can also find his "Throne of Amenkor" series and the "Well of Sorrows" series on the shelves. He is currently hard at work writing *Reaping the Aurora*, the third novel in the "Ley" series, and designing the kickstarter for the next Zombies Need Brains anthology project. You can find out more at www.joshuapalmatier.com or at the small press' site www.zombiesneedbrains.com.   Or   follow   him   on   Twitter   as @bentateauthor or @ZNBLLC.

Acknowledgments

This anthology would not have been possible without the tremendous support of those who pledged during the Kickstarter. Everyone who contributed not only helped create this anthology, they also helped solidify the foundation of the small press Zombies Need Brains LLC, which I hope will be bringing SF&F themed anthologies to the reading public for years to come...as well as perhaps some select novels by leading authors, eventually. I want to thank each and every one of them for helping to bring this small dream into reality. Thank you, my zombie horde.

The Zombie Horde: Danielle Ackley-McPhail, Carol J. Guess, J.R. Murdock, Brian Quirt, Greg Resnik, Emy Peters, Julia Haynie, Heather Fagan, Kristy K, Evenstar Deane, Andrija Popovic, Cheryl Preyer, Susan B, Evaristo Ramos, Jr., JP Frantz, Michael Skolnik, Joelle M Reizes, Lorena Dinger, Kathleen T Hanrahan, Derick Sweat, Sandra Ulbrich Almazan, Tony Finan, John P. Murphy, Sheryl R. Hayes, John McNabb, Fen Eatough, Megan Beauchemin, Karl Maurer, Al Batson, Lim Ivan, Teresa Carrigan, Sheryl Ehrlich, "Gorgeous" Gary Ehrlich, Diana Castillo, Keith E. Hartman, Duncan & Andrea Rittschof, Leah Webber, Claire Sims, Ruth Stuart, Sofie Bird, Halcyoncin, Jean Marie Ward, Jeff Gulosh, Henry Lopez, Kristine Smith, Sharon Stogner, John Sturkie, Tommy Lewis, Max Kaehn, Elaine Tindill-Rohr, Chris Loeffler, Kerry aka Trouble, John Sapienza, Kathleen Ferrando, Gary Phillips, Kathy Martin, Sally Novak Janin, Matt Keck, Lea Zane, Amanda Johnson, Holland Dougherty, Russell Ventimeglia, Roy Romasanta, Ed Ellis, Steve Lord, Terry Hazen, Nathan Hillstrom, David Hill, Fred Herman, Elizabeth McKinstry, Joanne B Burrows, Lisa Padol, Mia Kleve, Angie Hogencamp, Hisham El-Far, Eleanor Russell, Anthony R. Cardno, Sabrina Poulsen, Jenn & Drew Bernat, Patti Short, Christopher Mangum, Larisa LaBrant, Jenn Whitworth, Debbie Matsuura, Elizabeth Kite, Morgan S. Brilliant, Tina Noe-Good, Rosanne Girton, Juli, Wolf SilverOak, Marty Tool, Carey Williams, Jaime C., Chris Barili, Denise

Murray, Matt B, Scott Raun, Dino Hicks, Darryl M. Wood, Douglas Mosman, Peter Donald, R. Hunter, Steve Weiner, Krystina Harrington, Chris Brant, Andrew Neil Gray, Stephen Ballentine, Nancy Pimentel, Corey Terhune, Josie, Peter Thew, Ian Harvey, James Conason, Linda Pierce, Jeremy M. Gottwig, Ben Stanley, JE Chase, Jay Zastrow, Galena Ostipow, Sue C., Barbara Silcox, Michael J. D'Auben, Stephanie Lucas, Brad Roberts, David K. Mason, Dina S. Willner, Dustin Bell, Marsha Baker, Alice Bentley, Lisa Kruse, Jessica Reid, Helen Cameron, Pam Blome, Brenda Moon, Kate Nelson, Lex, Jo Carol Jones, Beth aka Scifibookcat, Janito Vaqueiro Ferreira Filho, Cyn Armistead, Lorri-Lynne Brown, Jason Palmatier, Dustin Bridges, Katherine S, Pat Knuth, Derek Hudgins, Cullen Gilchrist, Jonathan Collins, Ian Chung, David Perlmutter, Camron S, Keith West, Future Potentate of the Solar System, Amy E Goldman, Pat Hayes, Maggie Allen, Cathy Brown, Evan Ladouceur, Sue & Rich Hanson, Cheryl Losinger, Ragnarok Publications, Katherine Malloy, Kristie Strum, Elizabeth Inglee_Richards, Leann Rettell, The Hoose Family, Holly, H. Rasmussen, Anne Rindfliesch, Deborah Fishburn, M. Calistri-Yeh, Patrick Dugan, Steven Mentzel, April Steenburgh, Deanna Harrison, Shauna Roberts, Sara R Marschand, Katherine & Elizabeth Rowe, Bill Simoni, Elizabeth Vrabel, Wendy K Cornwall, Bonnie Warford, Robert Gilson, Chan Ka Chun Patrick, David Zurek, Sean Collins, Laurie Treacy, Jake, Chrissie, Grace & Savannah Palmatier, Steph am I, Chrysta Stuckless, David Decker, Rachel Sasseen, Sarah Liberman, Shannon Everyday, Robert Elrod, Crazy Lady Used Books, Will Carlson, Joey Shoji, Colleen R., Gayle, Liz Harkness, Svend Andersen, Vicki Colbert, Mandy Stein, Erik T Johnson, Patricia Bray, Eddy Black, Shawn Fennessey, Robby Thrasher, Chad Bowden, J.V. Ackermann, Brook West, James H. Murphy Jr., Sharon Wood, Ann Leveille, Jerrie the filkferengi, Stephanie Wood Franklin, Jo Dawn Good, Aurora N., Jef Ball, Sarah E, Keith Hall, Melanie McCoy, Malevolent Media, sam murphy, Rissa Lyn, Lark Cunningham, Clarissa Floyd, Barbara White, Crystal Sarakas, Danielle Shaw, Jonathan S. Chance, Craig "Stevo" Stephenson, Cynthia Porter, David Medinnus, Daniel S, Mark Hirschman, Simon Dick, Diane Bekel, Galit A., Sarah Cornell, Yankton Robins, Alexander "Guddha" Gudenau, M. Menzies, Michael Bernardi, Janet L. Oblinger, RKBookman, Fin & Fisher, Morva Bowman and Alan Pollard, Vamsi, SwordFire, Ash Marten, Annika Samuelsson, Michele Fry, Michael Kahan, Jerel Heritage, David Eggerschwiler, Alexander Smith, Jennifer McGaffey, Shirley, Mark Phillips, Gavran, Priscilla, Janet Yuen, Colette Reap, ARFunk, D-Rock, John Dallman, Megan Hungerford, Dina B., Lesley Smith, William Hughes, Justin, Karl

Jahn, Alexandra Garcia, Ilona Fenton, Andrew Taylor, Thomas Zilling, Lesley Mitchell, Mark Newman, James Spinks, Gabe, Alysia Murphy, Lirion, Robert Maughan, Beth LaClair, John Green, Adrian Cross, Chris Matosky, Lawrence M. Schoen, Jean-Pierre Ardoguein, Cate H, Nathan Turner, Eagle Archambeault, Sarah M Stewart, Leila Gaskin, Gilvoro, Todd V. Ehrenfels, Brendan Lonehawk, Kevin Winter, Elyse Grasso, Sarah Brand, Stephanie Cheshire, RiTides, Mandy Wultsch, Jen Woods, Mark Kiraly, Misty Massey, Hamish Laws, Jenny Barber, S Whitaker, Chris Gerrib, Lisa "Flaptain" Stuckey, Margaret St. John, John W. Otte, K. Hodghead, Kathryn Whitlock, Vicki Greer, Gail Z. Martin, Shawn Marier, Alon Ziv, Morten Poulsen, Epiphyllum, H Lynnea Johnson, Janet Armentani, AM Scott, Mike Hampton, Elizabeth A. Janes, Jen Edwards, Stephanie Louie, Kitty Likes, S K Suchak, Christian Lindke, Andy Clayman, Mollie Bowers, Leanne Wu, Aaron Canton, Michael Roger Nichols, J.L. Gerrard, Starr Iraklianos, Keith Jones, Sidra Roman, Kaitlin Thorsen, Karen Haugland, Evergreen Lee, Dave Entermille, Margaret C. Thomson, Adriane Hughes Ruzak, Mervi Mustonen, Laura F., Jeanne Hartley, Jody Lynn Nye, Melinda Hunter, William Pearson, Chris Huning, Damia Torhagen, Marti Panikkar, Tal S, T. England, Niall Gordon, Jörg Tremmel, David Drew, Kevin Niemczyk, Tiago Thedim Dias, Lee Dalzell, Lisa Mitchell, The Mad Canner, Wayne L McCalla, Jr, Paul Bulmer, Jill B, Tony Fiorentino, Elaine Walker, Iain Riley, Judith Mortimore, Jeffry Rinkel, Tanya Koenig, Sam Karpierz, Ty Wilda, Robert Farley, Axisor and Mike, Orla, Heather Parra, Donna Gaudet, Missy Gunnels Katano, Kathy Robinson, Silence in the Library Publishing, Peter Young, Katrina Knight, Harvey Brinda, Marc D. Long, Hugh Agnew, Leah Smith, Catherine Gross-Colten, Deirdre M. Murphy, Michelle L, Laura Sheana Taylor, Sarena Ulibarri, Patrick Thomas, Kelly Melnyk, P. Chin, Tory Shade, GriffinFire, Elektra, Jennifer Scott, Brian, Sarah, and Joshua Williams, Jeffery Lawler, Cliff Winnig, Ludovic Mercier, Rebecca M, Damon Eric English, Jules Jones, Felicia Fredlund, jasperoo, Mariann Asanuma, CE Murphy, Pete Hollmer, Michael Hanscom, Peggy Martinez, Deirdre Furtado, Zen Dog, Andrew and Kate Barton, David Rippere, Gina Freed, Amanda Power, Diego Comics Publishing, Dani Bednar, Stephen Leigh, Sandra Komoroff, Noah Nichols, Samuel Lubell, Fred and Mimi Bailey, Lennhoff Family, Thomas Santilli, Delanda Scotti, S Ruskin, Amanda Weinstein, Waylon Adams, Camden C, A fan of words, Leshia-Aimée Doucet, Yair Goldberg, Barbara Hasebe, Jennifer Berk, Marc Tassin, Phyllis Dennis, Heather & Zachary Jones, Kerri Regan, Lori Joyce Parker, Timothy Nakayama, Jamie FitzGerald, Nirven, Darrell Grizzle, Robert Parks, Limugurl, Shannon

Kauderer, Bobbie Heft-Eggert, WOL, Rhel ná DecVandé, Laura Wenham, Angela Butler, Belkis Marcillo, Erin Penn, Stephen Kissinger, TOM HAINES, Jenifer Purcell Rosenberg, Victoria, James Nettles, Liz H, Jenny Schwartzberg, Alien Zookeeper, C. R. Washington, Steven Halter, Chaddaï

Made in the USA
Monee, IL
16 July 2021

73750167R00177